PRAISE FOR *THE LAST AGENT*

"*The Last Agent* brings Robert Dugoni's latest stellar protagonist Charles Jenkins back to the page with spectacular results . . . More known for his psychological and legal thrillers, [Dugoni] seems to be channeling his inner Daniel Silva, or even John le Carre, here . . . Espionage writing doesn't get any better than Dugoni's shrewd take on the state of U.S.-Russian relations, as he proves to be not just a literary jack of all trades, but a master of all of them."

—*Providence Journal*

"In bestseller Dugoni's fast and furious sequel to 2019's *The Eighth Sister* . . . Dugoni writes with such immediacy that readers will feel as if they're standing alongside Jenkins as he contemplates his next death-defying move. Fans of espionage fiction are in for a high-octane thrill ride."

—*Publishers Weekly*

"Dugoni shows he can craft sensational characters and keep the plot moving along. Even behind enemy lines."

—*Mystery & Suspense Magazine*

"If you love international intrigue and spy thrillers, this heart-stopper is a must-read!"

—*Medium*

"If you're searching for a great international spy thriller, look no further. Stuffed with more action and espionage than most writers can cram into two books, Robert Dugoni's *The Last Agent* is fast, unflinching, and absolutely fantastic."

—The Real Book Spy

"The thriller equivalent of a *matryoshka* nesting doll: an outer layer of geopolitics; a deeper layer of intricate spycraft; and at its center, an unlikely CIA-FSB off-the-books alliance to save a brave Russian asset from the worst fate imaginable."

—Barry Eisler, *New York Times* bestselling author

"Fast paced and mesmerizing from start to finish, Dugoni flawlessly executes one of the best spy novels I've read in years. *The Last Agent* grabs you and doesn't let go—one twist and turn after the other had me tearing through the pages."

—Steven Konkoly, *USA Today* bestselling author

PRAISE FOR *THE EIGHTH SISTER*

"A gripping thriller . . . [*The Eighth Sister*] is destined to be a classic in the genre, and Dugoni is arguably one of the best writers in the field right now."

—Associated Press

"A great mix of spycraft and classic adventure, with a map of Moscow in hand."

—Martin Cruz Smith, international bestselling author

"Feels so fresh and authentic we could see the story breaking in the headlines tomorrow."

—Mark Sullivan, bestselling author of *Beneath a Scarlet Sky*

"With lean prose and spot-on local color, this plot-driven thriller pulses with tension and fraught escapes, the action capped by a courtroom drama as good as any from Grisham. A must-read for fans of legal thrillers and/or spy novels."

—*Library Journal* (starred review)

"Dugoni delivers an exceptionally gripping spy thriller that will keep readers on the edge of their seats."

—*Publishers Weekly* (starred review)

"[Dugoni] has outdone himself here, serving up a double-barrelled blast of action mixed with espionage in what's perhaps his most unputdownable thriller yet . . . Treason, moles, and plenty of misdirection . . . Robert Dugoni's *The Eighth Sister* is a high-stakes game between spies, and he doesn't take his foot off the gas pedal for a second."

—The Real Book Spy

"The perfect pacing and brilliant intrigue of [*The Eighth Sister*] result in a page-turning, intelligent tale that will keep readers engaged until the very last page . . . The perfect combination of espionage, history, and quick-witted characters—a rare feat in the thriller genre."

—New York Journal of Books

THE
SILENT
SISTERS

THE
SILENT
SISTERS

ROBERT
DUGONI

THOMAS & MERCER

Published by Thomas & Mercer, Seattle

www.apub.com

Amazon, the Amazon logo, and Thomas & Mercer are trademarks of Amazon.com, Inc., or its affiliates.

ISBN-13: 9781542029919 (hardcover)
ISBN-10: 1542029910 (hardcover)

ISBN-13: 9781542008341 (paperback)
ISBN-10: 1542008344 (paperback)

Cover design by Rex Bonomelli

Printed in the United States of America

First edition

To the real Charles Jenkins, my dear friend. God broke the mold when he made you. I said in law school that someday I would make you larger than life, but you were already.

Prologue

Charles Jenkins struggled to lift his chin from his chest. His head flopped to the left, then rolled to the right. The muscles in his neck could no longer hold the weight upright. He could see, with difficulty, out of his left eye; his right eye had long since swollen shut. The metallic taste of blood filled his mouth, and he could not breathe through his nostrils—his nose broken from the repeated blows. His tongue touched the sharp shards of what remained of several of his teeth. So much for all that dental work, and those braces he had worn as a child.

The woman stepped forward, the soles of her brown leather boots in the puddle of his sweat and blood on the finished concrete beneath where he dangled, from the meat hook, suspended by his bound wrists. On the hooks beside him hung large carcasses of meat, not yet halved—too big for cows, he recalled thinking before the beating began, maybe buffalo. He no longer felt the ropes biting into the flesh of his wrists or the strain of his weight on his shoulder joints. The bitter cold had initially exacerbated the pain of each blow his interrogators inflicted, but Jenkins had since grown numb.

He no longer felt much of anything.

"Do you know where we are?" The woman asked the question in heavily accented English, each word punctuated by a wisp of condensation.

He could guess at an answer to her question, but even if he knew, he didn't think he could form the words. No matter. Her question had been rhetorical.

"Like all American men, I'm sure you watched your Rocky Balboa use the sides of beef as punching bags. No? I stopped watching after the fourth picture show. The one in which Mr. Balboa defeats the Russian, Ivan Drago. It became . . . too far-fetched." Her lips formed just the hint of a smile. The two men who had taken turns punishing Jenkins laughed. A third man, his interrogator, sat stoically in a folding chair.

The woman turned her head and glanced around the expansive hall as if taking in the loading bays and finished concrete floor of the expansive room. "This is the largest meat processing plant in Irkutsk. On weekdays the refrigerated trucks arrive early each morning. When they come, you can feel the reverberation of the truck engines as the drivers back into place at the loading bays and the workers fill their shipping containers and satisfy orders all over Russia. Until then . . ." She glanced about the empty room again, took a deep inhale, exhaled a cloud of mist. "It is quiet. Peaceful. No?"

Jenkins tried to spit blood, but he could not generate the strength. His saliva dribbled down his chin. "Peaceful" was not exactly the word that came to his mind.

The woman took out a cigarette, holding it in her gloved hand. Her driver dutifully stepped from the parked SUV to her side and thumbed a flame on his lighter. She inhaled and blew out smoke. "Do you know how I know this?" she asked.

Jenkins's chin fell again to his chest. Just as quickly one of his punishers grabbed his hair and yanked back his head. "Pay attention, Mr. Jenkins," his interrogator, the eldest, said from his chair. "We are coming to the good part."

"My grandfather owned this processing plant," the woman said. "His name was not on the building, but he owned it. Each month he received a bag of cash for providing the plant with protection from its competitors. Each week my grandmother would come here for meat until our freezer at home was full. You see, Mr. Jenkins, when my grandfather was freed from Stalin's gulags, he came here, to Irkutsk, and built his business with men from inside those gulags—men loyal to him who hated the communist government. My father used to tell me stories about coming here as a boy, about seeing these slabs of meat. 'Thousands of them,' he would say. 'All hanging from hooks.' He loved to watch the conveyor belt in motion, hear it hum and shake as it pulled the meat along the track to the parked trucks in the bays. He told me he loved the simple efficiency of the operation. That is what my father taught me about business. He would say to me, *'Malen'kaya Printsessa,' Little Princess.* 'Simplicity is efficiency. Your profit margins will be higher for it, and your blood pressure lower.'" A thin smile. Wistful. "I loved my father as much, if not more, than any girl, and I passed his advice on to my son. I wanted my son to possess this same wisdom when it was his time to run the family business. Do you know what else I taught him?"

Jenkins spit, then rolled his head to the right so he could better see her. Attractive. Well put together. Not tall like his wife, Alex, maybe five five or six at most. Built like a gymnast. Light-brown hair fell softly to her shoulders. *Elegant.* That's how he would describe her, though maybe her beauty was just a contrast to the savagery surrounding them. Fine Slavic features. Oval face and eyes—blue, maybe green. Her skin, what he could see anyway, was the color of weak tea, her nose thin and straight, as were her teeth. Wealthy. He could tell not just from her appearance but from the car in which she arrived—a black Russian GAZ Tigr, which looked like an American Humvee. Probably $250,000. Four-wheel drive. Bulletproof windows. Tires that don't deflate. Secure.

Jenkins spit again and this time formed the words to answer her question. "How to treat a woman?" he said.

Her face soured. Her eyes shifted.

The blow to Jenkins's ribs was fast and hard. He felt only a dull pain. His punishers knew how to throw a punch, how to turn their shoulders and hips to deliver maximum force. Boxers, likely.

The woman stepped closer. She stared into his eyes. She didn't flinch at his battered appearance. She understood and was familiar with violence. "I taught him to be deliberate, to be careful, as my father taught me. I taught him to never leave behind evidence."

"Should have taught him how to treat a woman; we wouldn't be here if you had."

Jenkins braced for another blow, but the woman's eyes shifted to his punishers and she shook her head. "Perhaps," she said in a peculiar moment of honesty. "My son was too much like his father. He inherited his ill temper and his lust for the wrong women, but he was my son. Do you have a son, Mr. Jenkins?"

Jenkins thought of Alex and their son, CJ; their daughter, Lizzie. This was not supposed to end this way. He had expected to enter Russia this final time anonymously and leave the same way. In and out before the Russian FSB, the successor to the KGB, ever knew he had been there, his handler, Matt Lemore, said. Jenkins had screwed up.

He'd cared.

He should have just walked away.

"I'm not married."

Another smile. "You are a very good liar, but your FSB profile says otherwise. Born in New Jersey. A Vietnam veteran. America's Afghanistan, no? Central Intelligence officer stationed in Mexico City, though only for a short time. Then you disappeared. You did not resurface until decades later, in Moscow, asking to be a double agent. A ruse you somehow survived. You returned to Moscow a second time and managed to free a woman from Lefortovo Prison, which, I must tell you, is impressive. No one who enters Lefortovo leaves. So, you are a man of courage, principle, morals, ethics."

Jenkins grunted. "Doesn't do me much good now, does it?"

"Married to Alex Hart, also once a CIA analyst," she continued. "You have two children. A son, CJ, and a daughter, Elizabeth, not yet two."

Jenkins felt the adrenaline rush at her mention of his wife and children.

She dropped the cigarette and crushed it beneath her shoe. "So . . . you can understand my pain."

He shook his head. "No."

She looked up from beneath bangs and met the gaze from his one eye. "No?"

"Your pain is a mother's pain. A mother's loss. A father doesn't know that kind of pain."

His answer momentarily silenced her. When she finally spoke, she sounded emotional. A small burst of air preceded each word. "So, you do know."

"I did not kill your son," Jenkins said again, too many times to keep count.

"But you did cause his death."

Jenkins couldn't dispute that, nor did he believe this was the time to get into semantics. "What, then?" he said. "You're going to have Boris here kill me?"

"You have left me without choices."

"I'm sure we can think of some."

"Another thing my father taught me that has served me well. 'Never look weak. Others will take advantage.'"

"I won't tell," Jenkins said.

She chuckled. "No, Mr. Jenkins. You will not." She stepped away, checking the diamond-studded watch on her wrist. "Do you know what they do with the scraps of meat and the sides of beef they do not sell, Mr. Jenkins?"

"I can guess," he said.

"Yes. I am sure you can. But let me tell you. They grind the unwanted pieces into hamburger and sausage. Have you ever seen a slab of meat go through the meat grinder, Mr. Jenkins? No? The grinder crushes everything—the bones, the cartilage, the tendons, the muscle, the fat. Of course, the cow is already dead. It feels no pain." She considered him coolly; he could see now that her eyes were as blue as ice. "You will not be so fortunate."

Jenkins gave her a tired smile, then said, "Nor will be the person who gets a sausage made out of me."

1

Maria Kulikova pulled a brown paper napkin from the dispenser on the cafeteria counter and blotted the sweat beading at her temples. Her early morning Pilates class at the Ai-Pilates studio had been particularly challenging. The exercises activated the muscles deep in her abdomen, glutes, and obliques. She usually cooled down on her walk from the studio to Lubyanka, where she worked as the FSB's director of the Secretariat. But not this week. Moscow was enduring a September heat wave, and the morning meteorologist had again forecast temperatures of thirty-four degrees Celsius.

The bitter aroma of coffee teased her, as did the tempting odors of scrambled eggs, ham, and sausage, but those were luxuries not on her menu. Coffee made her jittery, and she followed a strict diet to keep her figure. She supplemented her three-day-a-week Pilates class with yoga to stay limber. At sixty-three, she could no longer run, though she had once been an Olympic-caliber long-distance runner who had held the Soviet record in the three thousand meters. Her years of training had worn out her knees.

It could have been worse. At least she had avoided the "supplements" her Soviet trainers imposed on other athletes, who now experienced heart and lung problems and various forms of cancer.

Maria had loved the competition, but that had not been the reason for her pursuit of athletics. Being a Soviet athlete had elevated her stature and given her access to people she would not have otherwise met. She exercised now for much the same reason. Her appearance. Her figure opened doors and provided opportunities. Her boss, Dmitry Sokalov, the FSB's Counterintelligence Directorate's deputy director, liked fit women with large breasts. The joke within the Secretariat, a ruthless rumor mill at Lubyanka, was that Sokalov liked the contrast to his own slovenly visage—he, too, had large breasts, to match his even larger gut.

Kulikova's appearance, and her decades-long position as Sokalov's mistress, provided her access to classified information, but it also subjected her to a degradation most could never imagine or stomach.

"Maria."

Kulikova turned at the familiar sound of the voice of her assistant, Anna. The poor woman looked flushed and sounded out of breath as she crossed the marble floor to where Maria stood in line at the "Prison" cafeteria. One of two staff dining rooms at Lubyanka, the Prison was in the building's basement, where the infamous KGB prison had once been.

"Thank God." Anna blew out a breath. "He is looking for you—again. Something about a file he cannot find. I don't know who or how many he has fired this time."

Maybe if Sokalov lost twenty-five to thirty kilograms, he could find things on his own, like his belt buckle. If not for Kulikova, Sokalov would have been fired years ago, childhood friend of the president or not. He drank too much, ate too much, and was too disorganized. He remained in power because he was ruthless.

She checked her watch; she had another fifteen minutes before she officially clocked in to start her day. Fat chance. She couldn't get away for ten minutes without someone, usually Sokalov, searching for her. Nights, weekends, holidays. As the Secretariat director, Maria was always on call. The government paid her handsomely and provided a luxury apartment close to Lubyanka that she and her husband, Helge, would have otherwise been unable to afford. In her position she served as the gatekeeper to all Lubyanka files, and absolutely no one in the FSB could do without her or her staff. The execution and completion of every FSB officer's work was dependent upon the women of the Secretariat. They typed, registered, and trafficked each document. They sent and received all mail. They booked vacations. If the Secretariat broke down, the Counterintelligence Directorate would grind to a ponderous halt.

Her position provided her the keys to every file in the directorate, as well as information too sensitive for files. Sokalov readily revealed such secrets during their role-playing sessions, when he pretended he was an FSB officer with classified information and encouraged Kulikova to bind, whip, slap, pierce, and drip hot candle wax on his fat body to extract the information—usually while he was so drunk he could not remember the night, let alone the information he had disclosed.

Information was power. Sokalov became drunk on it. And Kulikova was his drink.

She sighed. "Did the director say what he needed?"

"You!" Anna said. "He told me not to come back if I did not find you in the building. Thank God I know your habits. I'm sorry to interrupt your breakfast."

In addition to being a disgusting pig, Sokalov was a bully to those over whom he held power, including the women Kulikova directed.

"Don't worry about it, Anna, but do me a favor," she said with a practiced, reserved demeanor. "Get me a cup of tea, no cream or sugar, two hard-boiled eggs, and tvorog. Just put them on my desk." She handed Anna several rubles and made her way through Dom 1, one of two L-shaped buildings linked by a nine-story tower set in a large inner courtyard that gave Lubyanka the false appearance of being a single, square-shaped structure. At a bank of elevators, she used her secure card to summon a car. She had gone through metal detectors to enter the building and had her briefcase checked thoroughly—a Kremlin mandate. The president, a former KGB officer who had appointed himself czar, was obsessed with security and with punishing those who would betray Russia or him.

On the seventh floor, Maria hurried along windowless, poorly lit hallways. The soft parquet squares compressed beneath her steps. The low-grade pine constantly wore out, and workers perpetually circled the building adding new layers. A running joke at Lubyanka was that eventually there would be no space between the floor and ceiling.

To gain entrance to the Secretariat, Maria put her eyes to a scanner. A green light traced her irises and granted access. She pulled open the heavy door and stepped inside. The women seated at their desks gave a collective sigh of relief. The more experienced looked frazzled but not particularly concerned; they had been through many Sokalov tantrums. The less experienced looked terrified, which only fed Sokalov's ego—as massive as his appetite for food and sex. It took Kulikova just seconds to determine who had borne the brunt of Sokalov's latest tirade. Tiana, relatively new, wept at her desk as she packed picture frames of her children.

"Put your photographs back, Tiana," Kulikova said, passing by the young woman's desk.

"But the director . . . ," Tiana said.

"Is having a bad morning. Continue with whatever it is you were doing."

Karine, Kulikova's second in charge, quickly approached. She grabbed Kulikova's arm and spoke in hushed tones as they moved toward Kulikova's office door. "His Majesty is on the warpath again."

"I've heard. What this time?"

"Something about a meeting this morning and a file he needs."

Kulikova stopped outside her office door. "I'll handle the deputy director. You calm everyone. Tell them I said not to worry."

Kulikova stepped into her office and closed the door. She set her briefcase beside her desk, moved to her credenza, and exchanged her tennis shoes for a pair of black Christian Louboutin pumps, one of seven pairs she kept at work. She tipped a drop of Roja Parfums—a Sokalov present for her sixtieth birthday—on each wrist, then rubbed her wrists along her neck. She touched another drop to her index finger and ran that finger down her cleavage, then freed a button of her blouse. She peeled the yellow magnetic strip of tape that sealed her safe each night, entered a password that changed weekly, and exchanged her daily wristwatch for the Rolex, then slipped on a diamond-and-ruby bracelet—Sokalov gifts she also never brought home.

She found the file Sokalov needed inside her safe, exactly where he had told her to put it, then walked to the interior door that provided access to Sokalov's inner sanctum—an office that was a testament to his excess. The furniture and accoutrements were worth more than the GNP of some small countries, and the bar so well stocked it would rival the most popular in Moscow. She pushed open the door without a knock and stepped inside.

Sokalov paced the hardwood floor along the draped windows that provided a view of downtown Moscow while he spoke on his personal cell phone. FSB officers carried two cell phones: one for personal calls, and one encrypted and used only for FSB business. Kulikova waited alongside Sokalov's Louis XV desk while his wife, Olga, led him by his nose over his personal cell phone.

Olga Sokalov had something other women did not—a father who adored his little girl and his grandchildren, and whom Sokalov feared intensely.

Sokalov nodded to Maria, then rolled his bloodshot eyes. He wore his suit jacket in anticipation of his meeting. The tip of his tie rested on his protruding stomach, which tested the resiliency of the thread on his shirt buttons. The chemical odor of Sokalov's hair oil, used in a futile effort to protect what remained of his thinning hair, dominated the room.

"Yes. I have told you that I will be there. Of course, I will be there. No. Nothing will come up. Yes, I understand you do not wish to disappoint your father on his birthday. Yes, of course."

Olga's father was General Roman Portnov, the former head of the Foreign Intelligence Service of the Russian Federation, or SVR. "I have to go, Olga," Sokalov pleaded. "I have a meeting starting in minutes and I must prepare. No, nothing is more important than your father's seventy-sixth birthday, and I would be pleased to hear about all the preparations, just not this morning. Fine. Yes. This afternoon." He moved the phone away from his ear as he spoke. "Yes. Yes. Okay. Okay. Goodbye. Good . . ."

He lowered the phone and gave Kulikova an exhausted sigh, then lumbered to his desk. With thin shoulders and legs, and no butt to speak of, Sokalov looked like a pregnant Popsicle stick. "What could be more important than a man's seventy-third, seventy-fourth, and seventy-fifth birthdays? His seventy-sixth, of course!" He sighed. "She is exhausting. I have—"

"A meeting starting in ten minutes with Chairman Petrov, Deputy Director Lebedev, and General Pasternak." Kulikova held up the manila file folder Sokalov had given her the prior evening for safekeeping, but which alcohol had wiped from his memory. She had read and memorized it thoroughly, though it seemed incomplete. "The file was locked in the safe in my office, as you requested."

Sokalov reached for it like a parched man accepting a glass of cool water. He used a handkerchief to wipe the sweat from his forehead, despite his air-conditioned office. "Where would I be without you, Maria?"

She arched her eyebrows. "Abusing my staff, no doubt."

"This meeting has me anxious. Chairman Petrov has been particularly obtuse about its purpose. Does the file contain all of our recent operations and assets?"

"As you requested. Why are you so worried, Dmitry? You'll have Chairman Petrov's position soon enough." Petrov had announced his retirement as of the year's end.

"Lebedev is pushing hard for the position."

"Lebedev is only a stone on which you will step on your path to the Kremlin."

Sokalov smiled at the praise. His desire was to get out of Lubyanka and sit at a table at the Kremlin, and Maria had a vested interest in his reaching this pinnacle. He would insist that she come with him, giving her unprecedented access to the president, his inner circle, and their most classified secrets.

If Operation Herod did not disclose her true purpose first.

"With your help, no doubt." Sokalov stepped into her personal space so he could peer down her blouse and inhale her perfume. "Oh, if I could bottle and sell your fragrance, I would never have to work another day in my life."

"Yes. Yes. A wonderful fantasy, but now you must prepare for your meeting."

"I was hoping we could meet after work."

He kept an apartment just a few blocks from Lubyanka on Varsonof'yevskiy Pereulok where he and Kulikova could rendezvous whenever Sokalov had a good enough excuse to not immediately go home. The contents of that apartment would sicken most, a testament to Sokalov's perversions and fetishes.

Kulikova smiled thinly and lightly licked her lips. "Don't you have your father-in-law's birthday celebration this evening?"

"Bosh!" He grabbed the file and moved behind his opulent desk, sitting with a "hmpff." His leather chair groaned from the punishment. "The man has a birthday and Olga makes the world come to an end. It is worse than having another child."

"Yes, but you do not want to upset the general by upsetting his *Tsvetochek*." *Little Flower.*

"I wish for you to sit in on this meeting," he said. "I will tell the others you are taking shorthand. There is to be no recording."

No recording. Interesting. "Of course, Director. Whatever you desire," she said breathlessly.

Sokalov groaned.

2
■

The Island Café
Stanwood, Washington State

Jenkins stepped inside the Island Café in Stanwood determined to convince Matt Lemore there was just one six o'clock per day and it was not a.m. He surveyed the booths, surprised to find most already full and the café in express mode—both waitresses hurriedly delivering food and busing tables, cooks calling out orders over the cacophony of customer voices, the cash register ringing, and the clatter of forks and knives on porcelain plates.

Didn't anyone in this town sleep in?

"Coming through," Maureen shouted. The café's longtime waitress stepped around Jenkins carrying multiple plates of steaming hot food, which was what made getting up this early almost worth it. His stomach growled at the aroma of bacon, sausage, and the Island Café omelets. "You waiting for an invitation, Stretch? You don't seat yourself, you'll eat standing."

Charming as always, and Jenkins had been a regular for almost forty years. Maybe Maureen wasn't a morning person either. On the way to his booth, Jenkins gave a slight head nod to Jalen Davis, a sign of recognition between the two. He didn't know Davis well, but only a handful of African American men lived on the island.

Jenkins slid onto the cracked green vinyl of an empty booth and peeked out curtained windows at an awakening sky, orange and red draped behind gray storm clouds. It had rained something fierce the prior evening, a summer storm that no doubt had turned his horse pastures to slop. In the distance, jagged remnants of a wooden pier poked above the Stillaguamish River's muddy waters that separated Stanwood from Camano Island. The setting was picturesque, calm, and peaceful, in contrast to the bustle inside the café.

Maureen slapped a plastic menu on the table, drawing his attention. "You want coffee in that mug, or should I just pour it in your lap?"

"Mug would be less painful. Hopefully." Jenkins smiled up at her and turned his porcelain mug over on a paper doily.

"Don't be so certain. You haven't tasted it yet."

She poured. The coffee looked unusually dark. She raised her voice to be heard above the crowd and the bell pinging on the pickup counter. "Bruno thinks he knows what the customers want more than I do." Bruno was Maureen's longtime boyfriend and café cook. Most called him her spouse, but not Maureen. "I told him to take his best shot," she said. "That sludge in your mug is it."

She set the glass pot on the table and stared at Jenkins over the top of half-lens, bright-red reading glasses that nearly matched the color of her hair. For Maureen to stop moving, even for a moment, was serious. Jenkins sipped from the mug. The coffee was stronger than usual, and he detected the taste and the subtle odor of vanilla.

"Well?" she asked, hand now resting on her hip.

Jenkins made a sour face. "Bruno calls this coffee? Tastes like he scraped the mud off the floor and mixed it with water."

She nodded, vindicated, and departed. Jenkins never, ever upset the woman delivering his food.

The bells over the door rattled and chimed. Matt Lemore, Jenkins's CIA handler since his unexpected official return to the agency—and to Russia the previous winter—stepped inside the diner and wiped his boots on the floor mat as he unzipped his raincoat and surveyed the booths. Spotting Jenkins, Lemore smiled and waved like a kid greeting Santa Claus at the mall. Lemore *was* a kid. Though in his early forties, he looked ten years younger. His blond hair fell over his ears, and he frequently swept the bangs off his forehead. He removed his jacket as he neared the table, revealing an argyle sweater over a collared dress shirt. He tossed the coat on the seat before shaking Jenkins's hand, then slid into the booth across from him.

Lemore scanned the room and said, "I've been looking forward to the Countryman Special all morning."

"It's six a.m. What time do you get up?"

Lemore was on East Coast time. "Got in a five-mile run and a thirty-minute workout at the Anytime Fitness in town. They're open—"

Jenkins raised a hand. "Let me guess. Anytime?"

"You look like you shaved a few more pounds," Lemore said.

Jenkins had. With a son almost a teenager and a baby girl nearing two and already a handful, not to mention ten acres to care for, Jenkins got enough of a workout at home. He weighed 215 pounds thanks to Alex recently implementing a healthy diet of more vegetables and fruits and fewer chips and cookies. "I call it work," he said. "Gardening, feeding the horses, digging fence posts, splitting lumber. You want a workout? Come by the farm in the morning. Save you a boatload on fitness centers."

Jenkins still ran four days a week and lifted weights in his home gym. He had recently added a twice-a-week Krav Maga class—the Israel Defense Forces' attack-first training.

Lemore looked to the window. "What's with the rain in September?"

"For an intelligence officer I would have expected better research. It rains in Seattle. The month is irrelevant."

"Thought you said summers are beautiful here."

"Yes. As we like to say, 'God vacations here in the summer, but he gets out come October.'"

Maureen set down a menu and held the pot as if about to pour the coffee in Lemore's lap. Lemore quickly turned over his mug without being told to do so. He smiled up at her. "I remembered," he said.

"Well, la-di-da, Dennis the Menace. You're learning." She filled his mug.

Lemore raised it to his lips but said, "And I don't need a menu, Maureen. I've been thinking about this breakfast since I got up this morning."

"Most people do." She turned to Jenkins. "I can see now why he prefers decaf. I assume you want the special?"

"Extra gravy on the biscuits," Jenkins said.

Maureen looked to Lemore. "What have you been dreaming about, Gorgeous George?"

"Countryman Special with extra bacon." He sipped his coffee. Jenkins raised a hand. Too late. "Wow." Lemore smiled. "This coffee is fantastic. New blend?"

Maureen closed her eyes, shook her head, and departed.

"You were so close," Jenkins said.

"What did I say?" Lemore looked flummoxed.

"Next time we come to eat, you don't speak until we get our food."

Lemore set down his mug.

"I assume this isn't a social visit," Jenkins said. "The remaining sisters? Any news from Russia?"

He and Lemore had a conversation on his farm when Jenkins had returned from Russia after rescuing Paulina Ponomayova from Lefortovo Prison. Lemore had discussed exfiltrating the remaining four of the seven women who had spied on Russia for decades. The CIA operation had been named "the seven sisters" after the seven buildings Stalin commissioned following the Second World War to glorify the Soviet state. Taking a page from the KGB playbook, seven Russian women had been raised from birth to be American spies, what the KGB had referred to as "illegals"—deep-cover agents who blended in seamlessly with a target country's citizenry. Three sisters had been exposed by Carl Emerson, Jenkins's former CIA station chief turned traitor, and presumably killed. Over the prior six months, Lemore had advised Jenkins of the CIA's success in exfiltrating two of the remaining four sisters. It had not been easy. The Kremlin had authorized a secret branch within the Counterintelligence Directorate, a task force formed to find and terminate the remaining sisters.

"Operation Herod" was named for the Israeli king who, according to biblical accounts, feared the Christ child's birth and sent soldiers to kill infant Israeli males born in Bethlehem. The operation instituted a shotgun approach when the rifle could not find a target. Women sixty years of age and older working in the Russian government had been identified and were being extensively vetted. It sounded like an insurmountable task, except men still dominated most high-level Russian government positions, and even fewer women held such positions and were more than sixty years of age.

A similar task force, formed in 2008, had succeeded in identifying and assassinating prominent heads of *mafiya* families, as well as several powerful oligarchs the president considered a threat to his power.

Maureen set down plates containing heaping portions of eggs, ham, sausage, bacon, home fries, biscuits, gravy, and toast. "Anything else?"

"I think we're good," Jenkins said.

"More coffee?" Maureen asked Lemore.

Jenkins subtly shook his head.

"The coffee wasn't as good as I initially thought," Lemore said. "Leaves a bad taste in your mouth."

Maureen nodded. "I think 'bitter' is the word you're looking for." She left a check on the table and departed.

Both men dug in. "How are the two women you exfiltrated doing?"

"The NROC is helping them establish new identities and arranging new homes beyond Russia's wrath."

"NROC?"

"Sorry. National Resettlement Operations Center."

"Russia's reach is getting longer since they went after Alexei Navalny." Jenkins referred to the prominent Vladimir Putin opponent poisoned with a rare chemical agent before he boarded a flight from Siberia. Navalny had been hospitalized in Berlin, Germany, then imprisoned when he returned to Russia.

"They won't risk a poisoning on US soil," Lemore said. "There's too much at stake."

Jenkins ate a piece of ham with eggs and home fries. "I assume the two remaining sisters are the reason I'm sitting across the table from you at this god-awful early hour."

"They've recently gone silent."

"Meaning what exactly?"

"Meaning neither is responding to dead drops or phone calls."

"But still alive?"

"Still alive. We assume one sister's silence is the result of her knowledge of Operation Herod. We are uncertain about the reason for the second sister's silence. It could be she has detected some surveillance and had decided to go dormant."

The lack of specifics did not surprise Jenkins. Personal contact between a handler and a spy in Moscow was limited. The KGB, and now the FSB, intensely scrutinized Americans, especially those working at the US embassy. An experienced handler could utilize a brush pass, where the handler and spy passed one another, and the handler, using sleight of hand, provided a critical piece of information. They also utilized dead drops, a location known only to the handler and the spy where each could leave packages or messages without the two ever meeting face-to-face. To arrange these, the handler called and asked to speak to the agent, giving a wrong name that was actually code for the specific location. If the spy could meet, she would respond, "I'm sorry, you have the wrong number." If not, the spy would respond, "There is no one here by that name." Meeting locations could also be hidden in classified newspaper ads and, Jenkins assumed but did not know, through the use of computers. The spy would respond with a check mark on a certain bus stop, by opening a particular window of her apartment, closing a particular window blind, or placing flowers on a balcony.

"Is there a possibility either woman has turned?" Jenkins asked.

Lemore shoveled potatoes and eggs in his mouth. After swallowing, he said, "Can't be sure of the second sister, but the first sister is the person who provided the classified information on Operation Herod."

Jenkins, about to sip his coffee, set down his mug. "She's that highly embedded?"

"They're both that highly embedded, which is why I think they've gone silent. The second is in a position to know of Operation Herod or suspect something big is happening." Lemore shook his head. "If we lose them, it will be the greatest loss of classified information we've ever had access to in Moscow."

"Playing devil's advocate, each could be feeding us just enough information to make us think they're highly placed. Can't someone in Moscow figure out what's going on?"

"It's tricky," Lemore said. He told Jenkins of the minefield of surveillance that CIA officers and diplomats dodged in Moscow, how they couldn't leave the embassy to drive home without attracting multiple tails and satellite surveillance, not to mention some two hundred thousand facial recognition cameras throughout Moscow and a computer center programmed to match the faces of wanted individuals, of which Jenkins was one. Using a Russian asset could jeopardize that asset's exposure—and life.

"Can technology be used to reach them and find out what's going on?" Jenkins asked.

The last time they had met, Lemore told Jenkins about the implosion of the CIA's covert communications system used to converse with intelligence assets around the world. He said the implosion had been a textbook example of overreliance and naïve trust in digital security, especially in countries with cyber-savvy intelligence services, like Russia. As a result, the CIA had moved away from technology that could be hacked and had gone back to Cold War, tried-and-true spycraft methods their young officers weren't familiar with. That made Jenkins, once a boots-on-the-ground intelligence officer, of particular value.

"These women are also old-school. Both are in their sixties."

"Careful . . . ," Jenkins said, not willing to concede sixties was old.

"Because of their positions in the government, their cell phones and computers are closely monitored at work and at home. Each undergoes intense scrutiny every morning when she arrives at work, and evenings when she leaves."

They talked about the two women in greater detail, then Jenkins said, "What exactly do you need?"

"We need someone to observe both women, determine if either is under surveillance, determine what the problem is, if any, and why each has gone silent. If they're clean, we have an exfiltration plan, code named 'Red Gate.'"

"And someone over there can't exfiltrate them?"

"It gets tricky, as I said. They're old-school. They're paranoid. Because of their positions they know about the three sisters Emerson betrayed, as well as about how you got Ponomayova out of Lefortovo. They'll trust you."

Jenkins could tell by the disturbed look on Lemore's face, not to mention that he'd put down his fork, which until this point he had used as a food shovel, that there was something more bothering him. "What else?" Jenkins asked.

Lemore frowned. "According to information we received from this sister at Lubyanka, the remaining four sisters were put on a kill list signed off by the president."

"We knew that, didn't we?"

"We did."

"So . . ."

"So," Lemore said. "We've learned that you're also on that kill list. But as I said, I have a plan."

"A plan? Gives me the warm and fuzzies all over," Jenkins said.

3

■

Lubyanka
Moscow, Russia

Maria Kulikova stood off to the side as Dmitry Sokalov welcomed the three men into his office. Bogdan Petrov, National Antiterrorist Committee chairman, answered only to Vladimir Putin. Gavril Lebedev, the deputy director of Directorate S, led Russia's infamous foreign intelligence division. And General Kliment Pasternak led Zaslon, Russia's elite, highly secretive unit within Directorate S, the existence of which Russian authorities vigorously denied. Zaslon consisted of some three hundred highly trained operatives, each capable of speaking several languages without an accent, and each having extensive covert operation experience in secret units within Russia's military.

This was indeed an interesting development.

Zaslon operations included, among others, the poisoning death of Russian government critic Alexander Litvinenko six years after the former FSB officer had fled to Great Britain; the poisoning of Sergei Skripal, the former Russian military officer and double agent for the UK's intelligence services; and, more recently, the poisoning of Kremlin critic Alexei Navalny, just ahead of Russia's parliamentary elections.

Sokalov met the three men on the Persian rug beneath the tiered, crystal chandelier. Behind them the mahogany bookshelves held a collection of rare, antique books, but the officials were not interested in man-made opulence. Petrov's eyes found Kulikova, as they always did. He ogled her as a cat ogled a play toy.

"Ms. Kulikova." Petrov leered as he stepped around the maroon Chesterfield sofa to greet her. His gaze dropped to her breasts, and Kulikova leaned forward to allow him to kiss her on each cheek and to better peer down her cleavage. "Radiant as usual," Petrov said, alcohol on his breath. "To what do I owe this great pleasure?"

She didn't dare answer.

"Ms. Kulikova will take shorthand at the meeting and keep those notes in her safe," Sokalov said, stepping forward like a protective father. As if to assert his superior position, Petrov did not release Kulikova's hand.

"Out of the question." Lebedev moved his significant girth toward an end of the pressed-button couch. "The president was explicit; there is to be no recording of our meeting."

"And there shall be no recording." Sokalov adjusted the knot of his tie, a tic when nervous. "But the president will ask for an update, and I want to be certain *I* am accurate in providing one." Sokalov threw around what weight he had in this group—his long-standing relationship with the president. Otherwise, he was outranked on every level, which was why he was insistent on Kulikova keeping a record. As he liked to say, "Shit runs downhill." And Sokalov was at the bottom of this hill, holding a shovel and a pail.

"I do not feel comfortable with this arrangement," Lebedev whined. He shifted his girth to turn toward Petrov, who had not removed his gaze from Kulikova. She wondered if the old man expected her to just bend over the end of Sokalov's Louis XV desk and let him take her.

"Ms. Kulikova has worked for me for more than thirty years. Certainly you are not questioning her loyalties," Sokalov said.

"I am well aware of your *professional* relationship with Ms. Kulikova," Lebedev responded. He let his comment linger a moment.

Then he said, "I am only seeking to follow the president's instructions that there be no record."

Lebedev and Sokalov had one thing in common. Each sought the chairman's position and a seat within the Kremlin.

General Pasternak, a no-nonsense military man, waded into the turbulent waters. "Perhaps a compromise to move this meeting forward?" He looked to Petrov, who dropped Kulikova's hand, though not his gaze. She held it as long as she dared, not wanting to upset Sokalov, but also not wanting to offend Petrov. "Perhaps Ms. Kulikova can take notes, but her notes will be kept in the chairman's possession." Pasternak referred to Petrov.

"Ah, I understand your concern," Sokalov said, not willing to concede so easily. "A very good suggestion, but I don't believe the chairman wishes to be burdened with the obligation. I would propose, as an alternative, that Ms. Kulikova's notes be placed in my safe, and kept here in my office for safekeeping . . . were something to happen."

"Nothing will happen." Pasternak bristled.

Sokalov smiled, but he was not playing to the stand-in at this theatrical performance; he was playing to Chairman Petrov. "One can ride a train a hundred times without a problem, but the hundred-and-first ride and that train derails, without fault of the conductor, of course. All I am suggesting, a hypothesis if you will, is that *were* something to go wrong—and I cast no aspersions toward you or your unit, I can assure you—I am close to the president. He will listen to me when I tell him this meeting was held in the utmost secrecy."

Petrov sat on the opposite end of the couch from Lebedev. "I for one find Ms. Kulikova to be an aesthetically pleasing diversion from the horse faces I must otherwise endure at these meetings, my own included."

They all dutifully chuckled.

"Ms. Kulikova will note the proceedings. Dmitry will keep her notes in his safe here in his office. Now, let us move forward."

End of discussion, thought Kulikova, keeping her expression blank. As the other men found their seats, she moved to a chair Sokalov had placed to the side of his desk. Sokalov sat in one of two leather chairs; to sit behind his desk would be considered rude to his superiors in the room. Kulikova picked up her spiral notebook and flipped open the cover, noting the date and meeting participants.

She crossed her legs, which garnered the attention of everyone but Lebedev. At the same time, she reached a hand to her right breast and adjusted her bra strap, a move that also did not go unnoticed.

Petrov cleared his throat. "Ibragimov."

Petrov spoke of Fyodor Ibragimov, once a Kremlin insider on the periphery of the president's inner circle and a CIA spy. Ibragimov had been exfiltrated to America by the CIA after the US president revealed classified information that could have exposed Ibragimov. He had been America's highest known Russian asset and had provided classified information on Kremlin operations, including the Russian president's interference in America's presidential election.

Putin had been incensed not only at Ibragimov's betrayal, but that Ibragimov, his wife, and their two children had escaped to the United States. Heads had rolled inside the Kremlin, an extermination that officials privately likened to the purgings by Ivan the Terrible.

"The president believes sufficient time has now passed to take action. To not do so sends the wrong message to those who would betray Russia," Petrov said.

Kulikova kept her head down but ears perked. The president had a long-standing policy to rough up Americans in Moscow suspected of spying, and to seek retribution against Russian citizens who betrayed their country. He wanted traitors to know that his patience was as long as his reach.

"Ibragimov is in the United States," Sokalov said.

"Yes, a beautiful white house in Virginia with a picket fence and a garden," Petrov said with a spiteful tone. "It's all very lovely and not far from Langley. Ibragimov has refused CIA offers to go into hiding or to provide security. He believes he is more valuable as a symbol against Russian tyranny, an example that a traitor can find safety in the United States."

General Pasternak leaned forward. "He is thumbing his nose at all of us, daring us to do something."

"With all due respect, Chairman Petrov," Sokalov said, "it is certainly unfortunate that we missed an opportunity here, but—"

"No buts," Petrov said calmly but firmly. "I agree with the general. The longer Ibragimov goes unpunished, the more he becomes a symbol that betrayal and treason can be richly rewarded. There may already be others. His brazenness will only encourage them."

"What is it then that the president is proposing?" Sokalov asked.

"The president?" Petrov scoffed. His dark eyes pierced each of them. "The president proposes *nothing*, Dmitry. He knows nothing of this."

"Of course. My apologies," Sokalov said.

"He wishes only that we understand the depth of his concern, so that we can take whatever action *we* deem appropriate to discourage future acts of treason."

Kulikova's heart pounded in anticipation of what Petrov was about to propose.

"Does Ibragimov travel?" General Pasternak asked.

"Under the circumstances that would seem unlikely," Petrov said. "Wouldn't it?"

"Yes, of course."

"He has relatives here in Russia. We have—" Lebedev began.

Petrov cut him off with a wave of his hand. "Those relatives have been vetted and have conclusively demonstrated they knew nothing of Ibragimov's treason," Petrov said.

Meaning the relatives had been tortured and threatened until their interrogators were certain of their innocence. The thought made

Kulikova sick. She felt the air being sucked from the room by what was being proposed but left unsaid.

"This would be unprecedented," Lebedev said, speaking with a tone of doubt.

"Everything is unprecedented until it is accomplished," Petrov said.

"Yes, but United States intelligence has heightened its security since Skripal and Navalny," Lebedev said. "Sanctions have been increased."

"The sanctions have been nominal and will remain such, a placebo to appease the American population."

"Yes. But an assassination on American soil would force the American president's hand," Sokalov said. "Would it not? Given the recent history of poisonings, plausible deniability would be impossible."

"That is the point, isn't it?" Petrov said, and in so doing he confirmed the president approved the poisonings but did not want evidence that tied those poisonings to him. "Our actions will need to be well targeted to limit any collateral damage. Americans may express outrage, but that outrage will be tempered if the victim is only another Russian. A spy no less. Americans will consider it unfortunate but reason Ibragimov knew this to be a possibility when he betrayed his country."

"How do we limit collateral damage?" Sokalov asked. "With a radioactive agent we have little ability to limit who might come in contact with either the agent or the container in which it is delivered. Killing a Russian spy is one thing. Killing innocent Americans on American soil is quite another."

"Maybe not," Pasternak said.

The others looked at him as if he had misspoken. The general had the annoying habit of pausing between thoughts. *Was it for dramatic effect?* Kulikova had wondered. *Or did the general speak too quickly, then need the time to contemplate what he had said?*

The general shook his head. "Ibragimov's belief that he and his family are beyond punishment in America is also his biggest weakness."

They all nodded.

"As the chairman states, he has refused protection because he does not want his children to live as prisoners. I also agree with the deputy director that the use of a poisonous agent—a trademark now linked to Russia—will make plausible deniability impossible and could result in collateral damage."

"What is it then that you would have us do?" Petrov asked.

"What if we were to take a different tack, one that would ensure no collateral damage?"

"You have something in mind?" Petrov asked.

"One well-placed bullet."

At first no one spoke, all awaiting Petrov's comment. When he remained silent, Sokalov waded in first. "This is a dangerous game to play—sending Russian assassins to shoot someone on American soil would be . . ." Sokalov shook his head. "The Americans would immediately put their border guards on alert. If they located the assassins and identified them to be Russian, the end result would be the same. No plausible deniability. American public outrage would demand severe economic sanctions, and the Americans would influence their allies to do the same."

Pasternak shrugged. "Not if Ibragimov was the victim of an accident, or perhaps the criminal element so prevalent in the United States. A robbery perhaps."

"The danger remains—*if* the assassin were caught," Petrov said. "Unlike a toxin, which can take hours before symptoms occur, the bullet leaves little time for those responsible to slip away. Our intelligence advises that Ibragimov's movements are limited throughout the day. His wife rarely leaves the house except to take the children to and from school fifteen minutes from their home."

"What if the assassins had more time to slip away?" Pasternak said.

"How?" Petrov asked, clearly intrigued by the general's thinking.

"I am not yet certain, but something common—perhaps a traffic accident on the wife's return home from taking the children to school."

Sokalov looked at Pasternak as if he'd lost his mind. "A traffic accident? We are trying to eliminate any ties to a Russian agent, not hand one over."

"Not a Russian. I'm proposing we do to the Americans what the Americans have been doing to us with their seven sisters."

Kulikova fought not to react or show any indication she knew that code name. For years she had thought she was the only sister, until Sokalov advised that a CIA officer turned spy talked of seven sisters, three of whom the officer had betrayed and who had been tortured and killed.

"We activate an illegal living nearby and prepare a plausible reason for her to be in the area. She runs a stop sign at a designated moment and hits Ibragimov's wife's vehicle. They must stop to exchange information. A police officer is called to file a report. Perhaps an ambulance is needed to treat Ibragimov's wife's injuries and she is taken to the hospital. Time. It would give my men time to kill Ibragimov, slip across the Canadian border, and make their way home."

Pasternak's suggestion had legs, but no one would agree until it had the chairman's blessing. Petrov turned his attention to Pasternak. "I would like you to explore this further. Provide me with a detailed analysis I can take to the Kremlin." He shifted to Sokalov. "I think this calls for a drink."

They all stood. Sokalov moved to the liquor cabinet on the credenza.

Kulikova felt sick to her stomach but recognized an opportunity to do more damage to the administration. She moved toward the interior door leading back to her office.

"Ms. Kulikova," Lebedev said.

She turned and faced him. "Yes, Deputy Director?"

"Leave the notes, please." He glanced down at the notepad in her hand.

"Of course, Deputy Director." She set the notes and her pen on the edge of Sokalov's desk.

"Ms. Kulikova," he said. "I'm wondering if I might ask your age?"

Sokalov bristled. "One does not ask a woman her age."

"I only marvel that a woman—over sixty, I believe—remains in such good physical condition. You are older than sixty, are you not? Or have I offended you?"

"No offense, Deputy Director. Yes. I am over sixty."

Lebedev gave Sokalov a knowing look.

Kulikova stepped from the office and closed the interior door behind her. In her office she struggled to catch her breath. She felt the air conditioner's cool air on her damp forehead. She cursed Lebedev, the fat pig. "'Leave the notes'?" She smiled. "Gladly." And she reached for her bra to turn off the recorder.

The guards at the metal detectors no longer even bothered to question her when she set off the sensors, which she had dutifully done for years, until it became a common occurrence the guards expected. They believed a metal wire, sewn into Kulikova's bra to provide the support necessary for a woman blessed with her cleavage, set off their detectors. They never suspected she had sewn a voice-activated, wireless tape recorder, no larger than a paper clip, into her bra.

The game she had played for some forty years continued to become more dangerous. With the Operation Herod task force searching for sisters, Maria had gone into hibernation, neither responding to nor sending signals of a desire to meet her handler. Now she had no choice. She had to get this recording to her handler. This wasn't just about saving Ibragimov, though she felt for his wife and his two small children, it was for all those other Russians who detested the current authoritarian regime. If the regime succeeded in killing Ibragimov, it would scare others into silence, and Russia would slip further back to the dark age of authoritarianism.

She could no longer remain silent, though coming out could be a death sentence.

4
■

Jenkins sat at the head of the kitchen table enjoying his family, even if it was a bit like watching the food fight scene from the movie *Animal House*. Lizzie, currently their holy terror going through the terrible twos a few months early, alternately slapped at the macaroni on her tray, or picked it up with chubby fingers and flung it to the floor, where the dog, Max, dutifully cleaned it like a vacuum.

On the table Jenkins noted just a few stray noodles in the pan of baked macaroni. The bowls of corn and cherry tomatoes and cucumbers were empty. The chocolate cake for dessert was also now just a wedge. He'd first noticed how much CJ's appetite had increased when they went to their favorite New York pizza joint in Stanwood. They had always ordered the family special—a large pepperoni pizza and Caesar salad—and had invariably taken home a few slices of pizza and leftover salad. Not any longer. Their last visit Jenkins counted four pieces of crust on CJ's plate.

"Mom, can I have a cell phone?" CJ asked the question as he wiped his mouth with a paper napkin, crumpled it, and put it on his freshly cleaned plate.

"A cell phone?" Jenkins said.

Alex gave Jenkins the "look" and kicked him under the table. Then she asked CJ, "Why do you want a cell phone?"

"A lot of kids in my class have them," CJ said.

"What do your friends use their cell phones for?" Alex asked.

"Most just text. But they can also call home," he rushed to add before Jenkins had the chance to respond, an indication CJ had rehearsed this seemingly spontaneous speech. "Like Anna Potts got sick the other day at recess and called her mother. And I could call you if, like, Dad forgot to pick me up from soccer again."

"I didn't forget," Jenkins said. "I lost track of time."

"That's a responsible answer," Alex said to CJ. "But I would not want you to be on your phone playing video games or texting your friends when we're having family time, or when you should be doing homework. Perhaps we could make a deal that you could use the phone for emergencies and have a one-hour privilege to use it at home. Is that an agreement you could live with?"

"Sure." CJ smiled—a clear indication the boy had expected to be shot down, which Jenkins would have done if his wife had allowed him to speak. Jenkins was anti-technology. He thought cell phones turned anyone under eighteen into zombies. Kids no longer knew how to interact or to play. Not to mention cyberbullying.

"Why don't you let your dad and me talk about it after dinner? We'll make a decision together. If you're finished eating, you can clear your plate and get started on your homework."

CJ carried his plate, glass, and silverware to the sink, then went to the family room, where they kept the computer.

"Why'd you kick me?" Jenkins rose from his chair and gathered dirty dishes. He called out to the Alexa on the kitchen counter and asked for country music to keep CJ from eavesdropping on their conversation. Keith Urban's voice filled the kitchen.

"Because he's growing up," Alex said, keeping her volume soft. "He wants to talk with us, not be talked to. He asked in a reasonable way, and we can respond just as reasonably, and maybe get something out of it."

"You mean a reasonable way to say no."

"I would feel better connected if he had a phone with him. You did forget to pick him up that one afternoon."

"You show up late one time, and the jury here gives you the death penalty." Jenkins wasn't ready yet to have a teenager. It only made him feel older than he was, but there was no stunting CJ's age or his growth. With a mother five foot ten and a father six foot five, he was the tallest in his class and 115 pounds. His feet outgrew shoes before he wore holes in the soles. His voice cracked now and then, and he'd experienced his first pimples. Jenkins knew the difficulties the boy would soon face, if he had not already, being dark skinned in an almost all-white community. Jenkins had dealt with them himself when he arrived on Camano. People were guarded upon meeting him, some more than guarded. CJ would be perceived as an outsider and a threat. It would not be an easy talk for CJ to hear, but it was one that had to happen, as well as the talk every man needed to have with a son going through puberty. When CJ jumped in the car after soccer practice, Jenkins had to lower the window to air out the body odor. At home one evening, Jenkins had asked Alex what they should do.

"Don't include me in this. The birds and the bees talk is your responsibility."

Deciding there was strength in numbers, Jenkins found a sex education class through the local hospital. Afterward, he took CJ to a 1950s drive-up hamburger joint, figuring his son might have questions he didn't want to ask in front of his peers.

"I was just wondering how long it took. You know, the intercourse part."

Jenkins struggled with an appropriate answer. He finally talked with CJ about respect for the woman and concluded that the act lasted perhaps ten to twenty minutes.

CJ looked relieved. "Thank God," he said. "I thought it took like a week. I was wondering how the people got the chance to eat."

Jenkins nearly snorted strawberry shake through his nose. Upon their return home he told Alex, "We keep buying him pepperoni pizzas and I think we'll have a few years before we have to worry about sex."

"Charlie?" Alex stood at the kitchen sink giving him a funny look. "Huh?"

"I asked if you wanted cleanup duty or Lizzie duty."

He looked at Lizzie, who sat in her high chair covered in macaroni and cheese. Someday he'd wonder when *she* had grown up. "I think you mean cleanup duty or cleanup duty. I'll give Lizzie a bath."

"No bath," Lizzie said. "Cookie."

"Cookie?" Jenkins reached to tickle her belly sticking out from her stained undershirt. "You already have a Buddha belly. You want a bigger Buddha belly?"

Lizzie frowned and pounded the tray with her sippy cup. "No bath. Cookie."

"I think she's going to be a judge, the way she swings that cup like a gavel," Jenkins said to Alex. He removed Lizzie from the chair, holding her at arm's length. Pieces of macaroni fell to the floor, where Max, their aging pit bull, awaited and eagerly gobbled them up.

Jenkins flipped Lizzie onto her stomach and flew her from the room, making airplane noises. Once he put the bubbles in the bathtub, Lizzie's protest ended. She splashed and kicked, then didn't want to get out. He wrapped her in a large white bath towel, put her in a nighttime diaper and pajamas, read her three picture books, and lowered her into her crib with a bottle of water.

"Good night, baby girl," he said.

"Buddha." Lizzie laughed.

Jenkins tickled her stomach. "Buddha belly. Buddha belly."

He shut the door and went downstairs. CJ wore headphones while he worked at the computer in the family room. Jenkins caught Alex's attention and motioned to the sliding door to the porch. "I'm going to check the horse pastures. Got a fence down. Care to join me?"

"CJ?" Alex tapped their son on the shoulder to get his attention. CJ removed one of the earphones. "Dad and I are going for a walk. We'll only be gone a few minutes."

"You know, this is another reason for me to have a cell phone. It would be easier to keep track of you both."

The boy was laying it on thick. Maybe he would be a plaintiff's lawyer—or a politician.

Alex and Charlie walked the pastures and discussed CJ getting a phone, ultimately concluding they could do it on a trial basis and see how responsibly the boy behaved. A few more minutes passed in silence, both of them enjoying the evening. Summers, it remained light in the Pacific Northwest until late, but darkness began to fall earlier as September progressed, and Jenkins felt the chill of fall fast approaching. A breeze rattled the maple trees' leaves and caused the pines to shimmer, and the rain the prior night had softened the ground. Jenkins filled Alex in on his talk with Lemore while he fixed the pasture fence a horse had knocked down.

"Could their silence be related to the FSB operation to find them?" Alex asked.

"I would guess that's the reason," he said. "At least for the one at Lubyanka who revealed it. Not yet sure about the second sister."

"Anybody thought that maybe these women don't want to leave their country after sixty years?"

"Me," Jenkins said. "It's a weighty decision, especially if their positions have accorded them some luxury. Then again, if they're that high up, they know what happens to traitors. The other possibility is they turned, maybe years ago."

"How would you make contact without drawing attention? We've been over this. Russia's population is less than one percent Black; you don't exactly blend in here, much less in Moscow."

"Lemore has a plan and said the CIA is already at work on a number of disguises and passports, and I'd receive further training at Langley."

Alex didn't speak.

"I know you're worried," he said. "But Moscow is an enormous city—"

"With facial recognition cameras everywhere."

"I'll be in disguise twenty-four seven. I determine their situations and get them out, or I get out."

"Anything else I should know?"

Jenkins thought of Lemore's comment that Jenkins had been placed on a kill list. It wasn't new information; they had suspected that to be the case, but the confirmation was sobering. Still, Jenkins didn't intend to get caught. "That's it," he said.

"If either of these women has turned—and don't insult my intelligence and tell me Lemore can guarantee they haven't—one of them might be providing confidential information to lure you back to Moscow."

"I'll have the element of surprise."

"How do you figure?"

"Not even the Russians would think I was stupid enough to return a third time."

She shook her head. "Don't joke. This isn't funny."

They walked in silence, then Jenkins said, "We did talk about this. These women gave their lives. They helped us win the Cold War, and they've kept eyes on Putin. Three have already died because of Carl Emerson. I'd like to finish what I started and get the remaining two out. There are risks, but this time we can control the risks."

"Can we?"

"Anything gets squirrelly, I'll get out."

"I know you, Charlie; if you see an injustice, a wrong, you won't be able to keep your nose out of it."

"I can still take care of myself, Alex."

His comment stopped Alex dead in her tracks. "What does that mean? I hope this isn't something you're doing to prove you still can—some validation that your age is just a number."

"That's not what I meant," Jenkins said, but there was some truth to her comment. "I just meant Lemore has resources to help me."

He knew she suspected he wasn't telling her everything, that he was holding back information so she wouldn't worry. But he also couldn't deny that when he'd gone back into Russia to get Paulina Ponomayova out, he'd felt an adrenaline rush, the high that came with outsmarting people trying to outsmart him. The feeling had been intoxicating forty years ago in Mexico City, and even more so in Moscow, the darkest corner of the espionage world.

"Just remember one thing," Alex said.

"What's that?"

"Not everyone has your sense of duty and justice. Don't give yourself up thinking someone will repay the favor. Most people choose to save their own skin, even if you've given yours for them."

"I know," he said.

"You have responsibilities here at home to think about."

"I don't plan to get caught, Alex."

"No one ever does, Charlie."

Alex was quiet the rest of the evening, and Jenkins could tell she was upset. He let her be. She usually worked things out. This would take time. She sent CJ up to bed, and the boy was on his best behavior. Then she disappeared. Jenkins watched television alone, then turned it off and went upstairs. Before going to the bedroom, he went to Lizzie's room. He heard Alex rocking in the rocking chair beside their daughter's crib, the same chair she had used to rock CJ to sleep as an infant. In the glow from the lamp on Lizzie's nightstand, Jenkins could see tears lining his wife's cheeks.

5

■

Yakimanka District
Moscow, Russia

Maria Kulikova purchased the first bundle of fresh-cut flowers she saw at her customary street vendor, not bothering with the particulars or the price, then jumped on the Moscow Metro for the fifteen-minute commute to her home in the Yakimanka District—Old Muscovy. Her district was well known for Gorky Park, the Tretyakov Gallery, and its many churches, including the Cathedral of Christ the Saviour—the golden domes of which she could view from her bedroom windows. Being this close to Lubyanka was both good and bad. Good, because she hated commuting. Bad, because Sokalov mandated she be at his beck and call at all hours of the day and night.

Exiting the Kropotkinskaya station, she emerged aboveground on Volkhonka Street directly across from Christ the Saviour. She paused at the bus stop on the busy street as if to admire the cathedral's gold onion domes glistening in the fading dusk light. She took out her lipstick and her compact and used the mirror to check behind her and to each side, searching for anyone watching her or who looked purposefully disinterested. She used the lipstick to draw a check mark on the glass shelter of the bus stop, then pocketed both lipstick and compact, and crossed the street. She walked until she reached the Prechistenskaya embankment, which ran parallel to the Moskva River.

She crossed triangles of lawn and trees dissected by paved cobblestone walking paths lined by antique streetlamps, not yet lit. Muscovites lazed on blankets reading and enjoying picnics. Anything to stay out of an apartment baked all day by the unseasonably warm September weather. Fathers chased after young children, and shirtless men kicked a ball. It reminded Maria of the years when she and Helge used to picnic outside their small apartment. Helge would challenge young boys to a football match, not revealing that he played professionally in Russia's Premier League.

But a sad recollection accompanied each fond memory. She recalled the evening she told Helge she could not bear children. A lie, like so many others that so easily slid from her tongue. She had been taught to lie, without guilt or regret, to serve a higher cause. She could bear children. She was not willing. It would not be fair to the child. The decision had pained her, but she did not choose this life. Her parents had chosen it for her. Maria also never knew when she might have to flee, without leaving even a note to those she loved. She could not do that to children.

Her parents, both now deceased, had warned there would be sacrifices to defeat a communist regime, and now an authoritarian one. Kulikova never realized those sacrifices would compromise her to the very core.

In the marble lobby Maria greeted the doorman, and they exchanged pleasantries while she waited for the elevator. She rode the car to the twelfth floor. Their apartment was at the end of the hall, a two-bedroom, two-bath, nearly one-thousand-square-foot residence with a kitchen, dining area, and separate living room. The deadbolt was not engaged, meaning Helge was home. Where else would he be? Since his retirement he rarely, if ever, left the apartment. He stayed inside, drinking vodka, which would make her efforts to get away long enough to place the tape at a dead drop more problematic.

From behind the door Stanislav barked, and his nails clicked excitedly on the hardwood floor. She pushed open the door speaking to the small white ball of fur.

"Da, ya tozhe rada tebya videt'. Day mne snyat' pal'to. Seychas." Yes. Yes. I'm happy to see you also. Let me take my coat off. One moment.

Kulikova set her flowers down on the bench seat just inside the door, removed her lightweight summer coat and scarf, and hung them on a coatrack hook. She bent and picked up Stanislav, his body twitching and shaking as he licked her chin and provided unconditional love.

"Ty segodnya ne vykhodil? Poetomu u tebya stol'ko energii?" Did you not get out today? Is that why you have so much energy?

She had bought the Franzuskaya Bolonka from a breeder for Helge's retirement. She had hoped the little dog would provide him companionship and give him a reason to leave the apartment. Helge needed exercise as much as the dog. His body had deteriorated, but if she pointed out his need for exercise he bristled and returned the criticism. "Who do I have to look good for?"

She stepped into their living room. The arched, floor-to-ceiling windows provided a gorgeous view of the fading light reflecting off the domes of the surrounding churches and sparkling on the gray waters of the Moskva River. Helge sat, as always, in his white-cushioned chair facing the television, another football match. Within his reach on the side table stood a tall glass of vodka. Most nights he passed out in the chair and Maria helped him to bed.

Helge could never move beyond his unsuccessful attempt to make the Olympic football team, a failure that had quashed his spirit. Maria had helped him secure a job with the City of Moscow's parks department so he had something to do. He remained employed for thirty-five years, rejecting one promotion after another because the job would entail longer hours and greater responsibility. He used to come home from work and drink vodka and watch football.

"*Ty segodnya Stanislava ne vyvodil?*" *Did you not get Stanislav out today?* She smelled urine and found a puddle in the corner.

"*U menya net vremeni gulyat's etoy proklyatoy tselymi dnyami.*" *I don't have time to be taking the damn dog for a walk all day.*

"If you don't get him out, he piddles on the wood."

"You bought him. You clean up after him." He picked up his glass, taking a long drink.

She set Stanislav down and stepped to the back of Helge's chair, placing a hand on his shoulder. "I bought him for you, Helge. To keep you company in your retirement."

Helge ignored the hand. "Yes. At least the dog is home once in a while."

She sighed and went to the kitchen to grab paper towels, then opened a cabinet and removed a glass vase. She filled the vase with tap water. "You know my job requires long hours, Helge. It is a sacrifice for both of us, but it provides us this apartment, and other things."

"I am fully aware that you secured the apartment, as well as the *other things*." He threw a glance in her direction, which she ignored.

She arranged the flowers in the vase. In the living room she pulled open a balcony door to place the flowers on the small table there. Like the check mark on the bus stop, the flowers signified her desire to meet her handler.

When she turned, Helge watched her. "You have not bought flowers in months. What is the occasion? Or were those bought for you?"

She stepped past him, knelt, and cleaned up Stanislav's urine. "I felt like flowers to cheer me up."

"Are you depressed? Welcome to the club."

She fought the urge to fight. "I was hoping we could have a nice evening." She wasn't. She had hoped to find him passed out in his chair, so she could slip away. His failure to take Stanislav on a walk, however, had solved that dilemma for her.

"A nice evening . . . I don't recall one. Did we once share nice evenings?"

"Never mind," she said. "Watch your football. I will take Stanislav for his walk."

She went into the kitchen and deposited the paper towels in the garbage, which overflowed. She pulled out the liner and tied the top in a knot. As she did, she heard the phone ring in the living room. This would be in response to the check mark, the flowers, or both. She stepped into the living room but not quickly enough. Helge had moved to answer the call, smiling at her as he did. She turned back toward the kitchen but listened intently.

"Allo." Silence before Helge spoke. *"Nyet. Zdes' takih net. Vy oshiblis' nomerom."* No. There is no one here by that name. You have the wrong number.

Maria tried to appear disinterested and busy.

"Da." She heard Helge hang up the phone.

"A wrong number again?" she said. "I will speak to the phone company. Perhaps our line is crossed with someone else's, or we have their telephone number."

"Perhaps." Helge leaned against the wall leading from the dining room to the kitchen. "Except he never asks for the same person."

"Who did he ask for this time?"

"Anna."

"Anna?"

"Last time it was Tatiana. The time before that it was Sasha."

"Odd," she said.

"Yes," he said. "Odd."

"I'm going to take out the garbage and take Stanislav for a walk. Do you want to come with me?" She hoped the lure of his vodka and football would dissuade him.

"No. I do not."

"Do you want me to stop at Teremok and pick you up anything to eat?"

"I have eaten."

"I won't be long."

"Take your time," he said. "It's not like you're here even when you're home."

Again she sighed. "What would you have me do, Helge? Quit my job? What would we do for money? How would we live? Drink your vodka. Watch your football. I will take care of Stanislav."

Helge raised his glass of vodka as if to salute her. *"Priyatnoy progulki."*

She shook her head and left the room. At the front door she put back on her jacket, grabbed the leash, and clipped it to Stanislav's collar. The little dog was giddy with joy, shaking so violently Kulikova had trouble snapping the leash to the metal ring. *"Idi syuda, malen'kiy. My s toboy kak sleduet pogulyaem." Come. Come, little one. We will take a good long walk.*

—

Helge heard the front door to the apartment latch closed and hurried to the kitchen, dumping the remains of his glass of water down the sink. He removed the bottle of vodka from the cabinet and poured a small amount in the glass, swirling it, then hurried to the living room and again set the glass on the side table. He opened the window to the small balcony and looked over the side. Maria exited the building beneath the two light sconces and turned east, Stanislav leading the way.

Helge rushed to the hallway and pulled open the closet, removing the plastic shopping bag with the jacket and driver's cap he had purchased earlier that day at a charity shop. He slipped them on as he hurried out the door to the elevator.

When the doors opened on the ground floor, he strode across the lobby, acknowledging the doorman's greetings. *"Dobryy vecher, Helge. Smotreli segodnyashniy match?"* the doorman said. *Good evening, Helge. Did you see that game today?*

"Spartak played like crap," Helge said. "I won't be gone long. Just to get a pack of Marlboro Gold."

"Your wife just left."

"Yes, I know. She needs to walk the dog."

He turned in the same direction as Maria. Despite the fading daylight, Helge spotted his wife across the sidewalk, waiting while Stanislav took care of his business. He pulled the cap low on his brow and stuffed his hands in the jacket pockets as he surveyed two men at a chessboard.

When Maria continued walking, Helge crossed the street.

Maria turned on Akademika Petrovskogo Street, rather than take Stanislav through the park. Odd. She walked toward the Shabolovskaya Metro station and descended the stairs. Very odd, but also promising. Perhaps a visit to see her lover? He quickened his pace so as not to lose her in the Metro. He had suspected for some time that Maria had a lover. Since his retirement he was certain of it. The wrong numbers had been far too frequent to be coincidence, as had been the many late nights Maria worked. Acquaintances had also confided to him that they had seen Maria out at night, going into restaurants and hotels, which caused him to search the apartment and find the expensive jewelry stuffed at the back of her dresser drawer. Helge certainly had not purchased it for her. A good friend whose father had worked for the KGB told Helge the FSB would not be happy to learn Maria was having an affair, given her position as Secretariat director. They would want to know her lover's identity so they could vet the man and be certain Maria had not told him things she should keep to herself. His friend said if Helge played his cards correctly, turning in his wife before she made a critical mistake, there might even be a little something in it for him.

He descended the escalator, weaving between those people standing still. He located Maria on a platform just as the train arrived. She looked over her shoulder before she entered the car. Helge ducked his head and stepped onto a different car. He picked up a newspaper from an unused seat and moved to the sliding doors between the cars. He did not see Maria in the adjacent car. He slid open the doors and stepped past the seated and standing commuters, moving to the far end. Again, he peered through the doors between the cars. Though there was plenty of seating, Maria stood holding a hand strap, Stanislav sitting at her feet. Helge lifted the newspaper but watched her reflection in the Metro car window.

Maria exited at the Tyoply Stan station near the Yasenevo District. Helge lowered his head and hunched his shoulders, trying to melt in with the exiting commuters. Maria entered a store inside the station. Helge moved behind a shoe stand in the vaulted terminal as Maria spun a postcard rack. She appeared to be looking beyond it. Could she suspect that he had followed her? It seemed unlikely. She expected to find him passed out in front of the television.

She stepped to the counter, purchasing several items, then exited the store, the little white dog trotting along beside her. She walked along Novoyasenevskiy Prospekt. Light faded, night becoming more prominent. As there were fewer people on the sidewalk and fewer cars, he decided to pull back. He stopped at a bus stop and watched Maria cross the street, again looking over her shoulder.

She walked into a Teremok. Had she come all this way just to buy food? Helge did not know for certain, but it seemed there had to be a Teremok closer to their apartment.

Fifteen minutes later Maria exited the restaurant carrying a bag of food, but she did not walk toward the Metro. She turned into a parking lot with a single-story, white-brick building with two spires, a cross atop each spire. Helge was unfamiliar with this church, or its significance, if any, to Maria. He expected his wife to remain outside the building, perhaps for a designated rendezvous, but Maria surprised him again when she pulled open the green door and stepped inside.

Helge crossed the street to the church and settled outside a stained-glass window. Beyond a pane of red glass, his wife knelt before an icon—a woman holding a cross in one hand and a small bottle in the other. Helge stepped back to read the sign bolted to the building. Temple Martyr Anastasia. He did not know this martyr or her significance to Maria.

Maria remained kneeling, and Helge began to doubt she intended to meet a lover. Did she suspect Helge knew or had she seen him, making this visit to a temple an attempt to throw him off? After several minutes, the only other couple inside crossed themselves repeatedly, then departed, paying him no notice. When Helge looked back through the window Maria was no longer at the kneeler. He didn't immediately see her, but he saw Stanislav at the end of his leash staring up at someone behind the statue. Maria.

After a few seconds, Maria came out from behind the statue and moved without hesitation to the front door. Helge stepped from the wall to the opposite end of the temple. Maria quickly exited and crossed to the street. She stopped and looked back. Helge shrunk into the shadows and waited until his wife walked toward the Metro station.

Such odd behavior.

About to leave, Helge noticed the headlights of an approaching car. It parked beside the church and a man stepped out and walked to the church door. Was this Maria's lover? Had he missed their rendezvous? Did Maria have second thoughts? Or was this an innocent penitent? Helge stepped back to the window. The man gazed up at the same icon, crossed himself, then walked behind it. Moments later, the man reappeared, exited the temple, and departed in his car.

Uncertain what he had witnessed, Helge went inside the temple. He didn't have much time. He needed to catch a taxi and get home before Maria, or at least buy cigarettes to have an excuse for having left the apartment. Dozens of candles burned and flickered, emitting small spires of black smoke and the odor of melting wax. A click behind him caused him to turn, but it was only the door shutting. He caught his breath and walked to the icon, looking at the pedestal, then moving behind it.

"You there! What are you doing?"

A security guard in a blue uniform had entered the temple and stood inside the door staring at him.

"Nothing. I . . . I dropped my phone and was having trouble locating it."

The man gave him a disbelieving look, but since he had no real authority, he didn't inquire further. "The temple is closed now. You must leave. I am locking the door."

Helge held up his phone. "Good thing I found my phone then."

"Yes. Good thing," the man said.

Helge stepped past him and hurried outside in search of a cab.

6

Sheremetyevo Airport
Moscow, Russia

Two weeks after Jenkins had first entered Langley, he pushed and shoved against a horde making their way to the border guard seated behind the glass partition at Sheremetyevo Airport, the busiest of Moscow's three main airports.

Jenkins had spent those two weeks at CIA headquarters getting cross-trained in a variety of disciplines including how to use audio devices, detect camera and listening equipment, and how to communicate using a personal hot spot and an encrypted chat room to which only he and Matt Lemore would have access. He memorized the information on multiple passports and other documentation that identified him as anything from a white British businessman to an elderly babushka, what Langley's disguise division called "counterfeit people."

The division measured him in the same way a fine tailor measured a client—inseam, neck, sleeve length, waist, and chest. They photographed him from every angle, the lens capturing 360-degree images. They measured his shoe size, hat size, and hand size. They took hair samples and made wig patterns ranging from a bald man to a man with a full head of hair. He learned how to apply elaborate masks to disguise his face in under a minute, and how to go from a businessman carrying a briefcase to a grandmother pushing a shopping cart in just forty-six steps. He learned from the CIA's best that a disguise was not just a mask or applying makeup, but about creating illusions and deceptions so a witness would swear Jenkins had not been a six-foot-five Black man, but a five-foot-ten Asian man, for example.

At the airport it took Jenkins more than an hour to reach the border guard window and present his passport. The besieged guard held up the passport to better compare the photograph with the man standing on the other side of the glass. The young guard looked bored and indifferent as he scanned the booklet beneath an ultraviolet light. The code provided by the CIA would generate a number of visits to various destinations around the world, including Russia.

"And what is the purpose of your visit to the Russian Federation?" the guard asked, speaking monotone English.

The Border Guard Service was a department within the FSB. If Jenkins's papers or his disguise failed to conceal his identity, it would be a short drive to the front gates of Lefortovo Prison. Having been there once, he had no interest in returning.

"Business," Jenkins said in a British accent.

"What type of business?"

"Textiles. My company supplies the raw material used to manufacture uniforms, much like the one you are wearing. I'm here to visit manufacturers of machinery used in that process."

"You manufactured this uniform?" The young man held out the lapel of his military-green jacket and looked and sounded less than impressed.

Jenkins smiled. "Not the uniform. We provide the material to make the product—the cotton, wool, synthetic fibers."

"Polyester?" the man asked.

"Yes."

"Do me favor? Make the uniforms with cotton. Something that breathes. In summer I sweat like pig, especially if no air-conditioning."

"I will do what I can, young man."

"What businesses in particular you will be visiting?"

Jenkins furrowed his brow. "More than a dozen that make the various components of the textile machinery used in our factories. Would you like me to list them for you?"

"Place right hand on machine."

Jenkins set his right hand on the scanner and a light illuminated his palm and fingers. The guard's eyes shifted from the machine to his computer. "You've been to Moscow before, Mr. Wilson."

"Several times, actually."

The guard stamped Jenkins's passport and handed it back through the hole in the glass. He wasn't interested. "Have nice visit."

Jenkins hailed a taxi outside the airport and instructed the driver, in Russian, to take him to the Gostinitsa Imperkiy in the Yakimanka District. The driver turned and looked at him.

"Adres dadite?" Do you have an address?

Jenkins provided one. Unlike many hotels in Moscow's historic center, the Hotel Imperial was off the beaten track and did not cater to American and European travelers. It had been vetted by CIA assets in Russia, who confirmed that the rooms were clean, and without microphones or cameras, though there was a low-quality camera in the lobby.

Maria Kulikova lived in the Yakimanka District. Jenkins's hotel was within walking distance of her apartment, which would ease his surveillance until he determined the reason for her silence. Zenaida Petrekova, the second sister, worked in the State Duma and lived further north, a thirty-minute train ride to the Korolyov suburb where her husband had been an engineer in the Russian space program until his unexpected death from a heart attack.

Jenkins intended to watch Kulikova first. If he determined she was under surveillance, it would complicate communication and, ultimately, exfiltration. He would then move on to observe Petrekova.

The hotel clerk in the small, well-worn lobby was pleasant but reserved. After Jenkins presented his passport and credit card, the clerk handed him a key card for a room on the hotel's third floor. "Can you provide me the names of some of the trendier places to eat around here?" Jenkins asked, again in a British accent.

When the man did not respond, Jenkins spoke to him in Russian. The clerk handed him a sheet of paper from beneath the counter. A cursory review revealed the names of restaurants that delivered, a dry cleaner, several tour guide companies, and other services. Having been on an airplane for seemingly half a day, Jenkins did not want to eat in his room, but he also did not want to walk into an establishment on the tourist junket. He wanted something like his hotel, well off the beaten path. He made his way to the caged elevator and rode it to the third floor. He detected no camera in the elevator or in his third-floor hallway.

Inside his room, Jenkins shut the door but left the lights off. He scanned the walls and the ceiling, looking for pinpoints of green, red, or white light that could indicate a hidden camera or listening device. Seeing none, he turned on the light and put his suitcase on the bed. He removed a shaving kit and, from within, what looked to be an electric razor. He pressed a button on the bottom and walked the room. The device detected radio waves and magnetic field signals, as well as hidden camera equipment, mobile phone bugs, and GPS locators. When any of those were detected, an LED light illuminated and the machine vibrated.

Jenkins noted no response.

He returned the machine to the shaving kit and slid from his jacket. He undid the buttons of his shirt and removed it, then lifted off the fat suit that gave him the appearance of being forty pounds heavier, mostly in his belly. He peeled off the lightweight, synthetic gloves that extended nearly to his elbows and made his hands appear white, complete with liver spots, and provided the fingerprints for Mr. Charles Wilson, textile manufacturer. The gloves made his hands sweat in the unusually warm weather. He also removed the blue contact lenses that had dried out and annoyed his eyes on the plane and flushed them down the toilet. He left on the prosthetic mask. Moscow's facial recognition cameras were everywhere in the city and used extensively. The facial disguise was necessary because, if given the opportunity, the cameras would scan Jenkins's face, link it with his face in a data repository, and immediately alert the Moscow police and the FSB. The cameras would then track him throughout Moscow.

Fifteen minutes after departing his hotel, Jenkins entered the door to the Yakimanka Bar, set off a side street. The bar got an F for name originality and exterior and interior design, but an A for being exactly what Jenkins sought. Except for two men shooting Russian billiards at a ridiculously large table, the place was deserted and dimly lit. He didn't have to worry that his hands were darker complected than his face. The bar smelled of cigarette smoke and greasy food. Jenkins took a booth where he could see out the window onto the street.

One of the men playing pool shouted, drawing Jenkins's attention. The man looked to be in his twenties, with a fashionable haircut—short on the sides but long on top. His hair hung over the table each time he bent to take a pool shot. In between shots he strutted around the table, drinking from one of several beer bottles on the table's edge and verbalizing his next attempt to his large companion, a mountain of a man whose shaved head nearly touched the ceiling. The mountain looked bemused but not concerned.

The shooter was muscled beneath his white tank-top T-shirt. A thick gold chain hung from his neck. Jenkins noticed a long-sleeve shirt and suit jacket hanging on a wall hook near a pool-cue rack missing two cues. The man wore suit pants and dress shoes, but he did not strike Jenkins as the business type. A colorful sleeve of tattoos adorned his right arm from his wrist to his shoulder.

"Ya by na tvoem meste ikh ignoriroval. Yesli ty ne glup, uhodi." I'd ignore them. If you're smart, you'll leave.

Jenkins turned his attention to the bartender, who had come out from behind the bar. The man had a mane of graying hair and a bushy beard that covered most of his wrinkled face.

"Lobotomie," Jenkins said, ordering one of Russia's most popular beers.

The man shook his head, exhaled, and departed.

"Suka!" the pool shooter yelled. *Bitch. "Prinesi nam yeschche piva."* Get us more beer.

Jenkins had not previously noticed the woman seated on a bar stool in a dark corner near the table. A flimsy white dress barely covered her long legs or her cleavage. She stumbled when she stepped down, nearly falling off her red platform heels. The pool hustler laughed and swatted her backside with the pool cue, causing her to fall forward into the table, then onto the floor.

The woman was high. Something more powerful than beer. A narcotic of some kind.

The man poked her with the pool stick and lifted her dress, then looked to his friend for approval. The woman grabbed the edge of the pool table to rise, unsteady on her feet. She teetered toward the bar, this time falling from a step that elevated the room. She landed hard on the worn linoleum. The bartender looked at her but only briefly. He made no effort to help her. Jenkins nearly got up, then thought better of getting involved. The woman got to her feet and stumbled to the bar. She said something to the bartender, then turned and looked at Jenkins. Black mascara ran down her face, like a clown's tears.

Jenkins felt his heart sink. Having a daughter, he struggled to control his building anger at the woman's mistreatment. When Jenkins shifted his attention back to the two men, the punk leaned on his pool cue, giving Jenkins a hard stare. He stuck his thumb between his ring and middle fingers, the Russian equivalent of the finger.

Jenkins forced himself to look away. Punk.

The bartender returned with his Lobotomie. Jenkins took a sip and smiled up at him. The man turned to leave. *"Vasha kukhnya yeshche otkryta?"* Jenkins asked. *Is your kitchen still open?*

Behind the bartender the woman navigated the step to the pool table while carrying four bottles. As she neared the two men, a bottle slipped from her grasp and shattered on the linoleum floor.

"Vot der'mo," the bartender said under his breath. *Shit.*

"Suka!" The pool hustler swore.

The mountain took the remaining bottles from the woman.

"Priberis'," the punk said. *Clean it up.* He grabbed the woman by the neck and shoved her to the ground. *"Oblizhi ego kak sobaka."* *Lick it up like a dog.*

Jenkins gripped his bottle and looked to the bartender, who was clearly not going to do anything.

The punk squatted behind the woman and used the pool cue to simulate a sex act, then grabbed the woman by her hair and pulled her to her feet. He said something to the mountain and the two men exited with the woman through a door at the back of the bar.

The bartender's voice drew Jenkins's attention. *"Tol'ko rubili. Kreditnye karty ne prinimaem. Chto vy khotite zakazat'?"* *Rubles only. No credit cards. What do you want?*

Inside, a storm raged, but Jenkins spoke calmly, even managed a smile. *"Ya dumayu ty prav. Dumayu, mne luchshe uyti."* *I think you're right,* he said. *I think it best that I leave.*

Jenkins walked outside the bar but not in the direction of his hotel. At the building's edge he looked down an alley filled with garbage bags overflowing a bin, wooden pallets, and newspaper stacks. In a cone of light from a fixture above the bar's back door, the punk had the woman pinned against a wall, one hand at her throat. His other hand undid his belt buckle. The mountain stood watching the show, his back to Jenkins.

As Jenkins approached, the punk slapped the woman hard across the face.

"You don't want to lick up the beer, dog?" He slapped her a second time, just as hard. "Perhaps there is something else you want to lick. Huh?" He forced the woman to her knees, now gripping her hair. Blood trickled from her nose and the corner of her mouth. He unzipped his fly, but he swore when he struggled to pull himself free.

"*Vozmozhno, vy ne mozhete yego nayti, potomu chto on takoy malen'kiy,*" Jenkins said. *Perhaps you're having trouble finding it because it's so small.*

The mountain quickly swiveled. His hand moved to the bulge under his leather jacket, but the punk raised a hand, stopping him. The punk shoved the woman onto the ground and stepped from the cone of light, squinting as if having trouble seeing Jenkins.

"*Chto ty skazal, starik?*" *What did you say, old man?*

Jenkins kept one eye on the mountain's hands. "I said, perhaps the reason you're having trouble finding your pecker is because it's so small."

The punk smiled, but with uncertainty. He was no doubt debating whether the old man insulting him was drunk, simpleminded, or had lost his mind altogether. He looked to his companion, who also seemed perplexed. Then the punk laughed. The mountain laughed with him, but again, Jenkins knew it was nerves.

"You have some big balls, old man," the punk said. "The old man must have big balls, don't you think, Pavil?"

The mountain nodded.

Jenkins continued to watch the mountain's hands.

The punk grabbed the pool cue from the brick wall and stepped toward Jenkins. "Perhaps you'd like to show us your big balls. Huh?" He turned and nodded to the woman. "Perhaps you'd like to show her your big balls? What do you say, old man? Would you like a turn?"

Jenkins smiled. "Here's what I'd like. I'd like you two to go back into the bar and finish your beers and your game of pool. I'll even buy you a round."

The young man lost his smile. "You want her all to yourself, old man?" He made lewd gestures with his hands and his hips and spoke to his friend. "The old man does not wish to share, Pavil. So selfish."

"So selfish," Pavil said.

"Here I offer to share, and you want to take her all for yourself."

"The woman is going to leave. She's going to go home," Jenkins said.

"Is she?"

"You've had your fun. I'm asking you, again, to go back into the bar and finish your beers and your game."

The young man made a steeple with his hands and put the steeple beneath his chin, as if thinking. "What if . . ." He held up a finger. "What if . . . instead of us going inside, I stay here and fuck the woman while Pavil beats the shit out of you? How do you like that option, old man?"

"You know," Jenkins said. "I really don't like being called 'old.'"

"No?"

"No. You see, I believe age is just a mindset, that if we don't think of ourselves as old then we aren't."

"You are a philosopher," the punk said.

"No." Jenkins shook his head. "I'm a pragmatist. Take you, for example. You're what, twenty-five or six? But you have the mental mindset of a fourteen-year-old prepubescent boy who gets off beating up women."

"You insult me? Who are you?"

"Just a guy who wanted a little peace and quiet to enjoy a beer and something to eat before going to bed."

"Looks like you came into the wrong bar at the wrong time."

"We can all still win here. I'll go someplace else to eat. The woman goes home. And you and the mountain can go back inside and finish your game."

The young man broke the pool cue over his knee. "That is no longer an option." He tossed half the cue to Pavil. "I think we're going to finish this game right here. Right now."

The young man lunged and swung the pool cue. Jenkins stepped forward instead of back, so his shoulder absorbed the blow. He grabbed the wrist holding the stick with his left hand, spun, and struck the elbow, hearing a snap. The young man bellowed in agony and dropped to his knees. Pavil, much bigger, but slower, lifted the pool cue like an ax. Again, Jenkins stepped into the man and threw a quick jab, striking Pavil in the trachea. Pavil dropped the cue and grabbed his throat. Jenkins kicked him hard in the groin, then struck Pavil's chest, knocking him backward, off balance. Pavil toppled garbage cans as he fell into the debris.

The punk, one arm at his side, rose and came at Jenkins, slashing with a knife in his good hand. Jenkins avoided the first strike. When the knife crossed his vision a second time, Jenkins grabbed the arm with his left hand and snapped the wrist. The knife came free. He swung across his body with his right hand, striking the punk in the face and knocking him to the ground. He heard the clatter of garbage cans and turned. Pavil emerged from the debris, gun in hand.

At that same moment, the punk lurched to his feet, eyes burning with rage. He lunged at Jenkins.

The gunshot echoed.

The punk stumbled and fell into Jenkins's arms.

The bar door to the alley swung open. The bartender. He looked at Jenkins, then at the man slumped in Jenkins's arms, blood spreading from the wound, staining his T-shirt a burgundy red. The bartender's eyes widened and he quickly pulled the door shut. At the end of the alley, Pavil retreated, gun still aimed. He stumbled over debris, struggling to keep his balance. Then he turned and ran.

Jenkins set the punk on the ground. The bullet had pierced his back near the left shoulder blade. He checked for a pulse, didn't find one.

The woman cowered against the wall, looking both confused and scared.

"Seychas vy dolzhny uyti," Jenkins said. *You should leave now.*

She stared at the punk facedown on the pavement, then shifted her gaze to Jenkins. Her eyes momentarily cleared.

Fear.

"Chto vy nadelali?" she said. *What have you done?*

7

Yakimanka Bar
Moscow, Russia

When married, Senior Investigator Arkhip Mishkin of Moscow loved everything about being a criminal investigator except nights he was called out to a crime scene and had to leave the warmth and comfort of his bed and his wife, Lada. Her parents named their daughter after the Slavic goddess of beauty, and for thirty-six years Lada had been Arkhip's treasure. Since her death from breast cancer almost two years ago, Arkhip found little joy in life, but he no longer minded being called out to a crime scene in the middle of the night. His bed was cold. Most nights he fell asleep in his chair reading.

Getting called out was something to do.

Arkhip slowed his car as he approached a uniformed officer directing traffic, though few cars drove the streets at this hour. He checked his watch. Morning, actually. The officer vigorously waved at Arkhip to drive away. Instead, Arkhip lowered the car-door window.

The young officer looked angry. "What are you doing? Move along now or I will have you arrested."

Ah, youthful exuberance, though the young man's delivery needed work. *You got more bees with honey than vinegar,* his Lada liked to say. Arkhip smiled up at the officer and flashed his badge identifying him as a senior investigator with the Criminal Investigation Department for the Ministry of Internal Affairs. A mouthful, for certain.

The young officer raised his hands as if in surrender. He looked aghast. "My apologies, Senior Investigator."

"No need." Arkhip smiled again. "If you could just move those cones." The officer hurried to pick up the orange cones, then waved Arkhip forward.

Arkhip parked and stepped from the car. He put on his lightweight summer sport coat and brown porkpie hat. "Thank you, Officer," he said when the young man approached, looking chagrined. "If I might offer a word of advice?"

"Please, Senior Investigator."

"Smile more often. One gets more bees with honey." The officer tried, but the smile looked painful. "It will become easier with practice," Arkhip said.

Arkhip checked his jacket pockets, felt the familiar shape of his spiral notepad and pencil, then stepped into a throng of police, a seemingly inordinate number for a shooting at a bar. One would have thought the president of Russia had been killed here. Someone had made the mistake of painting the exterior of the bar red, which was like that other saying of Lada's . . . something about putting a dress on a pig. The peeling paint only drew more attention to the bar's dilapidated condition. In an area of Moscow rapidly undergoing revitalization, the bar was not long for the wrecking ball.

Arkhip flashed his badge, and officers kept passing him up the line to the front door. Inside the bar he was brought to an officer speaking to a middle-aged man with a mane of wild, black-and-gray hair and matching beard.

The officer squinted in the dull light to read Arkhip's badge. "Senior Investigator," he said.

Arkhip looked about the bar at all the uniformed officers and crime scene investigators. He hoped someone had a log to list all the people inside the bar contaminating his crime scene, but he doubted it.

"Senior Investigator?" the officer said a second time.

"Hmm?" Arkhip turned to the uniform.

The officer gestured to the man with the wild hair. "This is the bar owner."

Both men stood at least half a foot taller than the five-foot-six Arkhip, but that was not uncommon. His mother had told Arkhip that while God had not blessed him with physical height, his intellect scaled the tallest mountains. Perhaps, but football coaches and women didn't see intellect—except of course his Lada. Though she had also stood three inches taller, she made Arkhip feel like the tallest man in any room.

"One moment, please." Arkhip turned to the assembled group. "Excuse me. Excuse me." The officers continued jabbering uninterrupted.

"Hey!" the uniformed guard yelled, gaining everyone's attention. He gave Arkhip a nod.

Arkhip smiled. "Thank you, Officer." He raised his voice. "I am Arkhip Mishkin, senior investigator of the Criminal Investigation Department within the Ministry of Internal Affairs. If you are not a crime scene investigator, or a witness, please depart these premises immediately. Please do not touch anything. Provide your name and your badge number to . . ." He looked to a young officer at the door. "What is your name? Yes, you."

"Golubev."

"Please give your name and badge number to Officer Golubev so I can look for your detailed report of your time inside my crime scene this morning."

That cleared the bar. The officers loved having something to do at night but loathed having to fill out paperwork. As the bar cleared, Arkhip took in the worn booths and nicked and scarred tables, the low ceiling, and the scraped and worn linoleum floor. At the back of the bar, up one step, he noted a pool table with billiard balls. A game had been in progress. One cue stick lay on the table. He looked, but didn't see the second stick, though the rack on the wall was definitely short two. A suit coat and shirt hung on a wall hook near the rack. Multiple beer bottles lined the table's edge. A shattered bottle and beer, not yet cleaned up, puddled on the floor.

This was a drinking establishment. He could smell the beer permeating the air. People came here to get stinking drunk and forget their problems, perhaps their lives. Arkhip had seen this too often. A drunk dropped a beer. Another drunk took offense and said something. One thing led to another, and before anyone knew it, one of the drunks was dead. Likely a stab wound. The only question was—

"Where's the body?" Arkhip looked about the room.

"Excuse me?" the officer said. He and the owner exchanged a look.

"I was told there was a shooting. I'd expect to see a body." Arkhip smiled congenially at both men.

"The body is in the alley, Senior Investigator Mishkin," the officer said.

"Ah. They took their dispute outside?"

"Excuse me?" the officer said.

"The two drunks. They argued. One dropped a beer. The other took it as a tragedy of great consequence and they took their dispute outside. There it escalated. Someone said something to the other and . . . we have a body."

Again, the officer and the owner exchanged glances.

Arkhip used the eraser of his pencil to scratch at eczema he'd developed along the back of his head and down his neck. His doctor said it was stress related, likely due to his wife's death. He told Arkhip to take shorter showers and gave him some cream. He said it would likely abate when Arkhip retired at the end of the month, but as that day approached, the eczema seemed to spread, not abate. Arkhip turned to the man with the mane of hair. "You're the owner?"

"Yes," the man said.

Arkhip looked but did not see another employee behind the bar. "And the bartender?"

"Yes."

"You saw what happened? Perhaps you wish to tell me."

"Yes. Certainly. I was—"

Arkhip raised a hand. "Please." He reached in his jacket, removed the spiral notepad, and licked the lead tip of the pencil.

"Do you wish to record the conversation?" the officer asked. He held up his cell phone.

Arkhip looked to the officer. "Why?"

"To . . . document what is said."

"I'll have my notes," Arkhip said. "And you will take a statement at Petrovka. But please. Feel free. Now . . ." He turned to the owner. "Tell me what happened."

"Well. Two men entered the bar."

Arkhip chuckled. The bartender and the officer looked perplexed. "It's just that . . . the way you began . . . It sounds like the start of a joke." Neither man smiled. "Please continue."

"They were with a woman. They ordered beers and shots. They were drunk when they entered."

Again, Arkhip raised a hand. "You know they were intoxicated?"

"Know it?"

"Did they tell you?"

"No, of course not, but I have been a bartender for many years. I could tell from their behavior, the look in their eyes. It—"

"Ah. You surmised it."

"What?"

"You surmised from their demeanor and physicality that the men were drunk."

"I guess."

"Continue."

"Okay, well, they bought shots and beers and went to the back to shoot pool."

"Just the men or the woman also?"

"No. Just the men."

"What happened to the woman?"

"What happened to her?"

"Did she, too, play pool?"

"She is a prostitute," the owner said, seemingly baffled.

"She told you this."

"Well no, but . . . I *surprised* it."

"*Surmised.* You surmised it from her physicality and demeanor."

"More from what she was wearing, and she has been in before."

"You know her?"

"She goes by the name Isabella. I believe it is an . . ."

"An alias?"

"Yes."

"Please continue."

"Another man came in. He sat in that booth and watched the men and the woman. I surmised this also," he added quickly. "Because Eldar flipped him off."

"Eldar?"

"One of the men playing pool."

"You know him as well as the prostitute?"

"I know more of him. He comes into the bar to shoot pool."

Arkhip said nothing.

"So I approached the man in the booth. He ordered a beer, and I told him I thought it best that he leave."

"Why?"

"I sensed a problem. The man seemed too interested in the woman." The bartender's eyes shifted up and to the left.

A lie. The bartender was not telling the truth, or perhaps not the whole truth. Arkhip found it best not to confront a witness. It only made him guarded. He'd come back to the question. "What did your patron say?"

"He asked if the kitchen was still open."

"Did he eat?"

"What? No. When I returned with his beer, he looked at me and said he'd take my advice. He left through the front door."

"What happened next?"

"I heard a gunshot in the alley. I mean . . . I surmised it was a gunshot. When I pushed open the door—" He pointed to the rear of the bar, beyond the pool table. "The back door to the alley."

"Continue."

"I pushed open the back door to the alley and I saw Eldar leaning against the man from the booth. He'd been shot."

"When did Eldar go into the alley?"

"Just before the man in the booth left the bar."

"What of the other man and the woman?"

"They went into the alley with Eldar."

"Do you know why?"

"No." The man looked away.

Another lie. Arkhip would leave it for now and come back to it also. "They didn't finish their game of pool or their beers?" Arkhip asked.

"No."

"So this man . . ." He checked his notes. "This man, Eldar, and the other man and the woman went out the back door into the alley, for what reason we do not know. Shortly thereafter the man in the booth went out the front door, and we can surmise he walked around the side of the building to the alley, where you *believe* he shot Eldar?"

"I surmised it," the man said a little too forcefully.

"A good surmise." Arkhip smiled. It was important to keep a witness calm. Arkhip found it helped their recollection. "Where was the woman?"

"She was against the wall, to my left."

"And the other man?"

"What other man?"

Arkhip flipped back through his notes. "You said two men entered the bar. And I said it sounds like a joke . . . You said the two men appeared drunk—"

"Yes. Yes. I don't know where he was. I didn't see him."

"He wasn't in the alley?" That seemed odd.

"I said I didn't see him."

"You don't know."

"I surmised he wasn't there . . . because I didn't see him."

"Okay. Yes. What happened next?"

The man looked horrified. "What do you think happened next?"

"I can assure you I have no idea."

The bartender exhaled. "I shut the door. I didn't want to get shot. I shut the door and I called the police."

"Good thinking. Very good thinking," Arkhip said. He turned to the officer. "Were you first on the scene?"

"Yes. Me and my partner. He's speaking to people outside. Trying to determine if anyone saw anything."

"Was there anyone else in the bar?" Arkhip asked the owner.

"No. Everyone had left," the bartender said.

"Would you like to see the body, Senior Investigator Mishkin?" The officer moved toward the step leading up to the pool table. "I think it might explain some things."

"Yes, of course." Arkhip followed, then stopped and stepped back to the bartender. "One more question. You said the decedent was shot. How do you know this?"

The owner looked exasperated. "Because I heard the shot."

"When you opened the door, did you see the man from the booth holding a gun?"

"Well . . . No."

"You did not."

"But . . . I mean I heard the gunshot, and when I opened the door Eldar was leaning against the man. Can I surmise it?"

"Certainly." Until a good attorney tore him apart on a witness stand. Arkhip folded the cover of his spiral notebook and shoved it and his pencil back into his pocket. "You've been very helpful. The officer will come back and take you to Petrovka to give a statement," he said, referring to the Criminal Investigation Department in Building 38 on Petrovka Street.

"I cannot go home?" the owner said.

"No," Arkhip said. He turned to the officer. "The body, please."

The officer stepped to the door at the back of the bar. Arkhip followed. As he passed the booth where the bartender had indicated the third man had sat, a still-full beer bottle remained on the table, and a crime scene investigator awaited instructions. "Make sure you secure that bottle. I want it analyzed for fingerprints and possible DNA."

"Yes, Senior Investigator."

Arkhip followed the officer outside. The body lay on the ground beneath a white sheet. Personnel from the medical examiner's office huddled around it. Garbage cans near the door had been upended and piles of garbage scattered. He noticed half a pool cue on the ground. He looked for the other half and found it a good fifteen feet away. There had been a fight.

"The second pool cue," he said.

"What's that?" the uniformed officer asked.

"The rack on the wall is missing two cues. One was on the table. This is the second cue."

"Okay. The body—"

"There was an altercation here."

"Apparently."

Arkhip spoke to the officer's partner in the alley. "I want pictures, thorough pictures of this alley." He pointed at the windows in the buildings surrounding the alley. "Have patrol officers canvass the people living in the apartments around this alley to determine if anyone saw or heard anything. Also have someone determine what prostitutes work this area. I want to talk to the woman who was here. Isabella."

"Yes, Senior Investigator Mishkin," the officer said.

Arkhip turned and looked up at the light stanchions and telephone poles. Atop a light stanchion across the street from the bar was one of Moscow's facial recognition cameras, with four different lenses, one aimed directly at the alley. "And get me the number of that light stanchion," Arkhip called out to the officer.

He turned to the first officer on scene. "You indicated some urgency with my seeing the body?"

"Yes." The officer stepped to the side of the body beneath the sheet. The medical examiner handed Arkhip latex gloves, which he snapped on before squatting. The medical examiner pulled back the sheet. He had already bagged the victim's hands to preserve any blood or bits of flesh he might have under his fingernails from the altercation. Arkhip pulled the sheet lower to view the bullet wound. A hole was just to the right of the left shoulder blade. The bullet had struck the heart, no doubt. His death instantaneous. However, the puncture hole in the shirt was round, with minimal bleeding. This was most definitely an entry wound, not an exit wound. The bartender said he saw the decedent leaning against the unknown third man but he did not see a gun. With good reason. It seemed unlikely the man shot the decedent.

"Turn him over," Arkhip said to the two men from the medical examiner's office. They did so, confirming what Arkhip had surmised. The exit wound was larger, more jagged, with a lot more blood. "Hmm." He stood.

"Senior Investigator Mishkin?" the officer said. "We have confirmed the decedent's identity."

"Did you?" When the officer did not continue, Arkhip said, "Let's not hide it."

"This is Eldar Velikaya."

"Velikaya. How do I know that name?"

"He is the son of Yekaterina Velikaya. The grandson of Alexei Velikaya."

"The gangster."

"Mafiya," the officer said.

"Why didn't you tell me immediately?" Arkhip said. "This changes everything."

8

■

Yakimanka District
Moscow, Russia

Jenkins stepped into an alley that smelled of rotting garbage and urine, though that was not his focus. His focus was his appearance, and what had just happened. The bartender had opened the door to the alley. He saw the punk, shot, leaning against Jenkins. He had concluded, wrongly, but certainly understandably, that Jenkins had gone into the alley and shot the punk. The bartender could not have seen the punk's companion, Pavil, behind the open door.

He removed his leather jacket, ripped off his bloodstained shirt, and tossed it into a garbage bin, then put back on his jacket and zipped it closed. His mind spun. He should have walked away. Every instinct in his body told him he should have walked away from the situation, but every instinct wasn't as strong as that one pang of his conscience that wouldn't let him watch another human being be so brazenly degraded. He could not stand by as the woman was beaten and abused. It didn't matter that she was a prostitute. If anything, it made it all the more imperative that she be treated with sympathy. She certainly did not deserve to be mistreated by a two-bit punk.

Still . . .

What had the woman meant? *What have you done?*

She said the words with such clarity and . . . fear, and despite all the drugs pulsing through her system. Her fear had sobered her like a bucket of ice-cold water tossed on a drunk. The words came out in a haunting whisper, as if she could not accept what her eyes clearly saw and her brain, at least momentarily, registered.

What have you done?

Jenkins had miscalculated the two men's determination. In his experience and his Krav Maga training, most men, having been disarmed and so quickly incapacitated, would have run, and lived to fight another day. Most would have considered the woman not worth their pain and their suffering.

The big man got the point too late. The punk never did. And the punk was the person calling the shots. The fact that the punk did not stand down indicated he was not used to being confronted, not used to being denied what he wanted, and that he usually got away with such behavior. And that raised the more important question. Who was he?

At least Jenkins had worn the mask. He'd get back to the hotel and discard Charles Wilson forever—

He stopped midstride. He looked at his hands. Shit. He'd taken off the latex gloves. What had he touched? The bar door. The tabletop.

The beer bottle.

He looked back, contemplating if he had time to go back and . . . No. Definitely not. He needed to take his chances. Move forward. He had other masks and disguises.

Jenkins checked his watch; he'd activated the stopwatch as soon as he left the alley. He walked briskly, his hands in the pockets of his jacket. His head turned away from the streetlamps where he'd seen the cameras. He did not run. He did not want to appear guilty. He did not, however, have a lot of time. The police would check the facial recognition cameras and see the confrontation in the alley. They would identify Charles Wilson through his passport photo entered into the system at

Sheremetyevo Airport. Once they did, they would follow him from the bar to his hotel—the CCTV cameras, he had been told, were that good.

Even if they weren't, common sense would lead the police along the same trail, and they would reach the same conclusion. Jenkins had walked to the bar. A good detective would dismiss the possibility Jenkins had ridden a nearby subway or a bus to go to such a dive, especially one the bartender would confirm Jenkins had never before visited. A good detective would theorize Jenkins walked from a nearby motel or hotel for a quick drink and a bite to eat. The bartender would confirm this, and it would eventually lead the police from the bar to the Hotel Imperial, where the clerk had made a copy of Jenkins's passport. He would provide his guest's room number.

Charles Wilson was about to have a very short life.

The hotel clerk greeted Jenkins with a tired smile and wished him a good night. *"Spokoynoy nochi."*

Jenkins took a moment to talk to the man, to appear calm and rational and undisturbed. He told the clerk he had a pleasant meal and would sleep in tomorrow morning. He asked not to be disturbed. The clerk suggested Jenkins hang the "Do Not Disturb" tag on his hotel room door but said he would be sure to also leave a message for the maid.

In his room, Jenkins left the lights off, searching again for any pinpoints of light. Nothing. He removed his phone and plugged it into a black case that provided him a personal hot spot. He entered three random names that served as his username in the app, then entered a series of random numbers and letters that opened an encrypted chat room with Matt Lemore. He typed, then paused. He was rushing. He needed to think this through. He took a deep breath. He would ditch the hotel and Charles Wilson. He had several other disguises. No need to sound the alarm just yet. He typed.

I have arrived.

He hit "Send." It took a minute for Lemore to get the message and respond.

Arrival confirmed. Possible change in plans.

Jenkins had been about to type something similar. He decided to let Lemore play it out. He typed. Okay.

Red Gate 2 first.

The second sister, Zenaida Petrekova, would be extracted first. Jenkins typed. Problem?

After a minute Lemore replied. Advised Red One has made contact. Something in play. Proceed to Red Gate 2.

Jenkins considered the information for a moment. *Something in play.* Kulikova had made contact. It must have been something important for her to break her months-long silence, or could the Russians somehow know that Jenkins had returned and were setting him up? *Something in play.* Jenkins interpreted Lemore's text as an indication that exfiltrating Kulikova now could jeopardize whatever was in play or possibly put her in danger of exposure. He typed.

Red Gate 2. Confirmed. Out.

Jenkins checked his watch. It had been nearly half an hour since he left the alley. He disconnected his phone from the hot spot, then went into the bathroom and peeled off the latex mask. He set it, along with Charles Wilson's passport and other papers, in a burn bin that looked like a common metal water flask. He popped out an oxidizing tablet disguised in a packet of Tums, lit the tablet with a match, dropped it in the flask, and screwed on the lid. The fire would burn without oxygen and emit no smoke.

Back in his room, he lifted the hidden panel on the inside of his suitcase. The panel was lined with a material with a high rate of X-ray absorption that prevented screening by airport technology. He pulled out a second disguise, using the bathroom mirror to apply it methodically as he had been trained. When finished, the reflection of a middle-aged man of Bashkir descent, one of Russia's most common ethnicities, stared back at him. Zagir Togan had mild Asian features with dark hair and a goatee. Jenkins grabbed the corresponding passport and pulled up the information he had memorized at Langley—Togan's vitals.

He finished packing, went into the bathroom, discarded the ashes from the metal flask into the toilet, and flushed it. He checked his stopwatch. Fifty minutes since he left the alley.

Time to move.

9

Velikaya Estate
Novorizhskoye, Moscow

Yekaterina Velikaya stepped into her darkened office, the shades drawn across the cathedral windows. The only light in the room came from a green Tiffany desk lamp. The family—Eldar's blood relatives and people who had worked for her grandfather, father, and now for Yekaterina—gathered in the mansion's front room. Her father had the fifteen-thousand-square-foot mansion built on a five-acre estate in the Novorizhskoye suburb. All who arrived asked the same questions, though not of Yekaterina. Who would kill Eldar?

As the word of Eldar's death spread beyond the family, and it would, Yekaterina's actions would be closely monitored. Her gender would be an issue, even after all this time in power. Was she tough enough to act rationally but decisively? Would she meet violence with violence? Could she separate her personal feelings for her only child and act in a manner that protected the family business?

That depended on what had happened. First things first.

What Yekaterina did know was she would not mourn.

Not yet.

She had business to conduct. She needed information.

Pavil Ismailov stood across her desk alongside Mily Karlov, Yekaterina's longtime fixer—what Michael Corleone in *The Godfather* called his *consigliere*. Mily had come up through the ranks with her father and was like a grandfather to her. He was largely the reason that Yekaterina, Alexei's only child, had risen to the helm of his family empire instead of it splintering into a dozen rival factions. Her father had been obsessed with the *Godfather* movies, and he had modeled his own family on the Italian mafia structure, with its requirement of absolute loyalty and fidelity from those who worked for him.

Yekaterina nodded and the two men lowered into straight-backed chairs at the circle of light's edge, their faces cast in shadows. Pavil's leg fired like a piston. Yekaterina lit up a cigarette from a pack placed on her desk along with a fresh ashtray. She had quit, cold turkey, years ago, had every cigarette and every ashtray removed from the home and forbade anyone from smoking in her presence. Not today. Today she inhaled the nicotine, which calmed her nerves like a glass of Scotch, and blew smoke into the darkened room.

"Tell me what happened," she said, her tone calm and deliberate.

Pavil nodded. "We were . . ." He cried, choking on his sobs. Yekaterina did not yet know if they were sobs of grief or sobs of fear. She had seen both many times. Men pleading for their lives often sobbed not because they were sorry for what they had done, but because they were sorry they had been caught.

Yekaterina nodded to Mily. He retrieved brandy from a crystal decanter at the bar and poured it into a wide-mouth glass. He tapped Pavil's shoulder with the stem. Pavil took the glass, sipped the brandy, and regained some semblance of his composure.

Pavil had been Eldar's bodyguard and longtime friend. They had grown up together and trained together at the Russian Sportsmen Association started by Yekaterina's father. Like her father, Eldar had played hockey, though he was never as good as his grandfather. Alexei Velikaya had played professionally, then built his family business. A trumped-up extortion charge sent him to prison for the first time. Killing her father's accuser had been Yekaterina's first priority when she later became *comare*, the Italian word for godmother.

Eldar never had the discipline her father had, nor did he appreciate hard work. He quit too easily. He wanted things handed to him, and he usually got them.

Like Pavil as his bodyguard. When a knee injury ended Pavil's competitive weightlifting career, her son asked that his mother hire his friend as his bodyguard, and Yekaterina had complied. Though they remained friends, Eldar abused the relationship, as he abused all relationships.

"I know how difficult this is, Pavil," Yekaterina said. "I know how close you were to Eldar. But I need to know what happened. You will tell me."

Pavil nodded. "We went to the bar to shoot pool."

"Just you and Eldar?"

"Yes."

He dropped his eyes to his drink. His tell. His first lie. Pavil had been instructed to keep Eldar away from prostitutes. Two had ended up dead in Eldar's company, which created shitstorms Mily had to quickly rectify.

"A man came into the bar. An older man. He was drunk. He challenged Eldar to a game of pool and said he had money to bet. I told him to piss off and mind his own business."

Again, Pavil's eyes betrayed him, as did his tone. His sentences were too perfect. His cadence too calm and deliberate. He was not remembering a traumatic event. He was reciting an event he had re-created and practiced. A lie.

"What did he look like, this man?" Yekaterina asked.

"Older. Fifties or sixties."

"Describe him."

"I didn't get a good look at him. It was dark inside the bar."

"Do your best."

"He was tall. Well built for a man his age. Fit. I'm sorry I—"

"Russian?"

"He spoke Russian, but maybe he was Chechen. He was persistent. Eldar wanted to play him, to take his money and teach him a lesson, but I told him it was not a good idea."

"Why not?"

"Because . . . because there was something about the man. He was too sure of himself. Too . . . I don't know. I didn't like it. I thought perhaps it was a setup of some sort, like the man was deliberately trying to bait Eldar."

"What happened next?"

"I told the man again that we were not interested. I even offered to buy him a drink. Then I told Eldar to ignore him, but you know Eldar. When he gets his mind set, he is difficult to dissuade."

Her son was stubborn, also like his grandfather, but he rarely got his mind set on anything. He acted impulsively and often violently. He did not consider consequences because he rarely had to confront them. That, too, had been his father's problem—Yekaterina's husband. He cheated on Yekaterina because he believed he could. He'd been wrong. Yekaterina made sure he disappeared.

"Why was Eldar in the alley?"

When Pavil failed to immediately answer, she knew he was searching through the story he had concocted. "Why?" he asked. Stalling.

"Yes."

"I parked the car out back. In the alley."

"Why?"

"The door in the alley was a short distance to the car. And we . . . we wouldn't have to walk past this man who was seated in a booth near the front."

"I thought you said he was challenging Eldar to a game of pool?"

"He was. I misspoke."

"A wise decision on your part to leave." She nodded to the glass in his hand. Pavil took another drink. "Had you and Eldar been drinking?"

Pavil set the glass back in his lap. "We had a few beers and a shot at the bar."

"And before you arrived?"

"A cocktail at dinner. Some wine. Nothing excessive."

She doubted it. "What happened next?"

"We went into the alley. The man must have gone out the other way. He came around the side of the building. He had a pool cue in his hand and moved to attack Eldar, but I was able to deflect the blow. I knocked him down. I thought that would end it. I thought he would leave. I'm sorry. I wasn't as prepared as I should have been."

"Not prepared for what?"

"He had a gun. The man had a gun. I was too late." He sobbed again. "I'm sorry. I was too late to stop him."

When Pavil stopped sobbing and looked at her, she nodded again to the glass. Again Pavil sipped the brandy. "Where did he shoot Eldar?"

"In the gut."

"And how did you manage to get away without being shot?"

"The bartender must have heard the gunshot. He opened the door from the bar to the alley. I was behind the door, so I don't think the bartender saw me. When the man saw the bartender he ran."

"Where were you?" she asked.

"Where? Near the side of the building."

"The door on the south side." At her request, Yekaterina had received the building layout and photographs of the alley. She had them spread across the blotter on her desk in the cone of light.

"I don't recall the direction—"

"But you said you were behind the door when the door opened."

"Yes."

"So you were close to the entrance to the alley."

"Yes. I was. That's right. I remember now. I was."

"Why didn't you stop the man from leaving?"

"He . . . he had a gun."

"Did you have your gun?"

Pavil figured out the hole in his story and frantically tried to patch it before all the air leaked out. "It all happened so fast, Comare. And then . . . everything happened quickly . . . the bartender coming to the door . . . the man fleeing. I didn't know what to do."

"You left my son in an alley to die alone."

Pavil's eyes widened. "I . . . I thought it best that I not be there."

"Why didn't you come here? Why did I have to send Mily to find you?"

"I wasn't thinking straight, Comare. Eldar was my friend. I didn't know what to do." He sobbed again.

Yekaterina looked to Mily and nodded. Mily reached over and took the glass, then motioned for Pavil to stand.

"Go back to the front room," Yekaterina said. "Stay with the others, in case I have more questions."

"I'm sorry—"

She raised a hand. "Get out of my sight."

Pavil crossed the Persian carpet to the door, which Mily held open for him. He looked to Mily, who offered him nothing, then he looked back to Yekaterina. She did not acknowledge him. Mily closed the door behind him.

Yekaterina took a long inhale on the cigarette and held it. She exhaled slowly, smoke escaping her nostrils and mouth as she spoke. "Find out what really happened. Call our contacts at the Moscow police department and get ahead of this." She knew her son. Knew what he was, that he had likely provoked something. If he had been drinking, it had been a lot, and there was likely a woman involved. A prostitute. Drugs also.

Because that was her son.

And that had been her father—his grandfather.

They liked their booze and their clothes and their women. They liked to not just be seen but to be noticed. They were cheats and misogynists. They believed the family made them omnipotent, and that omnipotence allowed them to be cruel, especially to women.

But Alexei was her father.

And Eldar was her son.

And this was her family.

If another family had seen this as an opportunity and had gunned Eldar down, there would be a war, and she would win. And if it had been the government, killing Eldar like they had killed her father leaving a Moscow restaurant, she would cripple their construction projects with slowdowns, costing them billions of dollars. Someone would pay, in blood or in rubles.

"What of Pavil?" Mily asked.

"Let him mourn with the others for now. Make sure he doesn't leave the property or talk to anyone else about what happened," she said. "My son was not a good person in life, but like my father, I will do everything I can to see that he is remembered as one in death. Go. Bring me the information I requested."

10

Bolshevo Railway Station
Korolyov, Moscow Oblast, Russia

Early the following morning, Jenkins, disguised as Zagir Togan, stood sweating on the Bolshevo train station platform. Meteorologists predicted another sweltering Russian day. He had checked the newspaper that morning and listened to the news, but his confrontation at the Yakimanka Bar had not been reported. The prostitute's reaction, however, kept running through his head, along with her look of fear.

What have you done?

Jenkins shook the thought. He needed to focus. The matter immediately at hand was Zenaida Petrekova. During his time at Langley, he had memorized both Petrekova's and Kulikova's habits and their cues. Each weekday morning, Petrekova walked from her detached, redbrick home to this railway station to take the thirty-minute train ride to the Kazansky railway station in Komsomolskaya Square. From there she crossed the street and took the Metro, exiting at the Okhotnyy Ryad terminal and walking to the State Duma federal building.

When Jenkins got resituated in a new hotel, he had logged into the encrypted chat room using a different access code—it would change daily—and sought additional information on Petrekova. Lemore advised him that Petrekova had performed a Google search on her home computer the night before, looking for Friday's Moscow weather. She had deliberately misspelled Friday—indicating she desired to communicate. The CIA ran a series of paid advertisements on her weather page, and Petrekova clicked on the one for the Anteka A5 pharmacy, which brought up several ads for common pharmaceutical items. Petrekova clicked on two items, then exited.

Minutes later, she had posted a picture on her Facebook account. She sat in her home kitchen proudly displaying the meal she had cooked for supper—blini, pelmeni, and beef Stroganoff. She had switched on the light above her stove, to simulate the sun, i.e., daytime. The wall clock above the stove read 7:48. The time that she would be at the Anteka A5.

At precisely 7:12 a.m., Petrekova walked down the concrete platform dressed for work in a blouse, skirt, and tennis shoes, her eyes glued to her phone. In her other hand she dangled a cigarette, which she periodically inhaled. Jenkins recognized her from the many photographs he had studied. Midsixties, she blended in seamlessly with the other commuters, though better dressed, befitting her position in the State Duma. Petrekova's other cue was her scarves. Either she did not wear a scarf, meaning she had nothing to communicate and no need for a meeting with her handler, or if she desired a meeting or had information to pass, she wore a particular colored scarf, coordinated with the particular weekday. Yellow on Monday, red on Tuesday, blue on Wednesday, and so forth. To indicate a problem, she wore a different-colored scarf than the particular day called for. This morning, a Friday, she wore a lightweight blue scarf.

A problem.

Jenkins's job was to determine the problem, communicate to Petrekova her message had been received and that there was a plan in place to exfiltrate her out of Russia.

Petrekova raised her gaze from her phone and greeted another woman, who approached on the platform from the opposite direction. The two exchanged air kisses and Petrekova put away her phone.

Jenkins put his phone to his ear, simulating a call, but scanned the growing number of commuters gathering on the platform. A minute or two after Petrekova's arrival, a young woman walked down the platform dressed in business attire, a briefcase slung over her shoulder. But unlike Petrekova and the other women also dressed in business attire, this woman wore heels instead of tennis shoes. She did not regularly commute. Her eyes roamed the platform, as if looking up and down for the approaching train, but each time her head turned, Jenkins noticed the slightest pause when her gaze swept over Petrekova. The woman removed her phone from her coat pocket and considered it. She'd received a text message. She punched the keyboard on her phone, then lowered it. Jenkins watched the other commuters for a reaction. Seconds after the woman sent the message, a man, casually dressed in jeans and a black T-shirt, turned a cell phone over in his hand and read his text. He shoved a cigarette between his lips and blew out smoke, then tapped a reply. Jenkins shifted his attention back to the woman. She turned her phone over. Her partner had also arrived.

Petrekova had been accurate. She had a problem.

When the train arrived, Petrekova and her friend boarded, continuing to chat. Jenkins had to hand it to her. She never broke character, never looked about the platform or gave any indication of concern, though she clearly and rightly suspected she was being followed. The man and the woman entered the car through separate doors. One sat at the front and one at the back. Jenkins stepped onto the car and noticed the CCTV cameras in the ceiling. Big brother. With no seats available, he stood.

With each stop, additional passengers commuting to downtown Moscow boarded, and the car filled with the aroma of aftershave and body odor. At the fourth stop, the young woman in heels departed the train. Jenkins had not expected this. He watched to see if the woman made eye contact with any commuter entering the train, but he did not detect it. He looked behind him. The man remained on the car, on his phone. Jenkins looked at the other passengers, but if the man had texted a message to one of them, Jenkins couldn't pick out the person.

He swore under his breath. This could complicate things.

After roughly thirty minutes, they arrived at the Kazansky railway station, one of three major hubs in Komsomolskaya Square. Jenkins knew it well. He and Paulina Ponomayova had taken a train from the Leningradsky station to Saint Petersburg while being chased by the FSB.

Petrekova exited. So, too, did the man in the black T-shirt, and presumably an unidentified second tail. Petrekova said goodbye to her commuting friend on the platform and proceeded inside the opulent railway station, crossing marble floors beneath frescoes on the arched ceilings and hanging chandeliers. The hall included multiple businesses, coffee shops and shops with various sundries. Jenkins checked his watch. At 7:48 a.m. Petrekova stepped into an Anteka pharmacy and browsed the aisles. She would stay no more than three minutes.

Jenkins looked again. The man outside the pharmacy had his head tilted up, as if to read the elevated board listing the arriving and departing trains. Jenkins considered the other commuters, then scanned the patrons inside the store, but he could not find the second tail.

With a minute to spare, Jenkins entered the pharmacy and proceeded down the aisle with eye-care products. Petrekova came down the aisle in the opposite direction. Jenkins forced himself not to look at her. He stopped and picked up the first product Petrekova had clicked on the night before.

Visine.

It gets the red out.

Petrekova stopped beside him, picked up contact lens solution to acknowledge she had *seen* his confirmation. She put the solution in her basket. He noticed her hand shook, despite her polished façade. A good sign. She was afraid. If this had been a setup, she would have nothing to fear.

Jenkins paid for his item at the cash register, turned, and broke off surveillance. He had confirmed Petrekova had a problem and communicated her message had been received. That was the easy part. The harder part would be Petrekova shaking her tail long enough for the two of them to meet someplace and communicate in privacy.

He left the pharmacy and doubled back several times, entering and exiting stores to be certain he was not being followed.

Clean, he went to work on setting up a secure meeting location.

11

Directorate of the Ministry of Internal Affairs
Building 38, Petrovka Street
Moscow, Russia

Arkhip Mishkin arrived at his desk in the Criminal Investigation Department after spending much of the early morning feeling like a dog chasing his tail and losing ground. Uniformed officers canvassed the establishments and apartments near the Yakimanka Bar, especially those overlooking the alley. No one had heard or had seen anything. Like most Muscovites, they did not want to complicate their lives with a police matter. Arkhip had advised the officers not to mention it could also be a mafiya matter, which would have only exacerbated his predicament.

Upon the decedent's identification, Arkhip issued a gag order on the medical examiner's office and instructed that the ME's preliminary report be expedited and for his eyes only. He had issued a similar order to the Criminal Investigation Department's Technology Center. The video from the designated CCTV camera outside the bar was to be for Arkhip's eyes only. Despite these precautions, he suspected the decedent's identity would leak sooner rather than later.

It had been sooner.

Arkhip wiped his handkerchief across his brow. All the exertion that morning in the muggy Moscow air caused him to perspire profusely.

"You look like you could already use a shower, Mishkin," Faddei, another criminal investigator, said as Arkhip blew past his desk.

Arkhip smiled but did not slow.

Faddei turned and leaned back in his chair. "I heard you caught a homicide, and so close to your retirement. Maybe someone is trying to screw up that perfect record of yours, eh?"

In his twenty-five years as an investigator, Arkhip had not once left a crime unsolved. Some investigations took longer than others to resolve, but he fancied himself the tortoise more than the hare. Persistence and determination. The thought had crossed his mind, though, that this case, were it not quickly resolved, could delay his forced retirement.

"Anything of interest?" Faddei asked.

"Just a shooting in a bar." Arkhip pulled out his desk chair and sat.

"You need to learn to slow down, Mishkin. You move like a man getting zapped with a cattle prod. What will you do in retirement when you don't have a case to chase?"

He had no idea.

Arkhip removed his sport coat and porkpie hat, sat, and picked up the phone, hoping to dissuade Faddei from further questions for which Arkhip had no answers. He didn't have time to think about his future. Already he was behind. Veteran uniformed officers working the Yakimanka District had found the prostitute, Bojana Chabon, a.k.a. Isabella. Unfortunately, someone else found her first, though it had been made to look otherwise. Arkhip had climbed three flights of stairs in a dilapidated and soon-to-be-demolished apartment building only to find Chabon on a bed, a tube wrapped around her emaciated bicep, and a needle and syringe stuck in the crook of her arm. Having worked narcotics as a young investigator, Arkhip surmised the drug in the syringe had likely been heroin, and likely laced with a deadly poison such as strychnine or fentanyl. He'd know for certain when the labs were completed, though it wouldn't help his investigation any.

While at Chabon's apartment, Arkhip received a second call from uniformed officers who had obtained the address for Pavil Ismailov, Eldar Velikaya's bodyguard. Ismailov lived in an upscale condominium complex, also in Yakimanka, but light-years away from Chabon's apartment in terms of condition and cost.

Ismailov did not answer his door, though his neighbor in the adjoining apartment did open his door. The middle-aged man, holding a yappy dog, complained that Ismailov played heavy metal music at all hours of the day and night. After a three-minute rant, Arkhip got in a question and learned Ismailov was not at home, at least the man had not heard the music or Ismailov's footsteps late the prior evening or early that morning. He said it surprised him because Ismailov's car was in the underground garage and "The man clomps around like a draft horse."

Arkhip found Ismailov's car in the garage, an expensive black Mercedes. He found Ismailov in the trunk, with a bullet hole in the back of his skull. If Arkhip were a betting man, he'd wager Ismailov had been shot as he opened the trunk, then pushed inside, dead before he knew what had hit him. Much easier than trying to lift a man of Ismailov's size. Arkhip had the entire car, including the body, towed to the forensic team at Petrovka Street for processing.

Either Arkhip was in the midst of a mob war, or someone was cleaning up a mess. What mess, exactly, Arkhip didn't have a clue. But he would.

He always did.

—

Twenty minutes later, Arkhip waited in one of the Criminal Investigation Department's windowless, seven-foot-square interrogation rooms. A table and three chairs dominated the space. The chairs had nicked and scarred the pale-green walls, and years of traffic had worn the uneven linoleum squares. A high-powered fluorescent light bulb hung over the table, as bright as day. When left alone, a suspect could hear the tube buzz, like an annoying fly. Everything was intended to intimidate by simulating the cramped confines and loneliness of a cell. The room held the aroma of body odor and fear, poorly masked by a chemical disinfectant.

Arkhip could have opted for more comfortable surroundings—one of the division's conference rooms, or a table in the cafeteria—but it was well known the vory, Russian mafiya, had informants on their payroll working inside the Ministry of Internal Affairs, and the shit would hit the proverbial fan soon enough. The longer Arkhip could keep news from the press, the more opportunity he had to obtain information untainted by bribes and favors. As it was, two of his three witnesses had already been silenced. He needed to find the unknown third man quickly, but first he needed to better understand what he was up against, and that was the reason for this meeting.

The door pushed in without a knock. A man, balding in a horse-shoe pattern, stuck his head in the door as if uncertain he had the right place. "Senior Investigator Mishkin?"

"Arkhip, please. You must be Investigator Gusev. Please come in. I would stand but it seems that space is at a premium."

Gusev stepped to the side to shut the door, and the two shook hands. Gusev's eyes roamed the room as he placed a thick maroon file on the table.

"Ah. Good. You brought your file on the Velikayas."

Gusev smiled, but it was patronizing. "I would need to be a magician to bring you the files on the Velikayas. They would not all fit in this room. This is my personal file."

"Of course," Arkhip said. "Please take a seat." The linoleum squealed as Arkhip pulled the table toward his side of the room to allow Gusev space to sit.

"You have worked for the organized crime control department for many years?"

"OCC," he said. "And yes, for more than two decades."

"Then you are familiar with the Velikayas."

Another smile. Also patronizing. "We're all familiar with the Velikayas. It is Moscow's largest crime family," he said, as if it were an entity more than a family. Gusev adjusted his paisley tie and pressed it against his dark-blue shirt.

"Yes, of course. Perhaps you can give me a synopsis; I am interested in the hierarchy."

Gusev laughed. "How much time do you have?"

Since his wife's death . . . "All the time in the world, Investigator Gusev, but perhaps today a short version."

Gusev let out a breath. "Okay. May I ask what this is about?"

"In time." Arkhip offered nothing more.

After a few seconds of silence, Gusev got the hint. He chuckled and looked at his watch. "Do you want to record this?"

"Yes. Of course." Arkhip patted his sport coat and removed his notepad and pencil. "Thank you for reminding me."

Gusev grinned. "I meant do you wish to *record* our session?" He looked up at the camera in the ceiling corner. "Are we being recorded?"

"No." Arkhip smiled. "We are not. And my notes will be sufficient."

Arkhip learned early in his career that a tape recorder was a crutch. Investigators depended on the recording and failed to listen to a witness's answers. Without listening, there was no hearing; without hearing, one could not ask intelligent follow-up questions. Opportunities not taken were opportunities lost. Arkhip took notes and maximized his intuitive abilities. With years of practice, he could recall almost verbatim what a witness had said. "Please begin."

Gusev took a moment, then told Arkhip that the vory dated to tsarist times. The word meant "thief"—a general term used for an underworld member. The Velikayas emerged from the Khitrovka, a notorious slum just a ten-minute walk from the Kremlin.

"I've read about it," Arkhip interrupted.

"You have?"

"I've read many books on Russia's history these last two years. These places were crammed with lean-tos, shacks, tenements, and disease-ridden houses. The poorest of the poor."

"Criminalized enclaves for thieves and murderers," Gusev said without sympathy.

"Crime is the stepchild of poverty, is it not?"

"Perhaps, but the modern vory, which is who you are really concerned about, is anything but poor and was shaped in Stalin's labor camps."

"The gulags."

"Those imprisoned had a common enemy and vowed to never support the government. Sergei Velikaya spent years in one of these Siberian gulags. He was an audacious and ambitious gangster with a head for numbers and a natural ability to lead."

"Good qualities for a leader," Arkhip said.

Gusev scoffed. "He led by brutal and ruthless violence. His mistake was flaunting his status, promenading through Moscow in a cream-colored suit, bow tie, and straw boater hat, and currying favor with the public by throwing street parties with buckets of free vodka and food. His son, Alexei Velikaya, was educated in Moscow's finest schools and took over the family business when Sergei was killed in a mafiya war. Alexei moved away from the traditional vory of his father. He was fascinated by the American *Godfather* movies, specifically the Corleones' attempt to become a legitimate business family. He tried to blend in with the new elite and create a new breed of gangster-businessman, the *avtoritet*."

"The authority. It has a better ring to it than 'thieves,' doesn't it?"

"A thief is a thief, regardless of the label slapped on his backside. In the 1990s with all the chaos, Alexei Velikaya made a fortune in currency speculation and used the capital to buy real estate in Moscow."

"Part of his quest to become legitimate?"

"Thieves don't die that easily. He persuaded the elderly and invalids to sell their apartments. Those who refused disappeared."

"Oh," Arkhip said.

"He bought dozens of buildings for next to nothing, rehabbed them, and sold them at an exorbitant profit. Along the way, he established political connections. In return for their looking the other way, he ensured civic construction projects proceeded on time, and that labor was at a reasonable price. It allowed for unprecedented growth in Moscow, billion-dollar improvements to the Metro super trains, road construction and repairs, and airport expansion. Alexei Velikaya, however, was his father's son. His philanthropy made him a celebrity, and he thrived on the attention."

"I see where this is headed," Arkhip said.

"Yes. When President Putin took power, most of the *avtoritet* stepped back into the shadows. Alexei Velikaya did not. He believed his extensive business profile, network of informants, and beloved public persona would protect him."

Gusev paused here, not about to say more with a camera in the room, despite Arkhip's assurances they were not being recorded. The story of Alexei Velikaya's death was well known in Moscow. In 2008, during a campaign for a seat in the Duma, Velikaya was shot and killed, despite wearing a bulletproof vest and being surrounded by bodyguards. The government blamed rival gangsters until an oligarch exposed an FSB secret branch authorized by the president and within the Counterterrorist Directorate to kill him and other powerful oligarchs and mafiya family leaders.

"Which brings me to Yekaterina Velikaya," Gusev said. "His only child. *Malen'kaya Printsessa.*"

"The little princess?" Arkhip said.

"No longer. She is now—"

"Catherine the Great." Arkhip said the literal translation of her name. "A woman. That must be unique."

"Unprecedented," Gusev said. "The vory sexualizes or reveres women, but never respects them. Yekaterina had an uncle who said she didn't have the balls to run her father's business. They found him hanging in a warehouse, castrated, his balls shoved down his throat."

"She had something to prove," Arkhip said.

"Clearly. She's a chip off the old block. She has met every subsequent challenge with quick and decisive violence. She is also bright, like her father, and has legalized the family business while placating the Kremlin with its piece of the pie."

"How has she avoided her father's and grandfather's fates?" Arkhip asked.

"She hired former KGB officers and moonlighting FSB officers who inform her if the state intends to move against her or her businesses. And, unlike her father, she avoids all publicity."

"And does she have children?" Arkhip asked, knowing she did, of course, but wanting to hear Gusev's impression of Eldar Velikaya.

Gusev gave a short laugh. "A son. Eldar Velikaya. He is not his mother or his grandfather. He is a mental midget, which makes him dangerous. He runs around town spending money on hookers, gambling, and generally causing problems. There are rumors he has killed at least two prostitutes, but nothing has come of it. Now, Investigator Mishkin, do you wish to tell me what this is about?"

"Not yet. No."

"If this involves the Velikayas or any other mafiya family, then the OCC should be made aware."

"I will take that under advisement and consider it carefully. Thank you. You have been most helpful, and I am most grateful." Arkhip slid the table away, pinning Gusev in his seat and giving Arkhip the chance to stand and move to the door. "I will be in touch."

12

Manege Square
Moscow, Russia

Late that afternoon, Charles Jenkins, disguised now as an old man, sat on a bench in Manege Square, kitty-corner from the State Duma federal building on Ulitsa Okhotnyy Ryad. He'd spotted Petrekova's first tail, the same woman from the railway platform and commuter train earlier that morning. She'd changed her look, trying too hard to be decidedly younger in shorts, a T-shirt, and tennis shoes. She'd pulled her hair back into a ponytail and wore unflattering black-framed glasses.

At just after six in the evening, Zenaida Petrekova exited the federal building and stepped between rows of parked cars and over a chain designating a pedestrian walk. Per her routine each night, she gave every indication she would cross the street and descend to the Okhotnyy Ryad Metro station for her trip back to the Kazansky railway station. She did not look rushed or concerned, and she never let her gaze roam in search of her tail, though she knew she was being followed.

She proceeded across the street during a break in traffic to the Metro station stairs. A taxi sped forward and stopped in the far-right lane. A woman dressed similarly to Petrekova stepped out, moving to the stairs. Petrekova casually slid into the back seat just before the taxi merged into Moscow's heavy afternoon traffic.

On the sidewalk, near the entrance to the Metro, Petrekova's tail had her head down, reading her phone and smoking a cigarette. When she looked up, expecting to see Petrekova, she saw the woman from the cab, did a double take, and almost followed her down the steps. Almost. She studied the taxi merging with traffic, dropped her cigarette, and hurried into the street, her hand waving while she simultaneously glanced over her shoulder to track Petrekova's cab.

A car swerved around her, the driver honking his horn. Petrekova's taxi turned at the corner just as a second taxi pulled to the curb and the tail got in. Jenkins hoped the head start was enough to shake the woman, at least long enough for him and Petrekova to talk. Moscow traffic would help. Jenkins had an old-fashioned way to avoid it.

He got on a bike and rode around the block.

Arkhip descended an interior stairwell to the Criminal Investigation Department's Technology Center. Some days, descending and ascending the interior stairs was his only exercise. The Technology Center provided designated investigators with access to live and archived footage obtained from each of Moscow's two hundred thousand CCTV cameras. The footage was stored for five days at a centralized database at the Moscow Department of Information Technologies.

Computers were to Arkhip what holy water was to a vampire. It seemed every time he touched one something burned, then he would have a technician working at his desk for hours to resolve the problem. He had taken the training classes, and he had been personally tutored. He had improved, but technology remained a foreign language.

He pulled open the glass door and stepped inside the center.

"Mishkin. To what do I owe this great pleasure?" asked Vily Stepanov.

Arkhip smiled. Stepanov was a snake. He would sell his mother to make a dime. "I need some footage," Arkhip said.

Stepanov let out a burst of air, like a whale spouting through its blowhole. "How many times do we have to tell you that as a criminal investigator you have access to the information from your desktop computer?"

"At least once more," Arkhip said.

"Very well. It is your time, after all. You'll have to fill out the forms, though. Do you have the location for the video you wish to see?"

"I do. I have the light stanchion number and the time."

"You are on top of things, as always. Fill out the forms. It is a necessity to track who views the information."

"Yes, of course," Arkhip said. "We would not want unauthorized people viewing the information." The requirement was supposed to pacify the activists who protested that the cameras were an invasion of their privacy and used more to identify protestors who opposed the government than to catch criminals. No matter. The courts had approved the cameras, and they were here to stay. Arkhip filled out the form, a laborious process that almost made him want to learn how to access the information on his desktop. Ten minutes after starting he submitted the forms to Stepanov.

"Good. Thank you. Now, you can use that station over there." Stepanov pointed to one of several computer stations in a sealed room. "You will need to type in your identification and your password to gain direct access to the database. From there type in the camera locale and the date and time needed."

Stepanov was also lazy. "Why then did I bother to fill out the forms if I am only going to have to do it again at the computer terminal?"

"Why then did you come down here when you could have typed in the information from your desktop computer?" Stepanov countered. "We are required to log every request to ensure that users cannot reach outside of their sandbox and misuse the system."

"We wouldn't want that," Arkhip said, trying hard not to sound too sarcastic. He, too, considered the cameras a gross violation of personal privacy, but as his father liked to say, *You can sing that song all day long. No one is going to listen.*

Arkhip sat at the computer terminal and entered his name and his password. Following the prompts, he entered the database and typed in the required information. Within seconds he stared at four different camera angles that included the Yakimanka Bar, the alley beside it, and two views of the street on which the bar was located, one faced west, the other east.

Amazing. Incredibly intrusive, but amazing.

Arkhip hit "Play" and all four video images came to life in squares on the screen. Cars passed along the darkened street. Arkhip looked down at the keyboard and pressed the arrow to fast-forward the tape, stopping when Pavil Ismailov parked a large black Mercedes at the curb outside the bar. He let the tape proceed at regular speed. Ismailov exited the driver's side. Though the street was not well lit, that did not impact the cameras. Arkhip used the buttons on the keyboard to put a box around Ismailov's face and hit "Enter." Within seconds, a two-inch-by-two-inch picture appeared in a box on the screen above the name Pavil Ismailov and listed a criminal record for petty crimes—drunk and disorderly, driving under the influence, and solicitation.

Ismailov opened the rear passenger door of the car and a man emerged, followed by a woman. Eldar Velikaya and Bojana Chabon. Velikaya wore a light-colored suit, his tie removed, the buttons of his shirt open to his waist. He took a moment to pull his pants together, zip his fly, and buckle his belt. Chabon stumbled out on red platform heels, nearly falling. Her white dress concealed almost nothing. Arkhip didn't have to be a chief investigator to deduce what Velikaya and the prostitute had been doing in the back of the Mercedes.

The woman teetered on the sidewalk curb and reached out, grabbing the lapel of Velikaya's suit jacket to regain her balance. He slapped her hand away with an angry look and appeared to yell at her. Arkhip again stopped the video and centered on the woman's face. Within seconds her mug shot appeared below Pavil Ismailov's mug shot, along with her name, a list of known aliases, and multiple arrests for prostitution, possession, and solicitation of drugs. He repeated the process for Eldar Velikaya, but the database revealed no prior convictions.

"Doubtful," Arkhip said.

He hit "Play." The threesome entered the building.

He pressed "Fast-forward" until a man approached along the sidewalk and entered the bar. Arkhip backed up the tape and hit "Pause." He zoomed in and moved the square to the man's face. He hit "Enter." The computer did its magic, but this time it produced no photograph or record. *"Net sovpadeniy."* No match.

No criminal record, at least not in Moscow.

Arkhip used the computer mouse to snap a copy of the photograph and sent it to his desktop. He pulled up the camera angle that focused on the alley just west of the bar and fast-forwarded through the tape until the bar door to the alley swung open. The two men and the woman stepped outside. Arkhip zoomed in closer. Velikaya gripped the back of the woman's head. He pushed her up against the stucco wall, then gripped her throat, choking her. Pavil Ismailov stood with his back to the camera. Watching.

Arkhip took a deep breath. The abuse was difficult to stomach. On the second panel, the one displaying the bar entrance, the unknown third man exited and proceeded down the sidewalk to the alley. He certainly walked with a purpose. Remarkable, given that Velikaya was not small, and Ismailov a giant.

Arkhip leaned forward as the man stepped into the alley.

The screen went black, as if someone had pulled the plug on all four cameras.

Someone certainly had. This was not a computer error or an operator error. Someone had gotten to the tape, and that someone was likely Stepanov.

Arkhip left the terminal and returned to the counter.

"All done now, Mishkin?" Stepanov asked, a smug smile on his lips.

"No. I am not. I would like to know who checked out that film before me?"

"That particular film. The odds would seem less than likely."

"Yes, they would," Arkhip said. "Seem less than likely. Please confirm it."

Stepanov typed on his computer screen, then pursed his lips together and shook his head. "No one," he said.

Arkhip smiled. "That's very interesting, don't you think? Of all the cameras in all of Moscow, and the one tape of a murder is suddenly blank? What do you calculate those odds to be?"

"I don't know what to tell you," Stepanov said, still wearing his smug smile. "An unfortunate malfunction, it would seem. It is, however, well known that you have very poor luck with computers, which increases those odds substantially."

"So would a payment. A payment from the Velikaya family to someone within this office. Someone in this office early this morning. I don't see anyone else here but you, Stepanov."

"Go ahead," Stepanov said, shuffling papers and tapping them on the counter but looking a little less sure of himself. His face had become a crimson red. "File a complaint. See how far you get, Mishkin."

"I will. You see, I've already spoken with the organized crime control department and they expressed keen interest in any matter involving the Velikayas. They asked me to keep them informed," Arkhip said. "Be sure that I will do so."

Stepanov looked to be eating his words but said nothing. He stepped away from the counter to his interior office.

Arkhip left. He knew Stepanov was right; lodging a complaint would do little. He could only hope fear might motivate Stepanov a little more.

13

Do or Dye Beauty Salon
Moscow, Russia

Twenty minutes after Petrekova had slipped into her cab, Charles Jenkins, sweating beneath his disguise and the heat baking Moscow, climbed off his bike and carried it down four steps to the Do or Dye Beauty Salon's basement door. He hid the bike behind wooden shelves containing an assortment of supplies, then crept up narrow interior stairs at the rear of the salon. The room contained two deep sinks with extended nozzles for washing clients' hair. A Chinese folding panel separated the area from the remainder of the salon, which consisted of two stylist chairs on a black-and-white checked floor, a small waiting area, and a counter with a computer monitor. The salon smelled of hair chemicals.

The stylist, Suriev, shook his head to indicate Petrekova had not yet arrived. In a chair at one of two sinks sat a woman approximately the same height and build as Petrekova, with presumably the same hair color. She wore a maroon stylist robe snapped tight at the neck, her hair wrapped in a white towel. Her tennis shoes were the same brand and model Petrekova wore to work that morning. This double was a precaution in case Petrekova had not shaken her tail. Though Petrekova had for years had her hair cut and roots dyed by Suriev, she purposely kept no pattern to her appointments, nor did she ever use her cell phone, the phone in her office, or her home phone to make an appointment. The salon was one of the places she and her handler met.

Jenkins had communicated the meeting location in a call that afternoon. He asked to speak to Dasha, which was code for the salon. Petrekova had responded, "There is no one here by that name," to indicate she would make the meeting.

A gay man, Suriev hated the current Russian regime, which oppressed gay people and encouraged the population to persecute them by calling them "subhuman" and "devils." Suriev had been a CIA asset for years, hoping for a regime change.

Jenkins looked to the street. A cab pulled to the curb beside the salon's black awning. Petrekova stepped out and approached the ground-floor business in the four-story apartment building. Like most of Moscow, the area had undergone a revival, though they had kept the architectural character of the redbrick buildings lining both sides of the street.

Jenkins remained behind the divider, watching in a mirror as Petrekova pushed open the door. Chimes signaled her entrance. She greeted her longtime stylist with a kiss on each cheek.

"It has been too long," Suriev said, leading her to one of two salon chairs.

"I've had difficulty freeing myself from work," she said, her message deliberate.

"And today?"

"Today I was determined to do so, and I believe I have succeeded."

"I understand," Suriev said, playing with her hair.

"Can you save me before it's too late?"

Suriev smiled. "Of course. I think we need to trim your split ends while we are at it. They have become unruly."

"Whatever you say," she said. "I'm all yours."

Suriev directed Petrekova to the free chair behind the divider. She looked at Jenkins and the woman seated at the other sink, then sat and leaned her head back while Suriev washed her hair and kept up a steady flow of questions and comments in case someone listened in on the salon. He wrapped her hair in a white towel, then stepped to the look-alike and, using a second towel to partially obscure her face, led her back to the stylist's chair, rotating the chair so the back of the look-alike's head faced the salon windows. There was no mirror to reflect her image.

—

Dmitry Sokalov would have shrunk in his conference room seat at Lubyanka, if possible, to avoid Chairman Bogdan Petrov's stare. Gavril Lebedev sat two seats to Pasternak's left on the same side of the table and looked to also be inching himself as far away from the chairman as possible. Petrov stood with his palms planted on the table and peered up at the three men from beneath his bushy gray eyebrows. His gaze, for the moment, burned holes in General Kliment Pasternak.

"Tell me, General, how two of your most highly trained men could be apprehended by simple Virginia State Police officers." Petrov, a veteran of many clandestine wars, spoke evenly, though his eyes betrayed his calm façade and demeanor.

Pasternak blew out a breath and shook his head. "Everything was going according to plan, Chairman Petrov."

"Apparently not," Petrov interrupted. He straightened. His eyes never left Pasternak. A signal that the general's answer had been insufficient.

Pasternak tried again. "The wife left the house with the two children as scheduled. My men were to wait until they received confirmation of the traffic accident. Confirmation that did not come."

"Why did they not abort immediately?"

"Traffic is as bad in Virginia as here in Moscow. They thought perhaps . . ."

Petrov slapped the table, and his face blotched red. "They are not paid to think, General. They are paid to follow orders. Your orders. Apparently, you did not make *your* orders clear. At the first sign of anything out of the ordinary they should have immediately aborted."

"They did not have time to do so. Ten minutes after the wife left the house, she returned, with the two children still in the car."

Petrov paced the room. "Why did the wife come back?"

"I do not yet know. Perhaps one of the children became sick, or left something at home—homework or a school lunch. I don't know."

"Why did your men not leave immediately when the wife returned home?"

"That was the intent, but the police showed up before they had the chance."

"Who called the police?" Petrov asked.

"Again, we do not know. All I can suggest at the moment is conjecture."

"Which is?"

"That the wife saw the car and my men when she left and had a heightened sense of concern given recent poisonings of persons in similar circumstances as her husband. I can only assume she alerted the police, who also had been made aware of Ibragimov's circumstances, and they responded immediately."

"Where are your men now?" Petrov asked.

"We do not at present know. We are attempting to find out without divulging any link back to Lubyanka or the Kremlin. It is tricky," Pasternak said.

A sickening silence permeated the room. After nearly a full minute, Lebedev waded in with a question. "Have we any information from our diplomats? Perhaps the ambassador—"

"Can what?" Petrov's eyes shifted to Lebedev and nearly burned a hole through him. Lebedev looked as if he had melted into the leather. "Ask whether the Virginia police happened to arrest two men from Russia's most elite special forces division sitting in a car outside the home of a Russian traitor? On this General Pasternak is correct. The Americans will deny they have detained anyone and wait for us to ask about the two men. It would be a tacit admission that your men, General, were authorized by the Russian government to kill Fyodor Ibragimov."

"What then are our options?" Sokalov asked, his voice soft.

"Precisely," Petrov said. "What options can I take to the president?"

"My men will reveal nothing," Pasternak said, trying to sound defiant.

"Their presence has revealed enough," Petrov shot back.

Sokalov knew where this was headed. The president would need to be protected at all costs. Their job now was to provide an excuse to ensure plausible deniability by the Kremlin. It meant someone high up, someone no doubt seated at that table, would have to fall on his sword and admit that his office, without the Kremlin's knowledge or consent, had authorized the mission. In short, someone at the table would be the sacrificial lamb. The United States would never believe this explanation, but they would accept it if they could use it to their advantage, as both sides had done in the past, most likely for an exchange of spies in Russian custody. If the Americans wished to play hardball, however, they could take the matter to an international court and put Russia on a public stage of humiliation and embarrassment.

"Our job now is to protect the president," Petrov said, right on cue. "Our job is to find an alternative that will be satisfactory to the Americans, get our men back, and not result in a black-eye embarrassment to this administration."

No one at the table said a word.

After a moment Lebedev cleared his throat. "If I may suggest . . ."

Petrov glared at him. Sokalov knew that look. Whatever Lebedev had to say, it had better be good.

"If I might suggest that what has happened here is not a simple coincidence."

That comment drew Sokalov's and Pasternak's attention. Both knew what was to come.

"Meaning what?" Petrov asked.

"Meaning that the wife did not just happen to return home, and the Virginia police did not just happen to be in the area before General Pasternak's men could abort and flee."

Sokalov knew what Lebedev was suggesting and what the rat bastard was attempting to do. He was looking to place blame on anyone but himself, likely Pasternak.

"I am suggesting that perhaps the Americans intended this to appear to be a coincidence in order to protect a high-level mole within Lubyanka who leaked the information." Lebedev shifted his girth and looked directly at Sokalov.

Sokalov, initially surprised, took several moments to gather himself. He fumed. "If your suggestion is intended to implicate me, need I remind the deputy director that the president and I go back a very long way, to childhood in fact, that we have been friends for more than sixty years. So please, do not be discreet. Take your implication directly to the president and see how far it goes."

Lebedev smiled like the cat who had caught his prey. "You are too defensive, Dmitry." The use of Sokalov's first name, a sign of disrespect, was purposeful and did not go unnoticed. "I did not intend to implicate *you*. There was someone else from your office in our most recent meeting. Someone from your directorate whose presence you insisted upon, despite my objections. A woman, in power, over the age of sixty."

Sokalov fought against overreacting. "I will have you know . . . Gavril, that Maria Kulikova has worked for me for nearly four decades. Her parents were proud and prominent Communist Party members, and she has been vetted on a number of occasions with no findings of even the smallest stitch of impropriety."

"Perhaps you are . . . too close to Ms. Kulikova to be objective? Is it not your task force's job to interrogate Russian women over sixty years of age and in positions of power? And yet, she has not yet been interrogated."

Sokalov sought another way to defend and deflect. "Your comment is not only offensive to Ms. Kulikova and to me, it is an offense to my wife, Olga, and to her father, General Portnov." Sokalov did not like his father-in-law, but he was not averse to playing that card when it was to his benefit.

"We all know your father-in-law," Lebedev said, but with a tone of caution. "I'm asking why Ms. Kulikova has not yet been questioned by your task force."

"Perhaps you would like to bring something to his attention?"

"If you are through stabbing each other in the back, put your daggers away," Petrov said. "We have more important matters to deal with. General, I want a full update as soon as you have it. Dmitry, as charming as I find Ms. Kulikova, you will undertake an internal investigation to ensure nothing untoward has occurred." He sighed. "I have the unenviable task of breaking the news to the president. But let me make myself very clear, gentlemen. A head . . . or heads . . . will roll. And it will not be mine. I would suggest that you get busy finding the president an alternative he can use to save face if you wish to keep your heads attached to your bodies."

14

Do or Dye Beauty Salon
Moscow, Russia

Jenkins led Petrekova down the narrow staircase to the cramped storage room. Upstairs, Sergei increased the volume of the music. Jenkins turned a dial on what appeared to be an old-fashioned radio on a shelf. It emitted white noise.

"I did not pick up on a tail this afternoon," Petrekova said, speaking Russian.

"A young woman waiting by the Metro stairs. She followed you this morning on the platform, though she changed her appearance this afternoon. Shorts, a T-shirt, hair pulled back in a ponytail. Black-framed glasses."

"I spotted the woman this morning at the train, as well as a man. The woman got off the train two stops early." Petrekova wrapped an arm around her waist. In the basement she had dropped her guard. She looked and sounded frightened. "I have gone back over everything I have done the past six months. I can think of nothing to warrant this attention."

"When did you first notice that you were being followed?"

"Four days ago I picked up on the tail as I commuted to work. I was not certain, but I saw the same man that afternoon when I left the office. He communicated by cell phone to a woman, the same one as this morning. I did this for several days to be certain before I sent word to my handler."

"You didn't do anything wrong." Jenkins explained the president's authorization of Operation Herod.

"He's gone from a rifle to a shotgun then," Petrekova said.

"I'm afraid so."

"But I am an elected member of the Duma and have been for twenty years."

"Your position won't protect you. In fact, it probably pushed you to the top of the list. You have access to information others do not. They are undoubtedly checking to determine if any such information to which you were privy resulted in an asset or operation being burned."

"Then I guess this is over, isn't it? Do you have a plan to get me out?"

Jenkins nodded. "We do."

"When?"

Jenkins would not disclose any details in case Petrekova was a double agent. "You must be prepared to leave at a moment's notice." Petrekova should have known better than to ask, but he chalked it up to nerves. "You can bring nothing with you." He did not want her to be tempted to take something of sentimental value—a photo album, a piece of jewelry, or other items that would potentially alert authorities to her escape.

Petrekova paced the cramped quarters.

"I know you're frightened," Jenkins said. "I know it is hard to leave, but do as I say, when I say it, and everything will be fine."

Not all spies chose to leave their countries, frightened by an uncertain future in an uncertain country with a different language and different customs and without the support of family or friends. Some spies chose instead to remain and take their chances, retiring and going dormant. The problem with this option, however, had become abundantly clear when two American traitors, Robert Hanssen and Aldrich Ames, compromised hundreds of highly classified CIA assets within the Russian government, including many who had retired. Those assets had been immediately arrested, tortured for information, and executed.

Petrekova shook her head. "I am more afraid not to leave. Since my husband's death, I go home each night and rattle around in an empty house and an empty bed. I cook gourmet dinners for one, just to pass the hours. Weekends I spend in the yard, when the weather allows, or visit friends. Neither of my two children live in Moscow any longer, tired of the regime and the corruption. My son lives in Berlin with his German wife. My daughter lives in Canada, working for a high-tech company. Both have implored me to retire and to leave the country. It is time. I feel constantly sick, unable to eat or to sleep. This is no life for me—for anyone. I am ready to go."

Jenkins checked his watch. He had started the stopwatch when they reentered the basement. "You must leave everything in your home as it is—dishes in the sink, a bed unmade, a radio or television on, so as not to arouse any suspicion. Do you have plans on the weekends, things you do routinely?"

"No."

That would hopefully give them sixty hours before suspicions were raised when Petrekova did not appear at the train platform for her regular Monday morning commute.

"Is your house being watched?"

"I presume so, but I don't know."

Jenkins would have to determine this. "Any questions?" he asked. Petrekova shook her head. "It's time," he said. "You better get back upstairs."

She started up the stairs, stopped, and looked down at him. "Are you the man who came before, to stop the American spy divulging the names of the other sisters? The one who got the woman out of Lefortovo?"

Jenkins felt a pang in his stomach, his senses on heightened alert. He would have to be careful. "I know nothing of that operation or that man."

Petrekova took another step but stopped when chimes rang, indicating the front door had been opened. She glanced back at Jenkins, alarm etched on her face.

Jenkins raised a hand and motioned for her to descend. He ascended the staircase slowly, just enough to look in the mirror on the opposite wall reflecting the front door, and the woman from the Metro stop who had entered the salon.

15

Lubyanka
Moscow, Russia

Sokalov returned to his office, poured himself a stiff vodka that he swallowed in a gulp, then poured a second and paced along the windows that provided him a view of the Kremlin's red walls and spires. He felt his pulse slow and exhaled the anger he had toward Lebedev for attempting to throw him under the bus. Sokalov had given the better part of his life to his country, and he had always placed its interests above his own. Yes, he had a mistress; what man in power did not? Affairs had become more common in Moscow since the fall of communism and the prolonged consumer boom. For once, Russians could indulge their whims and their desires. Sokalov knew many men who engaged in anything from single-night trysts with prostitutes to parallel families, often with both wives' approval. What choice did the women have? Divorce? Slipping back to lower class? Raising their children alone? Not that his Olga had to worry, nor would she or her father ever tolerate such an arrangement. But if Lebedev wanted to throw stones, Sokalov had accumulated plenty to throw. He had a file documenting Lebedev's second wife and two children living in an apartment in the Voykovsky District whom Lebedev went home to twice a week and financially supported.

The intercom on his desk phone buzzed. "Deputy Director?"

His secretary. "What is it?"

"Someone here who wishes to see you."

He stepped behind his desk and considered the color-coded calendar he kept on one of multiple computer monitors, though he knew the calendar time slots would be empty since he had instructed his secretary to reschedule everything when he got the call to meet Petrov in the conference room. "I advised you to cancel all of my appointments for the remainder of the day."

"This is unscheduled. I'm told the man has been very persistent."

Sokalov thought it could be Pasternak, the general thinking there could be strength in numbers. However, he dismissed that possibility; at the moment, Lebedev held the better hand, and the wise move by Pasternak would be to hitch himself to the fat bastard and help Lebedev toss Sokalov under the wheels.

"Who is it?" Sokalov asked, ready to dismiss the intrusion.

"Helge Kulikov."

Sokalov froze. He had met Helge at multiple functions and found the man insufferable, unable to talk of anything except his career playing football, usually while drinking copious amounts of free vodka. The two men were cordial. In fact, Sokalov found a perverse pleasure in talking to the man, all the while banging the man's wife.

Vot der'mo. Shit.

Could the drunkard finally have realized Sokalov was sleeping with his wife—after all these years and at this very inconvenient moment? Maria had said Helge had recently retired and he was constantly at home, making it more difficult for her to get away. Sokalov wondered if Helge had come to confront him—security at Lubyanka made it impossible the man had a weapon, but . . .

Vot der'mo.

Sokalov decided it better to meet with the man to determine how much he knew and whether Sokalov could plausibly deny it. What better way to argue his innocence, if the fool were to accuse him, than to meet him here, in his office, with his wife right next door, as if he had nothing to hide?

And if Helge did know, so what? He was in no position to do much of anything.

He could tell Olga.

Der'mo. Der'mo. Der'mo.

Would the man do such a thing? A sickening thought crossed Sokalov's mind.

Had he done so already?

Better to find out now—information was power—and, if necessary, deal with the man's demands.

"Deputy Director?"

"Send him in."

Sokalov opened the top drawer on the right-hand side of his desk and disengaged the safety of his Makarov pistol, then slid the drawer only partially closed so he had easy access to the weapon, if he needed it.

The door to his office pushed in, and his personal assistant led Helge Kulikov across the throw rugs to the two chairs across from Sokalov's desk. Kulikov wore a suit, a size too small from the snug appearance, as well as a tie, though he had lowered the knot and opened the collar button to accommodate his extra weight. He did not look well. He looked pale and bloated. Nervous, but not angry.

"This is an unexpected surprise, Helge." Sokalov offered his hand and Helge took it. Another good sign. Kulikov's fingernails had yellowed from heavy tobacco use. His clothes smelled of cheap cigarettes, alcohol, and mothballs.

"Thank you for seeing me, Deputy Director."

"Please. Deputy Director is for employees. Call me Dmitry." He smiled. "We are both men, are we not?" He walked his assistant to the door and lowered his voice. "Tell no one of this meeting. Understood?"

"Yes, Deputy Director."

He turned back to Kulikov. "Can I offer you something to drink?"

"Yes," Kulikov said a little too quickly. "I mean, thank you."

Sokalov walked to the bar. So far this did not have any of the earmarks of a confrontation. He looked to Kulikov, who had his hands thrust in his suit pockets. "If I remember correctly, you are a Stoli man, are you not?" Sokalov had no clue what vodka Helge Kulikov drank.

"Yes. With one ice cube."

Sokalov poured three fingers, dropped an ice cube into the glass, and handed the drink to Helge. "I'm sorry to make you drink alone, Helge, but I have several late meetings."

"I'm sorry to take up your time."

Sokalov waved off the apology. "Please, sit." He gestured to the two chairs across from his desk. "I would offer you the couch where you could be more comfortable, but my back is sore today, and I need the support of my desk chair." Sokalov looked down at the Makarov as he crossed to his chair. He pulled the drawer out a little farther. "Tell me what it is I can do for you."

Kulikov took more than a sip of his drink and stared at the cube in his glass, as if he might ask for more. "This is difficult for me to say, Dmitry. For any man to say."

Sokalov casually rested his hand on the drawer. "My father always said when something is difficult to say or do, don't delay. Do it. Waiting only makes it worse."

"Yes," Sokalov said. "It is about my wife, Maria."

"What about her?" Sokalov reached inside the drawer and placed his hand on the weapon.

Kulikov sighed and finished his vodka. "I remember when Maria started her work here at Lubyanka. I was curious, of course; who in Moscow is not? There is so much history here. But Maria told me she could not discuss her day. She said it was not allowed, that a spouse could slip and say something . . . divulge classified information, endangering an operation, possibly lives."

"That is true, Helge. That is something we emphasize to all employees. To divulge confidential information, even to a spouse, is grounds for termination."

Helge sat back and took a deep breath. His shoulders shook and he lowered his head. Then he cried. "I believe Maria is having an affair."

Vot der'mo.

Sokalov feigned surprise but his right hand rested on the gun, finger on the trigger. "And why do you believe Maria is having an affair?"

Helge took a deep breath and seemed to gather himself. "I retired this year, from the parks department."

"I recall hearing that news. Congratulations."

Helge took another drink, but the glass was empty. The ice rattled. "Thank you. I am home nights. I noticed phone calls."

"Phone calls? From her lover?"

"No . . ." Helge shook his head. "I mean, I don't know. Not for certain. A man, but always he asks for someone different."

"A wrong number then?" Sokalov lowered his hand from the drawer. He had never called Maria's home. They communicated only at work, agreeing where to meet and when. Burner phones were used to text a change in plans, or regrets.

"That is how it is made to appear."

An odd assessment, Sokalov thought. "Whom do they ask for?"

"He. It is always the same man. I am very good with voices."

"Who does *he* ask for?"

"A different name each time, Dmitry. Never the same name. The other night he asked for Anna."

"Always they . . . he . . . asks for a woman?"

"No. Sometimes he asks for a man."

"I see." Sokalov felt jealousy roiling in his stomach. Could Maria be having another affair? "What do you tell this man?"

"I tell him he has the wrong number and he hangs up."

Sokalov found this odd, but he was now interested in the calls for a completely different reason. "Did you ask Maria about these telephone calls?"

"She claims she has no idea who this man is. She says it is possible our lines have been crossed, but if that were true then . . . I mean, the caller would ask for the same person each time, not a different name; would he not?"

"One would think." It was a plausible deduction. A good one. Maybe Sokalov had misjudged the man's acumen, then again even a broken clock was right twice a day. "Is there anything else causing you concern?"

From his jacket pocket Kulikov pulled out a watch and a bracelet and held them across the desk. Sokalov recognized both pieces, gifts he had given to Maria over the years, usually as an apology after one of his tirades and mass firings of her staff. Ordinarily Maria kept the jewelry locked in the safe in her office for this very reason.

"They are real, Deputy Director. I took them to a jeweler who confirmed it. Seven hundred and fifty thousand rubles, possibly more. I could never afford such luxury."

Sokalov took the pieces. "Hmm . . . ," he said. "Where did you find them?"

"In the back of her dresser. Hidden in a stocking."

"Did you confront your wife?"

"No."

"You didn't ask her where the jewelry came from?"

"I thought it best if she did not know I had found them . . . until I had something more. I have been trying to catch her with her lover. I did not want her to know I suspected."

Sokalov flinched. "How have you tried to catch her?"

"The other night . . ." He dropped his head, thinking. "Maybe two weeks ago, there was another phone call, another wrong number.

This time the caller asked for Anna. When I hung up my wife seemed interested in the call."

"What did she say?"

"She said she was taking Stanislav out for a walk."

"Your dog, I believe, a gift for your retirement."

"Yes. I thought maybe the caller was her lover and Maria was slipping out to meet him. I followed her, in disguise, of course." He looked to Sokalov for approval.

"Of course," Sokalov said.

"She took the subway."

"To walk the dog?" Sokalov asked. Again, this did seem like odd behavior.

Kulikov sat forward in his seat and put his glass on Sokalov's desk, his eyes wide, his voice again seeking approval. "That's what I thought. Odd, isn't it? I mean, we live in the Yakimanka District. There are many parks to walk a dog. We are not far from Gorky Park. So I'm thinking, Why would she take the subway?"

Sokalov leaned forward, lifted Helge's glass, and placed it on a coaster so as not to damage the wood. "And did you follow her? Where did she go?"

"First? First she went to Teremok."

Another surprise.

"She said she was picking up something to eat. After, she went to the Temple of the Martyr Anastasia. The temple is small and there was only one other couple so I remained outside."

"A temple? That does seem odd." Sokalov felt himself getting angry. "But how do you know she met a lover if you did not go inside?"

"I watched from a window. Maria knelt before an icon. She waited until the couple left."

"To do what?"

Kulikov raised a finger. "That is the odd part. She walked around the back of the icon." He arched his eyebrows, as if he'd just disclosed some nuclear code.

"To do what?" Sokalov asked.

"I don't know. I couldn't see. After a moment, she left."

Sokalov sat back, trying to hide his anger for having wasted precious time with this fool. "She picked up dinner, then went to a church where she knelt before an icon. Then she went behind the icon. Then she left?"

"Yes. I was about to go inside the church when a man arrived."

"Her lover?" Sokalov again became interested.

"I believed so, yes."

"You confronted him, then," Sokalov asked.

"No."

"No?" *Bosh! This man is a coward as well as a fool.*

"I could not be sure, not without Maria present, but I watched him and . . . he, too, went inside and he, too, walked to the back of the icon."

Sokalov had to admit, there didn't seem a ready explanation for this behavior. "Then what?"

"He left."

"And then you confronted him."

"No."

"You didn't confront the man you believe your wife is having an affair with? For God's sake, why not?" Sokalov caught himself. "I'm sorry. I just expected that you would."

"How could I confront them if they were not together? The man would have denied any knowledge of what I was talking about, and then he would have warned Maria that I was on to them. If he was her lover."

"What then did you do?"

"I went inside to see what was behind the icon."

"And . . ."

"A guard showed up and kicked me out to lock the temple for the night."

"So . . . you found nothing?"

"No, but don't you think that is odd behavior for one person, let alone two so close in time to one another?"

"Yes. It is, certainly." Sokalov pushed a button beneath his desk. A moment later his phone buzzed. Sokalov picked up the receiver and acted as if he were listening to someone speak. He hung up. "I'm sorry to cut our conversation short, Helge, but I have meetings, as I said. Let me cut to the chase here. What is it that you would have me do?"

"Maria respects you, Dmitry. She respects this office. I understand that affairs are forbidden so employees don't divulge classified information to a lover."

"As I said, it is frowned upon."

"I was hoping you might speak to her, in private, remind her of her responsibilities and the potential risk she is taking. This is a difficult thing for a man to ask . . . I was once a professional football player; have I told you that before?"

Sokalov tried his best to look grave. Inside he smiled. The man was asking Sokalov to spend time with his wife. Sokalov would certainly accommodate him. He'd spend time on top of and below Maria. "Yes, Helge, and I know you are a proud man, a proud Russian man. I promise you I will look at this from every possible angle. You don't need to trouble yourself or do anything more. If I learn of anything, anything at all, I will notify you immediately." He looked to the jewelry on the desk. "Let me keep these for when I speak to Maria. It will give me some credibility, don't you think?"

"Yes, of course." Kulikov sighed in relief.

Sokalov moved toward the office door. The two men shook hands. "Speak of this to no one," Sokalov said. "We do not want to ruin a woman's reputation . . . or yours, if this turns out to be nothing at all."

"Of course, Dmitry. I appreciate you being discreet."

Helge stepped from the office and Sokalov closed the door behind him. He nearly laughed out loud. He went back to his desk and picked up the jewelry. Thinking. Part of him wanted to call Maria into the office and spank her, then take her right on his desk . . . maybe with her husband watching. Maybe then the idiot would understand.

He caught himself and tempered his thoughts. Though relieved, he knew he had dodged a bullet. Maria's sloppiness bringing the jewelry home had nearly exposed them both, and the consequences for Sokalov were far more grave.

He also couldn't dismiss the wrong numbers and the excursion to a temple. Could Maria be having an affair with another man? Doing to him all the things she did for Sokalov? Did she even have the time?

Sokalov picked up the desk phone and pressed her call button. "Can you come in, please."

A moment later, Maria stepped into his office. "Yes? Did you need something?"

He flipped a switch, creating white noise in his office. "I need you. I've missed not seeing you," he said.

"You have been busy, and you must keep Olga happy, after all."

"Do not remind me. Were it not for her father, you and I could be together." That would never happen, but he hoped the possibility would keep Maria spreading her legs.

"I understand the situation and have for some time, Dmitry."

"Would you like that, to be with me?"

"Do not toy with my emotions."

No. He would leave the toying to her. "I had a visitor this afternoon. Do you know who?"

Maria shook her head.

"Your husband."

"Helge?" Her jaw dropped and she paled.

Sokalov placed the watch and the bracelet on his desk. Her shoulders slumped. "He believes you are having an affair."

She shut her eyes. After a moment she said, "Oh, Dmitry, I am sorry."

"He said he found these hidden in your stockings."

She sighed. "It was careless of me to bring them home. It was the night we went to the Bolshoi. I wanted to wear them out, Dmitry. I wanted to look good for you. I'm sorry. I didn't have a chance to put them back in the safe, so I hid them in my drawer. I forgot all about them."

"You must be careful. Helge is following you."

"Following me? Why?"

"He told me that you have been receiving telephone calls, wrong numbers—"

"Ugh." She turned away. Her voice became defiant. "He is obsessed with these wrong numbers, but he won't call the telephone company to find out why we keep getting them. Let me guess. He told you the calls are from my lover setting up secret rendezvous."

"That is exactly what he said. He said he followed you one night when you walked the dog."

Again, she shook her head to indicate she did not know what he meant. "I always walk the dog while he sits and drinks vodka."

"He followed you to Teremok."

She sighed. "I picked up dinner. I didn't feel like being home with him again when he'd been drinking." She shook her head. "And I stopped for a bit at the Temple of the Martyr Anastasia."

"Why?"

Tears pooled in her eyes. "I didn't want to go home. So . . ."

"Oh, *Zaychik*, I am sorry. Come here." He held out a hand. Maria stepped toward him and offered her hand. He felt the warmth and softness of her skin and thought of running his hand along the smooth contours of her body. He could smell her perfume and the scent of her; her vulnerability was Pavlovian. He felt himself becoming aroused.

Tears ran down her cheeks. Maria removed her hand to wipe them away and save her makeup.

"I find excuses to not be at home, but now Helge is retired, with nothing but time for these silly accusations."

"Not so silly. You do have a lover." Sokalov smiled.

Another sigh. "He thinks he is Porfiry Petrovich," she said, referring to the lead investigator in *Crime and Punishment*.

"He said you went behind the icon and, that after you left, a man went into the church and did the same."

She laughed lightly. "Extra candles are kept behind the statue. If you want to light a candle and leave a donation, that's where you will find them."

Sokalov laughed. "Maybe he is more Inspector Clouseau than Petrovich."

"Dmitry, I am so sorry he bothered you with this nonsense. How should I handle it?"

"Tell him that I spanked you a hundred times. You would like that, would you not? I know I would." He adjusted the crotch of his pants so she could see his arousal.

"I'm serious, Dmitry. What do I tell him to make him let this go? If I don't, he might very well catch the two of us and go to Olga. Then what would happen?"

"Yes," Sokalov said, the very mention of his wife's name sending a chill through his body, deflating him. He thought for a moment, then said, "Tell him that I confronted you with the jewelry, and I admonished you and reminded you of your duties and your responsibilities and that the matter is now over."

"Thank you, Dmitry. What would I do without you?"

He opened his knees to pull her closer. She placed a hand on his desk, bent her leg, and jammed her knee into his crotch. He flinched as she added more weight. "Why did you toy with me? Do you not trust me, Dmitry?" She jammed the knee against him a second time.

Sokalov groaned from the pain and the pleasure he derived from it. "It was silly of me. I was just having some fun."

She applied even more pressure, enough that he sat upright. "As if I have time for another man." She leaned in close. The aroma of her perfume intoxicated him. His Adam's apple bobbed. "Are you man enough for me, Dmitry?" She put her arms around his neck. Her shirt fell open, the gold chain and the crucifix dangling between her beautiful breasts. She nibbled his ear, a sensation that made his legs go weak. "Do you have time for me to show you now?"

He moaned. "Bosh! I cannot. Something has come up. A problem I must deal with before Chairman Petrov will have my head."

"Pity," she cooed. Her tongue traced the contours of his ear and she pulled his face deep into her cleavage. "Tell me you're sorry. Tell me." When he didn't immediately respond she jammed her knee again into his crotch. He winced, then felt himself release all the tension of the day, maybe the week.

He moaned. "I'm sorry."

16

Do or Dye Beauty Salon
Moscow, Russia

Charles Jenkins stepped down the back staircase to the storage room, hiding in the shadows but still able to watch the mirror on the salon wall, angled so he could see the store's front. Bells atop the shop door rattled. The young woman wearing shorts and a T-shirt who Jenkins had spotted outside the Metro station closed the door behind her. Jenkins looked to Suriev, standing behind the salon chair. He had shut his eyes, realizing too late his failure to lock the door and turn the window sign to "Closed" after Petrekova had entered.

Suriev opened his eyes and glanced over his shoulder, speaking casually. *"Ya vernus' k vam cherez minutu."* I'll be with you in a moment.

The woman stepped to her right to better view the person seated in the chair, not doubt to confirm it was Petrekova, but Suriev had also stepped to his right to block her view. When the woman took another step, Suriev reached for a jar on his tray, unscrewed the top, and applied green cream liberally to the look-alike's face. Then he approached the counter.

"Chem ya mogu pomoch' vam?" How can I help you?

"I'm thinking of a haircut," the woman said, speaking to Suriev, but looking past him to the chair. "Perhaps some highlights."

"Can you remove your hair band, please?" The woman did. Suriev stepped forward. "Turn around, please." The woman turned toward the street. Suriev played with her hair. After a moment he said, "I can cut your hair for you, but I wouldn't highlight it. Your hair has beautiful natural highlights as it is."

A beeper buzzed. "Suriev," the woman from the chair called.

"I'll be with you in a moment, Zenaida." He moved to the counter, looking at a computer monitor. "I could squeeze you in next week. Say, Tuesday evening at five thirty."

"I have an engagement this weekend. Can you do it tonight?" the woman said.

"I'm afraid not. Zenaida is my last client."

"Then I'll have to go somewhere else," the woman said. She moved to the door, glancing over her shoulder one last time before she departed. This time Suriev locked the door and turned the window sign, releasing a huge sigh.

17

Ministry of Internal Affairs
Building 38, Petrovka Street
Moscow, Russia

Arkhip returned to his desk following an hour-long meeting with his captain. He could no longer hide the news of Eldar Velikaya's death; the murder at the Yakimanka Bar had leaked inside the department and was being broadcast all over state TV. People would now be guarded about what they said—if they said anything. His captain wanted to know the status of Arkhip's investigation, whether Eldar Velikaya had been the victim of a mafiya hit and if the ministry should brace for a possible war on the streets of Moscow.

Arkhip assured him any such conclusion was premature and unsupported by the current evidence, which was admittedly limited. Though twenty years Arkhip's junior, and light-years behind Arkhip in experience, that didn't stop the captain from telling Arkhip how to do his job. He'd even suggested that, with Arkhip on the verge of retirement, the file be transferred to investigators with more vested interest in the outcome. Arkhip gently reminded the captain that he had a perfect record as an investigator, and he assured him he had a vested interest in seeing that the murder of Eldar Velikaya did not besmudge all that he had worked so hard to achieve. He would see the investigation through to its conclusion, and he preferred to remain active until his final day on the job, though if the resolution of this case lingered, he would willingly continue.

Arkhip's desk computer pinged, an e-mail from the medical examiner's office with an attachment for his eyes only. He opened the e-mail, then the preliminary medical report on the death of Eldar Velikaya. He picked up his reading glasses from his desk and slipped them onto the bridge of his nose, skimming the opening paragraphs, which provided details about where the body was found, its position, etcetera, etcetera.

Near the bottom he found what he was looking for.

Cause of death: trauma caused by a single gunshot wound to the abdomen.

Arkhip read the sentence a second, then a third time, not believing the words on the screen. He had seen the body. He had seen the bullet hole in the man's back and the ragged exit wound. He had seen the excessive bleeding on the front of the man's shirt, the pool of blood on the ground. The man had clearly been shot in the back. Any idiot with even a modicum of training and experience would know this to be true. Which left just one conclusion. This was no error. This was a deliberate fabrication.

He reached for his desk phone to call the medical examiner's office just as the phone rang. Caller ID did not come up on the digital register, and Arkhip did not recognize the number to be within Building 38, Petrovka Street.

"Mishkin," he said in a terse tone.

"Arkhip. It's Aaron."

"Who?"

"Aaron from the *car repair shop*. We have finished work on the car you brought us."

Arkhip needed a moment to grasp the complexities of the call, still focused on the ME's report.

"I'm afraid it is a bit more complicated than we suspected," Aaron continued. "Can you meet me at the repair shop in fifteen minutes?"

Things clicked. "Yes," he said. "Yes, I can."

The line went dead.

———

Ten minutes later, Arkhip departed Petrovka and stepped into another warm Moscow evening. Car and foot traffic on the streets and sidewalks was heavy. Muscovites sat at tables beneath awnings and umbrellas, drinking coffee or beer and getting a jump on the weekend. "Aaron" was Adrian Zima, who worked in the latent fingerprint lab within the ministry's Criminal Investigation Department. Whenever Adrian believed he had sensitive information to impart to Arkhip, he suggested they meet at the "car repair shop." The name was his code for the Pit Stop Café, which had once been a car repair shop before the owner fell victim to Moscow's robust renovation in advance of hosting the 2018 World Cup. The owner, in business more than forty years, was strongly advised to take a payment and find a more suitable area for his business. Like most receiving such offers, he took the payoff and closed his doors.

The Pit Stop was a ten-minute walk from the ministry, near the corner of Petrovka and Strastnoy Boulevard. The repurposing and renovations of the businesses along these blocks seemed to happen overnight. Though Arkhip found it sad to know so many people lost their businesses, the revitalization had accomplished what the government intended, bringing in younger and more vibrant crowds to the cafés, bars, and restaurants, and presenting the world with the modern face of Russia.

Out with the old, in with the new, his Lada would have said. Soon it would be Arkhip who received a not-so-gentle shove to the door. He had one foot on the threshold as it was. What then?

What will I do at home, without you, Lada?

Maybe he'd travel. Maybe he'd join one of those singles groups that took trips around the world. He'd stand on cruise ships in white loafers with dark socks and shorts and put on weight, telling everyone he should have retired years earlier.

He chuckled at the thought of what Lada would say to such a ridiculous suggestion.

You, stand on a cruise ship deck for days? You can't sit still for a minute. You'd lose your mind.

The Pit Stop had kept the repair shop's rolling, multiplaned glass door, and it had been rolled up so customers could sit outside at sidewalk tables, though apparently not to converse. Most had their heads down, their fingers rapidly punching their phone keys. Arkhip never understood such behavior. Why get together only to talk on your phone to someone else?

The young didn't yet understand time was precious. They thought time unlimited and themselves immortal. So had Arkhip, until it wasn't. Until his Lada wasn't.

Love is lost on youth.

Adrian sat at a table in the back corner. Arkhip would have preferred to save his money and not order anything, but he felt self-conscious walking past the counter without ordering. The rich aroma of coffee and the different tea blends, lemon and peppermint, filled the air. A young woman lifted her head as he approached, but she didn't greet him or even smile.

He smiled at her anyway. "Chamomile tea," he said. If he drank caffeinated tea or coffee at this hour, he would be awake all night—which he often was anyway.

"For here or to go?"

"I'm here. Am I not?" he said. She looked confused. He pointed. "I'll be at the table in the corner, sitting with the gentleman wearing glasses."

She rolled her eyes and pointed to a sign hanging above the counter. Arkhip looked up to read it: "Pick Up." "We don't deliver," she said.

"Then I suppose I'll wait." A moment later, after charging him far too much for tea, the woman handed him an oversized porcelain mug, and Arkhip carefully made his way to where Adrian sat waiting. Adrian was often melodramatic, but he had good instincts and Arkhip had come to trust him as one of the still-honest members of the Moscow police department.

Arkhip set his mug on the table and carefully sat so as not to spill the contents. "How have you been?" he said to Adrian.

"I've been better."

"You have been busy?"

"We are always busy, Arkhip. We are always backed up with DNA analysis."

"So then, to what do I owe this pleasure?"

Adrian leaned forward. "Your fingerprint in the case you pulled. You know the victim is Eldar Velikaya."

"I assure you I am aware," Arkhip said, hoping this wasn't the reason Adrian requested the meeting.

Adrian sat back. He looked hurt. Arkhip knew better. Adrian held information to play the role of investigator to as large an audience as possible, in this case only one, but still a performance.

"But I certainly don't have all the information," Arkhip added. "There have been some strange developments."

"They are about to get more strange." Adrian glanced to his left, then his right, though no one sat at the tables beside them. "I pulled the police report. That report indicates the fingerprints came from a beer bottle and were most likely left by a man who entered the bar and sat in a booth near the front. Facial recognition cameras identified the man as Charles Wilson, a British industrialist."

"I had not yet heard the name, but the details are accurate."

"Then something is seriously wrong . . . perhaps purposefully."

"What do you mean?" Arkhip asked, though "seriously wrong" would certainly fit with the evidence to date.

Adrian turned and pulled a sheet of paper from a briefcase beside his chair. He slid the paper facedown across the table while looking behind Arkhip at the others in the café. "Be discreet," he whispered.

Adrian was laying it on thick. "I will. I assure you."

Arkhip took the paper and discreetly turned it over. He stared at the face of a Black man. He read the vitals. Charles William Jenkins: 1.96 meters; 104 kilograms.

American.

Central Intelligence Agency officer.

"This is the fingerprint match?" Arkhip asked.

Adrian nodded his head.

"Are you certain?"

"More than sixteen matching points of identification," Adrian said. "Without doubt."

Arkhip sat back. He would have thought it a mistake, but too many other things—the missing facial recognition video, the doctored medical examiner's report, and the two eyewitnesses now dead—indicated this was no mistake. And that made it truly of interest. Arkhip had wondered why someone who had never been inside the Yakimanka Bar picked it that night. Now he wondered if the choice wasn't a coincidence at all.

But what did a CIA officer want with Eldar Velikaya?

"Does he work here in Moscow at the American embassy?"

Adrian shook his head. "I checked. The embassy denied knowing the name, and there is no one there registered under this name."

"A CIA officer," Arkhip said to himself.

"That is Lubyanka's designation, not the Americans'. As I said. This man does not exist."

Arkhip doubted it. Movies had romanticized spies. Most were far removed from the swashbuckling Hollywood creations of James Bond and Jason Bourne.

"Why would he come to the Yakimanka Bar?" Arkhip asked.

"It seems obvious, doesn't it?"

"What seems obvious?" Arkhip asked.

"Don't be thick, Arkhip. He came to kill Eldar Velikaya. What other explanation could there be?"

"What interest would a CIA officer have in killing Eldar Velikaya?"

"I don't know. If I had to place a bet, though, I'd place it on drugs. On the drug trade."

Arkhip thought of his earlier conversation with Inspector Gusev of the OCC and his statement that the Velikayas had moved toward legitimizing their businesses. The drug trade would be antithetical to such legitimization.

"But I'll bet this is going to set off all kinds of bells and whistles at Lubyanka," Adrian continued. He tapped the photograph of Charles Jenkins. "This man is wanted. I talked with my friend—"

"What?" Arkhip quickly looked up from the paper. "You talked to someone about an ongoing murder investigation?"

"You know me better than that. No. Of course not. I mentioned nothing of your investigation. I simply asked him to pull what information the FSB had on this man." Adrian again tapped the photograph with his index finger, causing the table to wobble. "Like you, I thought my friend would tell me this Charles Jenkins worked at the American embassy."

"What did he say?"

Adrian leaned forward, setting his palm on the photograph. "He said this man is a spy, that he has twice escaped pursuit by the FSB. The Counterintelligence Directorate has an entire file on him, and he is classified as being of the highest priority." Adrian leaned away from the table, resting an arm on the back of a nearby chair. He stared at Arkhip knowingly. "He is a big fish, Arkhip. A very big fish. If he killed Eldar Velikaya, you cannot reel him in on your own."

And therein was the problem. Arkhip did not believe the man had killed Eldar Velikaya. It was a possibility, but a remote one, at least based on what the bartender saw in the alley, and the medical evidence Arkhip had seen with his own two eyes. Arkhip also had it on very good authority that CIA officers did not carry weapons, not ordinarily. But all of that was putting the cart before the horse. Arkhip didn't care who the man was or what he had done in his past. He cared only that Charles Jenkins was a material witness to a murder. A murder Arkhip was tasked with solving. The decedent was far more complicated than an ordinary drunk killed in a bar fight, and now so was the murder suspect, but that didn't change Arkhip's job. His job was to close the file, as he had always done.

Still, he wondered what this man was doing in a dilapidated bar, in disguise no less. Did the CIA have some interest in Eldar Velikaya?

Perhaps they did. Perhaps Adrian was correct and Arkhip had finally landed that very big fish.

"Why are you smiling?" Adrian asked.

Arkhip didn't realize he had been. "No reason," he said.

"I should think not," Adrian said. "You need to walk away from this, Arkhip. Walk as far and as fast as you can. Retire. Something like this could linger for months, perhaps years."

Which is exactly why Arkhip had been smiling. He liked nothing more than a good challenge. If that challenge required that he stay in his employ as a chief investigator, well . . . so be it.

He didn't like cruises, and he didn't like white loafers.

What he liked, especially since Lada's death, was being kept busy and active. If he was going to be forced into a retirement he did not want, he would go *his* way, with a perfect record. To do that he needed to locate this man, Charles Jenkins, and find out what had actually happened.

And he would.

Maybe not as fast as some, but he didn't fancy himself the hare anyway. He was the turtle. Slow and steady. He'd close this file.

He always did.

18

Velikaya Estate
Novorizhskoye, Russia

Mily Karlov waited patiently in Yekaterina Velikaya's garden, holding a laptop computer. Her father had never showed any interest in the plants and the flowers. As with most things, Alexei Velikaya paid someone to take care of the garden. Yekaterina's love of flowers came from her mother, who had spent hours planting and pruning and consulting with some of Moscow's more prominent master gardeners. The gardens had been highlighted in countless magazines and newspaper articles and had won multiple awards.

Yekaterina ended all of that.

She would never allow her gardens to be featured in any magazine or newspaper articles. She did not garden for the accolades or the prestige. She gardened for the peace and the solitude. Yekaterina was an unwilling celebrity. She had never just been Yekaterina. She had been Alexei Velikaya's daughter, constantly surrounded by bodyguards whenever she left the compound to do anything: visit a friend, go to a birthday party, attend school. She never knew real life as a child. As an adult, she rarely went out to dinner, rarely attended social functions, not even for the charities to which she gave lavishly. The garden was the one outdoor place she could go on her own, where she could find solitude amid her Beauty of Moscow lilacs, roses, chrysanthemums, and orchids.

Mily respected her privacy—particularly given what had happened to her father and grandfather and now, perhaps, to her son. Was it also a government bullet this third time, a not-so-subtle message, perhaps, to keep Yekaterina in her place? She was head of the most powerful crime family in Moscow, and her business acumen only increased her wealth and her power each year. Was this a shot across the bow, a warning, or something else entirely?

Mily had no doubt about one thing. Yekaterina would find out.

With his help.

Mily had done what she had asked, what he had always done. He had gathered information, and he had spun it to reflect the best interests of the family. Guns and bullets could kill, but information could destroy. You controlled information two ways. One was to pay for it. The other was far less expensive but required far more effort. The Yakimanka bartender took the first option. Mily figured he would, given the condition of the bar. If called as a witness, he would recall Eldar and Pavil Ismailov arriving to play pool in his bar with the prostitute, but claim the prostitute left on her own, or that he did not see her go out the back door with the two men. The investigator, Arkhip Mishkin, would dispute this, but what evidence did he have to do so? The CCTV video of the alley would have supported Mishkin, but no longer. And the medical examiner's report would fit nicely into the story Yekaterina wished to portray. The prostitute and Pavil would also not support him.

The only wild card was the third man and, therefore, who could get to him first.

Mily turned at the sound of footsteps crunching the red gravel. Yekaterina approached with her eyes turned to her meticulous flower beds. Though it was dusk, the garden was well lit. Yekaterina carried a bucket of gardening tools and several plastic flats with sprouting plants nourished in one of her hothouses. She walked to a patch of plants that had died, knelt, and slipped on gardening gloves.

"What did you learn?" She pulled up the dead plants and shook the soil from their roots.

Mily recounted all that he had done. The prostitute, Pavil Ismailov, the CCTV tape and the medical examiner's report, the bartender's recollection. As he spoke, Yekaterina pulled several plants from their plastic containers and placed them in holes she had dug in the soil. Mily handed her the watering jug.

"The only loose end is this third man," Mily concluded.

"What do you know about him?"

"The bartender described him as big. Almost two meters and 100 to 105 kilograms. He wore a leather coat, but the bartender said he was well built. Gray hair, mottled skin. The bartender said he would guess early to midsixties."

She turned her head and looked up at Mily, as he thought she might. "And he took down Pavil and Eldar? Show me the video?" She sat back on her calves and removed her gloves, offering Mily her hand. He helped her to her feet.

"Are you sure you don't want me to just tell you what happened, Comare?"

She shook her head. "Play it."

Mily flipped open the laptop and hit the "Play" button on the keyboard. He handed her the computer.

Yekaterina did not use a computer—not a desktop nor a laptop. She did not use an iPad or a cellular phone. She did not use technology. It was too easily hacked, especially by the government. She learned from her father to conduct all her business orally and with a firm handshake. Her papers for her legitimate businesses were kept in a sealed, fireproof vault in the basement. The house had been fitted with devices to disrupt and jam directional microphones, as were her cars. Her business was her business. No one else's.

Mily stepped back to provide her with privacy.

"Did the bartender say whether Eldar or Pavil had been abusive to the prostitute inside the bar?"

Mily did not hesitate. "He said Eldar roughed up the woman when she dropped a beer. He shoved her to the ground and told her to lick it up like a dog."

She handed him back the laptop. After a moment to get her emotions in control, she asked, "Have you identified this man in the video?"

"He is not in the police system or in the Moscow Department of Information Technologies database."

She looked at him over the laptop screen. To be in neither was almost impossible in this new Russia.

"Russian?" she asked.

"The bartender said the man spoke Russian, but he did not believe him to be Russian. His speech was too formal."

"Chechen?"

"No. He said most likely American or British."

"But not a tourist?" she said.

"It would seem unlikely given his choice of bars."

"Did the bartender know why this man came?"

Mily shrugged. "For a beer and something to eat. He left a fingerprint on a bottle. I am awaiting a telephone call to find out if it provides any further information."

She gave this some thought as the video played.

"The bartender said he took an interest in Eldar," Mily said.

"In what way?"

"This man appeared to be bothered by Eldar's treatment of the woman. The bartender suggested to the man that he leave the bar, but this man initially declined. He reconsidered when Eldar took the woman into the alley."

Mily's cell phone rang. "This is my contact now. He may enlighten us," he said and turned away.

—

Yekaterina watched Eldar and Pavil exit the side door into the alley. Eldar dragged the woman with him and shoved her against the wall. A moment later the other man stepped down the alley. He must have said something because both Eldar and Pavil turned and looked at him. After a few moments when more words were likely said, Eldar and Pavil converged on the man with the broken pool cue. The man disarmed Eldar, likely dislocating or breaking his elbow, then disarmed Pavil and knocked him backward, into garbage. Pavil, with his gun in hand, came out of the garbage cans into which the man had knocked him. In that same instant, Eldar rose to his feet. Her son fell forward, into the man's arms.

Mily hung up the phone and returned his attention to her.

"Are there copies of this tape?" she asked.

"I am told there are not."

"This man is trained to fight," she said.

"Yes," Mily said. "I would say tactically trained."

"Military?"

"Maybe," Mily said. He held up his phone. "We have a positive identification. The fingerprint belongs to a Charles William Jenkins."

"American?"

"CIA."

"CIA?"

"And he is wanted very badly by the Kremlin. He is on a kill list."

Yekaterina paced the red gravel of her flower garden. She did not speak for nearly a minute. Then she said, "A CIA officer, tactically trained, just happens to enter a piece-of-shit bar late at night . . . a bar that Eldar frequented?" She turned to Mily. "I want to know who this man really is and who sent him. I want to know why he killed my son."

"You've seen the video, Comare. Pavil shot Eldar."

"Perhaps, but this man caused it. I want to know why. And I do not for a minute believe it was to protect some heroin-addicted prostitute. I have many enemies, Mily—many with an interest in seeing Eldar dead. Find this man. Bring him to me. I wish to find out for myself his purpose in killing my son."

19

Korolyov
Moscow Oblast, Russia

Sarafina Chernoff sipped coffee in the front seat of the Lada Vesta, parked in the shadows cast by the tree at the end of the street. She watched the redbrick house in the middle of the street—what ordinarily would promise to be a long and uneventful Friday night, except what had happened that afternoon did not sit well with her.

Petrekova had given every indication she intended to take the Metro to the train station, then quickly slipped into the back of a taxi-cab. It had happened quickly, without any delay, and the woman who had exited the cab had been dressed similar to Petrekova, with similar hair color, and similar in size. Chernoff had no information, from any source, that Petrekova had an appointment to get her hair dyed and cut, which also seemed odd. Popular stylists were often booked months in advance, though perhaps maybe not for a member of the Duma. Ordinarily this information would not have amounted to much, but in this instance, it had all the earmarks of a target evading a tail.

"You had a close call today," her partner, Dima Vinchenko, said in between sips of coffee. From the smell in the car, it was more than coffee, likely spiked with rum.

"I had to confirm it was her," she said. "I didn't want there to be any mistakes."

"I should think not. The deputy director would not look kindly on such a mistake," Vinchenko said with a straight face, though his tone sounded sarcastic.

Chernoff considered his comment and said, "Do you think she is one of them?"

"What? One of the seven sisters?" Vinchenko shrugged. "Personally, I think this is all an American farce to keep us chasing our tails—like their Star Wars program to defend against nuclear attack. I don't believe there ever were seven women trained from birth to spy on the Soviet Union. Think about it. What are the odds?"

"Equal to the odds of Russian illegals placed in the United States and raised from birth to be spies."

Vinchenko shook his head. "You are comparing apples to oranges. Russian illegals have long existed, and patience is part of the Russian way of life. Americans have never had that same strength. They are a consumer society. They want everything yesterday."

"But the women are not American. They are Russian."

Vinchenko opened his mouth as if to respond, then paused. Chernoff had made her point. After a beat he said, "Maybe, but the Americans elect a new government every four years. They lose focus and interest. Here, we have the same people in power . . . maybe for decades; it allows for continuity and long-term strategic planning."

Vinchenko's phone rang. He answered, listened for a few moments, grunted a reply, and clicked off. "She is coming. Nothing of interest. They have broken off their tail. It's just the two of us tonight."

"There." Chernoff pointed and raised the binoculars, watching Zenaida Petrekova walk down the dirt road to her home. Petrekova unlocked the door in the metal gate that allowed a car ingress and egress and stepped inside.

"What I wouldn't do for a detached home," Vinchenko said. He set his seat back. "Get ready for a long night of nothing."

———

Jenkins waited in Zenaida Petrekova's modest kitchen listening to each tick of the wall clock. He continued to wear the old-man disguise he'd worn earlier in the day and sat at a table pushed up against the wall and positioned beneath a ubiquitous picture of fruit on a tray with a darkened background. The setup seemed a sad commentary on the solitude of Petrekova's life. Meals at his home on Camano Island with Alex, CJ, and little Lizzie were lively affairs filled with laughter—most aimed at some Lizzie antic. His daughter was old enough to perform, and their laughter only encouraged her.

A window above the sink provided a view of a small but well-maintained yard with cared-for plants and flowers, though Jenkins had drawn the shade to prevent anyone from seeing in. A redbrick fence with a metal gate surrounded the yard. Each home on the street, which resembled more of an alley than a road in the United States—with no sidewalks—was surrounded by a fence of some type: corrugated metal, wood, even barbed wire. It reminded Jenkins of the road and the houses in Vishnevka on the Black Sea coast where he had departed Russia the first time.

He had provided Matt Lemore with an update through the designated chat room, and he advised that everything depended on timing. If things went as planned, Zenaida Petrekova would be out of Russia tonight and long gone before Monday morning.

If things did not go as planned, it could be fatal for them both.

The front door opened and closed. Jenkins moved to the wall behind the archway leading into the kitchen. Someone dropped things on the table on the opposite side of the wall. When Petrekova stepped to the archway she came to a halt, staring at the unfamiliar suitcase beside her kitchen table. When she stepped in farther, Jenkins put a hand over her mouth to keep her from screaming. She jumped, startled, but she did not scream. Her eyes widened like someone who had the wind knocked out of them. Jenkins slowly removed his hand from her mouth. He had not wanted to scare her, particularly not after what she had endured the past four days, but it couldn't be helped. He let her catch her breath.

Using hand signals, he directed Petrekova to turn on the television. She walked into the main room of the house, which contained two comfortable chairs and a sofa, and did so. Jenkins then indicated she should shut the blinds to her windows in the rest of the rooms on the ground floor. When she had finished, he invited her to take a seat at the kitchen table beneath the lamp.

She looked nervous, uncertain, and concerned. He smiled, hoping it would help her relax, then clicked open the suitcase. From the false bottom he removed Petrekova's mask and her clothing, as well as the makeup kit. The CIA disguise team and her Moscow handlers had done a masterful job preparing for this moment. Jenkins hoped he didn't screw it up.

He reached out with the makeup sponge and Petrekova nodded her consent. Something said on the television caught his attention. He slid back his chair and stepped into the front room. A reporter for the state media spoke of the shooting in the Yakimanka Bar, then put a picture up of the punk. Eldar Velikaya.

"Velikaya is the only child of Yekaterina Velikaya, long considered the head of the most powerful crime family in Moscow."

Jenkins felt his stomach drop. In his mind he saw and heard the prostitute. *What have you done?*

"Russia's Investigative Committee said the police are searching for this man." Charles Wilson's passport photograph appeared on the television along with his name, height in meters, and weight in kilograms. "Charles Wilson is a British industrialist who entered the country through customs at Sheremetyevo Airport yesterday evening. The Investigative Committee said facial recognition cameras identified Wilson at the airport and again entering the Yakimanka Bar. Wilson checked out of the Hotel Imperial in the Yakimanka District sometime after the shooting, and his current whereabouts are unknown. The Investigative Committee said Wilson is a person of interest wanted in connection with the shooting. Anyone with information on Wilson or his whereabouts should call the number at the bottom of your screen."

The reporter moved on to another story.

What have you done?

Jenkins now understood the prostitute's fear. This was going to complicate things, though he was not yet certain how. Charles Wilson no longer existed and never would again. He needed to take matters one at a time.

He turned back to the kitchen. Petrekova stood in the doorframe between the two rooms, watching him with an inquisitive look. He did not have time to explain, and there was no reason for Petrekova to know. They had work to do. He directed her back to the kitchen and sat beside her at the table, moving his chair close to apply the makeup as he had been taught at the Langley disguise division. As he did, Petrekova stared beyond him, with the same fearful look as the prostitute.

What have you done?

20

Lubyanka Building
Moscow, Russia

Ilia Egorov had stared at his computer screen for the better part of an hour.

"They say that can cause you to go blind," a colleague had said on his way out the door. "Among other things."

Egorov smiled, but he was in no mood for jokes. He faced a dilemma. Adrian Zima had been his friend for twenty years; they had forged a friendship as students at the University of Moscow studying criminology and science. They each wanted to work in law enforcement. Zima found his joy working behind the scenes, finding clues in the tiniest corners of a crime scene that could break a case wide open. Zima had always related his work to solving a puzzle.

Egorov liked the criminal sciences, but he didn't aspire to be a lab rat. He wanted to get outdoors, where the action happened. He didn't want to be hunting criminals through microscopes and spectrograms; he wanted to be chasing them down in fast cars. While Zima had remained at the Criminal Investigation Department, Egorov became an FSB officer. Being a federal employee certainly had its advantages, but Egorov soon learned the days of chasing down criminals in cars were quickly coming to an end. Now, most everything was done with computers and cameras. FSB officers were on their way to becoming the geeks Egorov had sought to avoid.

Egorov was currently sitting on a ticking time bomb, though, and it had been Zima who triggered the fuse. Zima had called and asked Egorov to run a name for him in the FSB database, a name that had come up from a latent fingerprint at a crime scene in the Yakimanka District, but for which the ministry did not have a match. Egorov and Zima had done favors for one another in the past, and Zima had let slip that the print could be related to the shooting of Eldar Velikaya. The death of the son of Moscow's largest crime family was big news.

The fingerprint had turned out to be even bigger news.

It was not every day you learned that one of the most sought-after men in FSB history was back in Moscow. Charles Jenkins was an international criminal. The Kremlin had put out a red notice and alerted Britain's National Crime Agency that Jenkins was wanted in Russia to stand trial on numerous criminal charges. Finding his fingerprint was like finding a gold nugget in a mountain stream. Extremely rare and extremely valuable—if Egorov played it correctly. Possessing information of this import could distinguish Egorov and help him to move up the FSB ladder, maybe into the counterintelligence unit.

He risked a lifelong friendship perhaps, but then, Zima didn't have to know he'd breached their confidence. And if Zima found out . . . well, Egorov could say simply he was only doing his duty. For the Kremlin and for Russia.

And if a little something extra were to fall his way as a result . . . could a good friend like Zima begrudge Egorov a morsel . . . or a nugget?

He picked up the phone. He did not intend to speak to just anyone, fearful someone might steal this golden nugget for themselves. He'd practiced his delivery. He had information for the director's eyes only. If he got any pushback, he'd tell the person to tell Sokalov that the information related to someone for whom the directorate had requested a red notice from the National Crime Agency. That would narrow the possibilities significantly. He dialed the number with visions of fast cars, fast women, and shootouts once again dancing in his head.

——

Maria Kulikova left her office at just after 6:00 p.m., careful not to appear rushed—or guilty.

What have you done, Helge?

Sokalov would be tied up in high-level meetings. For this, Maria could be thankful. The meeting and the tryst in his office would distract him from the conversation with Helge that afternoon. Over the past twenty years, Maria had learned which buttons to push, the fetishes the letch relished, and how to inflict pleasure and pain. She had learned that, when aroused, Sokalov was like a bull elk in rut. He thought of nothing but the sex, remembered nothing but the sex. For decades he had told her everything and remembered nothing.

But the information had come at a steep price.

Maria had allowed herself to fall to a depth of depravity and degradation that haunted her days and kept her awake at night. She feared she had lost her moral compass, the very essence of herself as a good and decent person. A person she could be proud of.

Upon leaving Lubyanka, Maria contemplated a taxi, but at this hour, on a Friday night, a taxi would take far longer than the Metro. One look at the snarling traffic confirmed it.

She needed to get home quickly.

What have you done, Helge?

The attempt to kill Fyodor Ibragimov had been thwarted, and though the CIA had attempted to make it look like a coincidence, a mother returning home to find two men seated in a car, Maria was not so naïve. Neither were Chairman Petrov or Deputy Director Lebedev.

They were also not blinded by her sexuality. Petrov perhaps, but certainly not Lebedev.

There had only been five people in Sokalov's office that afternoon. How many more knew of the operation? Maria would be closely monitored, if she was not already.

And now Helge had given them something else to consider.

He told Sokalov of the phone calls to their apartment, of the wrong numbers, and how he had followed her to the temple. Did Sokalov realize her actions were the same night, just after they had all gathered to discuss the operation? Did Helge tell Sokalov of the phone call asking for Anna? Would Sokalov be able to control his sickening urges long enough to put all the clues together?

She had made up the excuse about the candles on the fly. It was both brilliant and careless. Brilliant because it provided a viable explanation for both her and her handler's behavior. Careless because it could so easily be proven false—were Sokalov interested enough to send someone to the temple. There were no candles behind the statue, only a moveable stone in the pedestal—a dead drop used to pass things like microchips and cassette tapes.

Maria stepped onto her train and found a seat near the door. She studied the faces of the other commuters in case one chose to follow her. If so, she might already be too late. She could run, leave Russia, but Helge would see no reason to do so. And if Sokalov determined the truth about Maria, that she was one of the seven sisters and had spied beneath his nose for decades, he could never let her or Helge live. He could never let that information get out.

His father-in-law would kill him.

So, too, would the president.

What have you done, Helge?

—

Sokalov fiddled with a napkin at a table in the back of Vos'myorka s rulevym—the Coxed Eight. The bar was not far from his home in the Rublyovka suburb where many government officials and wealthy businesspeople lived. Homes cost up to $80 million. Sokalov had his father-in-law to thank for their 2.5-acre estate, ten-thousand-square-foot home, pool, tennis court, private movie theater, and gym. The general had received the home when communism fell and capitalism became a money grab. Things, like homes, were a way to pay those who had devoted their lives to the Soviet Union. Sokalov's estate came at a price, however.

His in-laws lived on the property, in the guesthouse.

The Coxed Eight was a far cry from those expensive homes, which was why Sokalov chose it for this meeting. The name was a tribute to the gold medal won at the 1985 World Rowing Championships by an eight-man Soviet boat from the Krylatskoye Sports Complex. The bar's dark interior, with tables shoved in nooks and crannies, made it a good place to have a private conversation.

Sokalov's hand shook with each sip of his brandy, which only exacerbated the pain in his stomach that four Tums had not helped. Nor had the alcohol. But he needed the alcohol ever since Ilia Egorov had been escorted into his office with news that Charles Jenkins was back in Moscow.

Alexander Zhomov stepped into the bar looking as though he might rob it. A block of a man, Zhomov, retired from the FSB, remained in exceptional shape. He lifted weights, rowed, and played eighteen holes, usually with wealthy clients. Zhomov got his start as a sniper in Afghanistan. His and Sokalov's relationship began when both later worked for the KGB and had a mutual interest in moving up the bureaucratic ladder. Zhomov eventually worked for Sokalov, and he had been a decorated and celebrated mole hunter who oversaw the arrest of, and took pleasure in, the torture of spies. He had once convinced the CIA that he sought to defect to the United States, and he learned how the US exfiltrated spies through ferry crossings into Finland. A true believer, Zhomov hated nothing more than he hated America, its capitalism, and its incessant meddling, which he believed had caused the fall of the once proud Soviet Union. He was not averse, however, to the pleasures capitalism could buy, like an expensive Mercedes.

Since Zhomov's retirement, Sokalov had employed him as a troubleshooter and torpedo—an assassin. Zhomov had been the torpedo Sokalov launched in 2008 to take out several mafiya family heads, as well as an oligarch, when the president deemed the men to be a threat to his power.

Zhomov sat across the table from Sokalov. The waitress appeared, but Zhomov—who did not drink—dismissed her with the wave of a hand.

Sokalov picked up his brandy, set it down again. He leaned back.

"The temple exists," Zhomov said, his voice deep and soothing, like a disc jockey on a classical radio station. "The kneeler exists. The statue of the icon exists." He paused, just the hint of a smile forming. "The candles . . . do not."

Sokalov felt the fire in his belly stoke. He took several quick breaths while using a napkin to wipe perspiration from his forehead. The waitress returned, setting a glass of water on the table.

"Napkins," Zhomov said.

The woman produced several dark-green napkins from the pocket of her apron and placed them beside the water glass before again departing. Zhomov handed a napkin to Sokalov. "Something else. There is a stone in the pedestal that can be removed. Beneath it is a hollowed-out area where messages and cassettes and such could be exchanged. A dead drop. No doubt. I have seen more than my share."

Sokalov closed his eyes, a burning rage running through his body. Helge Kulikov, the bumbling fool, had solved one of Moscow's most significant and long-standing security breaches. For decades Maria

Kulikova had spied directly under Sokalov's nose while plying him with alcohol and sex.

After his meeting with Egorov, Sokalov had slowly, reluctantly, fit the pieces together. The night that Helge Kulikov had followed his wife had been the night of the meeting in his office with Chairman Petrov, Gavril Lebedev and General Kliment Pasternak, the meeting in which Sokalov insisted Maria take shorthand notes. She had not been going out to walk the dog or to get dinner and spend time away from her husband. She had left the apartment to pass along information, information she had learned that afternoon, information about the Kremlin's plan to assassinate Fyodor Ibragimov. The wrong telephone numbers of which Helge had spoken had not been wrong numbers at all. They had been coded messages from a handler, advising Maria of certain drop boxes throughout Moscow. *Anna*, the name asked for that night, had been code for the Temple Martyr Anastasia.

Even more sickening, Lebedev, the leering shit, had been right.

Ibragimov's wife had not returned home by coincidence. The Americans only wanted it to look that way. It had been, as Lebedev had insisted, an effort by the Americans to protect a high-level asset who had disclosed details of the plan to kill Ibragimov. A high-level asset with access to what had been extremely restricted information.

Maria Kulikova.

Lebedev, smelling Sokalov's blood in the water, would have reason to demand an investigation, one that would no doubt reveal other information Sokalov had divulged to Maria during the past decades. But that was not the worst of it. Far from it. Lebedev would argue that, given the magnitude of and the protracted years of these revelations, Sokalov had to have been complicit, himself an American spy.

What other explanation could explain such a wanton breach?

What was Sokalov to say in his defense? That he was addicted to the sex? What evidence could he produce to defend himself?

He couldn't even recall everything he had divulged.

And what of the Polaroid photographs he had Maria take of him in various stages of bondage? The pictures were a testament to how muddled his thinking became, how misguided. He wanted the photos so he could look at them whenever he and Maria could not get together, or on those occasions when they could, to heighten his arousal.

Earlier that evening, after Sokalov had dismissed Egorov and admonished him to not mention the news of Jenkins's return to anyone, he had hurried into Maria's office. He had access to the passwords of every member of the directorate. When he finally opened her safe, he found only files. The jewelry he had given Maria over the years—and the photographs—were not there.

He would surely be executed, but only after he was tortured in Lefortovo. The president would see his betrayal as an egregious slap in the face, but that would be far better than what his father-in-law would do to protect his little girl and the family reputation.

Sokalov had returned to his office frantic, angry, and terrified of what awaited him. In time he had calmed enough to realize that the timing of Charles Jenkins's return to Moscow could also not be a coincidence, not with the creation of the clandestine FSB operation to find and terminate the seven sisters. Maria had access to this information as well, and she clearly had alerted American intelligence. Jenkins's return to Moscow could be for just one reason, to bring home the remaining sisters before they, too, were discovered and executed. To bring home Maria Kulikova, and whoever else remained out there in operation.

Maria fit the profile. Her age. Her position at work. Her access to confidential information. She had cultivated her relationship with Sokalov, playing on his prurient desires until he craved them as much as he craved her, addicted to the pleasure and the pain that she could so artfully administer. But in the midst of Sokalov's torment and despair, a flicker of clarity revealed itself, a flicker that provided perhaps his only hope, his only means to survive.

He could still save himself. Even now. He had always been able to save himself.

The FSB, like the KGB, was compartmentalized for security reasons. No one outside his division knew what happened within his directorate. Nothing was taken home. Not a tape recorder or a scrap of paper. At night, each agent locked his work in a safe in his office affixed with a personal seal broken only by that agent the following morning. The computer server was an internal network that only allowed officers to send communications to other officers within the Counterintelligence Directorate.

Operation Herod was known by fewer still. The president had entrusted the matter to Sokalov in complete confidentiality. Sokalov had handpicked the half-dozen members of the operation team, and they, too, had been sworn to secrecy under penalty of termination.

Sokalov replayed what Bogdan Petrov had last said to him, Lebedev, and Pasternak in the conference room.

But let me make myself very clear, gentlemen. A head . . . or heads . . . will roll. And it will not be mine. I would suggest that you get busy finding the president an alternative he can use to save face if you wish to keep your heads attached to your bodies.

And that was when Sokalov hit on the idea—just how he might manipulate his way out of this predicament. The arrest of General Pasternak's two men might very well prove to be a stroke of fortune, as opposed to a massive intelligence breach, that could save Sokalov's life. If Zhomov could kill Maria, her betrayals would remain hidden. If he could bring in Jenkins, the Kremlin could use him as the needed bargaining chip to exchange for Pasternak's two men. Sokalov would not look like a fool but a hero. He would eliminate one of the seven sisters—not that anyone would know Maria had been one—while reprising another biblical story of King Herod. He would bring the president the head of Charles Jenkins, though still very much attached to his body, and very much alive.

Zhomov sat patiently. He fingered the silver crucifix that hung around his neck, a habit when deep in thought, or interrogating a suspected spy. "Tell me what you need, Dmitry."

"First, I need a few loose ends taken care of," he said, so no one could ever talk of what Sokalov had allowed to happen, and with Zhomov's help, no one ever would. "Then I will need you to do what you do best—hunt down an American spy and bring him to me."

21

Korolyov
Moscow Oblast, Russia

As Jenkins applied Petrekova's mask and makeup, he could not shake the thought of FSB officers barging in the door to arrest him, could not shake the vision of spending years in a Lefortovo prison cell like the one Paulina Ponomayova had occupied.

The clock on the wall ticked. Jenkins turned his head when it emitted an annoying buzz, as if to find and smash a fly.

"It sticks," Petrekova whispered. She shrugged and smiled, but her smile had a sad quality to it. "You get used to it. When you live alone, noise can be comforting."

Petrekova's leg shook a nervous beat, and Jenkins had trouble applying her makeup because she was sweating, despite an oscillating fan they had placed on the counter to move the air and, along with the television, disrupt any eavesdropping. Jenkins derived comfort from the fact that Petrekova displayed nerves and looked around her home wistfully as she discussed what had been her life. She pointed out the photographs on the living room mantel of her deceased husband and her son and her daughter. Her family. Jenkins knew she did so because she wanted to take those photographs with her, another indication she planned to leave, that she did not have an intent to deceive him. Either that or she had missed her calling on the Russian stage.

He dabbed a bit more makeup with the sponge, then sat back to admire Langley's handiwork. He held up a mirror so Petrekova could see his creation. She gently touched the mask, then smiled.

"Slip on the clothes," he said, checking his watch. "I'll call for the delivery."

Petrekova did as he instructed, then paced the kitchen while Jenkins put the makeup kit away. When he had finished, there was a knock at the front door. Petrekova startled, then seemed to regain her composure with a few deep breaths. Jenkins nodded to her, hoping to give her confidence, but inside he felt his own nerves and braced for the worst.

Petrekova walked to the entry and looked through the peephole, then turned back to Jenkins and nodded. He stepped into a darkened corner of the living room as she opened the door.

—

Roughly an hour after Zenaida Petrekova had returned home, a car with a Domino's Pizza light attached to the roof drove down the darkened road past where Chernoff and Vinchenko had parked. The street, pitch-black and without streetlamps, was lit only by a few sporadic lights affixed to the fences and the ambient light from stars in a cloudless sky. Vinchenko remained behind the wheel, seat reclined, his eyes closed.

"Delivery driver," Chernoff said.

Vinchenko grunted.

"Have you tried it?" Chernoff asked.

"Tried what?" he said, without opening his eyes.

She looked over at him. "Domino's."

"No."

The Domino's driver stopped at the gate to Petrekova's home. Chernoff sat up, taking notice. She trained binoculars on the driver, face mostly hidden beneath a ball cap and shadows. "He's going to Petrekova's home."

"I guess she didn't want to cook."

"I think it's a woman," she said, adjusting the focus.

"Who?"

"The delivery driver." Chernoff gave this a moment of thought. "Does that seem odd to you?"

"I assume delivery drivers come in all shapes and sizes," he said, still not opening his eyes.

"That's not what I meant. Last night she posted a photo on Facebook after cooking a gourmet meal. Tonight, she is eating crap. Seems odd to me."

"She got home late from her appointment, is tired, and doesn't want to cook. What's odd about that?"

"I don't like it. With the fence and the window shades drawn we can't see enough to know what is happening."

"What's to see?"

"Something is odd to me."

"Are your spidey senses tingling?"

"What?"

"You have children. Surely you have seen *Spider-Man*."

"Why is it taking so much time to drop off a pizza?"

Vinchenko sat up and looked down the road. "I think you are starting to let your imagination run wild." The gate opened and the driver stepped out, walking back to the car. "There. You see. No big deal."

"I don't like this, Dima. I think we should check this out."

"How are we going to check this out? We are to have no contact unless certain, and I am far from certain."

Chernoff focused her binoculars on the Domino's driver, who got back into her car. Chernoff jumped when something sharp tapped on the passenger window. An old woman stood outside the car. They had seen her before. She walked her dog each evening.

"She's late tonight," Vinchenko said. "We should take bets on who dies first, her or her dog." He reached to lower the window from his driver's seat.

"What are you doing here?" the woman asked.

"We are waiting for someone," Chernoff said, keeping her eyes on the driver.

"Who? Who are you waiting for?" the old woman persisted.

"A friend," Chernoff said.

"Go on now. Walk your dog," Vinchenko said. "Go on. Move along."

"I am going to call the police," she said.

"Go ahead. Call. Tell them to bring coffee when they come."

The woman scowled as she walked off.

Red taillights illuminated and the pizza delivery car drove away from them. "I think we should follow the driver. I don't like this, Dima," Chernoff said.

"What's rattled your cage? The old bat?"

"This afternoon. Petrekova broke from routine."

"She went to a beauty salon."

"No. She walked toward the Metro. I turned my eyes from her for an instant and she was in the back of a taxicab. I think she knows she is being followed. I think we should follow the driver. If we're wrong we come back and continue doing what we're doing."

"Which is nothing," Vinchenko said.

"We are losing the driver," Chernoff said.

"Okay. Okay." He sat up and took a moment to adjust his seat.

"Hurry," she said. "Come on."

He started the car and drove down the alley, turning left at the end of the block, the same direction as the delivery driver. "You will find that ninety percent of this work amounts to nothing. You'll see. You spend weeks watching someone only to learn it was a false alarm. You will learn this. But for now . . ."

"There. Turning right," Chernoff said, spying the Domino's car's taillights.

"How long are we going to follow her?" Vinchenko asked.

"Pull her over on the next block," she said. She put a police light atop their car.

"And what will we say is the reason for pulling her over?"

"We don't need a reason."

The lights flashed and Vinchenko pulled close to the car, which slowed as if to allow him to pass. When Vinchenko did not, the driver pulled over and parked at the curb. Chernoff grabbed a flashlight from the floorboard and stepped out as soon as the car stopped. She approached the driver's side, keeping a hand on her gun. She stopped at the back window and reached to knock on the driver's window with the flashlight. The driver lowered the window.

"Did I do something wrong?" a young woman asked. Then, eyeing Chernoff more carefully, she asked, "Are you a police officer?"

"I'm sorry," Chernoff said. "We are looking for a car just like this one. Would you mind stepping out?"

"You are looking for a Domino's car?"

"Please, step out of the car."

"I'd like to see some identification. Why are you not in uniform? That's not even a police car."

"Step out," Chernoff said. Under no circumstance was she going to show her FSB identification. If word spread the FSB was in the area, Petrekova would certainly find out, if she didn't already know.

Vinchenko arrived. "We are working undercover," he said to the driver. "Please do as she says. This will go a lot faster, and you will be able to get back to delivering pizza and earning your tips."

The driver exited the vehicle. Chernoff lifted the flashlight to the woman's face. The driver squinted and looked away. "You are blinding me."

Chernoff lowered the flashlight and shined the light into the car's empty interior. "Open the trunk, please."

The driver hit the latch inside the car and the trunk popped. Vinchenko lifted the trunk. Empty.

"Do you have identification?" Chernoff said.

The woman produced a driver's license, and Chernoff reviewed it under her flashlight. She took a picture of the license using her phone before she handed it back. "It was a mistake. You're free to go."

Chernoff walked back to the car, stopping to take a photograph of the license plate before she got in the passenger seat.

Vinchenko slid into the driver's seat, chuckling.

"Better safe than sorry," she said, punching in a number on her phone.

"Who are you calling, the pizza police?"

"Domino's. I want to be sure the driver works for them."

Vinchenko pulled a U-turn in the middle of the street and drove back to the alley. Minutes later he parked again beneath the tree. The light in Petrekova's shaded kitchen window switched off. Seconds later, the light in her shaded living room window switched on. Chernoff could see the television flickering on the shade.

"She's going to eat watching television. We should be so lucky," Vinchenko said, sipping his coffee.

—

Two blocks from the redbrick house, the old woman shuffled along the darkened street to another parked car, her old dog obediently at her side. This time she did not knock on the window to get the driver's attention. She pulled open the back door and put the dog on the seat, where it curled up, seemingly happy to no longer be walking. Then she pulled open the passenger-side door—the interior light had been removed—and slid onto the seat. Charles Jenkins, still disguised as the old man, started the car and pulled gently from the curb. They looked like an elderly couple out for the evening.

Having Petrekova walk up to the tail had been a bold move, a move out of character for someone seeking to evade a tail. Jenkins could tell it had been nerve-wracking for Petrekova.

"Everything went all right?" he asked.

"What if my neighbor walks her dog?"

"She already has. That was another reason for you to get home later than usual."

"And if my tail gets suspicious?"

"We would have known of it already. The fact that they haven't makes it highly likely you'll have until Monday morning before you're missed. Depending on what happens from here, you might call in Monday and tell your office you are ill, to buy more time." He glanced in the rearview mirror for headlights but didn't see any. "Are you hungry?"

She gave him an inquisitive look.

Jenkins nodded to the pizza box in the back seat. "If you're hungry."

She shook her head and let out a nervous chuckle. "I don't think I will be hungry until we have left Russia. What now?"

"Information will be provided as you go. I set lights on timers within your home to turn on and off in the various rooms for the next few hours. Eventually everything will go black. Depending on how things go from here, you will be leaving Russia before the lights shut off in your bedroom."

Petrekova nodded. "What about the dog?"

"The dog will go back to its owner."

She placed her hands in her lap. Jenkins noticed the tremors. He reached inside the pocket of his jacket and pulled out the photograph of Petrekova with her family. He handed it to her.

She took it and grimaced. Then tears of joy rolled softly down her cheeks. "Thank you," she said, clutching the photograph to her chest.

Taking it was a risk, but Jenkins hoped thoughts of her family would calm Petrekova, which was equally important. She remained a bundle of nerves. She had a right. A year or so ago, Jenkins had done his genealogy. Not for himself, but for CJ and Lizzie, so that when they got older and curious, they would know who they were and where they had come from. Alex's family history had been well documented. She had a binder of materials about her ancestors in Mexico City. Jenkins's research revealed his ancestors had been slaves in Louisiana, until his great-great-great-grandmother escaped via the Underground Railroad made famous in books and movies. His relative had the courage and the moral fiber to repay her freedom by sending money to companies that helped others escape by processing forged papers and paying for train tickets. When he had learned of her heroism, Jenkins wondered if helping others to be free was somehow a genetic family trait he could not ignore.

Possibly. But he refrained from drawing a correlation between his ancestors helping others escape slavery and his helping Zenaida Petrekova to escape from Russia. He also didn't tell her about it.

Another of his relatives had also tried to escape, a young man.

He'd been captured and hung.

Jenkins drove until he arrived at the designated dead drop, though this time he would be dropping off a package very much alive. He had no further knowledge of Petrekova's journey. The driver of the second vehicle knew nothing more than her next designated transfer. It ensured Petrekova could not be betrayed. Jenkins wouldn't know the exfiltration had been successful until he returned home to the United States.

He had no sooner said his goodbyes and returned to his vehicle than his cell phone rang.

Lemore.

He was not using an encrypted number or chat room, which meant he was forsaking security for expediency.

Jenkins got a bad feeling that grew worse as Lemore spoke.

22

Yakimanka District
Moscow, Russia

The computerized woman's voice filled the Metro car, informing commuters that the train approached the Kropotkinskaya station. Maria departed the train with the mass of humanity emitting a cloud smelling of body odor, cologne, perfume, and cigarettes. Unable to push through the throng, she had no choice but to go with it. She considered those around her, their eyes. Was someone following her? Was someone already waiting to arrest her?

After forty years, she sensed her days of espionage coming to a sudden end, and she was glad to be done with them.

But also afraid.

They would come for her. They would come with a vengeance. Sokalov had let slip what had happened to the sisters who had been captured, the brutal torture and interrogations they had undergone. Their deaths must have been a blessing.

Sokalov had much to lose if the depth of Maria's betrayal were revealed. If the president did not kill him, his father-in-law surely would. Maria's one hope was that she knew everything about the man, the way he thought, his survival instincts. She knew Sokalov pulled the strings on the task force set up to find the sisters, and that the information had been compartmentalized and tightly controlled. Few knew of it. Sokalov would not order the task force to capture and interrogate Kulikova. She would destroy him. His only choice was to kill her and silence her before she could ever talk. To ensure she had not told others, he would also order the deaths of anyone he suspected might have knowledge of her betrayal or her infidelity.

Helge for certain.

If this was to be Maria's end, so be it. She had never believed she would survive this long, and she had long ago decided she would never allow those in power the gratification of her capture. She kept a cyanide capsule in the tip of a pen she had carried in her purse every day for thirty years. When the time came, she would not hesitate to bite down and end her life, taking to her grave the extent of her betrayal. Her death would be her greatest triumph; her only regret would be that she would not remain alive to witness Sokalov's punishment, which would finally bring *her* some pleasure.

Helge, however, was innocent, so much so that he had no idea the magnitude of his disclosure to Sokalov. He had no idea he had just signed his own death warrant. Perhaps Maria had underestimated the depth of the pain she had caused Helge, the damage to his pride, and the insult to his Russian virility. Perhaps Helge had gone to Sokalov to save face, hoping Sokalov would punish Maria for breaking one of the tenets of her position—to see her suffer, as he had suffered, all these years.

Maria emerged above ground across from the Cathedral of Christ the Saviour and again paused at the bus stop to go through the ritual of removing her lipstick and her compact mirror to scan behind her, searching again for anyone watching her. Seeing no one, she drew a check mark on the glass shelter, but this time she put a line through the stem to signify she was done. She needed to get out. She pocketed her cosmetics and hurried for home.

It had been a risk divulging the plan to kill Ibragimov to her handlers. When she had learned of Operation Herod, Maria had done what she'd been instructed to do whenever the Kremlin got too close. She'd cut off all communication with her handlers. She stopped making dead drops or responding to brush-bys. She stopped answering the phone at night or responded, "There is no one here by that name" to indicate her refusal to meet. She ignored the advertisements in the *Moscow Times* with hidden messages seeking to set meeting locations and times.

But she could not remain silent when she learned of the plan to brazenly kill Fyodor Ibragimov on American soil. It was not just about Ibragimov—or his wife and his children, who would mourn the loss of a husband and a father. His assassination would eliminate the final sanctuary for those seeking a better Russia. It would accomplish what the president had long sought to accomplish: sending an undeniable message that those who betrayed Russia were never safe. The repercussions would silence dissidents. Silence any opposition. It would send them into hiding and cause the country to hearken back to Soviet times.

The plan to kill Ibragimov had once again given Maria a purpose, and if finding her purpose cost her life, so be it.

But it should not cost Helge his.

What did you do, Helge?

In the building's marble entry, Maria greeted the doorman.

"A hot one today, was it not?" the doorman said. "I'm glad to be in an air-conditioned lobby."

Maria smiled and stepped past him to the elevator, repeatedly hitting the button to close the doors. She exited on the twelfth floor and rushed down the carpeted hall, her heart racing. She took a deep breath and inserted the key in the deadbolt. It was not locked. The sound tripped Stanislav's Pavlovian response. Helge's lightweight jacket did not hang on the coatrack. Maria stepped past the dog and called out her husband's name. "Helge?"

The chair in which Helge ritually sat was empty, a glass on the side table half-full. Maria had intended to suggest that he visit his older brother in Poland, with whom he was close and with whom he occasionally hunted. She had intended that Helge go away.

She turned in circles, uncertain what to do or where to go. The telephone on the wall rang. Maria answered it.

"May I speak to Ariana?" the voice said.

"I'm afraid you have the wrong number," she replied. Then, like the dash she had drawn in the check mark's stem, she added a phrase she had hoped she'd never have to use. "What number are you calling?" It, too, signified her need of immediate exfiltration.

"Sorry to disturb," her handler said, hanging up.

She didn't have much time. She would need to leave immediately. She could take nothing with her but the clothes on her back. She'd give Stanislav to the couple in the apartment down the hall.

Helge . . . Her conscience would not allow her to leave Helge to die. She had compromised so much of her moral fiber she no longer believed she was a good person at heart. To leave Helge to die would be to fall further into the depraved sewer, perhaps too deep to ever again be free. She expected she would pay for her depravity, if not in this life then when she reached the gates of heaven, but maybe, just maybe, God would show some mercy if she risked her own life to save Helge.

She reached for the notepad on the counter to leave Helge a message to call her immediately when he returned home. The pad was not on the counter where they regularly kept it. Nor was the ballpoint pen. She searched the kitchen counter and the table, did not find it, then turned to the living room. The pad and pen rested on the side table, beside Helge's glass of vodka.

She hurried to it, angled the top page beneath the lamp, and detected the faint etchings of the ballpoint pen, though she was unable to read the written words. This was a problem she had encountered before. Back in the kitchen, she rummaged inside the drawer by the phone and found a pencil. She lightly shaded the etched letters, seeing them form, faint but decipherable.

V . . .

Vr . . .

Vrat . . .

Vratar'—the Goaltender.

She pulled out her phone and punched in the name, obtaining the address for a bar near Moscow State University. She had never heard of it. She doubted Helge had. He had plenty of local bars at which to drink. This, she knew from experience, had Sokalov written all over it. Lure his prey someplace he was not known, would not be remembered.

She pulled up the Moscow Metro app on her phone as she moved back down the hall to the front door. The destination would require that she change cars twice and travel five Metro stops. She grabbed her pen with the cyanide capsule from her bag and rushed out the door with Stanislav. She dropped him at the neighbors' who had a child who loved Stanislav and came over often to see him, then hurried back toward the elevators.

She would not make her dead drop. She would miss her chance at freedom.

So be it. Better to die this way than to burn in eternal hell.

23

Ramenki District
Moscow Oblast, Russia

Helge Kulikov thought it magnanimous for Dmitry Sokalov to call and suggest they speak in private about Maria's infidelity. Sokalov said the delicate information was inappropriate for discussion over the telephone and better discussed in person. Could they meet?

Helge wished he had not drunk so much. He wished he had eaten something. The walk to the Metro station helped sober him, but the subway car had been hot and muggy, like all of Moscow, and he had struggled to stay awake. Back above ground, the two-block walk to the Goaltender, the bar where Sokalov asked to meet, again revived him.

As Helge approached the bar, he wiped the sweat dripping down his face and frowned. He had expected a significantly higher caliber establishment, one befitting the deputy director's status. The Goaltender was more of a *ryumochnaya*—the small basement bars in Moscow that served cheap alcohol and cheaper food. It seemed beneath the man, though the deputy director had told Helge over the phone that he wanted to be discreet. The Goaltender, tucked into a forested enclave at the end of a dead-end road, was certainly discreet.

"It has an assortment of football paraphernalia I thought someone with your extended résumé might find appealing," Sokalov had said.

Helge hoped only that it had the type of vodka he had drunk in the deputy director's office. He didn't drink Stoli often. Helge stepped into the bar and took a moment to allow his eyes to adjust to the dim lighting. The interior also disappointed. In the entry, young people sporadically populated the dozen or so upright tables, and the music played at too high a volume. The aroma of alcohol and fried food permeated the air.

Helge's eyes adjusted, but he did not see Sokalov. He walked through the entry to an interior room with traditional tables and seating. Sokalov sat at a table in a corner. The deputy director was certainly being discreet. He wore a dark jacket and a ball cap pulled low on his brow, which seemed not in keeping with the pompous man Helge had met at Lubyanka functions.

Sokalov raised his gaze and the two men nodded a greeting. Helge removed his jacket and draped it over the back of a chair before sitting.

"Thank you for coming, Helge," Sokalov said.

"Thank you for going to this effort, Dmitry."

"Yes, well, as I mentioned, the information I have uncovered so far is, I'm afraid, somewhat awkward to discuss over the telephone, and potentially embarrassing."

"I'm grateful for your discretion. How were you able to obtain the information, and so quickly?"

Sokalov smiled. "Gathering information is what I do, Helge."

"Yes, of course."

A waitress appeared at their table.

"Let me buy you a drink. Vodka?" Sokalov said.

"Yes, um . . . the vodka I had in your office."

"Of course. Stoli," Sokalov said to the waitress. "Over ice." The waitress departed. "Unfortunately, sometimes a man in my position must be the bearer of bad news."

"I'm sure it is one of many burdens," Helge said.

"And I'm sure a man of your standing, a professional football player, does not desire that I beat around the bush, so I will just come out and tell you."

Helge sighed. "Yes, please."

"I am afraid Maria is having an affair with an FSB officer. I understand from my sources that this has been going on for quite some time, years in fact."

Helge sat back. "I suspected her many late nights at the office and her weekends away were not all work related."

"No. I'm afraid not."

The waitress returned with the vodka and set it on the table. Helge eagerly sipped it, struggling to keep his hand from shaking. He would have downed the drink in a single gulp but decided it best to at least appear to be in control.

"That is the bad news," Sokalov said. "But there is some good news."

"Good news?" Helge said.

"Yes. Because this man is an FSB officer, he comes under my jurisdiction, and I have the ability to fire him from his position for violating one of the tenets of employment, adultery."

"He is married then?"

"With three young children."

Three young children. Helge hadn't thought the man would have a family. He only wanted to punish Maria. "And what of disciplining Maria?"

"That is up to you. I can't very well fire the officer and not fire Maria, as much as it would pain me to do so. But she, too, broke one of our tenets."

Helge gave this some thought. His retirement income from his work at the parks department was no more than a pittance. Without Maria's salary and her position, they would have to give up their apartment. Where would they live? Without her salary, how would they live?

"I don't think we need to go so far, Dmitry."

"No?"

"Perhaps you could speak to them . . . both . . . Warn them. Yes. Warn them. I think a warning from you would be sufficient to end it."

"That is magnanimous of you, Helge, I must say. I'm not certain most men could do such a thing. Too many would be blinded by jealousy and rage. I can certainly do as you suggested, and I wanted you to know that the officer involved has expressed his sincere apologies."

"Yes, well, I'm sure he is sorry," Helge said. Then, not wanting to sound like a pushover, he added, "But can we be certain he is sorry for what he did, or only sorry that he got caught?"

"Very wise of you, Helge, which is why I thought it important that you have the chance to confront him . . . to determine whether he is truly sincere."

"Confront him?"

Sokalov raised a fist. "I knew you would desire this, Helge, a man of your prominence, a professional football player. I have no doubt that once he meets you, and understands who you are, he will think twice about ever doing something like this again."

Helge sat a little straighter. The deputy director understood what Helge had achieved, what so many others had failed to understand. "Yes. Yes, I would wish this. Of course. If you provide me with this man's name and number—"

"He is here," Sokalov said. "I insisted that he come so you had the chance to confront him."

"Now?" Helge looked around the bar.

"He is in the alley in back, waiting in my car. Again, I wanted to be discreet and provide you with some privacy. I thought you might like to vent." Sokalov smiled. "I know I certainly would."

"I appreciate that, Dmitry, but . . ."

"Come. It is best to get this resolved and put it behind you so that you and Maria can move forward. I will talk to her, but I anticipate a stern talking-to from you would have more impact, no?" Sokalov stood from the table.

Helge did not want to confront the man. What would he say? This man was also an FSB officer, probably trained to fight. Still, he could think of no way out of the confrontation, not if the deputy director had arranged it. Not if Helge wanted to save face. Besides, he had Sokalov, and the threat of this man being fired to empower him. The FSB officer, after all, was the one who would suffer if Helge chose not to forgive. Helge held control over this man's livelihood, over the livelihood of his family. That alone should be sufficient to shame him.

"You know, Dmitry, I do want a shot at this man. I will do my best to be calm and rational, but I can't promise anything."

"I understand, certainly, and . . . If you decide you want to rough this man up a bit, just to get the point across . . ." Sokalov winked and smiled. "I wouldn't say a word to anyone." Sokalov pushed open the metal door and they stepped to the back of the building, where a black Mercedes had parked.

Charles Jenkins drove the Third Ring Road that circled downtown Moscow. He did his best not to speed, not wanting to get pulled over. Lemore had advised Jenkins that Maria Kulikova's handlers received an urgent message requesting immediate exfiltration, but Kulikova had failed to show at her dead drop at the designated time that evening. Lemore said a tap on Kulikova's home phone line had revealed a call from Dmitry Sokalov, the deputy director of counterintelligence, requesting Kulikova's husband meet Sokalov at a bar near Moscow State University to discuss a "delicate situation."

Lemore had no further information on whether the husband had somehow exposed his wife. The husband did not work for the FSB or any other intelligence office. He had been employed by the Moscow parks department and had recently retired. In other words, there was no professional reason for Sokalov to request a meeting.

As Jenkins took the exit, he spoke again with Lemore. "What would the deputy director of counterintelligence want to discuss with a parks and recreation employee?" Jenkins asked.

"I don't know," Lemore said. "It sounds like a setup."

"And you're assuming this meeting is somehow the reason Kulikova didn't show at her dead drop?"

"Again, that is not presently known, but further attempts to communicate with her have been unsuccessful. How far away are you from the bar?"

"Three minutes," Jenkins said.

"Do not engage unless it is absolutely necessary," Lemore said. "This could be an elaborate trap."

"I understand," Jenkins said. He remained in disguise, an old man, which should give him the ability to at least get into the bar and determine the situation. "And if she is there? What then?"

"Get her the hell out, by any means necessary."

"I'm going to need help."

"We're looking at all available options," Lemore said.

Whatever the hell that meant, Jenkins thought. He disconnected and checked the map on his phone. He was one minute away—from what, he had no idea.

Maria Kulikova exited the Metro station sprinting. Her Pilates and yoga classes had been about keeping in shape for the job she had to do, but now they might just keep Helge alive, if she could reach him before he got to the bar. Before he met Sokalov, or whatever henchman Sokalov had dispatched. She had her phone out, an app providing her directions. Previous attempts to call Helge had gone immediately to his voice mail.

She reached the end of a block, an intersection, and stopped to check her map. Her breathing was heavy, but controlled. She didn't know what she would do when she arrived at the bar, what she might say. She had no weapon.

She checked the map and realized she had run a block in the wrong direction. She swore and turned to her left, watching the blue dot with the arrow on her phone calibrate, then she again took off running.

Another block and she saw the red neon name lit up atop the single-story building like a beacon. The Goaltender. She crossed the street to a nearly vacant dirt-and-gravel parking lot, gravel crunching beneath her shoes.

Maria took a deep breath, pulled open the bar door, and stepped inside. A woman collected beer bottles and glasses from upright tables. *"Zakryvayemsya cherez desyat́minut."* *We close in five minutes.*

Maria ignored her. No one stood at the upright tables. She walked to the back of the bar, seeing empty tables and empty chairs. About to leave, she noticed a jacket draped over the back of one of the chairs.

Helge's jacket.

Her heart pounded.

She called out to the woman collecting bottles and glasses while pointing to the jacket. *"Vy videli cheloveka, kotoryy prishel v etoy kurtke?"* *Did you see the man who came in wearing that jacket?*

"He just left," the woman said. "Out the back."

"Alone?"

"No. With another man. Less than a minute."

Maria rushed to a metal door but pulled her hands back before they hit the bar. She didn't know what to expect, but she knew once she pushed the door open there would be no going back.

She shoved the handle. The door swung open.

Helge stood alongside Sokalov and two men she did not recognize, though one looked like Alexander Zhomov, one of Sokalov's and the Kremlin's most ruthless torpedoes.

Dmitry Sokalov placed his hand on Helge's back and pushed open the back door into an alley of dull light. A black Mercedes sedan, one of the pool cars FSB officers could check out of Lubyanka, sat parked beside a blue garbage dumpster. A form had been filled out that evening checking out the car to Ilia Egorov.

When they reached the Mercedes, Sokalov knocked on the window with his wedding ring. The driver looked up and Sokalov gestured to Helge. The man opened the car door and removed his seat belt, stepping out.

"Officer Egorov," Sokalov said. "This is Helge Kulikov."

Egorov nodded and put out a hand. "Mr. Kulikov, it is a pleasure to meet you. I look forward to speaking with you."

"What?" Helge asked, confused. He glanced at Sokalov, who had stepped back.

Alexander Zhomov stepped from the trees in a T-shirt, jeans, and black leather gloves. In his right hand he held a pistol fitted with a silencer. Zhomov raised the gun and sited a red dot on Egorov's chest, and pulled the trigger. The gun popped twice. Egorov dropped like a puppet cut loose from his strings.

Zhomov redirected his aim at Helge.

"Helge!"

Sokalov turned his head at the sound of the familiar voice. Maria stood in the doorway of the building. "Dmitry. No!"

Zhomov fired again. The bullet struck Helge in the temple, splattering blood and brain matter. Helge crumpled to the ground.

Zhomov never hesitated. He didn't even watch to confirm his second kill.

He turned the gun and his aim to Maria Kulikova.

24

Ramenki District
Moscow Oblast, Russia

Jenkins skidded to a stop in a deserted dirt-and-gravel lot in front of the stucco building. A single weak streetlamp illuminated a spot of ground like a fading spotlight on an empty stage. Jenkins thought perhaps he had arrived too late, or that he was in the wrong place, the wrong bar, but the neon light above the roofline clearly identified the establishment to be the Goaltender. The same name of the bar provided by Matt Lemore.

Just as he read the sign, the neon light switched off.

He stepped from the car, leaving the engine running, and waited a moment to determine if anyone emerged from the woods that surrounded the back side of the parking lot and the bar.

No one did.

Jenkins walked to the metal door and pulled it open, nearly bumping into a woman on the other side who held a set of keys, locking up.

"My zakryty," she said. *We're closed.*

Jenkins looked past her, scanning the empty tables. His gaze locked on the silhouette of a woman standing in a doorway with her back to him. Beyond her, in the dull light from the opened bar door, a man held two others at gunpoint. Before Jenkins had time to process the information, the gun puffed twice, and the first victim, a man in a dark suit, dropped to the ground.

"Helge!" the woman in the doorway yelled. Then, "Dmitry. No!"

Jenkins pushed past the woman with the keys, shouting at her as he did. *"Ukhodite. Bystro." Leave. Quickly.*

He rushed to the back of the bar as the gunman redirected his aim. The second man had turned his head toward the woman in the doorway. The gunman fired once, striking the man in the temple. He, too, dropped. As Jenkins neared, the gunman pointed the barrel at the woman in the doorframe. Jenkins reached beyond her and pulled the door closed, hearing two pings, bullets striking metal.

To his left was a janitorial cubby behind a black curtain. He grabbed a mop and jammed the handle in the door lever. The woman stared up at him, mouth agape, eyes glazed over. Shock. Maria Kulikova. He'd studied photographs of her while training at Langley.

Jenkins grabbed her by the shoulders. *"Poydem so mnoy, yesli khochesh' zhit'." Come with me now if you want to live.*

He pulled Kulikova across the bar, not seeing the employee, but hearing her on a phone, calling the police. The broom handle rattled in the door.

They would have just a few seconds.

He raced outside, Kulikova in tow, pushed open the passenger-side front door, and shoved her into the car, then ran around the hood to the driver's side and slipped behind the wheel. He threw the car into drive. The tires spit gravel. The rear window exploded. Kulikova screamed. He reached across the car and shoved her further below the seat, hearing bullets ping, then a loud pop. The car fishtailed, but Jenkins managed to correct the steering.

He'd lost a back tire.

They would not outrun anyone on three wheels.

Alexander Zhomov took aim at Maria Kulikova. He fired just after the old man had yanked the door closed. Zhomov stepped over Helge Kulikov and pulled on the door handle. The door rattled but did not open.

He walked back to the two bodies on the ground and wrapped Helge Kulikov's hand around the pistol, a cheap and readily available weapon on Moscow's black market. The fingerprint evidence would support that Kulikov had shot his wife's lover, then turned the gun on himself. Documents within the FSB would confirm Helge had recently spoken to Sokalov of an FSB officer having an affair with his wife, and Helge's desire for retribution.

Zhomov pulled his MP-443 Grach from its waistband holster at the small of his back as he moved around the side of the building, though with caution, uncertain if the old man who had saved Maria Kulikova was armed. When he reached the building corner, the only car in the parking lot lurched forward and spit gravel. He fired at the back window and heard it explode, then lowered his aim to the tires and gas tank, emptying the clip as the car pulled away.

He hurried back to his Mercedes, hidden in the forest, shouting at Sokalov to get in. "Do you know the old man in the bar?"

"No," Sokalov said, rushing to the passenger seat as Zhomov slipped behind the wheel.

"We will know soon enough. I shot out the back tire. They will not get far."

Zhomov threw the car into drive and sped to the double-lane road.

—

Kulikova sat up in the passenger seat and turned to the rear. Wind whistled in from the destroyed back window, and Jenkins could smell the burning rubber as the car thumped down the asphalt. *"Chto s mash-inoy?"* she asked. *What's wrong with the car?*

"On prostrelil zadneye koleso," Jenkins said. *He shot out a back tire.* Then, *"Ty govorish' po-angliyski?"* *Do you speak English?*

"Yes," she said.

Jenkins pulled the mask from his face and tossed it in the back seat.

"Charles Jenkins." Kulikova looked surprised, but Jenkins didn't have time to explain.

"We won't get far. The tire will come off and we'll be on the rim. We can't outrun them. I'm looking for a place to ditch the car and buy us some time. Our only choice is to hide in these woods."

She looked out the windshield. "Turn," she said. "Here, Mr. Jenkins. Turn!"

Jenkins did as she instructed, a hard right turn past signs for Moscow State University.

"You are well known by the FSB, Mr. Jenkins, particularly within the Counterintelligence Directorate. You have been put on a kill list."

"So they tell me."

"You are aware, then, that the president has begun a relentless campaign to find the seven sisters—a special division within the directorate with a singular purpose to find the remaining sisters. You should not have come back."

"Too late for that." Jenkins fought to control the steering wheel. The smell of burning rubber intensified. "Who got shot back there?"

"I believe one man worked within the FSB. The other was my husband, Helge."

"I'm sorry," Jenkins said. The woman stared out the windshield, intensely focused given her circumstances.

"Turn here," she said. Jenkins drove onto the campus grounds, the car thumping and banging as they passed tall buildings and near-empty parking lots.

"The man doing the shooting, is he part of the group tasked with finding the seven sisters, Operation Herod?"

"No. That man is Alexander Zhomov, one of the most celebrated torpedoes in the history of the Kremlin."

Jenkins knew the term meant "assassin." "What is his involvement in this?" The car thumped as if he had driven over a speed bump, then it dropped. Sparks showered the road. "We've lost the tread. We've got to ditch the car now."

"The parking lot." She pointed to a lot in front of a multistory building, and they slowly rolled in. "Drive around to the back of the building." Jenkins followed her directions, parking the car behind a blue garbage dumpster. "Hurry," she said, pushing from the car.

"Where?" Jenkins said.

"We don't have time for questions. Now it is my turn to lead and for you to follow. If you wish to live."

Jenkins rushed to the back of the car and popped the trunk, nearly gagging on the intense smell of burning rubber. Heat radiated from the tire rim.

"What are you doing?" she asked. "We don't have time."

He opened the suitcase and pulled out a plastic ziplock bag in which he kept over-the-counter medicines like ibuprofen, aspirin, and cold medications and emptied the contents. Then he removed the false wall.

"Mr. Jenkins, we have to go. Now."

Jenkins grabbed the passports, corresponding credit cards, rubles, and American dollars, crammed them into the plastic bag, zipped it closed, and shoved the bag into the interior pocket of his jacket.

"Go," he said.

She hurried forward, behind the buildings, which Jenkins deduced to be dormitories and classrooms. He looked behind them for head-lights. Trees lined the campus streets, which would help to hide them, but not for long. The sidewalks were vacant.

The woman crossed an inner courtyard surrounded by buildings and kept moving, as if she had a purpose.

"We need to get into the woods," Jenkins said, hurrying to her side. "We need to get out of sight."

"I know this campus. I went to school here, and I have had reason to study it extensively."

"Why?"

"Not now," she said. "Follow me."

Again, Jenkins had to give her credit. She seemed to have a singular purpose. She was also in good shape, not sounding the least bit out of breath, though she had to be close to his age. He was grateful for his early morning runs, and soon found his wind, his breathing becoming steady.

She came to what appeared to be the entrance of the school, dominated by an expansive lawn and divided by courtyards in front of a massive building Jenkins recognized from photographs.

"One of the seven sisters," he said, slightly out of breath. He recalled the distinct tiered neoclassical tower, one of seven built in the Stalin era. The central tower was nearly forty floors and flanked by four long wings.

"Ironic, isn't it?" She moved away from the building toward the courtyards. Paved with red bricks and lined with flower beds and tall trees, they might provide brief cover. Jenkins did not bother her with questions since she seemed to know where she was going and what she was doing. She rushed to a dry fountain in the southwest quadrant of the courtyard that looked like a multilayered wedding cake with a metal dish atop it. Gargoyle heads extended from the round basin, presumably to spew water. Like many things in Moscow, however, the fountain had fallen into disrepair. Several of the heads were missing, leaving pipes protruding from the pitted concrete. There was simply no money to maintain public landmarks.

Kulikova systematically walked around the fountain and pulled on metal grates beneath the concrete base.

"What are we doing?" Jenkins wiped perspiration from his face and looked behind them to the trees and the bushes, trying to discern car headlights.

"There is a ventilation shaft below the fountain. I don't have time now to explain. We need to get one of these grates opened and get inside."

Jenkins bent for a closer inspection. The decorative bars were part of a single grate with hinges at the top and a bolt embedded at the concrete base. The concrete had been drilled and the bolt epoxied into place, but the bolt had rusted, creating space. Jenkins yanked on the grate and the bolt head moved. He rattled the grate, and the noise echoed in the courtyard.

"I might be able to pry up the bolt." He grabbed the head of the bolt with his fingers and tried to force it up. It raised slightly, but not enough. He stopped. "I'm going to need to create some leverage."

He left the fountain for one of the surrounding flower beds and found a pile of rocks in a corner. He sifted through them until he found two that might work. Hurrying back, he dropped to his knees and angled the longer of the two rocks to put the flat edge under the bolt head, like a chisel blade. He used the second rock like a hammer. The bolt head raised slightly. He tapped again, and again, and again, each time raising the bolt millimeters. The woman kept watch. When Jenkins had raised the bolt enough to grip the head, he wiggled it, but again could not yank it free. He went back to tapping. He had no idea the length of the bolt, or how long it would take to dislodge it. He did know, however, they had very little time.

—

Zhomov drove slowly, searching the woods to the left and right.

"They could have hidden the car anywhere," Sokalov said.

"No," Zhomov said. "They could not. We would see the tire tracks and the bushes would be destroyed. They stayed on the road, trying to get as far as possible until the tire wore off the rim."

They came to a fork in the road. The main road continued back toward Moscow; the other took them to Moscow State University. "They would not risk taking the car back to Moscow. They would try to hide it someplace on the campus," Zhomov said.

He took the fork to the university, proceeding slowly, his head on a swivel, scanning the parking lots on each side of the campus. He slowed the car to a near stop.

"What?" Sokalov asked.

He pointed to the portion of the road visible in the car's headlights. The pavement looked like someone had dragged a spike down it. "He lost the rubber on the tire here. There," he said and pointed to torn rubber along the road's edge. "They cannot be far." He followed the scrape marks into the parking lot on the back side of a dormitory building and pulled behind the car with the blown-out back window, partially hidden behind a garbage dumpster. "They are on foot."

"They could be hidden in any of these buildings," Sokalov said.

Again, Zhomov dismissed it. "The buildings are locked," he said. "Call the CCTV center in Moscow. Throw your weight around. Tell them you want live footage of the campus, that you are looking for a man and a woman on foot, likely running. Tell them to have the computer system search for Maria Kulikova."

Sokalov took out his phone, made the call to Lubyanka, and was connected to the Moscow Department of Information Technologies. He provided them his access code and told them what he wanted.

"We have located them," the man on the phone said. "They are still on the campus, near the main building on Sparrow Hill. A woman and a Black man."

"Black?" Sokalov said.

"Is he an old man?" Zhomov said into the phone.

"Can't tell."

"But you're sure he is Black?" Sokalov asked.

"It is dark, but the man appears to be Black, yes."

"Can you estimate his size?"

"If the woman is of average height, the man would be about two meters. He is muscular, thick."

"Charles Jenkins," Sokalov said.

"Do you want me to see if I can capture his face and run him through the system?"

"No. Do not," Sokalov said.

The man provided the live feed and Sokalov recognized Jenkins from pictures on file. "I do not want them to be perceived as being together," he said to Zhomov.

"Then I would suggest we find them, quickly," Zhomov said.

Kulikova ran past the main building to an expansive courtyard, then disappeared behind trees.

"The coverage there is limited. I cannot see what they are doing," Sokalov said.

"Hiding while waiting for a ride," Zhomov said, taking out earphones, inserting one in his ear and attaching the plug to his phone. "I can move faster on my own. Stay here and monitor the feed. Advise me if you see them again or if a car arrives."

He turned and broke into a run, moving toward the large spire of the central building at the entrance to the campus.

25

Moscow State University
Ramenki District
Moscow Oblast

Jenkins gave the bolt another tap. He had raised it nearly three inches. He set down the rocks and gripped the bolt head, wiggling it back and forth as he applied pressure until it yanked free. He grabbed the grate with both hands and pulled. The bottom edge raised from the concrete but only about six inches.

"The hinges are rusty," Jenkins said, working the grate back and forth, raising it a fraction higher each time. The hinges emitted a screeching noise. He continued until he had raised it enough for a person to squeeze beneath it.

"Follow me," Kulikova said. She lay on her belly and shimmied under the grate, then carefully turned and braced her feet against the concrete on the far side so as not to fall down the shaft. She spun again, gripped the top of a metal ladder bolted to the wall, and descended the shaft.

Being considerably bigger, Jenkins had more difficulty wiggling under the grate, then maneuvering in the cramped space. He braced his hands and feet against the wall to turn. The rungs of a rusted ladder descended into darkness—to where, he had no idea. He looked back to the grate, which was open, and was about to reach for it when a man jogged down the path toward the fountain.

Zhomov, Maria had called him.

No time to close the grate. If it made a noise, it would draw Zhomov to him, and Jenkins would literally be the fish about to be shot in the barrel.

He stepped down the ladder rungs, moving as quickly as he dared. The lower he descended into the pitch darkness, the less he could see. He had to be sure his foot found a perch before he let go to reach down to the next rung. He likened it to rock climbing, or what he imagined rock climbing to be, trying to keep three points of contact on the ladder as he descended.

If he slipped and fell, he had no idea how far the drop, or if Kulikova was still beneath him.

—

Zhomov reached the courtyard in front of the building and slowed his pace, assuming the man who had come for Kulikova, Charles Jenkins, to be armed. He didn't know Jenkins, but he knew of him from Sokalov. He knew Jenkins had come to and escaped from Russia twice, the second time killing Adam Efimov, "The Brick," and one of Lubyanka's best torpedoes. The president had placed Jenkins on a kill list, and Zhomov would have liked nothing better than to appease the president, but Sokalov had been adamant that Jenkins be taken alive, a much more difficult task.

Zhomov removed the pistol from the holster at his back and held the barrel pointed at the ground as he walked and listened. He stopped, allowing his eyes to search the trees and shrubs for natural hiding places and unnatural colors. His ears listened for man-made sounds.

He touched his earpiece. "Anything?"

"No. They have not moved since they entered the courtyard in front of the main building. Do you see them?"

"*Nyet.*"

"They have to be close by."

"Yes. They do."

Zhomov took a step forward. He stopped when he heard a metallic tink. Tink. Tink. He tried to determine its location. He heard it again and stepped toward the sound, treading softly.

"Still—" Sokalov began.

"Do not speak," Zhomov whispered. He wondered if perhaps the sound was from one of the buildings, a mechanical system, then dismissed the thought. The noise had no pattern, making it likely man-made. It stopped. He heard a creaking noise, again man-made. Again, he moved toward the sound.

He stepped around a row of bushes and trees and came to the southwest courtyard dominated by a central, dry fountain. His eyes searched the shadows and natural hiding places, again seeing no one.

"Anything yet?" he whispered into the headset.

"Nothing," Sokalov responded.

They had to be here. Somewhere. He moved down a path toward the fountain and proceeded around it clockwise, looking left and right. No one.

Zhomov stopped. Listened. He did not hear anything, but something about one of the grates at the base of the fountain caught his attention. He moved toward it. The grate had been pulled open. A ten-centimeter bolt lay on the concrete. He felt scratch marks under the square head. It explained the tinking noise—someone prying up the bolt to free the grate. Carefully he leaned forward, holding out his phone, and used the light to look down into the darkness at a rusted ladder descending a shaft. His light was not strong enough to reach the bottom.

He pulled back and spoke into the headset. "They have gone underground. I am not far behind them and will follow. Have the center activate the cameras in the tunnels."

"I don't have time to explain, but there are no cameras in the underground."

"Then take the car back to Lubyanka and pull up a map with points of entry and exit. Find out where the tunnel beneath the fountain in the southwest corner of the courtyard goes. They have to come back above ground somewhere. Alert the Moscow police."

"Remember, I need Jenkins alive," Sokalov said. "Kill Kulikova and leave her body below Moscow so I can think fondly of her each time I drive to Lubyanka."

"I have no desire to be part of your fantasies, Dmitry. Do as I say. And do it now if you wish for me to succeed."

—

Jenkins stepped off the final rung and used the phone light to illuminate an enormous underground bunker with multilevel labyrinths of tunnels and rooms. It reminded him of the tunnels beneath Oslo that he and Ponomayova had used to escape. Those tunnels had been built so leaders of Oslo could move around the city while it was under Nazi rule. But these tunnels were many times the size of those tunnels.

"What is this?" he asked, keeping his volume low.

"The underground city," Kulikova said. "Ramenki-43. Built in the 1960s and '70s to withstand a nuclear attack. It can house up to fifteen thousand people, some say for thirty years."

Jenkins swore. "You people really are paranoid."

"You have no idea. We need to move," she said.

Jenkins followed. "How do you know this place? Do others know of it?"

"Some," she said, moving down an arched brick tunnel, the light of her phone illuminating no more than a few feet in front of them. "In college a friend found this shaft. He brought me and others underground to explore the tunnels at night. When the Soviet Union collapsed, he created an organization called Diggers of the Underground Planet and gave subterranean tours. The tours stopped when Putin came to power."

The ground was moist, slick, and uneven. Jenkins felt his shoes slip. "This is all in anticipation of a nuclear war?"

"Don't sound so surprised, Mr. Jenkins. During the Cold War, Great Britain and your country also built special underground bunkers where their respective leadership could seek refuge. The Soviet Union built up its underground system far beyond what was built by your country or Great Britain, but as you said, we are more paranoid. Down here you will find bunkers, underground factories, even tank tunnels."

"How big is it?"

"I don't know. I have, however, seen the plans. There are twelve levels running beneath Moscow. A few of the passageways date back to the 1300s. Ivan the Terrible expanded the tunnels during his reign in the sixteenth century, fearing he might have to someday flee the Kremlin. The largest tunnel is an underground subway system, known informally as Metro-2 and officially as D-6. It has been an ongoing project since the 1940s and is used only by high-ranking government officials, all of whom categorically deny its existence. You will not find a map or a document to substantiate it anywhere except at Lubyanka and, because of me, at Langley."

Jenkins's foot slipped and he reached out to the wall to regain his balance. The wall, too, was moist, and unlike above ground, where Moscow was hot and muggy, the passageway was cool and musty. Jenkins felt a chill on his arms beneath his dampened shirt. He estimated the temperature to be no more than forty-five degrees Fahrenheit. Their breath hung in the light from his phone.

"How do you know so much about it?" he asked.

"Because an issue came up as to who should be responsible for the tunnels. During the Soviet Union, it was run by the Fifteenth Directorate. When the Soviet Union collapsed, the directorate in charge of the tunnels was renamed the Main Directorate of Special Programs of the President, or GUSP. GUSP's sole purpose is to maintain and expand these tunnels and keep their absolute secrecy. Sokalov was at one time the director, but he is lazy. He had me study the map and provide him with the details. I was glad to do it."

"Do you have a photographic memory? How do you know where we are going?" Jenkins asked. They had ignored multiple side tunnels.

"I am following the main communication cable." She tipped her phone so Jenkins could see a series of cables, like tree roots, anchored along the brick wall. "It will lead us back to Moscow. From there, I assume you have a plan to get us out."

"I *had* a plan to get us out," Jenkins said. "At the moment I'm improvising." He checked his cell phone but, as he suspected, he had no reception. "Are there security cameras or motion detectors we should be concerned about?"

"The government has tried, but the underground belongs to the Diggers and subterranean explorers, and they do not like the government. They have clashed over access to the tunnels. Cameras and motion detectors don't last long down here. The government has given up spending the money. Walk behind me," she said. "The passageway narrows."

Jenkins stepped behind her and they slowed their pace. Walking on the slick, concave bricks was like walking inside a pipe. "I asked earlier: What is Zhomov's involvement in this?"

She turned her head to speak over her shoulder. "Sokalov brought in Zhomov to try and keep this quiet. He and Zhomov have a history."

"Keep what quiet?"

"His and my affair. Sokalov is deathly afraid of his father-in-law. If word of his infidelity were to get out, his father-in-law will kill him. If they learn I was one of the seven sisters, the president will kill him. Either way, he is a dead man."

"Who's Sokalov's father-in-law?"

"General Roman Portnov," she said, providing Jenkins with a quick biographical sketch. "He has the means and the ability to kill Sokalov. And this was not just any affair. I went to great lengths, at great costs, to make sure the details of our relationship would be an extreme embarrassment—one the president and the general would never let surface."

"Can Sokalov do it; can he keep the affair secret?"

"He can if Zhomov finds us." She explained to Jenkins that the Counterintelligence Directorate was self-contained, and Sokalov might survive were he to kill her. The tunnel widened. "You wore a disguise."

"To trick Moscow's CCTV cameras."

"How then could they have known of your return to Moscow?"

Jenkins told her of the confrontation in the bar.

She stopped and looked back at him. "Eldar Velikaya?"

"You know him?"

"Everyone in Moscow knows what happened to Eldar Velikaya, Mr. Jenkins. You killed him? Why?"

"I didn't kill him, but I was there when he was killed. It's a long story. In short, I likely left a fingerprint on a beer bottle or the surface of a table in the bar."

They followed the tunnel of white light cast by Kulikova's phone. After a few minutes she said, "This is starting to make sense."

"What is?"

"How Sokalov determined my betrayal. My husband followed me when I made a dead drop, to provide information on the attempt to kill Fyodor Ibragimov in Virginia."

"Hang on. You're saying Lubyanka attempted to kill Ibragimov on American soil?"

"I took notes at a meeting between Sokalov and others. When the assassination failed, they must have looked for the leak. I would be the primary suspect."

Jenkins realized now what Lemore had meant last night when he said there was something "in play" and told Jenkins to proceed to exfiltrate Petrekova first. The CIA did not want to exfiltrate Kulikova until after they had arrested the two assassins.

"Sokalov confronted me about it," Kulikova explained. "But I am very good at diverting his attention. He must have learned of your return to Moscow and decided it was all too big a coincidence."

"We have to assume Sokalov knows I'm here."

"And if that is true, I assure you the Velikayas also know you are here. They have many ears and eyes inside the Moscow City Police, as well as at Lubyanka. Yekaterina Velikaya will be hunting you with as much vengeance as Sokalov harbors for me. So, I guess we both now have a problem."

"We'll deal with the Velikayas if we have to," Jenkins said. "Let's focus on Zhomov. You're saying he might be the only one within the FSB we have to be concerned about?"

"You say that like it is a good thing. Let me assure you, Mr. Jenkins, Zhomov is more relentless than a dozen FSB task forces, and more deadly. He made his reputation as a sharpshooter in Afghanistan, and recorded more than one hundred and fifty kills. Since then he has served the Kremlin and is responsible for the deaths of twice as many."

Jenkins thought of Viktor Federov and of Adam Efimov, who had hunted him on his first two trips inside Moscow. "Seems like the FSB has a whole warehouse of those guys," he said.

Jenkins heard a noise and tapped Kulikova on the shoulder, stopping her. He put a finger to his lips. "Shh," he whispered. He had her hold her cell phone light against her body. He watched the darkness behind them and heard drops of water falling from the vaulted ceiling. Zhomov could not follow them in the dark, not unless he had brought night-vision goggles with him, which Jenkins doubted. He'd also need to use a light. Jenkins counted silently two full minutes. As he was about to step forward, a faint reflection of light illuminated a tunnel wall. Jenkins watched it for a moment to be sure he wasn't imagining it.

"Vot der'mo," Kulikova said.

26

Moscow Underground
Moscow, Russia

Zhomov walked at an uneven pace. He had no choice; the bricks beneath his feet were slick and the tunnel concave, sloping toward the middle, likely to facilitate drainage. He walked in pitch-black but for the few cones of light descending from the street above. He kept the light on his phone facedown, spotting the ground so he could see where he was going, but not giving away his position, and so he could better discern any artificial light in the tunnels ahead of him. The tunnels, however, twisted and turned, and it was possible he wouldn't see a light until he was on top of Jenkins and Kulikova, if he was even going in the right direction. He followed the communication cables along the tunnel walls, figuring they would be the best guide for someone not intimately familiar with the tunnels to find their way.

Zhomov knew of, but was not familiar with, the labyrinth of tunnels beneath Moscow. In 2002, he had been part of a special forces unit that freed 850 hostages held by Chechen rebels at the Dubrovka Theater. Their problem had been how to get into the theater and neutralize the threat before the hostages were assassinated. The resolution came from an unlikely source, the head of the Diggers of the Underground Planet. He provided Zhomov's unit with a detailed map of the tunnels, including an entry inside the theater. Zhomov and his men used the underground passage to storm the theater, killing all forty of the stunned Chechens.

Zhomov had been hyperfocused at the time but was now amazed at the vastness of the tunnels and how they spoked from a central tunnel. Each time he came to an intersection he stopped, listened, and searched the intersecting tunnels for a glimpse of artificial light. Seeing none, he followed the cables.

He picked up his pace as his eyes adjusted to the dark and his footing became more sure, but he remained information blind, with no cell phone reception. He needed to either find Jenkins and Kulikova or conclude they had left the tunnel, in which case he would go back to Lubyanka and search footage to determine where they had surfaced.

He turned at a bend in the tunnel and thought he detected a flicker of artificial light. It was quickly extinguished. He doused his own light and used a hand on the wall to feel his way forward. The light appeared again, this time more than a glimpse before it was extinguished.

Zhomov needed to get closer before he fired his weapon. Not knowing the bends and turns in the tunnels, he could fire the gun with no chance of hitting Jenkins or Kulikova but alerting them to his presence. He decided to keep his light off and use only his hand to guide him, hoping to get close enough for a decent shot.

—

"What is it?" Kulikova whispered.

Jenkins shook his head. He was looking behind them. "I thought I saw a light."

"I don't see anything. Are you sure?"

"No. I'm not sure."

"It is not likely Zhomov knows about the tunnels, and unlikely he could find the entrance," Kulikova said.

Jenkins paused. He did not want to panic her and tell her he had seen Zhomov near the fountain before he had time to pull the grate back in.

"Mr. Jenkins?"

Jenkins kept his eyes on the tunnel walls behind them. "Let's move," he said. A man flashed beneath a tube of light descending from above, like a flickering image in a black-and-white film. "Shit," Jenkins said just before a shot rang out.

The bullet pinged off the bricks, kicking up dust and nearly hitting him. Jenkins and Kulikova took off in a dead run, Kulikova turning left and right with the bends in the tunnels. When they came to a ladder, Jenkins told her to climb. He would wait until certain Kulikova reached the level above. On the ground he at least had the chance to perhaps surprise Zhomov.

Footsteps pounded the pavement.

A silhouette rushed past the side tunnel in which they had taken refuge.

Kulikova was approximately thirty feet up the ladder, climbing quickly. Then her foot slipped on one of the rungs and she dropped but managed to grab a bar and keep from falling. Her phone, however, which she had wedged in the waistline of her pants, came free. It pinged against the ladder once, then a second time, before it hit the ground and shattered.

The sound of feet pounding the pavement stopped, then started again. Zhomov returning. Jenkins looked up and watched Kulikova go through a hole. Momentarily safe. He quickly climbed. The ladder was more rusted and less stable than the one they had descended. He climbed as fast as he could, trying not to think of Zhomov shooting him. If he did, Jenkins hoped he was dead before he hit the ground.

Zhomov had no depth perception in the dark and did not know if he was ten meters or a hundred meters behind Jenkins and Kulikova. Uncertain he would ever get a clear shot, he broke his established protocol and sprinted forward, then dropped to a knee, steadied his aim, and fired at the light, someone running, their phone in hand.

The light continued to swing wildly. He'd missed.

He rose and sprinted, lost view of the light, turned, and saw it again. Jenkins and Kulikova were turning left and right, hoping to confuse him. Hoping to lose him. But he heard footsteps pound the bricks and splash in puddles of water. Zhomov stopped. Listened. Followed the sounds. Stopped again. Listened. Then ran.

He stopped a third time but this time he heard nothing. About to go forward, something metal pinged once, then a second time. The sound came from behind him. He was close.

He pivoted and ran to another T. He stopped, listened. Nothing. He stepped to his left. This time he heard metal thrumming. Someone climbing a ladder. They were attempting to exit. He ran down the tunnel. A cone of light from above illuminated Jenkins on the ladder rungs, nearly to the ceiling.

Zhomov knelt, took aim, and fired.

—

Jenkins was ten feet from the top rung of the ladder, moving as quickly as he dared. He briefly diverted his attention to glimpse down to the T where the tunnels met, and stepped up. The rung snapped under his weight and he slid down several rungs before his hands regripped, but not before he hit his chin hard on a rusted crossbar. He winced in pain, saw stars, and felt blood trickling from his chin. With pain in both hands, he resumed climbing, careful not to put weight on the broken rung. Kulikova leaned over the opening above him, urging him on.

"Don't look down. Just climb. Climb."

He looked up at her and could see her gaze focused down the tunnel. Her eyes widened again. Zhomov.

"Climb," she urged him. "Climb."

Jenkins reached for the top rung, and Kulikova pulled him from the ladder as shots rang out, hitting the metal rungs. Jenkins rolled on top of Kulikova in case the bullets ricocheted through the hole.

Unhit, but with blood dripping from his chin and his hands, Jenkins scrambled to his feet. "Go. Go." He pushed her forward. The ground beneath his shoes was no longer brick but gravel. A rail track with crossbars centered in the tunnel made it more difficult to run, requiring them to pick up their feet, like football practice in high school.

This had to be Metro-2, the tunnel Kulikova said was used to transport those in authority. He hoped the trains were infrequent.

The tunnel was decidedly narrower than the lavish Metro system that transported millions of Russian commuters each day. Jenkins searched for a way out, a door or a ladder. With Zhomov armed and in pursuit, and with nowhere to run except straight ahead, it was just a matter of time before one of his bullets found its mark, or they reached a tunnel that had been sealed off. Dead end.

At a Y they took the tunnel to the left. From the condition of the rails, it looked to be older, the walls dingy and not as bright. He kept Kulikova in front of him, running behind her. He had to give her credit. She just kept motoring.

He looked behind. Zhomov emerged at the Y, paused, then started down the right tunnel. Maybe it would give them a reprieve. They continued for another minute until Jenkins reached out and grabbed Kulikova by the shoulder, stopping her. He bent over, hands on knees. Condensation clouded their faces with each breath.

"I think we might have lost him," Jenkins said in between breaths. He looked up at Kulikova, then past her, seeing a bright light on the wall of the tunnel just before feeling a sudden rush of wind. Kulikova turned, eyes wide.

An advancing train.

Jenkins searched the tunnel walls for a doorway or cutout in the stone, anyplace where they could press their bodies.

He saw none.

With no time to consider, and no options, he grabbed Kulikova and started sprinting back toward the Y. Halfway there, he stopped. Zhomov appeared at the far end, searching. Two steps ahead, Jenkins noticed a manhole cover with holes in it. The wind behind them increased in intensity. The lights brightened on the tunnel wall. Jenkins dropped to a knee. So, too, did Zhomov. Jenkins shoved Kulikova down onto the tracks and reached into the manhole cover holes, gripping the metal disc. It lifted, then slipped back into place. Jenkins couldn't duck to avoid Zhomov's bullets. He needed to remain upright for the leverage. The first bullet whizzed over his head. No matter how good a shot, Zhomov was firing a pistol from a considerable distance. He would, however, adjust.

Jenkins pulled again. This time the disc budged, and he yanked it to the side so it wouldn't slip back to its original place.

Another bullet grazed the shoulder of his leather jacket. Zhomov had risen and rushed toward them. With each step closer, his aim would become more accurate.

Jenkins wedged his fingers into the small gap on the right side of the disc and shoved it to the side, revealing a hole two feet in diameter. He strained to lift the disc on one end and use it as a shield. Behind Kulikova the train lights brightened. The wind increased. Another bullet hit the metal disc.

Jenkins peered down the hole into darkness. He had no idea how far the fall.

The train came around the corner.

Lights shined directly on them.

Wind blew back Kulikova's hair.

He assumed Zhomov was running back to the Y, though he had no time to look.

Kulikova wasn't waiting. She moved to the hole, dropping through. With the wind intensity, Jenkins didn't hear her land. It was like being inside a vacuum.

The train lights aimed directly at him. Jenkins fit his legs into the hole and dropped just before the subway train passed overhead. Falling felt like minutes but was certainly only a few seconds. He braced for an impact that never came. He hit water, splashed, and plunged beneath the surface. The freezing water caused him to gasp and open his mouth. He sucked in water.

Instinct took over. He kicked to the surface, gasping and choking. The water current shoved and pushed him, a torrent not unlike rafting rapids. He lifted his head, gulped for air, and tried to get his heels pointed downcurrent.

Up ahead, Kulikova screamed, piercing and sharp.

A second later, Jenkins felt himself free-falling, as if shot from a cannon. He again plunged beneath the water. This time, when he reached the surface, he felt no current. The lights of downtown Moscow lit up the sky and reflected on the surface of what must be the Moskva River. The Kremlin, St. Basil's, and other landmarks oriented him. He put his head down and swam toward Kulikova, who had reached a ladder attached to a concrete embankment.

They stumbled across the embankment to a park and fell to their knees, retching and coughing up water. Eventually Jenkins caught his breath long enough to ask, "What the hell was that?"

"The Neglinnaya River." Kulikova struggled to suck in air.

"A river under the city?"

"Covered over many years ago," she said. "It passes beneath Moscow, under Red Square, and empties into the Moskva."

"Well, thank God it does."

"Zhomov?" she said.

Jenkins shook his head. "I don't know. But we can't stay here. It's a little too close to the Kremlin and Lubyanka for my tastes."

"I know of a place," she said. "It is a risk. Sokalov and I used to go there. And you will have to get even closer to Lubyanka."

"As long as I don't have to go inside the building," he said. "Lead the way."

27

Department of Information Technologies Center
Moscow, Russia

Early morning, Sokalov paced the carpet of a darkened room at the Moscow Department of Information Technologies control center on Zhitnaya Street. He drank coffee from a Styrofoam cup and spoke on his personal cell phone, talking his wife off a ledge.

"I cannot tell you everything, Olga," he said. "You know that. But it is an emergency, and I am doing my best to handle it."

He listened to her rant, accusing him of spending the night with another woman. He looked through a glass partition into what resembled a command center on a science fiction spacecraft with numerous computer terminals, monitors, and blinking colored lights.

He flexed his head to the left, then to the right. The kink in his neck worsened with stress. Caffeine didn't help, but he needed the jolt to stay focused; he was operating on no sleep and his brain felt sluggish. He really didn't need her lecture.

Sokalov had awakened the chairman of the Information Technologies Center, Maxim Ugolov, at his home and told him urgent state business demanded his attention at the center. When Ugolov arrived, Sokalov stressed to him the need for discretion, then provided him pictures of Jenkins and Kulikova. He told Ugolov, "This man is an

American spy. We do not, however, want to alert anyone in the media that we are hunting him or if and when we capture him. We do not want the Americans to know he has been apprehended. We will need unfettered time to interrogate him. Therefore, I am counting on your discretion and the discretion of the technician you bring in to assist on this matter. And I will hold you both personally accountable."

Ugolov had been appointed to his position by the government and well understood that Dmitry Sokalov's displeasure would bear considerable weight on Ugolov's continued employment. He advised Sokalov he would bring in one of his senior and most trusted technicians.

"Yes, I will call you as soon as I am able, Olga. I don't know. Maybe tonight. At present I simply can't say, but I can assure you this is no picnic. Your father? Why would I want to . . . No. Olga?" Sokalov sighed and looked to the door as Alexander Zhomov walked into the room, his eyes glaring and focused. "Good morning, Roman," Sokalov said into the phone. "Yes, it has been a long night, and I apologized to Olga that I did not call her. No. This is an emergency I am not at liberty to discuss . . . Surely you understand . . . Tonight? I will do my best, Roman."

Sokalov looked at the phone. His father-in-law had disconnected the call, but not until making it clear he expected Sokalov to return home and provide a better accounting of his evening.

"Did you bring the map?" Zhomov asked Sokalov. "Dmitry?"

Sokalov looked at him.

"Did you bring the map?"

"Yes." Sokalov pointed to a rolled-up tube on one of the tables. Zhomov unrolled it and studied the maps of Moscow's underground tunnels, including those that accommodated Metro-2.

"What happened?" Sokalov asked.

"Too long a story to get into now," Zhomov said. He carried the map to where the technician sat at his terminal. His fingers rapidly stroked the keys on his keyboard and punched buttons. In the upper right corner of his computer monitor was a picture of Charles Jenkins.

The computer screen rapidly clicked through thousands of images taken by CCTV cameras.

"Stop typing," Zhomov said from behind the man.

The man's fingers dutifully silenced. He sat ramrod straight, eyes on the screen, fingers poised to begin.

Zhomov studied the map and told the others his intent was to find the most likely places where Kulikova and Jenkins could have exited the tunnels, then review CCTV camera footage in those areas to find them. "Pull up a map of downtown. Zoom out." The man complied. Zhomov leaned over the man's shoulder, pointing to the Moscow State University campus. "Give me a live feed here." The man clicked keys and the camera view switched to a live feed of the campus. "Closer here," Zhomov said. Again, the keyboard clicked, and the monitor zoomed in on the courtyard directly in front of the main campus building. "Go back in time on the camera feed . . ." Zhomov checked his watch. "Four hours."

The man did as instructed. After several starts and stops, the camera focused on two people, Jenkins and Kulikova hurrying into the square toward the fountain and eventually to the back side, where the fountain obscured them. "This is where they entered the tunnels, beneath this fountain."

"Ramenki," Sokalov said, referencing the underground city beneath Moscow State University.

"Do you have cameras in the underground?" Zhomov asked Ugolov.

"No," Ugolov said. "We have tried, many times, but the Diggers destroy them and the motion sensors. We are working—"

Zhomov raised a hand. "Stop." Ugolov did. Zhomov studied the map. The technician remained at the ready. Sokalov assumed that, like most people in Moscow, the technician had no real knowledge of the Moscow underground and certainly no information of its extent. To most Muscovites, the underground was more rumor than reality.

After a minute, Zhomov lowered the map and pointed over the technician's shoulder. "We proceeded northeast for approximately one hour. A man generally walks five to six kilometers an hour." Zhomov looked to be calculating in his head. "Draw me a line roughly four kilometers northeast of the fountain." The technician typed on the keys and used the mouse, drawing a straight line that further along the map roughly intersected Gorky Park. Zhomov alternately studied the map and considered the live feed on the computer monitor. "Draw me another line northeast roughly three kilometers." Again, the technician complied. Zhomov provided additional directions and the technician drew lines as instructed until Zhomov's finger touched the screen for Zaryadye Park.

"Pull up the CCTV feeds from cameras in this area and along the streets surrounding it," he said, drawing a circle on the map. "Go back one hour and have the cameras search for the photographs you have been provided. With few people on the street at that hour this should not take long, if my calculations are correct."

Zhomov stepped back and the technician went to work. Zhomov motioned Sokalov over to one of the tables, where he set the map. "They climbed up a level to Metro-2," he said, keeping his voice low and using a finger to draw lines on the map of the underground. "I was close, but a train came and they disappeared down a storm drain cover." He pointed to a winding waterway.

"The Neglinnaya," Sokalov said. "Could they have drowned?"

"Maybe," Zhomov said. "The river empties into the Moskva River here, here, and here. It is also possible they survived and are in this general area. They will not ride public transportation because of the cameras. More likely they will walk or take a taxi. Kulikova will not return home. It is too risky. They will not go to a hotel because their clothes, wet and soiled, will draw too much attention. They need to go to a place that provides privacy. No cameras."

As Zhomov spoke, Sokalov felt a sick burning in his stomach. The apartment he kept for his trysts with Kulikova was on Varsonof'yevskiy, within walking distance of the park. Kulikova also knew Sokalov had the camera on that street removed to provide secrecy. Revealing the existence of the apartment was not his concern, though. His concern was the contents of the apartment, what Zhomov would find upon entering it.

Zhomov stared at him, his eyes no doubt reading Sokalov's facial expressions. "You know where she went?" Zhomov asked.

Sokalov nodded. "If she exited at the park then yes. Most likely to an apartment, but, Alexander, there are things in that apartment—"

"I don't give a shit about what you may have done there, Dmitry, or about any of your prurient interests. That is your business. You are paying me to do mine. Where did she go?"

"An apartment on Varsonof'yevskiy."

"Give me the address. Then stay here. Call me if and when they are spotted on the cameras."

28

Varsonof'yevskiy Pereulok
Moscow, Russia

Kulikova punched in an access code on the keypad mounted to the right of the thick wooden exterior door. The entrance to the apartment building was beneath a small iron pergola. The buildings on this block were high-end, built before the rise of communism and its cheap, box-shaped, uniform construction. Each had a stone façade with ornamental details—sconces, alcoves, small balconies surrounded by wrought iron, and modern, white vinyl windows. At this hour of the morning, the sidewalks were devoid of people and only a few cars passed on the streets. A man walked a dog on a leash in a small park surrounded by a six-foot fence, a place to take children to get outdoors and for a dog to relieve itself.

Kulikova and Jenkins stepped into a central courtyard reminiscent of apartment buildings in France and climbed an interior stairwell to the third floor. Kulikova pressed the buttons on another keypad and entered the apartment through a dark wood door. She paused in the entry. She looked pained.

"Are you okay?" Jenkins asked.

"What you are about to see, Mr. Jenkins, is not Maria Kulikova. What you are about to see is the personality I had to become to do what I had to do." She looked up at him, eyes watery but jaw set. "Do you understand?"

"I'm not here to judge you," he said. "I'm here to get you out."

Jenkins followed her inside a small entry to a well-decorated front room that spilled into a kitchen modest in size but with high-end appliances. "Wait here," she said and departed down a dark hallway.

The apartment had a peculiar smell to it. It didn't smell lived in. Jenkins did not detect the odor of food or cigarettes or even perfume. It had a musty smell to it, like a cabin that needed to be aired out after a long winter. On the coffee table Jenkins noticed magazines of hard-core pornography, mostly sadomasochism. He wondered if the odor he had detected was human perspiration, perhaps lotions.

When Jenkins looked up, Kulikova stood in the hall wearing a plush robe and holding another. She looked embarrassed, and he was embarrassed for her. She handed him the robe. "Give me your clothes. I will put them in the dryer." Jenkins took the robe and stepped from his clothes.

He pulled the plastic ziplock bag from his coat and checked their passports, credit cards, rubles, and American dollars. They were dry. His phone, however, which had been in his pocket when he fell into the Neglinnaya River, had shut off, likely for good.

Kulikova returned, using a towel to dry her hair. Down the hall, Jenkins could hear clothes tumbling in a dryer. It was the first chance Jenkins had to really see her. An attractive woman, Kulikova had auburn hair, Slavic features, and a full figure she no doubt kept in shape given the rigors they had just endured.

"Phone's dead," Jenkins said.

Kulikova stepped past him and into the kitchen. She pulled open a drawer and handed him what looked like an old-fashioned flip phone. "Burner phone," she said. "It has an app that redirects the contact information to a random phone number in Moscow so it cannot be traced.

Sokalov insisted we use these phones in case one of us was detained or could not make an arranged meeting."

Jenkins figured, given what was at stake, Sokalov would have gone to some lengths to ensure the phone was secure. He also did not have a lot of choices. They needed help. He flipped open the phone and called the number he had memorized. The number went through an internal switchboard at Langley, where it was also scrambled and redirected so, if traced, it, too, would lead to a random phone number somewhere within the United States.

If a call was an internal call, Lemore answered "Lemore." If it was an outside call, he answered "Hello."

"Hello?"

"I'm calling about the two love seats to be reupholstered," Jenkins said. "I'm going to need some help."

After no more than a beat, Lemore replied. "Yes. What about them?"

"I'd like to change the fabric we picked out, something that will better conceal their current appearances. Can you deliver two different fabrics for me to consider, one feminine and one more masculine?"

"Certainly."

"I've also changed my mind and wish for you to make arrangements to pick up the two chairs, but tell your driver to be discreet. This is a surprise for my wife."

"Your address?"

Jenkins provided the address. "Tell your driver to ask for Nicholas, the superintendent in 3C. If my wife is out, I will respond '*spasibo.*' If she is home, I will respond '*nyet.*' Do you know how long this will take? My wife indicated she would be out no more than half an hour."

"We'll do our best to be there before she returns."

Jenkins disconnected. He slipped the phone into his pocket, then thought better of it. If Sokalov suspected Maria might use the apartment, he might also consider the phone and somehow be able to track it. He put the phone back in the drawer and spoke to Kulikova. "I have disguises and transportation on the way, but I assume they will be nothing as elaborate as what I originally was given—likely just a change of clothes, something to conceal our hair, perhaps wigs and facial hair." He moved to the window and pulled back the curtain, peering down at the street emerging in the dawn light. "I'm assuming that at some point one or both of us will be identified on the CCTV cameras and those cameras will track us back to this apartment building."

"Sokalov had the camera on this block removed to better conceal our meetings. That might buy us a few more minutes," she said. "But not many. If he tracks us moving in this direction, he'll deduce we chose this apartment for the reasons you just explained."

Jenkins hoped they'd be long gone before that happened.

29

Velikaya Estate
Novorizhskoye, Russia

Mily Karlov hung up his desk phone, left his office, and walked to the other wing of the house, to where Yekaterina Velikaya kept her office. He rapped softly on the door three times.

"*Voydite.*"

Mily entered. Yekaterina spoke on the phone in the light of her desk lamp. Out her arched windows dawn broke through the dark sky, offering muted blue-gray light. Steam rose from a cup of coffee beside a slice of toast. Both looked untouched. Mily deduced she was discussing funeral arrangements. After a few more sentences, Yekaterina hung up and stared vacantly across the room. "Eldar will be buried with his grandfather in Yekaterinburg," she said, her voice soft. "I am arranging to have a similar marble statue erected in his honor."

Mily had never understood the desire to erect grandiose statues or slabs of marble depicting a decedent to mark that person's grave. In Yekaterinburg Cemetery it seemed the mafiya families tried to one-up one another, erecting sculptures with the decedent's fingers bearing large jewels, or his body standing beside expensive cars and lavish homes. Mily understood the display was intended to represent that the deceased would lead just as grand a lifestyle as the person had lived in life, but he found them to be gauche and a waste of money. They only reminded him that the men who died had been too young.

He didn't believe in the afterlife. If there was one, he'd know soon enough. Until then, he'd enjoy this life as much as he could.

"I'm sure it will be lovely, Comare," he said.

"You have information," she said.

"I just spoke with Maxim Ugolov at the Information Technologies Center. Mr. Jenkins has surfaced in Moscow, and it seems we are not the only ones interested in him."

"The police, I am sure," she said.

"And the FSB," Mily said. "Dmitry Sokalov was in Ugolov's office early this morning along with another man tracking Mr. Jenkins. They are considering CCTV footage now to find him."

Yekaterina's face hardened at the mention of the name of Dmitry Sokalov, the man she held responsible for her father's death, along with the president. She paced near the windows, half her face in shadow.

Mily knew Yekaterina had, on more than one occasion, contemplated killing Sokalov, as she had evened the score with others who crossed her father, but she did not make rash decisions. To kill someone of Sokalov's stature would start an all-out war with the government and potentially Sokalov's father-in-law, the former leader of Directorate S. It was a war Yekaterina could not hope to win.

"You have told Ugolov the importance of this information to me?" she said, her voice controlled.

"He assures he will advise me before he advises the deputy director, if he gets a hit for Mr. Jenkins."

She paced, turned, and looked out the window. "Did Ugolov identify the second man with Sokalov?"

"He did not, but he said it was clear this man was in charge, that Sokalov deferred to him."

She gave Mily a quizzical look. He, too, had thought the information odd. "Did Ugolov know this man's name or tell you what he was doing there?"

"Only that Mr. Jenkins and a woman used the underground tunnels to avoid capture and he was directing their search to surface streets. Something else Ugolov said of interest."

Yekaterina waited.

"Sokalov told him any information regarding Mr. Jenkins was highly classified and not to be shared with anyone. Sokalov was even concerned with Ugolov's choice of technician to review the camera footage. Ugolov said they did not alert the Moscow police or any other FSB officers."

Yekaterina gave this a moment of thought. "Given what we know of Mr. Jenkins, that he is on a Kremlin kill list, one would have assumed all of the FSB would have been alerted, would one not?"

"One would, but it is not the case. I have made multiple telephone calls to those who work for us," Mily said, meaning the FSB officers on Yekaterina's payroll. "Ugolov is correct. They know nothing of Mr. Jenkins's supposed return to Moscow, and they are unaware of any general order from Sokalov about him."

"Sokalov is keeping this quiet. Why?" She paced again, in and out of the shadows from the windows. "Who is the woman?"

"Maria Kulikova," Mily said.

Yekaterina stopped and faced him. "Director of the Secretariat. Sokalov's longtime lover."

The Velikaya family had, for years, maintained files on key government officials, information they could use to blackmail the person. Sokalov had been a priority. Mily's men had secured photographs of Sokalov with Kulikova, though always in public, where Sokalov had always been discreet. He and Kulikova never rode together in the same car, never walked Moscow streets together, held hands, or showed any other public displays of affection, even when dining out in restaurants.

Every photograph Mily and his men had filed away, Sokalov could explain as a business meeting.

Yekaterina smiled. "The little bitch," she said.

"Comare?"

She looked to Mily. "If Kulikova is running *with* Mr. Jenkins rather than *from* him, then what must we conclude? She is a spy."

Mily felt his jaw go slack. How did he miss it? This was information he should have brought to her.

"And if Kulikova is a spy, then she has been spying under Sokalov's nose for years." Yekaterina laughed. It sounded out of place in the darkened and somber room given what had transpired over the last few days. "Sokalov is not trying to keep this quiet because of Mr. Jenkins, Mily."

"That would not make any sense," he agreed.

"The FSB would have a manhunt seeking to arrest Mr. Jenkins," Yekaterina said. "The fat pig is keeping this quiet because the little bitch has been spying on him between the sheets, and if such knowledge were to become public knowledge, Sokalov is a dead man. They will be lining up to kill him—his father-in-law and the president. If we can produce such evidence, they may even allow me the honor of killing him."

Mily's cell phone rang. He pulled it from his suit pocket, considered the caller, then smiled at Yekaterina. "Ugolov."

"Sokalov will kill Kulikova to keep his secret hidden. We cannot allow that to happen, Mily. You need to find them both and bring them to me, alive. I wish to determine from Mr. Jenkins what business he had with Eldar. As for Kulikova, I have an entirely different use in mind."

30

Arkhip Mishkin used the eraser of his pencil to rub at the eczema spot on the back of his head. His itch got worse with each passing minute, and with each passing minute he seemed to get farther and farther away from a resolution in the Charles Jenkins matter. No doubt the latter caused the former. He was running out of options. He had made several attempts to speak with Yekaterina Velikaya, but the mother of the victim was said to be in mourning and would not be speaking to him or to anyone else. It was a polite way of telling Arkhip to go screw himself, and Arkhip didn't have much recourse.

He'd gone back to speak to the bartender at the Yakimanka Bar, but the man had gotten a rapid case of the three monkeys. He no longer could see, hear, or speak of the shooting. It was a wonder the man even remembered that Eldar Velikaya and Pavil Ismailov had entered his establishment. Arkhip tried to charm the man, but charm was no match for fear as a motivator and, Arkhip suspected, it didn't pay nearly as well either.

He'd spoken to the medical examiner, but the ME politely told Arkhip that his visual perception of the wound had been mistaken. As the report clearly stated, Eldar Velikaya had been shot in the stomach and died from massive hemorrhaging. Arkhip warned that he would have a second autopsy performed, and if the results were to the contrary, he would have the man brought up on charges—a hollow threat. The department would never pay for a second autopsy, and the medical examiner knew it. He told Arkhip to proceed in whatever manner he deemed best. Oh . . . and in case Arkhip was interested, he could find Eldar Velikaya's body, or at least his ashes, at a certain crematorium in east Moscow.

In the midst of all this, Adrian Zima had requested another meeting at the repair shop, during which he told Arkhip his source at the FSB, who had provided information on the return of Charles Jenkins, had gone missing. Zima spoke to the man's wife, who said her husband had called late the prior afternoon to tell her he had an important meeting with the deputy director of counterintelligence, and he hoped the meeting would lead to a promotion. That was the last she had heard from him.

In short, Arkhip was getting screwed more ways now than when Lada had been alive.

He looked at the picture of his wife on his desk. "Sorry," he said.

He leaned back and stared at his notepad. Beside it, his cup of tea had gone cold. He was dog tired. He didn't know how much he'd slept the past few days. He'd napped, more off than on, in one of the interrogation rooms. And he'd eaten, more crap food than healthy, in the cafeteria. If Lada had been alive, she would have warned him about burning the candle at both ends and filling his stomach with junk; how it could shorten his life the way cigarettes could, had he not quit upon her urging.

What did he care? He might even pick up the nasty habit again once he retired. What did he have to lose, after all? Or maybe the better question was, What really did he have to live for once they retired him?

He flipped through the pages of his notes and checked off items on his to-do list until he flipped another page and came to nothing but neat, blue lines. He'd run out of items to check. He envisioned a doctor standing over a patient holding shock paddles and staring at that electronic device—whatever they called it—seeing nothing but thin blue lines.

Call it. This patient is dead.

He blew out a breath while tapping his fingers on the table. Then, resigned, he reached and turned off his computer screen, which they said saved energy and increased the screen life. Whoever took over Arkhip's desk and terminal wouldn't really give a rat's ass, but Arkhip did it anyway because, well . . . because it was the right thing to do. He grabbed his jacket off the back of his chair while giving himself a pep talk. He'd had nights like this over the years, but he'd always gone home to Lada, and she'd always found a way to cheer him. She'd tell him something would break in his case; some witness would be unable to bear the weight of a guilty conscience and would give Arkhip the information he needed to move his case forward. *Just watch,* she'd say. *It'll happen.*

It always did.

He smiled. Even in death that woman could make him smile.

The telephone on his desk rang.

Arkhip picked up the receiver. "Mishkin," he said.

"Have you stopped reading your e-mails now as well? Why are you so opposed to technology, Mishkin?"

"Who is this?"

"Come down to the technology department. I have something I think will interest you."

Stepanov hung up. Arkhip stared at the receiver, then at the picture of Lada on his desk. "Nah," he said. "It's probably nothing."

A man who looks at a glass as half empty will always be half full, Lada said.

Arkhip stepped inside the Technology Center, about to ring the counter bell when Stepanov came out of his office. "Follow me." He looked very much like he had secrets to hide.

"Where?" Arkhip asked.

"Don't be obstinate. Just do as I say, Mishkin."

Arkhip followed Stepanov into one of the computer rooms, whereupon Stepanov locked the door and lowered the blinds. He typed at one of the computer terminals.

"What are you doing, Stepanov?"

"Preserving my retirement, which, unlike you, I am very much looking forward to, and financially planning to afford." Stepanov hacked at the keys, then sat back. "There."

"There what?"

"Don't be thick, Mishkin. Look at the screen. What do you see?"

"I see a man and a woman."

Stepanov closed his eyes and shook his head, clearly frustrated. "You are as thick as butter, Mishkin. How you have solved every one of your cases is beyond me. Who were you searching for *yesterday* when you came into my office?"

"I was searching for—"

Stepanov raised a hand. "Don't say his name." He pushed his chair back from the desk. "I know nothing. You know how to move the video forward and backward and how to zoom in and out, I presume?"

"Yes, of course. But who is the woman?"

"The file, Mishkin. The file." Stepanov motioned to the file on the desk. He sighed and moved toward the door, gripping the door handle.

"Stepanov."

Stepanov did not turn to face him. "Do not thank me, Mishkin. This was no act of heroism or duty. It was an act of self-preservation. I am not worried about you turning me in, but if word somehow got back to the Velikayas that I had somehow discussed . . ." He sighed. "I would not have to worry at all about my retirement. I am hoping this will be sufficient."

With that, Stepanov stepped out, shutting the door behind him.

Arkhip didn't know what to think. Could it have been his Lada who found a way to get Stepanov to redirect his moral compass and do the right thing? Or was it just as Stepanov had said—conscience be damned, this had been another selfish act. Arkhip wouldn't know, but it felt better believing his Lada was somehow involved.

Don't question the motivation for the act, Arkhip, just accept the act as one driven by motivation.

Yes, Lada.

He opened the manila file folder on the desk and found an official-looking photo of Charles Jenkins, along with his vitals and the various crimes he had supposedly committed inside Russia justifying the Kremlin seeking a red notice from the National Crime Agency, and making his apprehension of the highest priority. It was all very interesting, but perhaps not as interesting as the fact that Adrian Zima said his friend who had provided the information on Charles Jenkins's return to Russia was now missing.

It could not be a simple coincidence, but who would want to kill an FSB officer? And why?

Arkhip set aside the photograph and found another, this of a beautiful woman, that gave him pause. The only other woman to cause this type of visceral reaction had been Lada. This woman was well put together. Her auburn hair had been cut and styled and fell to just above her shoulders. Her face practically levitated off the page. Straight white teeth, fine features, and inviting green eyes behind thick lashes. Arkhip looked to her vitals, her most important feature—her height. Five feet seven inches.

Maria Kulikova. Sixty-three years of age.

"Hmm."

He read more about her. His mind churned. Kulikova was director of the Secretariat within the Counterintelligence Directorate. Another coincidence? Unlikely. Arkhip knew enough about Lubyanka and the FSB to know the Counterintelligence Directorate belonged to Dmitry Sokalov, and he knew Sokalov to be one of many elevated to a high place within the government because he grew up with the president in Saint Petersburg.

Arkhip hit "Play." Jenkins and Kulikova walked the streets of Moscow. They looked like they had just stepped from a shower, their clothes wrinkled and wet, Kulikova's hair straight and flat. Jenkins did not appear to be forcibly taking Kulikova anywhere. Arkhip reasoned what that could mean.

Arkhip would double-check to be sure, but he had not seen any bulletin seeking the arrest of either Jenkins or Kulikova. Why not? Could it just be too big an embarrassment for Sokalov and Lubyanka? Was Sokalov seeking to suppress this matter and handle the discipline internally?

This sounded very much like someone, or some persons, working hard to cover their asses. Or maybe Arkhip was just predisposed to think such a thing because it seemed to be a genetic trait found in all political figures. Or maybe it was because Arkhip was in the middle of an investigation in which everyone seemed to be covering their asses.

Jenkins and Kulikova turned the corner. The video coverage ended. Again, an oddity, but in a case filled with oddities, perfectly fitting.

Still, it was something.

And something was better than what Arkhip had before, which had been nothing.

He walked away from the video to the door. He'd do what he'd always done. He'd follow this lead and see where it took him.

31

Varsonof'yevskiy Pereulok
Moscow, Russia

Charles Jenkins leaned against the wall and peeked from behind the window curtain. A white van had parked at the front entrance to the building, and a man got out wearing white coveralls and a black baseball-style cap pulled low on his brow. He was tall—Jenkins estimated several inches over six feet—and dark skinned. The man moved to the back of the van and opened the doors, removing a handcart. He put a large cardboard box on the cart and wheeled it to the front door beneath the pergola.

The buzzer on the intercom rang. At the front door Jenkins pressed the button. "Hello."

"Mogu ya uvidet' Nikolaya?" Is Nicholas in?

"Spasibo," Jenkins responded, and buzzed the man in.

He turned to tell Kulikova to hide in the back room until he was certain the man was legitimate. Kulikova, in the doorframe between the hall and the living room, held a gun, the barrel pointed at Jenkins.

Jenkins froze.

"Just to be sure," she said.

"Where did you get that?"

"I've hidden it here in the apartment for many years. I can't tell you the number of times I wanted to shoot Sokalov with it."

Jenkins let out a held breath. "Hide in the bedroom in back. If you hear me say 'Kremlin,' come out. If I say 'Saint Basil's,' do not."

Kulikova stepped back into the shadows.

Someone rapped three times on the apartment door. Jenkins opened the door an inch, keeping his foot braced behind it.

"Nicholas?" the man said.

"Spasibo." Jenkins looked behind the man to be certain he was alone before opening the door and letting him inside the apartment.

The delivery driver wheeled in the box and set it beside the coffee table in the living room. "There is a man in a black Mercedes parked in the alley across the street," the driver said in heavily accented English. "I blocked the front door to obstruct his view. You may be able to go from the front door of the building to the van."

Jenkins walked to the front window as the man spoke. He stepped to the side and peered down, seeing the grill and hood of the Mercedes. He scanned up and down the block. His gaze fixed on a second, expensive black car, a Range Rover, parked on the same side of the street as the building. Jenkins detected movement inside the car's tinted windshield, and a stream of cigarette smoke spiraled from the tiny opening on the driver's side.

"Kremlin," he said. Kulikova emerged from the back bedroom.

The delivery driver opened the box and removed articles of clothing. "You didn't give us much time. We put together what we could."

He handed Jenkins baggy pants and a sweater. To Kulikova he handed a long skirt and black knit sweater. Ziplock bags contained what looked like grey facial hair and wigs. It was far from the intricate masks and disguises Langley had prepared for them, and the passport photographs would not match their disguises. Jenkins would deal with that later.

Kulikova slipped on her clothing and took the ziplock bag to a mirror in the hall. She tried on several wigs and eventually chose a gray wig that, with the clothing, transformed her into an elderly babushka.

The man pulled out a pair of white coveralls still in its sealed pack and removed the black cap from his head. He handed both to Jenkins. "Extra large. I hope they fit." He then held out the keys to the van and an 8½-by-11-inch manila envelope. Jenkins reviewed what was inside the envelope as the man spoke. Rubles and four train tickets to board the Trans-Siberian Railway. It was clear the man expected Jenkins to switch places with him and wheel Kulikova in the box back down to the van. This was not likely. Not with the man in the Mercedes watching.

"This is where I must leave you," the man said. He turned to Kulikova. "Get to the Yaroslavsky rail terminal. It is less than three kilometers directly down—"

"I know where it is," Kulikova said.

"Ditch the van. Catch the 322 train, which goes all the way to Vladivostok. We have booked you first class, a family of four—in case Lubyanka checks the airports and train stations. After security, go directly to your train. No need to go to the ticket counter. Cut it close so the matrons don't have time to review your passports too closely. Until then, the less you are seen, the better." The man moved toward the front door, leaving the box and the dolly. "There is no other way out of the building except the front door. I will ditch my coveralls in the garbage bin and wait until you are gone. Good luck."

"Hold on," Jenkins said. With the Mercedes already in place, they couldn't get out of the building by walking out the front door to the van, which made the van useless to them, except as a decoy. He handed the man back the keys and the hat and put the white coveralls back in the box.

"Take that chair," he said, pointing. "Put it in the box and wheel the dolly back to the van. Act as if you are transporting heavy cargo."

"How will you—"

"Do it," Jenkins said. "When you get to the ground level, wait five minutes before you go out the door."

The man looked at Jenkins like he was crazy. "All right. Good luck, then," he said. He lifted the chair and set it in the box, then departed with the box on the dolly.

Jenkins went back to the window. "Get the burner phone," he said to Kulikova. "You're going to make a call." He explained what he wanted her to do as he changed into the clothes, and put on the wig and facial hair.

32

Varsonof'yevskiy Pereulok
Moscow, Russia

Zhomov drove down Varsonof'yevskiy Pereulok, a narrow one-lane road with cars parked on each side of the street that made it more narrow. The apartment buildings were pressed tightly together—the only respite from the concrete and stucco being a small strip of green behind a wrought-iron fence. Zhomov spotted an alley just to the north of the park where he could watch the front door of the yellow sandstone building to which Sokalov had directed him.

Once he was parked, however, a white van pulled to the curb, blocking Sokalov's view of the front door. A tall man with dark skin exited the van in white coveralls and a black baseball hat. He removed a handcart and used it to wheel a tall cardboard box toward the front door. Unable to see, Zhomov got out of the vehicle and stepped to the building corner. When the deliveryman entered the building, Zhomov almost rushed the door, but he decided to wait. Fifteen minutes passed before the door opened and the man emerged, though Zhomov could not see his face and confirm it was the same man. He wheeled the cardboard box back to the van.

Zhomov approached. He pulled the gun from the holster hidden beneath his coat and held it behind his back. When he was within six feet he said, *"Proshu proshcheniya." Excuse me.*

The man ignored him. Zhomov could not get a good look at his face. He stepped closer, bringing the gun down by his leg. *"Proshu proshcheniya!"*

The man looked over at him. "Are you talking to me?"

"Remove your hat."

"What for?"

Zhomov raised the gun. "Do it."

The man raised his hands. "I deliver furniture. I don't have anything of value."

Zhomov ripped the hat from the man's head. Not Charles Jenkins. He looked to the box. "What do you have in the box?"

"A chair to be reupholstered."

"Open it."

The man pulled open the box, revealing the chair.

"Freeze!" someone shouted. "Drop your weapon. Drop your weapon."

Zhomov shifted his gaze to a short man in a sport coat and porkpie hat holding him at gunpoint. In the other hand he held a badge and identification. "Do not move again unless I tell you to do so. I am Arkhip Mishkin, chief investigator, Moscow Criminal Investigation Department. Drop your weapon. Now."

Zhomov shifted his gaze back to the delivery driver, then to the windows of the apartment building.

He placed the gun on the ground.

—

Mily Karlov and two of his associates surveyed the apartment buildings on the street to which Ugolov said the CCTV footage had tracked

Jenkins and Kulikova. A gap in the coverage, for reasons Ugolov did not know, prevented him from identifying which apartment building Kulikova and Jenkins had entered. Ugolov assumed they had hidden in a building when he did not find footage of Jenkins or Kulikova emerging at the opposite end of the block or the intersecting alley. That limited where Jenkins and Kulikova could be at present to a dozen apartment buildings and dozens of apartments.

Mily's driver inhaled his cigarette and blew smoke out the window. "What do we do?"

"Be patient. See what develops," Mily said.

A delivery van drove down the street toward them but stopped and parked. Mily watched the driver closely.

"We have company," he said. A good sign they were in the right place.

Minutes after the driver had entered the apartment building wheeling a large box on a dolly, he exited with the same box. Mily reached for the door handle, but a man approached down the sidewalk and, as he passed beneath a streetlamp, Mily saw him remove a handgun from a holster at the small of his back.

Mily's heart skipped a beat. "Zhomov," he said. The man suspected to have pulled the trigger and killed his boss, Alexei Velikaya.

Mily felt his anger build, the chance for retribution strong. He reached for the gun in its holster beneath his left armpit and moved to get out of the car.

The driver reached across the seat and gripped Mily's arm. "No. Police."

Mily looked back to the windshield. A short man in a tweed sport coat and brown porkpie hat approached Zhomov from the side, gun in one hand, a badge and identification of some kind in the other. Zhomov had clearly been caught off guard.

"A setup," the driver said.

"We need to go," Mily said. "Now."

The driver started the engine. Police sirens wailed a split second before blue-and-white Moscow police cars rounded the street corner at the far end of the block, lights flashing.

"Back up." Mily looked over his shoulder just as more police cars emerged at the opposite end of the block and stopped behind their Range Rover. Police exited their cars in combat position, doors open, submachine guns resting on the open window frames.

Mily looked back up the street. Zhomov had placed his weapon on the ground and kicked it away. He knelt, hands on his head, eyes staring up at a window. Police officers moved forward and cuffed Zhomov's hands behind his back, then shoved him face-first onto the ground and went through his pockets.

Police officers shouted at Mily and his men to exit their car with their hands raised over their heads. Mily nodded to the others to comply. As he stepped out, Zhomov, now on his feet, shifted his gaze and their eyes met.

An elderly man and woman emerged from the apartment building's door and scurried down the sidewalk. Mily studied their faces. Jenkins and Kulikova, he presumed, though in disguise.

The elderly man's eyes shifted, for just a beat, but met Mily's gaze.

Mily smiled and gave the man a nod. He would see them both again.

33

Varsonof'yevskiy Pereulok
Moscow, Russia

Police sirens. The man heard them also, and although he looked momentarily hesitant to do as Arkhip had commanded, the sirens—and the sudden appearance of police cars hurtling around the corner from both ends of the block at high rates of speed—seemed to convince him. He carefully placed his gun on the ground, kicked it away, and knelt, hands behind his head.

Arkhip reasoned that this man had either done this before, many times, or he had instructed others to do it.

Uniformed officers exited their cars and took defensive positions. Arkhip held up his badge for all to see, though in the early morning light that was anything but a certainty.

"I am Arkhip Mishkin," he shouted. "Senior investigator with the Ministry of Internal Affairs."

As officers approached and handcuffed the man on the ground, police officers at the other end of the block removed three men from a Range Rover.

A uniformed officer approached Arkhip. "What do you have, Senior Investigator?"

The question surprised Arkhip. He had no idea how or why the other police cars had arrived. "What do you mean? What do you have, Officer?"

"We received an emergency call of armed men in the process of robbing a delivery driver. One man in a black Mercedes and three men in a Range Rover."

"Who made the telephone call?"

"A woman."

"What was her name?" Arkhip asked, thinking it Maria Kulikova.

"She wanted to remain anonymous. Why are you here? And how did you get here so fast?"

Arkhip wasn't sure until the door to the apartment building opened and a tall man with a woman emerged. They looked at the scene, then hurried down the block away from him. They looked older, but Arkhip's memory, well conditioned from his years of practice, was certain the man and woman were the same two people he had watched on the CCTV cameras, now in disguise. He took a step toward Jenkins and Kulikova, then reconsidered. He looked to the man he had in custody. He, too, stared at the couple. Arkhip looked to the three men down the block. Their gaze also fixed on the man and the woman hurrying past them.

The three men in the Range Rover were likely Yekaterina Velikaya's men. The man in the Mercedes was more likely an FSB officer, or had been, given his familiarity with the arrest process. It raised still more pressing questions.

The FSB had sent just one officer for a man and a woman wanted so desperately?

The only logical explanation was, as Arkhip had suspected, to keep this matter quiet. If that were the case, were Arkhip to arrest Jenkins and bring him to Building 38, Petrovka Street, he doubted he would even have the chance to interrogate Jenkins about the fight in the alley that led to Eldar Velikaya's death, and that was Arkhip's only real concern.

The FSB would snatch Jenkins, and Kulikova for that matter, before Arkhip ever had the chance to open his mouth. As for the presence of Velikaya's three men in the Range Rover, it proved, once again, that there were more holes at Building 38, Petrovka Street, than a slice of Swiss cheese.

Arkhip would get no answers from the three men or the man he had arrested. They were sophisticated enough to know they didn't have to answer his questions. The FSB would bail out the Mercedes driver, and Velikaya money would bail out the other three.

And Arkhip's investigation would be screwed yet again, and he had already been sufficiently screwed this day, thank you very much. He might not get another chance at Jenkins, not if the FSB got a hold of him first.

What he needed was what Charles Jenkins and Maria Kulikova needed, why they had likely perpetrated this scenario. Arkhip needed time.

"Chief Investigator?"

Arkhip removed a business card from his coat pocket and handed it to the officer. He then removed his hat and his sport jacket, and he also handed them over. "Do me a favor," he said. "Place my hat and jacket on my desk at Building 38, Petrovka." He provided the man detailed instructions. "You can do this for me, yes?"

"I will take care of it, but—"

"Take the four men to Petrovka. Book them on suspicion of armed robbery and illegal possession of weapons. Keep this one separate from the other three."

"What are you going to do?" the officer asked.

"I am a chief investigator," Arkhip said. "I am going to do my job."

34

Yaroslavsky Rail Terminal
Moscow, Russia

Jenkins and Kulikova kept to side streets and, when possible, alleys. They moved as quickly as they could without looking suspicious. Jenkins checked his watch. They had forty-five minutes to get to the train station and through security. Jenkins had been told that while the Yaroslavsky rail terminal had CCTV cameras, the Trans-Siberian trains did not. Just the same, once on board, he and Kulikova would need to stay within their cabin and mostly out of sight. The ticket purchased for them was for a family of four traveling to Vladivostok, the end of the line. Seven days. Jenkins didn't expect to ever see the end of the line, however. He expected Lemore would somehow get word to him to get off at a designated location, where alternative travel arrangements were being made for them. How Jenkins was going to retrieve those messages with a water-damaged phone, he had no idea, but he'd solve one problem at a time.

"How much farther?" Jenkins asked, grateful at least that Moscow had awakened, and they could better blend with the crowd emerging on the sidewalks. Buses and cars spewed diesel fumes.

"Not far," Kulikova said.

"We'll split up when we get there," Jenkins said. "But stay within eyesight and meet on board the train. This is what I would suggest when we get to—"

"Mr. Jenkins," Kulikova interrupted. "I have spent my life hidden, real or imagined. Yaroslavsky is Moscow's busiest railway station, with many shops in which we can hide until our train departs. Do not worry about me. Worry about yourself. A man of your skin color and height is rare in Moscow. I'm surprised you have survived this long. You must be very good at what you do."

And lucky, Jenkins thought. "I assume the man in the Mercedes was Zhomov?"

"Yes," she said. "And I am assuming the three men in the Range Rover were Yekaterina Velikaya's men. All four will be detained, but not for long. Hopefully long enough for us to get on the train."

"How are Velikaya's men getting their information?" Jenkins asked.

"Ordinarily, I would say from FSB officers. Yekaterina pays many, and the pay is more than what they earn as federal employees. But if Sokalov is keeping my betrayal and your return quiet, then Velikaya's information must be coming from the Moscow police, who have access to the Information Technologies Center."

"That's the agency that runs the CCTV cameras?"

"And stores the information collected."

"Did you recognize the plainclothes officer who approached Zhomov?"

"I did not get a good look at him. I assume he is Moscow police, likely an investigator."

"Why would an investigator respond to an emergency call of an armed robbery?" Jenkins asked.

"This I do not know."

They came within sight of Komsomolskaya Square, a bustle of activity with four different train stations and trains departing to dozens of destinations and people walking in all directions. Jenkins and

Paulina Ponomayova had caught a train to Saint Petersburg from the Leningradsky station across the square. Jenkins scanned the sidewalks behind them but did not see anyone who appeared to be following them. Then again, he didn't have a lot of time to watch. A stream of passengers entered and exited the Yaroslavsky rail terminal, enough people, he hoped, for the two of them to become lost. The terminal looked like a cathedral of white stone, with thick columns, narrow windows, and a tall steeple.

Jenkins walked to a drain basin in the street curb and bent down as if to tie his shoe. He removed the gun Kulikova had given him from his coat and dropped the magazine down the drain, then dropped the gun. He would have preferred to have kept it, but that option was not possible with metal detectors scanning every person and every piece of luggage entering the railway terminal.

He followed Kulikova to the front door, both keeping their heads down. Inside the terminal, Jenkins veered to the right, to a line moving toward a metal detector. Kulikova veered to her left. Voices of commuters echoed and blended with the computerized voice broadcasting from loudspeakers to announce arriving and departing trains. Jenkins focused on the people around them, the men and women falling into line behind them, and the police officers watching from the other side of the metal detectors. No one seemed particularly interested in him or in Kulikova, and, unlike his excursion with Ponomayova, the police were not considering their phones or comparing a picture to the faces of the passengers stepping through the scanners. Because neither he nor Kulikova had luggage to scan, they stepped to the front of the line and went through the machines, meeting on the other side, though without acknowledging one another.

Jenkins moved quickly toward the interior shops, scanning the various sundries until he found what he sought. He purchased two hats, one a baseball-style cap with a logo, the other a blue beret. He also picked up two extra-large sweatshirts with hoods, one a bright red, the other gray, and a navy-blue scarf. He purchased a backpack, paid with rubles, and shoved everything in a large plastic bag.

Inside a restroom stall he removed the gray wig and mustache and pulled on the red sweatshirt. He pressed the baseball cap so the brim fit low on his head and the bill obscured much of his face. He raised the hood over the hat, slipped the wig and mustache into the backpack, and, before he exited the restroom, remembered the training he had received at the Langley disguise division about creating a counterfeit person. A disguise was not just about masks and makeup but about creating illusions in the way one walked, stood, or gestured, and taking on a character's role.

Jenkins exited into the terminal with the quick and confident gait of a much younger man late for a trip. He dashed toward the swinging glass doors leading to the outdoor platform, but he did not immediately exit. He moved to the side as people came and went, and pulled out his ticket as if to consider the platform, but kept his gaze outside the glass doors. He searched for anyone watching the doors as well as for the CCTV cameras. He found one camera with four lenses high up a light stanchion, no doubt providing platform coverage. In the center of the outdoor platform was another kiosk with multiple stores that looked to carry similar merchandise as the interior shops. He searched the stanchions on the other side of that kiosk for another camera but didn't immediately see one. That didn't mean there wasn't one.

Jenkins checked his watch. Thirteen minutes until their train departed.

He stepped outdoors and moved quickly to the far side of the kiosk. In his peripheral vision he spotted Kulikova. She had ditched the black sweater for a colorful scarf, and somehow had managed to lift her long skirt above her knees. She had also changed from walking shoes to heels and she had removed the wig. She had put her hair up beneath a fashionable hat that looked like something a 1950s newsboy would wear selling newspapers on the street corner. The most intricate part of her disguise, however, was not her clothing but her company. She strolled alongside a man and two young children, keeping her head turned away from the light stanchion as she crossed the platform. Jenkins looked for the man's spouse but didn't see one. The young-looking Kulikova completed the family picture—a mother possibly, but more likely a grandmother.

35

Varsonof'yevskiy Pereulok
Moscow, Russia

Arkhip hurried but did not rush. He did not want to look as though he was in pursuit. As he passed the Range Rover, he studied the faces of the three handcuffed men and committed them to memory. One of the men, the oldest looking of the three, wore a tailored suit and dress shoes that would likely cost Arkhip his annual salary. As Arkhip passed, the man looked up at him, gave him the tiniest thin-lipped smile, and tipped his head, as if to say they would meet again.

Arkhip did not return the gesture.

He turned the corner in the direction Jenkins and Kulikova had walked, blending in with the emerging crowd on the sidewalks and congregated in the cafés and at coffeehouse tables. The crowds were not as dense as on weekday mornings, but sufficient for Arkhip, at five foot six, to not stand out.

He spotted Jenkins and Kulikova in the far distance just before they turned another corner. Arkhip needed to close in but not get too close. He contemplated what would be Jenkins's and Kulikova's first priority. Getting out of the country, definitely, but how best to do it? Transportation? Certainly. What method?

He considered his location. Were Jenkins and Kulikova walking to a designated rendezvous site where a car would pick them up? Perhaps, though that would be potentially risky for all involved, especially the person providing aid, given the depth to which Jenkins and Kulikova were wanted.

Arkhip felt his cell phone buzz and removed it from his pants pocket. He noted the number for the Moscow police department.

He answered the call. "This is Chief Investigator Arkhip Mishkin."

"Chief Investigator, this is Officer Orlov. We spoke at the crime scene."

"Yes, Officer. What do you have for me?"

"Well, nothing, I'm afraid."

"Nothing?"

"The man's name is Zhomov. Alexander Zhomov. But when I ran his name through the customary databases on my car's computer, I came up with nothing. His file has been sealed."

So it wasn't nothing. It was very much something. "On whose authority was his file sealed?" Arkhip asked, though he suspected he knew the answer.

"Lubyanka. My inquiry produced a telephone number for us to immediately call."

"Have you made that call?"

"I thought it best to call you, as instructed."

"I will make the call, Officer Orlov. If a head is to roll, I would prefer it be mine. I'm close to retirement, anyway."

"Thank you, Chief Investigator." He could hear the relief in the officer's voice.

"Take Mr. Zhomov to Petrovka and detain him as I advised until you hear back from me. Do not let him make any telephone calls until then."

Arkhip disconnected, slipped his phone back in the pocket of his slacks, and smiled. What were they going to do to him if he didn't call? Fire him?

He drew closer to Jenkins and Kulikova but continued to maintain a comfortable distance. Cars and buses filled the streets with the smell of diesel and the sounds of the awakening city. They neared Komsomolskaya Square. The trains. Of course. Moscow had more than nine terminals with a multitude of different platforms at each. If Jenkins and Kulikova could avoid CCTV detection and get on one of the trains, they could get a long way from Moscow, and there were far fewer, if any, cameras. Arkhip paused when the two stopped. Jenkins bent down. From his angle, Arkhip could not tell why. Just as quickly Jenkins rose, and he and Kulikova entered Yaroslavsky rail terminal. Here, Arkhip could not delay. If he lost them inside the station, he would not know the train they boarded, and he doubted Stepanov would again be so charitable, or that cameras would be available in the smaller towns where Jenkins and Kulikova might be headed.

He used his identification to move past the line and enter the railway terminal. He didn't immediately see either Jenkins or Kulikova, then spotted the old man he presumed to be Jenkins passing through one of the metal detectors. He spotted Kulikova at a different machine, still in disguise. They had split up. A smart move. He decided to follow Jenkins, since he was Arkhip's person of interest. He again flashed his badge and stepped past the metal detectors. Jenkins had entered a store within the terminal. Arkhip sat on a bench near lockers and waited for him to emerge. Jenkins remained in the store for about five minutes. He exited carrying a large plastic bag and went into the restroom on the other side of the terminal.

Arkhip watched the door. Men came and went, but he did not see Jenkins, the old man, emerge. What would be the purpose of the bathroom—the usual, of course, but then why go into the store and what would he buy? Other disguises?

He looked about the terminal and noted a man at the doors leading to the platform studying his ticket. He wore a red sweatshirt with the hood pulled over a baseball cap, obscuring much of his face, and a backpack. It was not just the hood and the hat that concealed Jenkins; if this was Jenkins, he had seemingly transformed his whole persona—the way he stood and, when he pushed open the door and moved to the platform, the way he walked: quicker, shoulders slumped, head down. He appeared much younger, a man rushing to catch his train.

Arkhip followed. The man crossed to a kiosk in the middle of the platform and moved to the far side. Arkhip looked back and gazed up at the CCTV cameras on the light stanchion. The man sought refuge from the cameras. On the other side of the kiosk, he seemed to be looking to the terminal doors, as if searching for someone. Arkhip could not get a clear look at his face.

Minutes later the man stood in line to board a train car while the *provodnitsas*, female attendants in red berets and dark-blue uniforms, checked tickets and passports. This time Arkhip got a look at his face. Jenkins.

Arkhip went to the ticket counter and flashed his badge. "Where does the train on platform eighteen go?"

"The end of the line is Vladivostok."

"I will need a private cabin," Arkhip said. He'd never ridden on the Trans-Siberian Railway, though he had read about it. Like most Muscovites, it was one of those bucket-list items he and Lada never got around to accomplishing. He'd do so now, using his expense budget. While he still had one.

No sense wasting his retirement funds. Not just yet.

36

Lubyanka
Moscow, Russia

Dmitry Sokalov stood at the windows of his office staring across Moscow to the Kremlin and ignoring the ringing of his cell phone. He sipped heavily on a glass of vodka and turned to the sound of his office door opening. Zhomov stepped in. He had spent most of the morning at the Moscow police station. The arresting officer had apparently refused to allow him to make a phone call or to even enter his name into the computer. Had he done so, a prompt would have informed the officer to release Zhomov without any questions. Zhomov had apparently said enough buzzwords to finally reach a captain in the Criminal Investigation Department and get him to run a background check. When he did, Zhomov was released immediately. "We are going to have a problem," Zhomov said.

"Just one?" Sokalov asked.

"The three men arrested work for Yekaterina Velikaya," Zhomov said. "What is their interest in this?"

"That is what I have been trying to figure out these last several hours."

"It looks like you've been drinking," Zhomov said.

"Yes, a fair amount of that also."

"So . . . What have you learned?"

Sokalov told Zhomov how Charles Jenkins's fingerprint came up on a beer bottle in the Yakimanka Bar where Eldar Velikaya was killed, and he didn't think it could be a coincidence.

"It appears Yekaterina used her influence to have the CCTV tape outside the bar expunged, and the prostitute and the bodyguard have been killed."

"The bartender?"

"Is no longer talking."

"Who is the investigator who arrested me?"

"Arkhip Mishkin," Sokalov said. He opened a folder on his desk and tossed an eight-by-ten photograph across the table at Zhomov.

Zhomov nodded. "How did he know Jenkins was at the apartment?"

"I don't know. I can only assume someone advised him when Jenkins was spotted on the CCTV cameras."

"You have a leak."

"I will deal with that after you find Jenkins and Kulikova."

Zhomov smiled. "So Jenkins has the Moscow police and the Velikayas after him, as well as the FSB. One could end our problem for us."

"No. They will make it worse. If the Moscow police arrest them, word of Kulikova being a spy will spread too fast for us to stop it. And Yekaterina Velikaya's interest is directly contrary to mine. She holds a grudge from the killing of her father, and Kulikova possesses the kind of information to destroy me. Yekaterina will kill Jenkins for his role in her son's death, and we . . . I will lose the opportunity to use Jenkins as I must. I need Kulikova dead and Jenkins alive. I need you to find them first."

If Zhomov could pull off both, Sokalov's position as chairman and his seat at the Kremlin table awaited him. It would arm Sokalov in his battle with his father-in-law, should the general ever learn of the affair with Kulikova. With Sokalov as chairman of the National Antiterrorist

Committee, his father-in-law would tell his daughter to forgive and forget—for the sake of their children, but really for the general's sake. Having someone so high up in the government would allow him to gain favors not currently within his reach, and while General Roman Portnov loved his daughter, he also loved the luxuries his title could accord him.

"Do we know where Jenkins and Kulikova have gone?" Zhomov asked.

"The Information Technologies Center says they are working on it. We have to assume what they learn will be passed on to the Velikayas also, maybe before it is passed on to us."

"What do you want me to do, then?"

"Stand by," Sokalov said. "I also have men watching the Velikayas. They may have some value yet. They will go after Jenkins. When they do, I will notify you."

37

Yaroslavsky Rail Terminal
Moscow, Russia

The train to Vladivostok wasn't one of the sleek, white bullet trains that sped between Moscow and Saint Petersburg, among other places. These cars were significantly older, with years under their belt, and slower. This train wasn't about getting from one place to the next as quickly as possible; it was about the experience, about the journey. The cars were painted bright colors—dark blue, bright red, a vibrant yellow, and a pea-soup green. Jenkins hoped the train choice would throw off those searching for him and Kulikova, that they would focus on quicker means of getting out of Russia and not think two people in a hurry would travel for days on a train.

Jenkins walked behind the kiosk and removed his sweatshirt and ball cap, shoving them into the backpack and exchanging them for the blue beret and scarf. He looked across the platform. Kulikova did not change her clothes or her appearance. Her disguise was more elaborate, and its success was premised on the man and his two small children welcoming her presence, looking like a family about to take a trip on the historic railway. Kulikova approached one of two provodnitsas, who checked passenger tickets before boarding. The provodnitsa did not ask to see a passport, a good sign.

Jenkins walked to the other end of the car and mingled with another group of passengers, keeping his face turned away from the CCTV cameras and slouching as much as he could. A male attendant, a *provodnik*, was not as easygoing as the two women, asking passengers for their passports and slowing Jenkins's progress. Jenkins reached into his bag and retrieved a passport prepared at Langley. In his photograph, he was a Black man from Germany with facial hair.

The provodnik took Jenkins's passport and ticket, considered both from behind round glasses, then held the photograph up to better compare it with Jenkins.

"*Vy pobrilis'.*" *You shaved.*

Jenkins squinted as if he didn't understand Russian.

"I said, 'You shaved.'" The provodnik spoke in heavily accented English and rubbed a hand over her chin.

"My wife did not like the beard. For her, I shaved," Jenkins said in broken English but with a German accent.

"Where is the rest of your party?" The provodnik looked past Jenkins, presumably for his fictitious wife and their two children—or grandchildren.

"There." Jenkins pointed down the platform to where Kulikova stepped onto the train after two small children. "I stopped to pick up souvenirs."

The man considered Jenkins's outfit and handed Jenkins back his passport and ticket. "Enjoy your trip. If there is anything I or my partner can do to make your trip more enjoyable, do not hesitate to ask."

"*Danka* . . . I mean, *spasibo.*"

"*Pozhaluysta,*" the provodnik said.

On board the train, a matron took Jenkins's ticket and pointed out the toilet and washbasin in a room at the back of the carriage, then led Jenkins down the narrow corridor, exterior windows on his left and carriage-room doors on his right. They passed four cabins and stopped at a door in the center of the carriage. The matron advised that inside his cabin he could lock the door, but only the matron, or a provodnik or provodnitsa, could lock and unlock the door from the outside. He thanked the matron, handed her ten rubles, and ducked inside the cabin. He tossed the bag containing his backpack on a luggage rack above two berths and turned sideways to step between them to the curtained window. He searched for anyone on the platform who looked familiar.

Moments later, the cabin door opened. Kulikova turned her back to Jenkins. She laughed as she finished a conversation with a man, presumably the father of the two children with whom she boarded the train. She shut and locked the door. Kulikova's façade disappeared. She looked drained, pale. She sat on one of the berths, which were not much wider than a bench seat, and looked up at Jenkins with tired eyes. Neither of them had slept in more than twenty-four hours.

"Everything all right?" he asked.

Kulikova nodded. Then she said, "I have been invited to have a drink before dinner."

"That was smart, to appear to be together."

She shrugged. "Seducing men comes naturally to me, Mr. Jenkins. Do you know how many men in my lifetime have offered to buy me a drink? Nor do I. But I do know how many I accepted because I wanted to get to know the man better. Not one." She sighed and quickly moved on. "Do you think we were spotted?"

"I don't know," he said. "I'm sure you know more about the capabilities of the CCTV cameras than I do. We hear everything, from the system being filled with glitches to being so accurate it can identify a suspect even if he's wearing a mask."

"The cameras are very good. They measure the distance between the eyes, the nose, and mouth, and record the shape of the chin, among other things. The government would like us to believe the cameras can detect a person even if that person's face is partially hidden, but that technology does not yet exist, at least not in the cameras of which I am aware. Once the calculations are made, the camera uses algorithms to compare that face with the calculations for the millions of faces stored in police and other government agency databases."

"I guess we'll know soon enough how good they are," Jenkins said. "When's the last time you slept?"

Kulikova shrugged. "I haven't slept a full night in years."

"Why don't you lie down. Are you hungry?"

"No." She shook her head.

"I think it best we stay out of sight, until we know the lay of the land."

"Lay of which land?"

"It's an expression. It means, 'Until we know more.' I'll buy drinks and snacks when the trolley service comes by." Jenkins held up his phone. He pressed the button on the side, hoping it had time to dry out. The device powered up, but he could tell it was glitchy. "At least it works."

"Yes, but the Wi-Fi and the Internet do not." She was right. He had no service. "So at present, we are on our own."

Jenkins opened an interior door to the adjacent cabin.

"Are you married, Mr. Jenkins?" Kulikova asked.

He turned back. "Charlie, please. And yes, I'm married."

"Children?"

"Two. A twelve-year-old boy and a daughter almost two years old."

Kulikova squinted as if not understanding him. It was a look he got often. "So young."

"I got married late in life. My wife is twenty-four years younger."

"Do you love her?" Kulikova asked in a quiet voice.

"I do," he said. "More than anything in this world."

Her smile looked rueful. "I have never known love." She sounded as fatalistic as Paulina Ponomayova had sounded the night they spent at the beach house on the Black Sea coast, the way Zenaida Petrekova had sounded the night Jenkins exfiltrated her, which was only a day but felt like a week ago.

"I know this has been a very hard life for you."

She smiled again, wistful. "You have no idea," she said.

"I'm sure I don't. You were married."

She nodded. "Helge. For appearances. Not for love. My parents told me it was better that way—if I did not love him. They were right, I suppose, but Helge deserved better. He sensed I had a lover. There were too many late nights. Too many trips away. It hurt his masculinity deeply, I'm sure. He did not deserve to die." She wiped at tears.

"Life will be better in the United States," Jenkins said, trying to raise her spirits. "The relocation center will provide you with a new identity, and you will have the chance to start again. Maybe you will know love yet."

"It sounds wonderful, but excuse me when I say that I don't believe you. The Kremlin's reach for spies is like an octopus. Many arms of much length. I could not put someone in such danger. Especially not someone I truly loved."

"Get some sleep," he said. "We still have a long road ahead of us."

He did know what Kulikova was going through—not the details of her life, but the guilt and the shame, certainly. As Kulikova lay down atop the blue blanket, Jenkins thought of the many years he had lived as a hermit on Camano Island, unable to forgive himself for what he had been a part of in Mexico City, the people who had died because of his work as a young CIA officer. He had been unable to comprehend that he would ever be forgiven. Then Alex had unexpectedly stepped into his life, and she had rotated it 180 degrees toward the better. She'd helped Jenkins to forgive himself and to love again.

Jenkins hoped someone would do the same for Kulikova.

38

Arkhip found his way to his carriage. Two berths. It made him think of Lada. He placed the bag containing the two shirts he'd just purchased before boarding on the bed, sat at the window, and watched the remaining passengers board with suitcases and backpacks. Some were older, like him, perhaps checking off an item on their own bucket lists. Some were young, with large backpacks, off on an adventure before life sucked them in too deeply. None were alone. They all had someone to share the experience with.

His telephone rang. His captain.

Arkhip answered. "Senior Investigator Mishkin."

"What exactly are you doing?" his captain asked.

"I am not understanding you," Mishkin said. "You will need to be more specific."

"Do you have any idea who the man was that you arrested?"

"None," Arkhip said, lying.

"He is a former KGB and FSB officer who now works special projects for the Kremlin."

"And what exactly is a special project? Painting?"

"Don't be insolent, Mishkin. I just got off the phone with Lubyanka and was told that you had interfered with an FSB operation to capture a man of the highest order."

"How could I have known such a thing? With whom did you speak?"

"The deputy director of counterintelligence. He advised me that you are to close your file and not to interfere in this operation again."

"Which operation?"

The captain groaned. "The operation to bring in an American spy, Charles Jenkins."

"I have no interest in Charles Jenkins the American spy. However, Charles Jenkins is the only man who can tell me what happened the night Eldar Velikaya died. I cannot close my file until I speak to him."

His captain's voice rose and Arkhip could hear the frustration with each word. "Eldar Velikaya was shot by Charles Jenkins, Mishkin. We have the medical examiner's report."

"The medical examiner's report is a fabrication. I saw the body. Velikaya was shot in the back, not the front. Therefore, the shooter could not have been Charles Jenkins."

"That is no longer your problem, Mishkin. It is a Lubyanka problem."

"How am I to close my file?"

"Consider it closed. Do not interfere again, Mishkin. Let Lubyanka handle this matter and retire in peace, or I will consider terminating you. You don't want that now."

No, he did not. But he also could not retire, not if he wished to retire in peace. Not without speaking to Charles Jenkins. "What of the other three men who were arrested?" Arkhip asked.

"A case of mistaken identity. They were waiting for a friend in one of the apartments."

"With weapons?"

"I know nothing of any weapons, Mishkin."

"Where are they at present?"

"How should I know? I told you they were released."

How very convenient, Arkhip thought.

The brakes of the train hissed. Arkhip felt a jolt as the train moved backward, then rolled forward. "Where are you now?" his captain asked.

"At home, of course."

"What is that noise in the background?"

"The kettle. I am making a cup of tea."

"Listen, Mishkin, you don't have long and then you will be retired. You have earned it. Relax. Take it easy until that day arrives."

Take it easy, Arkhip thought. *And do what, exactly?* "Thank you. I think I will take the next few days off. I believe I have accrued enough vacation days to do so. Yes?"

"Good. See. Already you are learning how to relax. Don't think about work. Think about all the things you are going to do once you are retired. Maybe take a long-awaited trip."

Arkhip looked out the window as the train pulled from the station. "Maybe sooner than we both know," he said. He disconnected the call and removed the fur hat he had also purchased in the kiosk, then put it back on his head and considered his reflection in the mirror mounted on the inside of the cabin door. The hat added another two to three inches in height. He could hear Lada now, a chuckle in her voice. *A man who wears a hat to look taller is hiding a certain failing in another area.*

Arkhip quickly removed the hat.

39

Trans-Siberian Train

Maria Kulikova awoke with a start. She quickly sat up, confused by her surroundings. Her heart raced, and she had soaked her shirt with sweat. She looked to the clock on the nightstand, but the nightstand wasn't there.

She was not home in her bed.

The gentle rocking of the carriage and uneven sound of the train rolling on the tracks pulled her back to the present. She took deep breaths and looked to the window. It was dark outside. Night.

She looked at her door. Jenkins had applied the deadbolt. Through the interior door to the adjacent cabin, she saw that Charles Jenkins slept on his side on one of the two berths, his face turned toward the wall. He looked like Svyatogor, the giant warrior in Russian mythology and folklore, trying to sleep in a child's bed. Heavy, rhythmic breathing. She envied him; it was a rare night Maria slept so soundly, or until morning. The good nights, she slept in spurts, awakened by her thoughts, but most nights she was able to keep those thoughts from spinning out of control. Reading sometimes helped, as did exercise.

The bad nights, such as this, she awoke in a panic, her shirt drenched in sweat, her heart racing, unable to slow or rationalize her thoughts that she had been discovered, that men were coming for her.

She slept with her pen beside her and, on more than one occasion, she had contemplated biting down on the capsule concealed in the end.

She had lost her pen in the Neglinnaya River. She felt naked without it.

She looked at the small confines of her room and concluded that exercise would be cumbersome and likely wake Jenkins. Chamomile tea helped, and the samovar was just a few doors down in a cubby at the front of the carriage car. She looked again at Jenkins and thought about what he had said, about a better life awaiting her in America. She wanted to believe him. She wanted to believe that maybe, once forever free of the person she had allowed herself to become, she would find her true self again. She felt the onset of tears but pushed them back. Maria Kulikova, she told herself, was a good and decent person, and she would find her again.

If she made it out of Russia alive.

She thought of her earlier conversation with Jenkins and the way his face had lit up when he spoke of his wife and his family. She had been surprised to learn he was not only married but had two young children. It made her realize that he, too, had sacrificed, maybe not for as long as she had sacrificed, as each of the seven sisters had sacrificed, but perhaps just as deeply, maybe more so. Maria never had anything to lose, except her sense of self. When the time came to end her life, she would be comforted by the thought that no one would miss her. Her parents were gone. She had no siblings. No children. Helge would have missed only the luxuries she provided, the apartment and the clothes. He would not have missed her.

Her lack of family made her realize that Jenkins, despite having a wife and two small children he clearly adored, was here, in a country that had placed him on a kill list, to rescue a woman he did not know. So perhaps his risk was greater, as was his need to succeed and get back home. He had people to live for. She concluded that he must be a man of very high moral character and ethics. It was one thing to do your job.

It was another to risk your life for the life of another, especially with so much to lose.

Maria slid on the pair of cheap slippers beside her berth, unlocked the cabin door, and stepped out into the hall. The train chugged along the tracks, the carriage shaking gently, but the ride relatively stable. A man holding a cup to the samovar had his back to her but turned as she approached.

"It is good to see I am not the only one who cannot sleep," the man said. He looked about her age. Midsixties. Short, with thinning hair and round glasses on a face her mother would have called genteel. His soft blue eyes invited conversation.

Maria smiled but did not respond.

"Can I buy you a drink?" he asked.

Maria closed her eyes, then shook her head. "I don't drink," she said. "Not with strangers."

"I'm sorry," he said, sounding remorseful. "It was meant as a joke. A poor joke. I meant, Can I get you a cup of coffee or perhaps tea?"

She studied him, his face. He sounded sincere. "Tea, please. Chamomile."

"A good choice," he said. "Soothing. Sometimes if I have a cup, I can get back to sleep. Sometimes not." The man grabbed a cup and filled it with hot water.

"You also have trouble sleeping," Maria said. "What is it that keeps you awake?"

"Many things. Common troubles." He handed her the cup of hot water and stepped to the side so she could choose a tea. "Mint soothes the stomach," he said.

She stepped forward, considered her choices, and chose peppermint.

"My name is Arkhip." He extended a hand. "So we do not have to be strangers."

"Maria," she said, still not certain about him.

"The dining car is closed, but I believe the sitting car is open." Arkhip gestured behind him. "So you don't have to drink alone in your room. A nasty habit if one can avoid it. I know this myself." He smiled but it waned. "Another poor attempt at humor."

Maria laughed.

"A laugh. Maybe not so poor an attempt."

"Sure," she said.

He looked confused.

"The sitting car." She figured there was little trouble she could get in while on the train, and she did not wish to sit in her room and ruminate on all the things that could go wrong. "Lead the way."

Arkhip slid open a door between the carriages, and they stepped into a brightly decorated sitting room with upholstered seats, intricate woodwork, and stained-glass windows. "It doesn't lack for color, does it?" he said.

"No," Maria said. "It certainly does not."

Arkhip turned a chair and waited for Maria to sit, then turned a second chair to face her. "I hope you did not think of me as too forward," he said.

"No. I just misunderstood you."

Arkhip sipped his coffee. "Where are you heading, Maria? All the way to the end? Vladivostok?"

"One doesn't know," she said, deliberately vague. "And you?" She lied easily and without remorse, and she was a quick judge of character. She could quickly assess what someone wanted, especially men. She did not get the sense Arkhip wanted anything but a little companionship. If he were FSB, unlikely, or a Velikaya, even more unlikely, she got no such sense.

"To the end, of course," he said. "My first time riding the Trans-Siberian. I may not get to do it again. I am no spring chicken."

"How old are you, Arkhip?"

"Sixty-four. I will retire shortly."

"What is it that you do?"

"I work security for an industrial firm in Moscow. And you?"

"I am a secretary."

He pointed to her finger. "I see that you are married."

She, too, pointed. "And you as well."

"No," he said, spinning the ring on his finger. "Not anymore. I am widowed."

"I'm sorry. Was it recent?"

He seemed to give her question some thought. "To me, yes. Two years."

"You must have loved your wife very much."

"More than breathing," he said. Then he smiled and sipped his tea.

"That's nice," she said. "A nice sentiment to love someone so much."

"Yes, though it makes it all the more painful to lose them, I suppose."

"You still wear your ring?"

"Yes." He cleared his throat. "Your husband has no trouble sleeping then?"

He had changed the painful subject. "No, he does not. He snores like a bull." She kept guarded about her personal life, but they spoke on a variety of subjects: Russian politics, travel, hobbies, the world. Maria relaxed. She found herself enjoying the conversation, though she remained on guard. Arkhip sounded very much like his work had become his life, especially since his wife's death from breast cancer. He expressed several times that he had been a fool to put off until tomorrow what they could have done today.

They spoke until Maria's remaining tea had turned cold. "I should be getting back—in case my husband wakes and wonders where I am."

Arkhip rose and gave a slight bow. "Thank you for indulging me and my poor humor."

Maria smiled. "Thank you for not taking offense at my response."

"None taken. I'm sure you are asked quite a bit."

"By men far less kind than you," she said. She started back to her carriage.

"I would enjoy the chance to meet your husband, Maria," Arkhip said.

She didn't answer. She just smiled.

—

A click awoke him. The door to the adjacent cabin opened. Jenkins startled, sat up quickly, and hit his head on the luggage rack over the bed. He fell back. Stars flittered in and out of his vision and he tried to shake them away. Maria Kulikova entered the compartment. He exhaled a held breath, wincing in pain.

"Where did you go?" he asked.

"Tea," she said, holding the paper cup. "I could not sleep."

"Did you see anyone?"

"Just a lonely widower unable to sleep."

Jenkins let out another held breath and rubbed the top of his head. Under the circumstances he figured this was as good a time as any to leave the cabin.

"Are you hurt?" she asked.

"Only my pride." He pulled a timetable from the unused bed and studied it. "We will arrive in Perm tomorrow and then Yekaterinburg. I will get off at each stop in case someone is trying to pass us a message, and to try to get an Internet connection on the platform. Hopefully, I'll get more information and we'll both know what to expect going forward. I don't like traveling blind like this."

"At least, Charlie, we are traveling. It could be much worse."

40

Velikaya Estate
Novorizhskoye, Moscow

Two days after they lost Jenkins and Kulikova, Mily stepped into Yekaterina's darkened study. He smelled cigarette smoke. A cigarette burned in an ashtray alongside several spent butts, the smoke spiraling languidly toward the ceiling. Yekaterina sat behind her desk, spotlit in one incandescent circle of light as she spoke on a cell phone, one of many burner phones she used and frequently discarded. The shades had been pulled across the two arched windows, the air inside the room so still Mily could hear the static in his ears.

Yekaterina picked up the cigarette and inhaled deeply, like giving a hug to an old friend after a long absence. She had stopped smoking when information on the correlation between smoking and cancer could no longer be refuted. She'd simply removed the cigarettes from the house, forbade anyone from smoking in her presence, brought in cleaners who sprayed various aromas to remove or mask the smell, and quit cold turkey. Because he spent so much of his time in her presence, Mily, too, had to quit, though not as easily. He still occasionally smoked at home.

She picked up the cigarette and inhaled as she turned her head to the sound of the door handle clicking shut behind him. Yekaterina looked to Mily as if she had aged ten years over the past three days. Her hair seemed to have more gray, and the lines in her skin—what his mother had called "worry lines"—appeared to have been etched deeper, like paper cuts. In this instance he disagreed with his mother's characterization. These were not worry lines. Yekaterina mourned. Mily suspected there was nothing less natural than a child passing before a parent and nothing as painful.

Yekaterina disconnected her call and set the cell phone gently on the desk. Mily noticed the rise and fall of her chest, as if it pained her to take each breath, to go on living. Eldar had been an ass, spoiled, self-centered, and intoxicated by power and money, neither of which he had created or earned. But Mily knew Eldar had not always been that way, nor were those a mother's memories now. Yekaterina remembered the baby boy to whom she had given birth, the still-innocent child she had cared for and loved, the young man who had showed so much promise before the drugs and the booze unleashed a genie she hardly recognized—cruel, angry, bitter, and vengeful.

"You have news?" she asked softly and without emotion.

"Ugolov has located Jenkins and Kulikova," he said, referring to the director of the Moscow Department of Information Technologies.

"Where?"

"The Yaroslavsky rail terminal in Moscow. They boarded a Trans-Siberian train, 322, two days ago."

"They could be anywhere."

"No," he said. "Ugolov and his technician worked around the clock reviewing video of the platforms and tracks between Moscow and Novosibirsk at the time the 322 was designated to arrive. They have not departed the train."

"Where is the train now?"

"It will be arriving in Krasnoyarsk at 8:24 this evening and departing at two minutes after nine. The flight there is more than four hours, and it will take time to get to the airport and then from the airport in

Krasnoyarsk to the railway terminal. However, the train's next stop is Irkutsk at 3:47 a.m. We can be there. We can meet the train."

"And what if Mr. Jenkins and Ms. Kulikova again do not depart in Irkutsk?"

Mily smiled. "I have a plan, Comare, but if we are going to act, I must move now to get everything in place. I will call you when I have Mr. Jenkins and Ms. Kulikova on the plane back to Moscow."

The faintest smile curled a corner of Yekaterina's lip, the first Mily had seen in days. "No, Mily. I have no intention of sitting here."

Mily shook his head. "I must disagree. Let us bring them back here on the plane. It is safer here on the estate where we can protect you and keep you out of view of the many cameras."

"My father spent years in Irkutsk after his father's release from Stalin's gulags, Mily. I know it well, and I know just the place to bring them. Besides, the farther we keep them from Moscow, the farther we keep them from Sokalov. This is the smart thing to do. Go, get everything prepared. I will change clothes and meet you at the car."

41

Trans-Siberian Railway
Novosibirsk, Russia

Jenkins and Kulikova spent two days and nights largely out of sight as the train chugged east, passing through miles of forests and muddy villages, past the towns of Yaroslavl, Kirov, Perm, and Yekaterinburg, and finally through the Ural mountain range into Siberia, though the mountains had been no more than foothills. The cities seemed to come and go, indistinguishable from one another, gray and gloomy. In between the cities spread a vast nothingness, grazing for cattle, marshland. Jenkins and Kulikova did not leave their compartment except to use the bathroom at the end of the carriage. They purchased food and a deck of cards from the trolley service, ate in their cabin, and played card games to occupy their time.

"If I eat another cup of noodles I might throw up," Jenkins said at one point.

With each of the prior stops, Jenkins spent all but a few minutes of the allotted time peering out their carriage window at the people on the platform. He looked for anyone lingering beneath the canopy, or standing near the Victorian-style iron lampposts seemingly without purpose. With each stop, dozens of passengers waited to board the train, and dozens more poured off to buy food or goods in the railway terminal stores or from the men and women who set up tables beneath the terminal canopies. Nicotine-starved passengers hurried from the train to smoke, which was not allowed on board and subject to a heavy fine.

Someone associated with the Velikayas or Sokalov could have already boarded the train, but Jenkins did not think so. Nor did Kulikova. They agreed the best opportunity the Velikayas or Sokalov had to grab Jenkins and Kulikova without drawing significant attention was when the duo departed the train, whenever and wherever that might be.

Jenkins still did not know, and he did not like being in the dark. He needed to find a way to contact Lemore.

Five minutes before the train was scheduled to depart a depot, Jenkins pulled on a sweatshirt and his baseball cap and lifted the hood over his head to cover as much of his face as possible. He stepped off the train holding a cigarette from a pack he had purchased at a terminal stop, lit it, and checked his cell phone. He had no Internet access as the train traveled between cities. He did have access at the depot stops, but his phone remained glitchy since his plunge into the Neglinnaya River. He either could not get a signal or the signal would fade in and out. Mostly out. Watching others on the terminal, their gazes glued to their phones, he deduced the problem wasn't the signal but his phone.

Each time he returned to his cabin, Kulikova shrugged and said much the same thing. "What can we do? It is what it is, Charlie. At least neither of us is in a cell at Lefortovo." He wasn't sure if she was being pragmatic or fatalistic. Maybe both.

On the second day, after his attempt at the Novosibirsk depot failed, he asked the provodnik if any stores at the upcoming terminals sold cell phones. The provodnik did not know for certain but said Jenkins's best bet was at the Krasnoyarsk station. The government had spent billions to upgrade the depot station and the city in advance of the 2019 Winter Universiade, a sports competition between youth from more than sixty nations. If not Krasnoyarsk, the provodnik suggested the terminal in Irkutsk, a city that had, at one time, been called "the Paris of Siberia."

"If the terminals do not have a store, check the stores in the nearby plazas, but be aware that those two stops are for only one half hour, and you would have to go through security to get back into the station. If there is a line, you might not make it. The train will leave as scheduled."

Kulikova echoed the provodnik's warning. "Russian trains were once notorious for delays, but that has changed in recent years. They are now religiously punctual. The train will leave on time, with or without you, and we cannot risk it leaving without you."

Jenkins decided he had no choice but to at least try the Krasnoyarsk station. If he had time, and the terminal was not busy, he would chance the stores in the plaza outside the station. Kulikova wanted to divide the task and search the station stores while Jenkins tried the ones in the plaza, but he dismissed that idea out of hand. He did not want to put her at any risk.

When the train stopped at nearly half past eight that night, Jenkins quickly exited, this time wearing the wig and mustache that aged him, and moving as an old man up the steps into the terminal with the other passengers. He shifted his gaze left to right, looking for anyone shadowing him. He searched the stores on one side of the station and then the other. He entered several and asked if they carried prepaid cell phones. None did, but the employees kept suggesting other stores in the railway terminal. By the time he had checked each store recommended, it was 8:52. He looked out the windows of the station to the stores in the plaza, saw a pharmacy, and, beside it, the retail store Svyaznoy, one of the larger cell phone retailers in Russia.

He checked his watch. The train would leave in ten minutes. He looked to the metal detectors at the entrance to the station. A line spiraled down the steps. Kulikova's warning filled his thoughts.

The train will leave on time, with or without you.

Maria Kulikova paced her cabin. Four steps to the window. Four steps to the door. Each time she reached the window she looked to the platform and the commuters smoking furiously or standing in the shadows beyond the reach of the light from the decorative lamp poles. Charles Jenkins had disappeared up the steps of the railway station. She had wanted to go into the terminal with him, to divide the responsibility, but Jenkins had rejected that idea. She understood his commitment to his job, his duty to bring her home alive, but she didn't like feeling helpless. Her desire to help was also pragmatic. What would she do if Jenkins did not return? Where would she go?

She took a deep breath and brought her thoughts under control. She'd do what she'd done for the past forty years. She'd find a way to survive.

She looked again to the terminal, then checked her wristwatch: 8:59.

Someone knocked on her door, startling her. Her heart skipped. It was not the code she and Jenkins worked out before he left. The wheels of the traveling cart squeaked in the hallway. Someone, the matron, perhaps, knocked a second time. Maria knew the matrons, as well as the provodnik, had a key to her carriage. She pressed her ear to the door and heard a different sound. She looked down at a piece of paper being slipped under the door.

She stepped back. The deadbolt remained in place. The door handle did not rattle. The wheels squealed as the cart continued down the carriage. Maria bent and picked up the slip of paper.

Get off the train in Irkutsk.

Look for a friend.

She stared at the note, not knowing whether to believe what had been written. It could be a trap. Then again, the deliveryman who came to the apartment had provided the train tickets. Jenkins's contacts would therefore know which train Jenkins and Kulikova boarded, as well as their carriage number. But information could also be bought—and the Velikayas had money to burn—or coerced through the power of an office, and few had more power than the deputy director of counterintelligence.

While she debated the meaning of the note and its legitimacy, she felt the train lurch, then begin to slowly leave the station. *Charlie.*

They no longer needed a phone.

She shifted her gaze from the note to her watch: 9:03. She rushed back to the window and searched the platform and the steps leading up to the station.

Charles Jenkins was not there.

Another rap on the cabin door startled her, but this time the knocking came in code. Two knocks, then four, then one. Maria stepped to the door and unlocked it.

"There was a Svyaznoy store across the plaza," Jenkins said as he stepped inside. "I didn't have—"

Maria hugged him. Then she stepped back and held up the note. Jenkins opened it and read the words. "Where did it come from?"

"The cart matron slipped it under the door."

"You're sure?"

"I am not sure. But I heard the cart passing. The matron knocked. Then someone slipped the paper under the door. What do you think of it?"

Jenkins smiled. "My contact told me to think low tech again when high tech failed or could be compromised. This certainly fits that scenario. We'll need to be careful. We'll disembark in Irkutsk separately, as we boarded, until we can be certain."

"Who is 'a friend'?" she asked.

"I don't know," he said. "But it must be someone I will recognize or who will use those words to make him or herself known."

42

Trans-Siberian Railway
Outside of Irkutsk

Maria Kulikova checked her watch—12:42 a.m. She had tossed and turned on her berth, unable to sleep, for several hours. Their train would arrive in Irkutsk at 3:47 a.m., the early hour perhaps the reason why she and Jenkins would depart the train at this platform. The darkness would help to conceal them. Jenkins had told her to get some rest, but that was not likely. She sat up. As before, he slept soundly in the other cabin.

She put on her slippers, unbolted her cabin door, and looked down the train carriage to the samovar. No one. She walked down the narrow corridor, her legs balancing with the rocking of the train. At the samovar she filled a paper cup with hot water and chose a peppermint tea bag, along with several napkins. She looked through the glass partition into the adjacent sitting car. Arkhip sat alone, staring out the window, his gaze fixed to the glass, his thoughts seemingly far from the carriage. She wondered if he thought of his wife—if her death was the reason he did not sleep. She wished she shared his pain. She wished she had felt the same way about Helge as Arkhip felt about his wife. It might help ease the horrible burden Maria felt for Helge's death—if she had loved him the way Arkhip had loved his wife, still loved his wife. She saw the love in Arkhip's moist eyes, heard love in the tremor in his voice, deduced it from the fact that two years after his wife's death, he still wore his wedding ring. Maria wanted to grieve Helge's death, but she could not lie, at least not to herself.

Her pain was more guilt than sorrow.

She had not loved Helge.

She walked down the aisle, but Arkhip's gaze never shifted from the window. "It must be——" she said.

Arkhip startled. He knocked over his tea, what was left of it. The liquid pooled and spilled over the table edge and dripped onto the carpeted floor.

"I am so sorry." Maria handed him a few of the napkins she'd grabbed at the samovar. She bent to blot the carpet, smelling peppermint and honey.

"No. No worries," Arkhip assured her. "Clumsy of me. There was not much left anyway, and it had gone cold." He cleaned up the spill and righted the cup. "Please," he said and offered her the chair across from him.

"I was going to say, it is either a very complex problem you are solving or a memory you recall vividly."

"It would seem we are the only two awake on the train, again. I wondered if you might come."

She sipped her tea and stalled, considering his comment. The train rocked and gave an occasional jerk when the car came to a turn, but, overall, the ride was pleasant and the sound of the train peaceful. Had Arkhip been thinking of her? She dismissed the thought; in a few short hours she would leave this train and her country and never see this man again. "So, what was it?"

"What was what?"

"A complex problem you were trying to solve or a memory you recall vividly."

He smiled but did not provide an answer, at least not with his voice. His eyes, however, were telling. She had learned to read men's eyes. He had been thinking of his deceased wife. "What brings you out here again?" he asked to change the subject.

"The same as you," she said. "I can't sleep. I don't like to just lie in bed where my thoughts can do more damage than good."

"I haven't seen you during the days," Arkhip said. "Are you and your husband enjoying the trip?"

"It has been very relaxing, thank you. And you? Is the trip everything you thought it would be?"

He seemed to give her question some thought, and his blue eyes sparkled again. He smiled. "I needed the time to think," he said. "We don't take enough time to really think, do we?"

"About your wife?" she asked.

"Yes. And my job. About retiring."

"I was surprised when you told me. You are still young."

He smiled, but this time pensive. "Some don't think so, I'm afraid. The decision has been made for me. Those in power see me as an old dog unable or unwilling to learn new tricks. They want computer nerds."

"What will you do?" she asked, then sipped her tea.

He glanced out the window before redirecting his attention to her. "I don't know. That is the problem. I do not desire to sit in an empty apartment alone. Perhaps I will travel more if this trip turns out to be enjoyable."

"Was this trip then a trial run, in anticipation of your retirement?"

"You might say that it was," he said.

"I see. I am retiring as well," she said.

"Are you?"

"And it was not exactly my idea either."

"You know, then, how I feel. What is it you will do, in your retirement?"

She realized she, too, had no idea. Not a single thought came to her. "I don't know. It's scary, isn't it? Not to know."

"Yes. Some would call it a great adventure. I'm not one of them."

"Nor am I. I suppose I will take my retirement as I have lived my life. One day at a time."

"A sensible plan," he said. "Very wise."

They talked for another half hour and found they had still more in common. Neither had children. His wife could not give birth; they had contemplated adoption, but in the end chose to live as just the two of them, and they had found it surprisingly pleasant and fulfilling. Maria had not. She had always wished for children. They each had no siblings, and their parents were deceased. "A team of one," Maria said, describing herself.

"Not much of a team," Arkhip said. "Are we?"

"No," she agreed. She checked her watch. They would approach Irkutsk soon. "I'd better be getting back." She stood. Arkhip also moved as if to stand. "Don't get up," she said. "I'm sorry to have disturbed your thoughts."

He stood anyway. "I would say 'brightened.'" He bowed gently. "And a man who does not stand when a beautiful woman enters and departs will forever sit alone."

She saw affection in his gaze and in the gentle tone of his voice. She didn't know the last time she had received an unconditional compliment from a man. She felt it in her stomach and fought the urge to cry. "That's a beautiful sentiment, Arkhip. Who said that?"

He smiled. "Will I see you tomorrow evening?"

He wouldn't, she knew, and a part of her felt disappointed. "I hope so," she said.

43

Trans-Siberian Railway
Outside of Irkutsk

Charles Jenkins tensed when the cabin door clicked. He had awakened earlier to use the washroom. When he had returned, he took a peek into Kulikova's berth. When he didn't find Kulikova in her berth he felt his blood pressure surge. He had been about to rush out to look for her when she stepped in their cabin door.

"Where did you go?" he asked.

"I'm sorry," she said, clearly reading the concerned look on his face. "You were sleeping. I just went for a cup of tea and a chance to sit for a moment someplace other than this cabin. I feel claustrophobic."

"Did you see anyone? Anything suspicious?"

"No. No one."

He should have told her they needed to devise some code when she left the cabin to get tea, a sticky note on the door . . . something, but there was no point now. They would exit the train when it pulled into Irkutsk in a little less than an hour. "We need to talk about how we're going to handle things when the train stops."

She sat on her berth. Jenkins sat across from her but further up the bunk to make room for his knees. "I'll exit the front of the carriage and look for 'a friend,' whoever he or she is. If I find the person on the platform and everything is okay, I'll drop my backpack onto the ground. That will be your cue to exit from the other end of the car. If I don't drop the backpack, don't depart. Stay in the compartment and lock the door."

"I understand," she said. "But unless this friend has purchased a ticket, he won't be on the platform. He'll be on the other side of the train station, waiting in the parking lot."

She was right. Jenkins had not considered that possibility. He gave it a moment of thought, then said, "If I don't see anyone on the platform, I'll continue into the terminal. You'll need to follow, but try to blend in, as you did when we boarded. Again, if I get outside the terminal, meet a friend, and everything is okay, I'll drop the backpack. If not, use your ticket to get back on the train. It is good to Vladivostok."

Kulikova nodded stoically, but Jenkins could see her nerves in the slight tremor of her hands, which she held in her lap. She projected a strong image, and Jenkins surmised that she had done so for many years. He thought of her telling him that every day, for decades, she had gone to work thinking that day could be her last, that every day she had thought she might bite down on her pen and crush the cyanide capsule, taking her life. He had no doubt of her strength, but even the strongest person would get weak-kneed when they got this close to the finish line, this close to being free. He knew this was the moment when panic could set in. Training and planning often went out the window. His job was to project confidence and to hold things together—for both of them.

"Whatever happens," he said, "stick to the plan. If something goes wrong, get back on the train. If they could get us a note once, they can do it again. We just have to stay positive."

"I will try." She looked down as if in thought, then glanced up at him. "Tell me what my life will be like in the United States."

Jenkins deduced she'd changed the subject to calm herself. "Initially, you'll spend some time being debriefed with CIA officers. After that, the relocation center will work to provide you with a new life—a new name, new identity, new background. You'll be treated well, given a nice house in a nice neighborhood."

"And then what?" she asked.

"You'll be free," he said.

"To do what?" She asked a simple question, though Jenkins realized it was anything but. She had never been free. She'd always been trapped within the confines of her spying. It had occupied her every waking moment and thought.

"Whatever you want," he said.

"I wish I knew, Mr. Jenkins. For years my day was predetermined to the minute, and many of my nights as well. When I wasn't working, I thought of work, of the things I had done, and that I would have to do. I prepared for the possibility that each day would be my last. I fear I won't know what to do without that burden that took up so much of my life, that filled my every waking hour."

He wanted to tell her he had lived for many years just as she had lived, alone with his guilt. He wanted to tell her how Alex had popped into his life and changed everything. He wanted to tell her that age was just a number, that old dogs could learn new tricks. But it would just be words. She needed to find out for herself.

"Don't try to think too much about what is to happen," he said. "My mother used to tell me that life is a lot like reading a book. You don't know what is going to happen next unless you turn the page and read to the ending. That's the beauty of reading. The journey."

"I hope, Charlie, that your mother was reading a good book. One with a happy ending. I would like that very much."

"So would I, Maria." He checked his watch. "It's almost time." He tried to smile, to project confidence.

She reached across the aisle and squeezed his hand. "It's going to be okay," she said. "Let us turn the page together, Charlie. And see what happens next."

—

Jenkins looked out the window as the train neared Irkutsk, but at just before four in the morning the view remained pitch-black, not a glimpse of the sun yet on the horizon. According to the brochure, the train snaked along the Angara River, which flowed through the middle of the city from the southern end of Lake Baikal, the deepest freshwater lake in the world. Of the hundreds of rivers that flowed into Baikal, the Angara was the only one that flowed out. Jenkins hoped that served as an augury, that he and Kulikova would also get out. The train station was built along the river, several miles from the lake.

Jenkins put on the gray sweatshirt, pulled the baseball cap low on his brow, and lifted the hood over the hat. He slid the backpack onto his shoulder and tightened the straps. He stepped to the window as the train rolled into the Irkutsk train station, the platform illuminated by streetlamps. He surveyed the faces of the people waiting on the platform as the train rolled past. Irkutsk was a main hub on the Trans-Siberian Railway, and a considerable number of tired-looking people waited to board the cars. The train lurched to a stop. Jenkins slid between the bunks to the door and turned back to Maria. "Remember. If I take off the backpack, we're good. If I don't—"

"I'll get out of there as fast as I can." She smiled and he knew it was to calm him.

He pulled open the door. Despite the early hour, sleepy passengers trudged down the train toward the exits, dragging rolling suitcases behind them. Jenkins shut the cabin door and heard Maria lock it from the inside. He shuffled into the line. At the exit he looked out at the faces on the platform. No one he recognized. He felt the cool morning air, a strong breeze blowing in from the river. The provodnik advised each passenger to watch his or her step. On the platform Jenkins walked with the mass of travelers toward a covered stairwell, again searching for a familiar face and waiting for someone to approach and tell him they were "a friend."

He speculated whether the friend could be Lemore, but just as quickly concluded such a scenario was far too dangerous. More likely the friend was an asset who intended to remain anonymous. He hoped it wasn't a trap, but that was a possibility too.

To his right, across the tracks, the Irkutsk train terminal looked like a two-story, turn-of-the-century palace with bright-green paint and white trim highlighting the arched windows and elaborate molding. Jenkins followed the commuters to the covered stairwell and descended to a tunnel beneath the tracks. The wheels of the rolling suitcases echoed off of the tiled walls, a hum that sounded like jet engines. The travelers kept their voices to a minimum, exhausted by the early hour. He ascended a stairwell on the other side of the train tracks and paused, again looking for "a friend," but also to give someone time to approach or to make eye contact. Seeing no one, he entered the train terminal. He kept his head directed forward, but his gaze shifted left and right. He looked for men seemingly taking an interest in the passengers, maybe wearing concealed earpieces. He looked to their mouths to see if their lips moved. If this was a trap, there would be more than one, and they would communicate with one another.

Again, he saw no one.

No one approached him.

He neared the exit. He stopped for a moment and bent to tie his shoelace, taking the time to look for Maria. He did not see her.

He stepped through the exit but remained atop the step to scan the parking lot. Lamps on stanchions illuminated a bus at the bus stop across the lot and the parked cars. The commuters exited the depot and crossed the lot.

Jenkins kept his gaze roaming.

Headlights flashed on a black Citroen in the parking lot. A moment later a man pushed out of the car into the light of dawn.

Jenkins couldn't believe what he saw. Nor could he suppress a smile. He did not know how Lemore had arranged this, but he was certain he'd find out soon enough, and in great detail. He departed the step into the parking lot, about to slide the backpack strap from his shoulder.

—

Maria Kulikova waited several long minutes, as instructed, inside her cabin. She felt a rush of adrenaline but fought to control it before she pulled open the cabin door. She held her bag of clothing in one hand. Without her pen with the cyanide capsule, she felt naked and exposed. She had never put herself in a position that would allow Russian forces to capture her, and that prospect now terrified her. She knew what had happened to the sisters betrayed by the CIA informant Carl Emerson, the months of psychological and physical torture they had endured before being executed.

She stepped toward the opposite end of the car, away from the exit Jenkins had taken. The man and his two children whom she had met on the platform in Moscow approached the same exit from the attached train car. The man smiled and waved enthusiastically, an indication he had been looking for her on the train. His two children trudged forward as though he had just gotten them out of their beds, which he certainly had. The boy and girl wore pajama bottoms beneath their jackets and pulled their roller bags behind them like prisoners dragging heavy stones. The boy's bag clunked against the side wall several times.

"Ya dumal, vy yedete do konechnoy stantsii, vo Vladivostok," the man called out across the exit. *I thought you were traveling to the end of the line, Vladivostok?*

"One never knows one's plans for certain," Maria replied. "A woman is free to change her mind, no?"

The two children stepped down onto the platform, their suitcases clunking on each step, as well as the concrete. The man gestured for

Maria to go before him. "I didn't see you on the train. We looked for you in the dining car."

"The time zone changes have played havoc with my sleep," she said, relying on the six time zone changes from Moscow to Vladivostok as an excuse. "It is the middle of the night, and I am wide awake. I don't think you can say the same about your two children."

"Getting them up was like raising the dead," he said, the four of them walking forward with the crowd. "What are your plans? A little sightseeing then?"

She looked for Jenkins. His hoodie bobbed above the others, though he had done well to make himself look shorter. "Perhaps, yes. I have never been to the Paris of Siberia." Her eyes danced between the faces of the people on the platform waiting to board.

"I would love to take you," the man said.

"That would be kind," she said, keeping her gaze moving. "But it looks like you need to get these two back to bed before they fall asleep on their roller bags." The two children smiled and wiped their eyes. "Here, let me pull your case," she said to the little girl, who willingly handed Maria the handle of her roller bag.

She stayed close to the man and to his children as they descended the interior stairwell and crossed beneath the tracks. Up ahead, Jenkins ascended the staircase. Moments later, she and the family ascended, entered the terminal, and crossed toward an exit to the parking lot. As they neared the exit the man asked, "Do you have a ride?"

"A friend is picking me up," Maria said.

"Perhaps I might call you while you are here, to show you around Irkutsk?"

"Thank you," Maria said. "Why don't you give me your cell phone number, so it doesn't look like I'm the type of woman to give out her number to every attractive man?"

The man provided his number.

Maria thanked him and said her goodbyes. She paused, then stepped out the exit into the parking lot. To her right, at a second exit, she spotted Jenkins atop the step. He fiddled on his cell phone, but she could tell he was surveying the lot. She moved behind one of the pillars and waited. In the parking lot a car's headlights flashed and a man stepped out. Jenkins moved from the platform, then reached to slide the backpack strap from his shoulder.

He had found "a friend."

—

As Jenkins started toward the friend in the Citroen, he heard the throaty roar of a car engine and caught a glimpse of a fast-approaching car a moment before it cut off his path and stopped beside him. The doors flew open, blocking his escape. Just as quickly two men popped out from the front and back seats. Choreographed. Each held a weapon, the muzzle pointed directly at him. Jenkins thought briefly of fleeing. He thought of fighting. Instead, he raised the backpack to sit firmly on his shoulder. In that split second the man behind him clubbed him in the back of the head with the butt of his pistol. As Jenkins fell, he was shoved onto the floorboard of the back seat.

The doors closed, and the car sped forward.

After a moment, the man in the front passenger seat spoke. "You are a popular man, Mr. Jenkins."

Jenkins tried to shake the cobwebs and the stars. He felt plastic ties cinch one wrist and then the other. His ankles were similarly bound.

"Tell me, where is Ms. Kulikova?" the voice asked.

"Who?" Jenkins said.

His response generated a series of kicks with hard-sole shoes to his ribs. One smashed his face.

"Do not play games, Mr. Jenkins. It would not be wise. Where is Ms. Kulikova?" the man in the passenger seat repeated.

The metallic tinge of blood filled his mouth, and his right eye felt as if it were swelling shut. "I told you, I don't know who or what you're talking about. I traveled alone."

His response generated more kicks and a few punches. He felt the impact of each blow.

The man in the passenger seat continued. "I can see we are going to have to do this the hard way. So be it. We will find Ms. Kulikova, with or without your help."

One of the men in back shoved a black bag over Jenkins's head. Their feet held him in place, and an occasional kick kept him groggy and unable to think clearly. He hoped "a friend" had found Maria before others hunting her. As bad as Jenkins expected to be treated, each kick a confirmation, he knew Maria could expect far worse if Sokalov got a hold of her.

44

Irkutsk Railway Terminal
Irkutsk, Russia

Maria saw the car approach Jenkins at a high rate of speed and brake to a stop. This was not the "friend." Jenkins readjusted his backpack onto his shoulder as two men exited the vehicle and, in very short order, struck Jenkins in the back of the head, then shoved him into the back seat. She fought against panic, but her legs felt numb and rooted to the concrete. A thought struck her. She quickly turned and searched for the man and his two children, seeing him across the parking lot, his children already in the back seat of a waiting car. The man slammed the trunk shut and moved to the passenger door.

"Wait," Maria called out, struggling to get her legs, which felt leaden, to move. The man ducked into the passenger seat. "Wait. Please," she called again.

The door pulled shut and the car drove from the lot toward the street.

What now?

Stick to the plan. Get back to the train.

She turned toward the train terminal but saw a tall man with a shaved head quickly approaching from between parked cars. She looked to her left. A second man, this one shorter, but stocky, also approached. Clearly not "a friend." Definitely not Zhomov.

Velikaya's men.

A strong hand gripped her bicep and pulled her in the only direction she could go. "There you are. I have been looking all over for you." Arkhip had appeared out of nowhere. "The bus leaves in less than a minute. We'll have to hurry."

They cut between another row of parked vehicles, illuminated in headlights. The sound of engines and odor of diesel fumes filled the air. Maria allowed Arkhip to lead her, wondering, if perhaps, he had provided the note, if he could be "a friend."

Another car cut across their path and stopped, preventing their escape to the bus. She could see the driver's face through the windshield. Alexander Zhomov. The car interior illuminated as Zhomov slid from the vehicle holding a weapon. He took aim.

"Down." Arkhip shoved Maria to the pavement between the parked cars just before a shot rang out. The bullet sparked off a car's side mirror. Zhomov fired again. Again the bullet hit a car, puncturing its tire.

For a moment, none of the other commuters moved, paralyzed by fear or confusion. Their minds tried to place the sound, perhaps wondering if a car had backfired. Arkhip squatted between the row of vehicles, looking for a way out. The two Velikaya men advanced. Zhomov blocked Maria's and Arkhip's escape in the other direction. Either way, they were sitting ducks.

In the second it took Maria to process their situation, the retort of automatic weapons and the spray of bullets punctured metal and shattered glass. Pandemonium ensued. No mistakes now as to the sound. The commuters scurried in all directions. Some, too scared to move, remained crouched behind cars. Others fled back to the train terminal.

Zhomov returned the shots. One of the Velikaya men fell. The second sprayed Zhomov's car with more automatic gunfire and moved to assist his fallen comrade, finding refuge behind a vehicle; Zhomov's only option under the barrage of return fire was to also retreat behind his car door.

Arkhip used that second to their advantage. He pulled Maria toward the train terminal. At the final row of vehicles, their last cover before the six meters of open space to the terminal doors, he paused, reached inside his coat and removed a pistol. Maria wondered again if he could be "a friend." Was that the reason he had first approached her on the train?

"When I say, 'Go,' you run for the terminal." He glanced behind him. Zhomov lifted his head above the car door. Arkhip fired a shot, forcing Zhomov to retreat.

"Go," he said.

As Maria scurried into the unprotected divide, another car skidded to a stop and cut off her approach to the terminal. The passenger door flung open. The man behind the wheel reached his hand across the seat. "Get in, Ms. Kulikova."

Maria hesitated, confused. She knew this man. She knew him from years working at Lubyanka, but she had trouble placing him here. Then it clicked. "Viktor Federov," she said.

"Get in, Ms. Kulikova. I am a friend."

Maria felt Arkhip's hand push at the small of her back and they rushed for the car. Federov aimed the barrel of a pistol at Arkhip. "I don't think so," he said.

"No," Maria said. "It's all right."

No time to debate, Federov swore and lowered the weapon. Arkhip pushed inside and slammed the door shut. Maria looked over her shoulder. Zhomov hurried back inside his car as Federov punched the accelerator, swerved between cars and around pedestrians, and made a hard right turn onto the main road, tires squealing.

Maria gripped Arkhip, who held the door handle to keep from toppling over.

Federov reached across her and again pointed his gun at Arkhip. "Tell me who you are?" he said.

Maria reached to lower Federov's arm, but it was rigid. "He's a friend from the train," Maria said.

"I don't think so," Federov said, his gaze dancing between the rearview mirror, the windshield, and Arkhip. "For one thing, your friend is carrying a gun. Tell me who you are, *friend*, or I will shoot you and leave your body along the side of the road."

"I am Arkhip Mishkin, senior investigator with the Moscow police department."

"You're a police officer?" Maria said, stunned and feeling betrayed.

Arkhip glanced at the side mirror. "The other car is coming," he said. "I suggest you turn, frequently, if you desire to lose him."

Federov drew back the gun and checked his side and rearview mirrors, swearing repeatedly. He turned the car multiple times, weaving down alleys and streets without hesitation. Within a minute, Maria did not see Zhomov's car in the side mirror.

Federov drove down a narrow alley, sending garbage cans flying over the hood and roof of the car. Just before the end of the alley, he pulled into a bay of a two-car garage in a concrete-block building. A car occupied the second bay, in the process of being pulled apart. Federov got out and quickly rolled the door shut.

Back at the car, he waved the gun at Arkhip and Maria inside the vehicle. "Both of you, get out."

Maria and Arkhip did so. Light inside the concrete room came from fluorescent tubes in light fixtures suspended by chains from the ceiling. Spare car parts littered a wooden workbench along with tools. The aroma of oil and gas permeated the air.

Federov held Arkhip at gunpoint. "Remove your weapon slowly and hand it to me," he said. Arkhip did so.

"You are a police officer? You have been following me?" Maria said again.

"Not a police officer. A senior investigator. And I was not following you, Ms. Kulikova. I was following Mr. Jenkins. I am sorry for not telling you the truth on the train, but I assume you can understand why."

"How did you even know we were on the train?"

"I followed you from the apartment building in Moscow to the Yaroslavsky station. When you boarded the Trans-Siberian train I had no choice but to follow."

"What is your business in this?" Federov asked.

"My business is the murder of Eldar Velikaya," Arkhip said. "My business is speaking to Mr. Jenkins."

Federov laughed. "Well, you've bitten off a lot more than a murder, Investigator Mishkin."

Arkhip looked to Maria and spoke calmly. "Yes. It appears that I have."

"On the train . . ." Maria struggled to find her words. "I don't understand. Why didn't you just arrest Mr. Jenkins? Why take the train all the way to Irkutsk?"

Arkhip didn't immediately answer but his look was telling. He had not been following Maria, but he had been anticipating their meetings. "My situation is complicated, as is yours, Ms. Kulikova. As I said to you the other night, I am being retired. I might already be retired. This is the thanks I get for three decades of service, a pat on the back as I am ushered out the door. I am trying to come to terms with forced retirement, but not before I close this case. Not for them—they have already removed me from it. For myself."

Maria looked to Federov and they all collectively exhaled. "What do we do now?" she asked.

"He stays with us for now," Federov said. "We can't very well let him leave; and killing a Moscow police officer will generate more interest, and we have enough as it is."

"I assure you. I have no interest in this except in speaking to Mr. Jenkins. If I cannot leave on my terms, at least I will leave with a perfect record. It is a small thing, and it isn't."

"What is your interest in this, Viktor?" Maria said. "Are you a CIA asset?"

Federov chuckled. "No. I am not CIA. I am no longer FSB. I have no affiliation with government organizations any longer, nor do I wish to be so affiliated."

"Then why are you here?"

"Money," Federov said. "It pays better to be an independent contractor."

"You approached the CIA and offered your services?"

"No. The CIA, Mr. Jenkins specifically, approached me several months ago and asked for my services."

"You helped him get Paulina Ponomayova out of Lefortovo Prison and out of the country."

"Yes," he said. "For which I was paid very well."

"Then why are you here now . . . It doesn't sound like you need the money."

"One can always use more money, Ms. Kulikova." He shook his head. "But no. It was not the money. Mr. Jenkins's handler found me in Paris. It seems the CIA has followed me for some time, my alias anyway. They seek to turn me." He looked to Arkhip. "But like you, I will do this on my terms, nobody else's. Mr. Jenkins's handler told me the situation. I said it was of no concern of mine. He offered me money; I told him I had money. Then he offered me something I didn't have."

"What?" she said.

"The chance to spit in Dmitry Sokalov's face is a once-in-a-lifetime opportunity, is it not?"

"The man who fired you."

"Yes. Besides, Mr. Jenkins's handler told me his plan to get you out, and I am from Irkutsk. I was born and raised here. I have many friends, and I know this city like the back of my hand."

"You sent the message about 'a friend.'"

"Yes. But as it always seems to be with Mr. Jenkins, nothing is simple, is it? The men who grabbed him, do you know who they are?"

"They work for Yekaterina Velikaya," Arkhip said.

"*Vot der'mo,*" Federov said. "When Jenkins gets himself in trouble, he really gets himself in trouble. And the other man?"

"Alexander Zhomov," Maria said. "He—"

"*Vot der'mo,*" Federov said again, sounding exasperated. He let out a held breath and ran his hand over the stubble atop his head. "I am well familiar with Alexander Zhomov, and his reputation."

"Who is he, exactly?" Arkhip asked. "FSB, no doubt."

Maria explained.

"This is getting more and more interesting," Federov said, continuing to rub his stubble as he paced.

Maria told him the conclusion she and Jenkins had reached. Why Sokalov wished to keep her apprehension quiet.

"It makes sense," Federov said. "Then can I presume that the rumors of your relationship with Sokalov being more than professional are true?"

Maria glanced at Arkhip, then redirected her focus on Federov. "Yes. They are true."

Federov chuckled. "Don't look so surprised, Ms. Kulikova. There were many rumors inside Lubyanka."

"Mr. Jenkins would be a very big fish for Sokalov to land," Maria said. "His goal has always been to be chairman and to work at the Kremlin."

"True. But Jenkins is on a kill list."

"He is," she said, "but Sokalov would have another purpose for him."

"Which is what?"

"To provide the Kremlin with someone they could exchange for the two members of Zaslon recently arrested in a failed attempt to kill Fyodor Ibragimov."

Federov's eyes widened. *"Tvoyu mat',"* he said. *Holy shit.* "When did this happen?"

"Recently. The Americans have not yet acknowledged it, or that they are holding the two men."

"They're waiting for the Kremlin to act first," Federov said. "An admission would be a huge embarrassment, especially if the Americans can prove the president was aware of the operation."

"Yes, it would," Maria said. "Not to mention justifying a condemnation and the imposition of strong sanctions other NATO countries would join. If Sokalov can deliver Mr. Jenkins, he provides the Kremlin with a powerful bargaining chip to get the two men returned quietly."

Federov looked to Arkhip. "It seems you and the Velikayas are not the only ones who want Mr. Jenkins, Senior Investigator Arkhip Mishkin."

"It would seem not," Arkhip agreed.

"As I said, when Mr. Jenkins steps in the shit, it is deep. Tell me, Mishkin, about the death of Eldar Velikaya and why you wish to speak to Jenkins. We may be able to use this to our advantage. But be quick about it. I don't believe Mr. Jenkins has much time."

45

Irkutsk Meatpacking Plant
Irkutsk, Russia

Jenkins had hoped for a long drive; he had hoped to be pulled from the car and placed on a plane, to be flown back to Moscow; he had hoped even for a cell in Lefortovo, because then it would have meant he had been picked up by the FSB. Had that been the case, he would have the slightest chance of remaining alive. Yes, he was on an FSB kill list, according to Matt Lemore and Maria Kulikova, but even kill lists weren't certain death. He could expect to be tortured, interrogated, and kept in isolation for as long as Moscow believed he had information to offer, something of value he could provide. It would be precious time Lemore would need to work on his behalf, if Federov could get word to him that Jenkins remained alive. An unwritten code existed between hostile nations. You expel our diplomats, and we'll expel yours. You capture one of ours and accuse him of spying, and we'll do the same to one of yours, regardless if the person is actually a spy. Then we will exchange them. According to Maria, the CIA currently held two members of Zaslon, Russia's elite and highly secretive special operations unit that Moscow would not publicly acknowledge. That meant Lemore had assets to bargain with.

All of that, however, became moot when the car into which Jenkins had been forced stopped just minutes after departing the train terminal, and the two men pulled Jenkins from the floorboards of the back seat and deposited him on hard ground. These men were not FSB. These men worked for Yekaterina Velikaya. Mafiya. They had no interest in negotiations or trades, and probably not even in enormous sums of money.

They had just one interest. Vengeance.

The men grabbed him beneath his armpits and dragged him, presumably into a building, from the temperature change. Inside, he was lifted off the ground and felt an increased strain on his shoulders. They had suspended him in midair. Not good.

They would interrogate him, but not likely for very long. They had just one question. Why had he killed Yekaterina's son?

It changed the game.

He hoped Federov, the "friend" at the Irkutsk railway terminal, had reached Maria and taken her to safety. Maria had to then let Lemore know the Velikayas had Jenkins. And Lemore had to then somehow get word to the Velikayas that killing Jenkins would be frowned upon by the CIA, which would launch an all-out war on the Velikayas' business interests.

Again, it was a lot to hope for, and it would require time, probably too much time. Given the force of the kicks and the blows Jenkins had endured already, he'd likely be beaten to death before Lemore could get involved.

Jenkins's goal, however, remained the same. Stay alive—for as long as possible. Alive, he retained the faintest chance, the smallest hope, that everything might fall in place, and he could get out of this situation and get home to Alex and his two children.

Jenkins had to give Matt Lemore credit. Federov made sense. He didn't know how Lemore got in contact with Federov, although Lemore and the CIA had a thick file on the former FSB agent and knew the alias Federov lived under, Sergei Vladimirovich Vasilyev. Lemore likely traced Federov to somewhere in Europe tied to Viktor's substantial bank accounts. Lemore also knew Federov had been born and raised in Irkutsk, that he had grown up in the Paris of Siberia, and Lemore likely assumed Federov, a very good former FSB officer, remained well connected.

At least Jenkins hoped so.

The chill in the room spread quickly over Jenkins's body, the temperature some forty degrees less than the temperature outside. The cold caused the kicks and blows to hurt more when the men struck him. The pain shattered his skin like splinters of broken glass passing through his body. Jenkins's limbs became numb, and not just from a lack of circulation. Had he been placed in a freezer of some kind?

He detected a distinct smell, an aroma he had, unfortunately, become familiar with over the years. Warm blood, tinged with iron, but the faintest odor of bleach.

Suspended from a chain that moved. A freezer. Warm blood. Bleach.

A slaughterhouse.

Another chill, this one running through Jenkins's entire body, independent of the cold and the lack of circulation in his extremities. Fear.

He could only imagine what the Velikayas had planned for him.

46

Vasin Estate
Irkutsk, Russia

Maria Kulikova stared at the ornate iron gates at which Viktor Federov had stopped the car. What looked like an insect of some sort had been designed into each gate, which hung from thick brick columns and spanned an expansive entrance to a long, paved road. A guard, armed with an assault rifle and a German shepherd on a leash, stepped from a stone guardhouse and approached the gate. A second guard within the guardhouse spoke over a speaker and asked Federov to identify himself and to state his business.

Federov did so and within a minute the gates pulled open. Federov drove forward and the gate closed behind the car. The guard ran a mirror on the end of a long telescopic stick beneath the body of the car, while the dog sniffed and panted. After circling the car in both directions, the guard waved them through.

Unlike the front entrance, which conjured images of a prison, decorative lawn lights outlined the contours of the road as it cut between manicured lawns, pristine flower beds, and sculpted fir and birch trees that gave the property a softer feel.

"This home belongs to Plato Vasin," Federov said. "He is a childhood friend of mine."

"What does he do?" Arkhip asked.

"The Vasins are to Siberia what the Velikayas are to Moscow, and there is no love lost between the two families. Alexei Velikaya got his start here in Irkutsk but left when he became rich and successful. He tried to run a lucrative heroin trade from Moscow, but the Vasins would have none of it. Eventually they came to a bloody truce. The Vasins control much of the heroin trade through Siberia."

"What is the design on the gate?" Maria asked. "It looked like an insect."

"It is. A fly. When Plato was a young man he specialized in burglaries of small stores and warehouses. A Siberian mob boss said Plato Vasin was nothing but a nuisance, a fly he would squash. Before killing him, Plato made the man eat a bowl full of dead flies."

"Oh God," Maria said.

"He keeps the name to remind others of their fate if they cross him."

"And that is what you call him?" Arkhip asked. "'Fly'?"

"Only his friends call him 'the Fly.' He embraces the name, as you will see from the décor; so much so he once tried to have a fly tattooed onto the tip of his penis but gave up when it proved too painful. He settled instead for flies throughout his home, including the tiles of his shower and the headboard of his bed."

"His wife must love that," Maria said.

Federov smirked. "His first two, not so much. His third has come to terms with it. Plato likes to say: 'Love and wives are more easily exchanged than flies cast in iron or stone.'"

Maria didn't know whether escaping the clutches of one mafiya family for another was wise, but she also had no choice but to trust Viktor Federov. She had known him to be an excellent and thorough FSB officer, one who had become a scapegoat when Jenkins avoided capture. Sokalov had, in effect, offered up Federov's head on a platter.

Perhaps Federov's desire to do the same would be enough, though she worried it would not be in time to save Charlie.

"Whatever we intend to do, we must do it quickly, before the Velikayas kill Mr. Jenkins."

"I will be as quick as I can," Federov said. "But one does not rush Plato Vasin when asking a favor."

Eventually the road came to a circular drive and a mammoth house perched on a hill. The high ground. It looked like an expensive hotel, bright-yellow stucco with a promenade, columns, and balconies. More armed guards waited atop the staircase.

Before pushing from the car, Federov turned and spoke directly to Arkhip. "I would not volunteer your profession, Chief Investigator Mishkin. Or you may find yourself sitting in front of a bowl full of flies. Please, allow me to do the talking."

"With certainty," Arkhip said.

47

Irkutsk Meatpacking Plant
Irkutsk, Russia

Jenkins felt each blow, like wedges of sharp ice crashing into his skin, penetrating his body, then splintering into millions of shards that ran up and down his torso and into his extremities. They started with the body, which made sense since blows to the head would possibly knock him unconscious or senseless and unable to answer questions. They wanted him to feel every punch. They had also removed the black bag, wanting him to see each blow delivered.

His assessment had been accurate. They had brought him to a slaughterhouse. He hung from a hook attached to a conveyor belt in a long room that seemed the size of half a soccer field. All around him hung the carcasses of animals stripped of their fur; what remained of cows, sheep, goats, pigs, and buffalo. The two men from the back seat had meted out his punishment and were adept at doing so. They resembled boxers or wrestlers in training, wearing sweatpants and sweatshirts, their hands taped to keep them from breaking a knuckle while they delivered maximum impact. The man from the passenger seat, older than the others, sat comfortably in a chair, his legs crossed, his body bundled in a long wool overcoat, gloves, and an ushanka. He looked like a wealthy grandfather.

"I can assure you, Mr. Jenkins, this will end much more quickly if you simply tell me where to find Ms. Kulikova." Condensation punctuated each word.

Jenkins didn't know what the Velikayas would want with Maria, but if it meant more time, he would use it. Every second of every minute was another he remained alive. He had no idea where Maria had gone, or, even if she remained alive, but he wasn't about to tell them. "I told you. I don't know a Maria Kulikova."

The man nodded and the two men swung their fists, taking turns delivering blows, like men on the railroad line alternately swinging sledgehammers. The blows came so quickly Jenkins couldn't catch his breath, and when he did, it burned in his chest. After a dozen more punches, the seated man raised a hand and the two men stopped the punishment. "Do you really wish for this to continue?" he asked.

"What is your interest in this Ms. Kulikova, and why do you believe I would know where she is? I thought your interest was in Eldar Velikaya."

"We will come to him soon enough," the old man said. "My employer wishes to question you about him herself. Now, we are fully aware that you helped Ms. Kulikova to escape from Moscow, Mr. Jenkins. Our interest here is leverage. You see, we have a common enemy in Dmitry Sokalov. Ms. Kulikova can give him to us."

So that was the answer. "What's your beef with Dmitry Sokalov?"

"Unfinished business."

"You're going to have to be a bit more specific for me to believe you."

"Mr. Sokalov ordered the assassination of my boss. I now work for his daughter."

"No doubt upon the president's orders?"

"No doubt. But the president is not a realistic target. Not while he remains in office, anyway. My boss has waited many years for this opportunity. She does not intend to let it pass. So tell me where to find Ms. Kulikova and we can stop this nonsense."

Jenkins chuckled. "Am I to believe that you intend to let me go?"

"That would be foolish. But I could expedite your death."

"You're a real pal. I wish I could help you, but I have no idea where Ms. Kulikova is. I would assume she is a long way from here. She left the train before we arrived in Irkutsk. I'm a larger target and I tend to stand out. I was a decoy. I guess it worked."

The seated man nodded and the other two resumed delivering sledgehammer blows. After half a dozen he raised his hand and they stopped. "A lie," he said. "Ms. Kulikova was spotted in the train station parking lot by two of our men. Tell me your plan to get her away."

"Why would the men who took her away tell me that? It would only give you the opportunity to beat it out of me. I'm as ill informed as you."

"A shame, then, for you."

The fists struck again, this time moving up the body, likely cracking ribs and tearing cartilage. Each blow knocked the wind from him, and Jenkins had to struggle not to panic when he could not breathe. He clenched at the blows and fought to recapture his breath.

When the punches stopped, he said, "I thought you Russians were sports oriented. Why don't you cut me down and let the three of us go at it? Or are you afraid one American would beat you both?"

The man in the chair smiled. "I am well aware of your abilities to fight, Mr. Jenkins. I watched the videotape of your fight with Eldar and Pavil. I was impressed. You are well trained. Tell me, did you learn to fight in the CIA?"

Jenkins shook his head. "I'm not CIA. I'm an independent contractor. A mercenary."

"Then there is no one who would bargain to get you back or care if you should die. Pity."

Shit. Jenkins hadn't considered that logic. "You'd be surprised. If it's a war you want, they'll bring you one," he said.

"What form of combat did you use to take down Eldar and Pavil?"

"Krav Maga," he said.

"The Israel Defense Forces. I am told they are badasses."

"Have your boys cut me down and we'll have a go of it. You can see for yourself."

"Why did the CIA send you to kill Eldar?"

"I told you, I'm not CIA. And if you watched the videotape, then you know I didn't kill anyone."

The man gave a flick of his head. "Here's what I watched, and what I know. A man in an elaborate disguise walks into a . . . how do you Americans say it? A dive bar? Why, unless he has business inside?"

"Or he's in disguise because he's trying not to get noticed and chose the dive bar for the same reason."

"Which would make killing Eldar a poor choice."

"I told you. I didn't kill him. And yes, it was a poor choice to get involved."

"You watched him. You took an interest in him—"

"No. I took an interest in the woman he was beating the shit out of and treating worse than a dog."

The man shrugged. "She was a prostitute. Why would you care?"

"The fact that you would ask me that question tells me everything I need to know about you," Jenkins said.

"Really? Then tell me, Mr. Jenkins. Let us see if your powers of perception are as strong as you believe."

"You're a yes-man. You say yes to your boss whether you agree with her or not. You're also either a psychopath, like Eldar Velikaya, who takes pleasure in others' pain and suffering, and have no empathy for human life, or you have your head so far up your boss's ass that you will ignore your own morals, which makes you just plain sad."

One of the other men threw another punch, a circular loop that landed with a dull thud, but before the second man could do the same, the seated man raised a hand. "Stop." He uncrossed his legs and stood.

Then he walked to where Jenkins hung, staring at him with a blank expression though his lips looked as if they were holding back words. He inhaled deeply through his nose and blew out a heavy breath that turned to mist in the cold air.

"Before I kill you, I want you to know that I watched the videotape. I want you to know that I watched Pavil shoot Eldar in the back, as Eldar attacked you. I want you to know that Eldar Velikaya was a shit who could have never taken over the family business. His mother of course knew this . . ." He paused here, perhaps to choose his words. "But she is his mother. And yes, she is my boss. You see, but for your interference, there would have been no shooting and Eldar would still be alive today. Pavil might have pulled the trigger, but your interference pulled out the gun. Tell me why?"

"I told you why," Jenkins said. "This is getting us nowhere."

"The Good Samaritan?"

"Do you have children?"

"Whether I have—"

"Do you have a daughter? What are you afraid of, that I'm going to get out of here and kill your family?"

"I can assure you. That is not going to happen."

"Do you have a daughter?" The man didn't answer him, but Jenkins could see in his eyes that he did, and that he understood why Jenkins had done what he had done, not that it was going to be any help to him now. "So you know. You just won't acknowledge it, but you know. Which means I was right in my evaluation. You're not a psychopath. You're just sad."

"Unfortunately, Mr. Jenkins, Yekaterina Velikaya has no daughters. She had only one son. So, it would be my suggestion that if you don't have a good reason for killing her son you come up with one."

"Is it going to save my life?"

"No. Most assuredly it will not. But it may cut short your punishment." He smiled. "You see, I can have sympathy."

48

Vasin Estate
Irkutsk, Russia

Federov stepped from the car and approached the V-shaped, ornate staircase. He removed a handkerchief from his pocket and wiped his brow. A heat wave across Russia had made the Irkutsk weather unseasonably warm. Once atop those steps he looked across the manicured lawns to wooden gazebos and several guesthouses with views of the Angara River. Further out, he took in the shores of Lake Baikal, a view he recalled from as far back as childhood, when he and the Vasin brothers attended school together. Federov had been best friends with Plato Vasin's younger brother. Their fathers had also been childhood friends in Irkutsk, though Federov's father, a mechanic, had never been tempted to become part of the Vasin family business, and he did not want the allure to tempt his son. He shipped Federov off to a boarding school in Moscow with an admonition. "Money is like an attractive woman. Everyone wants it, which makes it very hard to keep."

Odya Vasin, the father, had died from a car bomb. Some blamed the war with the Velikayas. Others said the death, in 2008 and just a month after Alexei Velikaya had been shot, was part of the president's plan to kill those who threatened his quest for absolute power.

Federov had played in this house, but that had been many years ago and before the renovations. A fly had been designed in the stained-glass windows of the front door. A guard posted outside the door patted down all three of them, Maria Kulikova more so than necessary, though Federov could certainly understand why. When finished, the guard knocked three times and the door pulled open. Plato's little brother, whom they called "Peanut" because he grew as big as an African elephant and had a penchant for eating the shelled nut, stepped out wearing shorts and flip-flops but no shirt. The black hair on his chest was as thick as a wool sweater and seemed to be one with his beard and mane of long hair.

"Viktor!" Peanut embraced Federov in a bear hug and lifted him off the ground. Though Federov was just shy of two meters and more than ninety kilograms, he felt as small as a child in Peanut's arms.

"Hey, Peanut."

"How long has it been?" Peanut asked, his eyes wide. He put Federov down.

"Too long," Federov said.

"You never come to visit your old friends in Irkutsk anymore." He gently slapped Federov on the cheek. "What, you got to be too good for us?" Peanut waved his palms and cooed. "A Moscow FSB officer. I'm scared." He laughed loud and long, as if Federov were his son or his kid brother.

When Peanut saw Maria Kulikova, he brushed Federov aside. His eyes ran up and down her body as he spoke. "Is this the cargo bound for Vladivostok? You never told me it was exquisite." He offered his hands and Maria reciprocated with one of hers. Peanut gently kissed the back of her hand, then each of her cheeks. He looked to Mishkin. "And is this—"

Federov spoke quickly. "An associate of mine. I'm afraid we've run into a problem. Is the Fly home?"

"Plato is in the pool in the backyard with his kids."

"More kids? How many does he have?"

"With this wife? Three. Altogether, seven. Come on. I'll take you there. Can I get you something to drink?"

"Nothing for now, Peanut. Thank you."

"And the beautiful woman," he said, looking to Maria. "Would you care for a drink?"

"Nothing for me, Peanut," she said.

Peanut feigned a swoon and leaned close to Federov's shoulder but spoke loud enough for Maria to hear. "You sure she has to leave? I could fall in love with this one."

They walked through Plato Vasin's garishly ornate house, which indeed included a fly motif. He had flies fabricated from different materials on the mantels and shelves, and embedded in the marble floors, the expensive throw rugs, and the paintings hanging on the walls.

Federov knew Plato had learned from his father's death. He remained elusive and inaccessible to the public, though for friends he was always available. His reputation in criminal circles had become almost mythical. Had he not been the eldest son of a mafiya kingpin, he probably would have become a powerful public figure, maybe an oligarch. As it was, his boyhood had schooled him as thoroughly in street-mean survival as any university could have honed a leader of the apparat—those in authority. He was also a contradiction. Despite his viciousness, the Fly was known for his integrity and fairness. To those he employed, the Fly was God. He'd earned their devotion and expected it returned in spades. Those in his employ lived by strictly observed rules and values, the code of the vory.

Federov had grown up privy to the vory's system of favors, obligations, and punishment, and though he did not join in their criminal activities, he had stood with them and by them in his early years. The Fly had become King of Irkutsk, and when Viktor joined the FSB, they did occasional favors for each other. Viktor could provide the Fly with connections and information when the Irkutsk FSB office was about to clamp down, or when another gang tried to make inroads.

The favor Federov was about to ask, however, would test the bonds of their friendship. Unlike Peanut, who loved Viktor unconditionally, the Fly did not love. He looked at people as chessboard pieces to be moved and manipulated to his benefit.

Peanut led them to a backyard that looked like a miniature Disney World. The pool was three tiered, with waterslides and waterfalls cascading from one level to the next, and a lazy river that meandered around the expansive yard. The pool interior included several well-stocked bars. And tiled on the pool bottom was a huge fly. A lush, green football field lay adjacent to the pool, and smoke rose from a barbecue area beneath a cabana with seating that looked like it could fit a royal wedding party.

Despite it being morning, the Fly lay in the pool on a large green flotation device. The salt-and-pepper hair on his chest, as thick as his brother's, did not keep the sun from coloring his skin an uncomfortable-looking pink. His entire body looked slick with oil. He wore sunglasses and spoke on a cell phone. Another flotation device bobbed close by and held several glasses of half-finished energy drinks, for which he had a penchant, and two additional cell phones. As a boy, the Fly had always been on the go—always making a deal, no matter what kind. He loved the art of negotiation, the ability to manipulate others without them knowing he was doing so. Federov had never seen him stop moving for more than a few minutes.

His third wife, twenty years his junior, stretched her lean and well-toned body on a chaise lounge along the side of the pool, her face covered beneath a floppy hat and large sunglasses. When Peanut introduced them, she gave Federov a lazy wave.

The Fly flipped his phone closed, tossed it onto the flotation device with the two others, and smiled at Viktor, who waited patiently at the side of the pool. After friendly greetings, the Fly said, "I didn't expect you to come to my home, Viktor. Though I welcome you and invite you to stay."

"Thank you, Plato. I apologize for coming unannounced and disturbing your time with your family."

"For an old friend, a friend of Peanut's, I am always available."

"*Spasibo.*"

"Tell me why you are here?"

The plan had been for Viktor to pick up Jenkins and Kulikova and deliver them into the arms of the Fly's men, but not to meet with the Fly. The largest heroin supplier in Siberia, the Fly shipped his stock by rail, plane, and boat to partners in Mongolia and Kazakhstan for distribution worldwide. Jenkins and Kulikova would be put into a railcar and delivered to a distributor in Mongolia, who would see them to the shores of the East China Sea, where a cargo vessel would take them to the United States. For this, the Fly would be paid an exorbitant sum.

"I have just one of the shipments."

"One? It looks like two to me, Viktor."

"This is Arkhip. He is an associate of mine."

"You are taking on partners now, are you, Viktor? Business must be good. I heard you left the FSB and are working on your own. What about me? Why am I not your partner?"

"We have lost one of the cargo," Federov said.

"'We'?" The Fly rolled from the raft into waist-deep water and stepped from the pool. A man handed him a large white robe and another green energy drink. "I did not lose anything, Viktor. Your job was to deliver the cargo. My job was to transport it. That was the deal, was it not?"

"That was most certainly the deal, Plato. And I do not want to take advantage of our friendship."

Plato chuckled. "But you're going to do so anyway, aren't you?"

"I'm afraid so. It seems the Velikayas have taken an interest in our cargo and picked him up at the train station."

The Fly lowered his sunglasses and looked at Viktor over the rims. "The Velikayas?"

"Yes."

After a beat, the Fly said, "You always were a good chess player, Viktor." He led them to the shade beneath an awning and invited them to sit in plush outdoor furniture. Another man handed the Fly a plate of gigantic shrimp and put a glass bowl of cocktail sauce on the table. The Fly dipped one of the shrimp into the sauce and ate it to the tail. "Are you bluffing, Viktor, to gain my favor?"

"I would never play you, Plato, unless it was straight up."

"This I know. The Velikayas have come into my backyard without asking my permission. Who is it?"

"I don't know for certain, but I am told that Yekaterina has taken a particular interest in the capture of this man."

The Fly's eyes widened. He stopped in mid-dunk of a second shrimp, leaving the tail protruding from the cocktail sauce. "Who is this man, Viktor? You told me he was CIA."

"He is most certainly CIA, Plato, or at least in their employ."

The Fly sipped his energy drink and set it down on a silver platter. "For Yekaterina to return to Siberia uninvited after so many years, this man must be very important. Why does she want him?"

"She believes, wrongly, that this man killed her son, Eldar."

It was clear from the flat expression on Plato's face that he was well aware of the news. "Did he?"

"No," Mishkin said. Federov turned his head at the sound of the chief investigator's voice, dismayed by the intrusion.

"And you are again?" the Fly asked.

"Arkhip Mishkin. I am an associate of Mr. Federov."

"What do you know about the death of Eldar Velikaya?"

Mishkin filled in the Fly on the details of his investigation, but deftly, careful not to use that term or indicate police involvement.

"And why do you know so many intimate details of this murder, Mr. Mishkin?"

Federov started to jump in, hopefully before Mishkin stepped in a pile of dog shit and found himself sitting before a large bowl of flies.

Mishkin, however, spoke first. "Please, call me Arkhip, Mr. Fly."

The Fly glanced at Federov out of the corner of his eyes while Mishkin continued. "Mr. Federov asked that I inform him fully. I took that responsibility seriously and used all of our contacts to obtain the information I have provided you."

Federov had to give Mishkin his due. He'd handled it well, and it wasn't a lie.

"Why did you not tell me of this potential complication, Viktor?" the Fly asked.

"I did not learn the details until a short while ago. Besides, I did not think the Velikayas would have the temerity to come into Siberia without first seeking your permission, Plato."

"Don't placate me, Viktor. It is unbecoming." The Fly thought for a few moments, then said, "This man, and what he is accused of, is no business of mine. I have no desire to get involved. Get him here and I will ship him. That was the deal. Otherwise, she goes alone." He rescued the second shrimp from the sauce and popped it into his mouth.

"I understand," Federov said. "It's just that . . ."

The Fly leaned forward for a third shrimp but stopped and considered Federov, again over the top of his sunglasses. "It's just what, Viktor?"

"I just wonder what the other families in Siberia will think when they learn the Velikayas came into Irkutsk without permission or repercussions."

The Fly leaned back in his chair and stared at Federov for what felt like a full minute.

Peanut, standing off to the side, said, "It may make us look weak, Plato."

The Fly shifted his gaze to his brother, then back to Federov. "As I said, you were always a competitive chess player." He gave Federov a hard stare before smiling, then laughed. "Make me look weak? Hardly. What is it you really want? Why is this man important to you, Viktor?"

"This man is a friend of mine, Plato. He has done me several favors in my lifetime and, as my associate has detailed for you, he is innocent. I want to get him back for his wife and his children."

"When did you get to be sentimental, Viktor? It is unbecoming."

"Perhaps, but possibly lucrative for you."

"Really? Tell me how," he said, not sounding convinced.

"I will be sure the CIA is made aware that it was only because of your graciousness that we were able to recover Mr. Jenkins."

Federov could see the wheels spinning in the Fly's head. The CIA had its fingers all over the heroin trade, and it would not be bad to have them owe Plato a favor.

"What I will do is out of respect for our friendship and the friendship of our fathers, not for any expectations. Is that clear?" the Fly said.

"Absolutely."

"What do you need?"

"I'm going to need your resources to find out where he has been taken."

"What makes you think he is here and not in Moscow?"

"Sokalov also wants this man. Why bring him back to Moscow and give Sokalov the chance to take him from them? The Velikayas will hide their kill here. Once we determine where, I will need your manpower to get him back."

"And potentially start a war with the Velikayas; I don't think so, Viktor. It's bad for business."

"No. The Velikayas will give Mr. Jenkins back willingly. Without bloodshed."

"Is that a promise, Viktor? I warn you, do not make promises you cannot keep."

"It is a promise, Plato." He returned the Fly's hard stare. "On this I swear."

After a moment Plato said, "The cost for shipment has doubled. Call your contact and get approval. If you do, I will take it as a showing of good faith and give you what you need." He looked to his brother. "In the interim, Peanut, make some phone calls. See where the Velikayas have taken this CIA man."

"Thank you, Plato," Federov said.

"Don't thank me, Viktor. Get on the phone. Get me my money. Then you can thank me. Otherwise, I might offer you something other than shrimp." With that, the Fly rose, cinched tight his bathrobe, and departed inside the mansion.

Federov turned to Mishkin. "When Peanut finds Mr. Jenkins, I assume you have a contact in the ministry who will leak the information to the FSB."

"Indeed, I do," Mishkin said. "Vily Stepanov would sell his mother for the right price."

"Use him, then. If he doesn't already know it, tell him that Mr. Jenkins is on the president's kill list, which will make Mr. Jenkins considerably more valuable. Leak also that Velikaya's men have captured Maria Kulikova."

Federov was playing a hunch. At the railway station, Alexander Zhomov had every opportunity to shoot and kill Charles Jenkins. He knew Zhomov had been a sniper in Afghanistan as well as when called upon by the government. He could have positioned himself in the parking lot or the rail terminal, or on the hillside above it, but he had not done so. That told Federov that Zhomov didn't want Jenkins dead. His job was to bring him back alive, likely for the very reason Maria Kulikova had said. Jenkins was worth more to Sokalov alive than dead. He was Sokalov's potential ticket to the Kremlin and, if Kulikova's betrayal ever came to light, Jenkins might be the chit that kept Sokalov alive despite his having divulged classified information.

Irony was such a powerful tool. Federov would use Sokalov's penchant for self-survival to likely get him killed. If he could pull this off.

"Won't that lure Sokalov to wherever Mr. Jenkins is being held captive?" Kulikova asked.

"One can only hope," Federov said.

49

Lubyanka
Moscow, Russia

Sokalov sat at the conference room table, the cat about to swallow the canary, but only after chewing on him and breaking every bone in his body. Lebedev and Pasternak took seats across the table. Petrov stood at the head. Minutes before entering the room, Sokalov had hung up the phone with Alexander Zhomov, who had spoken directly with their contact at the Ministry of Internal Affairs. He had it on good authority that Mr. Jenkins had been taken by Yekaterina Velikaya's men from the Irkutsk train station to a slaughterhouse on the shores of the Ushakovka River. He said the men had also succeeded in capturing Maria Kulikova. Zhomov told Sokalov he was en route to the slaughterhouse and would kill Velikaya's men and, if she was present, Kulikova. He would bring back Jenkins alive.

All of which meant this was working out better than Sokalov had hoped for. Within hours he would hobble the most powerful crime family in Moscow, kill the woman who could ruin him, and solve the president's more pressing issue: how to get back the two would-be assassins and save face on a world stage. In return, the president would direct Petrov to name Sokalov his successor as chairman of the National

Antiterrorist Committee, whereupon Sokalov's first order of business would be to fire Gavril Lebedev.

The purpose of this meeting was to discuss the options each man had come up with to get back Pasternak's two unsuccessful assassins, and by default, identify whose head would roll. American intelligence still refuted any suggestion they held Pasternak's men, which left hope the CIA would be open to negotiations, once advised Russia held Mr. Jenkins.

"I am told this matter is now well up the Kremlin chain of command," Petrov said gravely. He sucked on a cigarette and laid the butt in the ashtray. "Our diplomats have been of little help. They are like young men with their first woman, feeling around the edges to determine how she will respond, and so far the Americans have been cold and uninterested."

"Why have the Americans not responded?" Lebedev asked rhetorically. "This information would go a long way toward impugning the Kremlin, and this type of opportunity does not come around very often."

"Perhaps they are doing so because they hope to negotiate for something important, but do not yet know what that is," Sokalov said. "In which case our time would be better spent undermining whatever it is they are seeking to do by eliminating the potential the Americans have to embarrass us all on a world stage."

"I believe we should take a different tack, an offensive tack," Pasternak said, speaking like a true general.

"Which is what?" Petrov asked.

"The Kremlin can publicly accuse the Americans of improperly detaining two Russian citizens, claim the weapons allegedly confiscated were planted, and demand that the Americans either release my men or provide solid evidence to support their allegations," Pasternak said. "By making a bold first statement, we have the opportunity to direct the flow of information and plant the seed that this is nothing more than

American hypocrisy, another attempt to impugn the Kremlin. We can then disavow any information the Americans release as false or misleading and designed to spin world opinion in their favor."

"A bold plan, General," Petrov said. "You would be poking the hornet's nest with a stick and hoping not to get stung. We cannot be that naïve, Kliment. The Americans have more than enough evidence to do significant damage to Russia's reputation."

"Has anyone determined the source of the leak that led to the men's capture?" Lebedev looked directly across the table at Sokalov.

Sokalov smiled. "Do you have some evidence that something untoward has occurred in my directorate, Gavril?"

"I've heard that Ms. Kulikova has not been in the office for several days," Lebedev said.

"Yes, that is true, but it is certainly no mystery," Sokalov said directly to Petrov, deliberately dismissing Lebedev. "Ms. Kulikova is having female issues. I have sent someone, in an abundance of caution, to her apartment to ensure her well-being. I am told she is contemplating a hysterectomy."

"Then let us hope her recovery is speedy so she can come back to Lubyanka," Lebedev said, dripping sarcasm. "How ever are you managing without her?"

"Perhaps," Sokalov said, "your time would be better spent directing your division's attention to finding a solution, rather than casting aspersions, Gavril. That is, after all, what the chairman asked of us."

"And do you have something?" Lebedev asked, falling directly into Sokalov's trap.

"As a matter of fact, I do," he said, and again directed his attention to Petrov. "My office is currently monitoring classified communications that indicate we just may obtain something the Americans would consider valuable enough to trade for the general's two men and keep this matter strictly confidential."

"And what is that?" Petrov asked.

"Not what, but who," Sokalov said, now the cat playing the three mice. "Charles Jenkins."

For a moment the announcement was met with silence. Lebedev looked like he had deflated.

"He has returned?" Petrov asked.

"It appears so," Sokalov said, empowered by the information. "My office has worked diligently, as you asked, Director Petrov, to find a solution the Kremlin can use. The task force formed under my command to identify and capture any remaining American assets known as the seven sisters has picked up communications through an encrypted chat room that indicate Mr. Jenkins is in Russia."

"Why was my office not made aware of this development?" Petrov asked.

"With all due respect, Director, I believed it wise to keep knowledge of this development to a limited few within my department to ensure the proper management and dissemination of the information. My intent was to provide you with a complete debriefing when Mr. Jenkins was in hand."

"Mr. Jenkins has been in Russia twice before . . . that we know of," Lebedev said, puffing air back into his deflated torso and looking to Petrov for support. "And he escaped. Russia is a large country. Knowing he is here and capturing him are two different things."

"Yes. A good point, Gavril," Sokalov said. "But I have it on very good and reliable authority that Mr. Jenkins has been traced to Irkutsk, that we have eyes on him, and that his capture could be imminent."

"Do you wish to provide us the specific details of this operation?" Lebedev asked, not sounding convinced.

"I would. But as you said, Gavril, we seem to have a leak in the chain of information, and I am concerned that leak could result in someone tipping off Mr. Jenkins and result in his fleeing at this very critical time. In the interest of protecting the president, and those within the Kremlin, as well as the chairman, I opted to handle this matter internally."

Lebedev looked as if he was chewing on a piece of bitter leather.

"When will you have information on Mr. Jenkins's capture?" Petrov asked.

Sokalov made a showing of checking his watch. "Within the hour, I would say. I will monitor the situation closely and advise you when it has been accomplished."

"Do so," Petrov said.

With that, they moved toward the conference room doors. "But understand, Dmitry," Petrov said, drawing their attention. He wore a thin, malevolent smile. "That your decision to act alone means that you alone will receive the Kremlin's praise and gratitude when the operation succeeds, perhaps even this very position as chairman."

Sokalov deflected the praise. "I do not wish—"

Petrov cut him off. "And you and you alone will suffer the Kremlin's wrath and castigation if you fail."

50

Irkutsk Meatpacking Plant
Irkutsk, Russia

Alexander Zhomov found the Irkutsk Meatpacking Plant in an industrial area of the city, across the Ushakovka River. A U-shaped building, it had loading bays perpendicular to the water and a butcher shop
accessed from the street that sold fresh meat to the public. Zhomov
dismissed the butcher shop as a likely holding place of Charles Jenkins
and Maria Kulikova and focused on the two building wings. A quick
surveillance revealed the black car into which Charles Jenkins had been
forced, which was now parked outside a bay door alongside the car that
had taken Kulikova away from the train station.

Zhomov sat in his car and studied a 3D exterior layout of the
building he accessed from his laptop. To the east of the slaughterhouse
was a mall. To the west, a vacant lot with grazing cattle and sheep. A
stockyard. The stockyard included electrical towers with lines extending
to the building. On the back side of the building facing the stockyard
were two-story high windows, some boarded over. At the end of the
building was a metal staircase ascending to second-story doors. Neither
was an option. He would be too exposed.

Zhomov had called Sokalov and asked for the interior layout of the
building so he could determine the best location to have maximum and

efficient firing power. He would have no trouble quickly killing six men, which was the number he counted at the Irkutsk train terminal—the two who got out of the car, the driver, and Mily Karlov, plus the two with Kulikova. If Yekaterina had come to face the man who killed her son—and that seemed likely given her temperament and because the men had not flown Jenkins back to Moscow—Zhomov would kill her also and cut off the head of the most powerful crime family in Moscow, with no waiting successor.

But first things first.

Zhomov studied the interior of the slaughterhouse while watching the exterior happenings. Even from a distance he could smell the stockyard and the slaughterhouse—the odor of manure, blood, and chemicals.

He observed men in blood-splattered white coats, hairnets, safety goggles, and white hard hats entering and exiting the loading bays to have a smoke and was glad for the diversion the men would provide. The second key was to look like he belonged. That's where the layout came in. The stockyard led to the lairage, where cattle and sheep rested after transportation. He knew you did not want to kill a highly stressed animal. The hormones ruined the meat. From the lairage a corridor led to various rooms where the animals were stunned, killed, hung on hooks, eviscerated, and bled. Workers skinned their hides and dissected their carcasses. Their heads and hooves were sent by conveyor belts to specific rooms, and the hanging carcasses were transported to a room where the meat could be inspected. From there the conveyor-belt hooks transported the hanging carcasses into the long slaughter hall and, after slaughter, to the chilling and deboning rooms, and ultimately to cold storage.

Zhomov found what he was looking for just off the utility block. Male changing rooms with lockers and disinfecting stations. He would need to move with a sense of purpose, a sense of belonging.

With the layout memorized, Zhomov concluded there was no good place to lie in wait and snipe the men. He also could not think of a way to easily get his rifle into the building, even if he disassembled it and reassembled it once inside. He decided instead to rely on his Makarov pistol, which was deadly accurate and held a magazine of twelve bullets. He could bring additional magazines in a backpack, though he didn't anticipate having to use them.

Zhomov drove to the building and parked in what appeared to be the employee parking lot. He grabbed a backpack from the back seat of the car, tugged a cap low on his head, and walked toward the employee entrance. He was counting on there being no security presence. Who, after all, would want to walk into a slaughterhouse if not required to do so? If there was security, he would state that he was newly hired and looking for the office to complete his paperwork.

He pushed through a swinging door and continued down a corridor. No security. A few men dressed in white coats, hard hats, and safety goggles moved about the floor. What appeared to be a skeleton crew. Zhomov found his way to the employee locker room. He moved from locker to locker, finding most, but not all, padlocked. Odd. He moved toward the showers and found what he was looking for—spent coats, face shields, and goggles, presumably discarded from an earlier shift. He quickly put them on and found a hard hat above a row of lockers. In a bathroom stall he removed the pistol, chambered a round, put a second magazine in the pocket of his jacket, straightened his protective goggles, and walked out.

Just being in the slaughterhouse gave him the thrill of the kill.

Zhomov continued down an empty corridor toward the entrance to the slaughter hall. The corridor was also surprisingly devoid of employees. It gave Zhomov pause, but he dismissed it when, through a thick glass panel in a swinging door, he saw a black SUV inside the slaughter hall. To its side, Charles Jenkins hung by his wrists from one of the meat hooks alongside slabs of beef on a conveyor belt. Jenkins did not look good, his face a bloody pulp, a puddle of blood and sweat beneath him. The Velikayas would indeed kill him, if they had not already done so. Zhomov saw three men near Jenkins. Standing among them, Yekaterina Velikaya and her bodyguard.

He would kill her first.

Zhomov removed the pistol from beneath the white coat, stepped toward the door, and pushed it inward. "Like father, like daughter," he said.

Zhomov felt himself becoming weightless, the door and the floor pulling away from him. "What the hell?" he said.

He had been picked up and hurled backward, into the concrete wall. The hat dislodged from his head and the gun slipped from his hand, both clattering across the floor. Zhomov had the presence of mind to lunge for his weapon, but a boot struck his back and pinned him against the ground. Hands gripped his wrists, pulled his arms behind his back, and quickly applied zip ties. Duct tape was wrapped around his mouth and the back of his head, and a harness was fitted around his torso. Then he was again suspended in air, this time hung from one of the empty hooks, his shoes two feet off the ground.

A setup. An elaborate setup. But who?

The man who had lifted him so readily wore a white coat and hard hat. He was as big as one of the slabs of meat. A second man, familiar somehow, stepped forward dressed in an expensive suit and tie. It took Zhomov a moment to place the face, one he had not seen in several years.

His eyes widened with recognition and confusion. He had seen the face at Lubyanka.

"I see you remember me, Colonel Zhomov. I am flattered," Viktor Federov said. "And I am delighted that you have decided to hang around to see how this all turns out. No pun intended, of course."

51

Irkutsk Meatpacking Plant
Irkutsk, Russia

Yekaterina Velikaya considered Charles Jenkins, battered and beaten, but not yet broken. Remarkable. Most men caved at just the thought of enduring such pain. Those who considered themselves tough enough gave in after less than half the beating Jenkins had endured. It had convinced her that Jenkins had not been part of any CIA operation to kill her son, but rather had simply been in the wrong place at the wrong time. It did not change the outcome, though. Because Jenkins had chosen to become involved, Eldar was dead. Jenkins might not have been the bullet, but he had been the gun. The former could not be deadly without the latter.

Under other circumstances she would have offered a man with such fortitude a job. Men with such conviction, such unquestioned belief in their principles, were rare and became more so with each passing year. But Yekaterina had no further use for him. He would not tell them Maria Kulikova's whereabouts, or he did not know. If the former, he was the toughest son of a bitch she had ever encountered. It didn't really matter.

She stepped away, again checking her watch. She needed to leave. They needed to find Maria Kulikova some other way.

"Do you know what they do with the scraps of meat and the sides of beef they do not sell, Mr. Jenkins?" she asked.

"I can guess," he said.

"Yes. I'm sure you can. But let me tell you. They grind the unwanted pieces into hamburger and sausage. Have you ever seen a slab of meat go through the meat grinder, Mr. Jenkins? No? The grinder crushes everything—the bones, the cartilage, the tendons, the muscle, the fat. Of course, the cow is already dead. It feels no pain." She turned and considered him, eyes as blue and cold as ice. "You will not be so fortunate."

Jenkins smiled at her, but without a hint of arrogance or defiance. He smiled as if he knew her pain, and he was sorry for it. Then he said, "Nor will be the person who gets a sausage made out of me."

A joke.

It almost brought a smile to her face. Almost.

Yekaterina turned and addressed Mily before she lost her nerve. "Advise me when this is finished. I will meet you at the plane." She did not want to stay and watch. She'd learned long ago, when her father had died, that vengeance did not bring satisfaction. It didn't even temper the pain of death. It would not temper the pain of Eldar's death. It only let others know that killings would come at a heavy cost. Retribution. An eye for an eye.

Heavy is the head that must wear the crown, she recalled her father saying.

"Something else, Comare?" Mily asked.

She thought of Jenkins's family, of his wife whom she would make a widow, and his two children who would grow up without a father. What was worse, she wondered, to grow up without a father or to grow old without a child? She thought the latter, if only because it was against the natural order. "No," she said.

She climbed into the back seat of the SUV and took one last glance at Jenkins. She could not help but think he looked Christlike, hanging dead on the cross, arms straining from the weight of his body, no longer able to hold himself upright. Her driver started the car and dropped the engine into drive, moving across the finished concrete floor toward one of the rolled-up bay doors. The driver slowed. Then he stopped, causing her to look up from her thoughts. "What is the problem?" she asked.

"I don't know. A worker just rolled the bay door shut and has padlocked it."

"What?" She leaned forward to look through the windshield. The worker disappeared behind strips of plastic. "Try another bay."

Her driver did as she instructed. Again, as the car approached the bay, a worker rolled the door closed and padlocked it. Once was chance. Twice was coincidence. She pointed to a third bay, but before she could get the words out, the door rolled shut. Three times is a pattern.

All around the warehouse she heard the bay doors rolling shut, slamming when they hit the ground.

The lights to the building dimmed, everything now cast in the red glow of the emergency lights near the exits.

The driver put the car in reverse and hit the gas, tires spinning on slick concrete, smoke filling the air. He swung around and returned to Mily and the other men, who had pulled automatic assault rifles and stood back-to-back.

Yekaterina stepped from the car. Her bodyguard moved to shield her.

"What is happening?" she asked Mily.

"I do not know, Comare."

She looked around the room. The men who had locked the bay doors had vanished; there was nothing but the slabs of meat hanging from the hooks.

A metal door opened, then shut, the sound echoing. A man's dress shoes clicked against the concrete floor. He emerged from between the hanging carcasses, bathed in the red light, like a ghostly apparition. He did not rush. He walked deliberately across the hall. As he neared, she saw he wore a suit, an expensive brand, and carried something beneath one arm. The driver aimed his weapon, as did Mily and the other guards.

The man stopped a few meters from the group, opened a chair, and set it down across from the folding chair already there. He held open his coat to show he was not armed. Then he offered Yekaterina a seat.

She did not know this man. They had never met. He was not the head of one of the other families, certainly not in Moscow. She doubted he ran a family in Irkutsk. She would have known.

This man, whoever he was, had a quiet confidence about him. His face wore a thin, but not smug, smile. Unlike other men he also did not rush to speak. He waited, politely, for Yekaterina to sit.

Curious, she did so.

—

Viktor Federov unbuttoned his suit jacket and crossed his legs. For this to work, he had to project an air of confidence. If not, he'd be riddled with bullets. Plato Vasin had made it clear he did not want a war with the Velikayas, and Federov had given him his word he would not provoke one.

"My apologies for the theatrics, Ms. Velikaya. When you have a child in the theater, you become attentive to making a favorable impression upon entry and exit." One of the guards stepped toward him. Federov stopped him with a cold gaze. "I can assure you that will not be necessary. I'm unarmed."

Yekaterina waved the guard to step back but kept her gaze on Federov. Good. She was curious. That was the first step if this was going to work. "Who are you?" she asked.

"Allow me to introduce myself. I am Federov, Viktor Nikolayevich."

She stared at him as if waiting for more. When Federov added nothing she asked, "Is that name supposed to mean something to me, Federov, Viktor Nikolayevich?"

"No. No, I'm sure a woman of your stature has no idea who I am. But you do know my friend."

"And who is your friend?"

Federov nodded to Charles Jenkins. "I see you two have met. Intimately, one might say. Nice of you to hang around, Charlie."

"Fuck you, Viktor," Jenkins whispered.

Federov gave a small shrug. "He gets angry when he isn't fed."

"What is it you want, Mr. Federov?"

"I have a problem."

"Yes, you do. Do you know who I am?"

"Certainly. You are Yekaterina Velikaya, the most powerful woman in Moscow."

It was her turn to smile. "You flatter me, Mr. Federov. Yet, you hold me captive against my will."

"As I said, I apologize for the dramatics. My daughter is an actress, so perhaps theatrics runs in our veins."

"Or stupidity."

Federov smiled. "No. Stupidity is only me. My daughters are very bright. They take after their mother." He uncrossed his legs. "I needed to make an entrance to capture your attention."

"And so you have."

He nodded. Beneath the borrowed suit he was sweating bullets, but he continued to project serenity, as if he were in charge. Maybe he had missed his calling and should have pursued theatrics, like his daughter. "Thank you. You see, Ms. Velikaya—"

"Call me Yekaterina, Mr. Federov. Your stunt here has earned you that right. It might, however, be your last."

"And you will call me Viktor. You see, Yekaterina, I am being paid a significant sum of money to get Mr. Jenkins out of Russia, and I will not be paid unless and until I do so. So you can understand my dilemma."

"No. I fail to see how your dilemma is of any concern to me."

"Another problem," Federov said. "No doubt."

"No doubt. So unless you would like to be hanging on a hook beside Mr. Jenkins, I would suggest you walk out of here while you still have two legs to carry you, and tell whoever locked the bay doors to open them. Or I will make you my problem. Do we understand one another?"

"Indeed. It is a fair proposal," Federov said. "May I counter?"

Yekaterina chuckled. "Why not?"

Federov put a hand in the air and twirled his finger. The sound of machine guns being racked echoed all around the warehouse, and no less than fifty men in white coats and white hard hats stepped out from behind the hanging slabs of meat, each bathed in the red light. Federov waited a beat, and this time it was indeed theatrical. Mily and the other bodyguards raised their weapons, but it was a ridiculous response.

"Here is my proposal. You wish to be vindicated for the loss of your son, so much so that you would kill an innocent man."

"How do you know he is innocent?"

"Because I know all the evidence."

"Which is what?"

"I could tell you, and you would think I was lying, no?"

"Probably."

"Then would you indulge me and allow my associate, someone who knows firsthand what happened, to tell you the evidence?"

Yekaterina nodded.

Federov remained seated but waved behind him. The door from which he had entered opened. Arkhip Mishkin stepped into the warehouse and crossed the floor. He also carried a folding chair. His shoes clicked on the concrete as he approached. Velikaya's men again raised their weapons.

When he arrived, Mishkin bowed slightly to Yekaterina. "My name is Arkhip Mishkin."

"Chief investigator," Mily said.

"Yes," Mishkin said. "May I first offer my condolences to you and your family on the loss of your son. I had hoped to do so in person earlier but was unable to secure an interview."

Another nod from Yekaterina. Then her eyes shifted to Federov—even more curious.

Mishkin unfolded his chair and sat. "It is my job to close the case involving the death of your son, Ms. Velikaya. And I will need Mr. Jenkins's testimony to do that. In my career, I have never not closed a case. I have been one hundred percent successful."

Yekaterina looked puzzled. "And that is why you are here?"

Mishkin did not immediately answer. After the pause, he said, "It must seem strange to you, a chief inspector here in this position. My circumstances have changed in the past few days, but not my desire."

"And what is your desire?"

"Justice," he said.

"Tell me what it is that you know, Chief Investigator."

Mishkin sighed. "Since my wife's death two years ago, I have had a heavy heart. I don't sleep well. For this reason, I told my captain to give me the murders that occur late at night, so that I might have something to do. Your son's murder is one of those cases."

Mishkin went through the evidence from the moment he arrived at the Yakimanka Bar until his arrival at the slaughterhouse. "You see, my notes and my personal observations make it clear that your son was shot in the back, not in the front, and that Mr. Jenkins did not kill him."

Yekaterina, whom Federov assumed already knew this information from viewing the CCTV footage, did not look impressed. "That is all very interesting, Chief Investigator, but the fact remains my son is dead because Mr. Jenkins stuck his nose in a place where it never belonged."

"Or perhaps he stuck his nose in a place exactly where it did belong, but where few men have the courage to do so. We can debate this for many hours, I am sure. But let me ask you a simple question, if I may? Do you sleep at night, Ms. Velikaya?"

"What business is that of yours?"

"None. I ask only because I want to ask next whether you have obtained any satisfaction from the beating and the torture of Mr. Jenkins. Do you believe it will help you to sleep at night?"

"What is your point, Chief Investigator?"

"Perhaps I can answer," Federov said. "You will not sleep because you know it would be a hollow victory to kill a man who did not kill your son, and you would get no satisfaction from this. It would not alleviate your grief or your pain. You know this because you have been through this before, have you not?" She did not answer, but Federov knew she understood. "The unresolved death of your father in 2008."

"It is only unresolved to the general public."

An answer that gave Federov hope. "Yes. So my point . . . Kill Mr. Jenkins and you will still have to live with the pain of your son's death, just as you have had to live with the pain of your father's death, without any recourse against the men responsible."

"I am tiring of this game. What is it that you are offering me, Federov? You said you had a counterproposal. Make it or unlock the bay doors."

"I am offering you the chance to right a wrong, something very rare in these times. I am offering you the chance at more than a hollow act. I am offering the chance to once again sleep soundly at night."

"And how will you do that?"

Federov again raised his hand. This time the slabs of meat hanging all around them quivered and shook, then moved along the conveyor belt. The slabs came to a right turn and each piece of meat spun, nearly 180 degrees, just behind Federov's shoulder. From around that far corner of the room came a man hanging from a hook, with his back to the circle as he proceeded around the track. When he reached the right turn, he spun and faced them.

The blood drained from Yekaterina's face. "Zhomov," she said, her voice barely above a whisper.

"The man who shot your father," Federov said.

She waited a beat, staring at Zhomov, her eyes emitting pure hatred. She looked to Federov. "You can prove this?" Yekaterina said. "Without doubt?"

"I not only know of the operation, Yekaterina, but I was a member of the task force. I can say with certainty that Alexander Zhomov shot your father. But my counterproposal includes more."

She gave him a quizzical look.

"I am not just offering you the man who killed your father in exchange for Mr. Jenkins. No. I am offering you the man who ordered your father's assassination."

"You are going to produce Dmitry Sokalov? I doubt it."

Federov raised his hand and again circled his finger. The door from which both he and Mishkin arrived clicked open. This time, Maria Kulikova stepped through and approached. Kulikova knew much about Yekaterina Velikaya from her years working with Sokalov at the FSB, including the operation that had led to the assassination of Alexei Velikaya. As she and Federov had discussed, the trick would be to get Yekaterina to trust that Kulikova could essentially deliver Sokalov—not physically, certainly, but in a manner that would destroy him.

Kulikova stopped alongside Mishkin. "I am told that your father was a fan of the *Godfather* movies, that he ran his family based upon the fictional Corleone family," she said.

Yekaterina's eyes narrowed. "This is true."

"Then I believe, Ms. Velikaya, that I can make you an offer you can't refuse."

52

Irkutsk Meatpacking Plant
Irkutsk, Russia

Jenkins didn't know how long he'd been suspended from the meat hook. He'd lost all sense of time, certain he had passed out more than once, his only reprieve from the pain. After awakening a second such time, he decided it best not to focus on the present, on each blow, each prick, each electric shock. It was better if he let them blend together, let time pass unimpeded as he got closer to the end. His punishers had hit him like well-trained prizefighters, attacking the body first to weaken his will. When that didn't cause him to provide information, they had moved to his face. The beating had stopped long enough for Yekaterina Velikaya to interrogate him, but the pain, the excruciating pain, continued. He had thoughts of Alex, and of Lizzie and CJ. He'd wished he'd taken the time to have the talk with his son, to better prepare him for what was to come, being a large Black man in America.

He saw Maria Kulikova enter the warehouse and cursed silently, wondering what game Federov was up to. Maria looked calm, relaxed. She nodded to him, as if to let him know everything would be all right. When he heard Federov tell Velikaya that Maria could provide Dmitry Sokalov, things began to fall into place.

Before Maria spoke, however, Federov requested that Yekaterina remove Jenkins from the meat hook, which he called a sign of good faith. She had agreed. One of Federov's men, a behemoth Charlie's height but as thick as a redwood tree, lifted Jenkins from the hook as if lifting a child, Jenkins grimacing in pain, and gently sat him in a chair.

"Spasibo," Jenkins said, struggling to catch his breath. He could barely sit upright. His rib cage burned as if someone had lit it with an acetylene torch. The question wasn't whether he had fractured ribs, but how many. He hoped one of those cracked ribs hadn't also collapsed a lung. He labored for each breath, but mainly from the excruciating pain. He had spit out more than one tooth, and now his tongue traced the jagged remains of several others. He couldn't breathe through his nose, a clear sign it had been broken; so, too, was the crunch of cartilage when the men struck him. It sickened him. He didn't want to look in a mirror.

Maria faced Yekaterina Velikaya and provided the intimate details of her relationship with Dmitry Sokalov. She did so as if reciting some bizarre sexual behavior that she had observed, not that she had participated in. Her voice remained soft and even-keeled, rarely rising in volume or displaying any emotion. Jenkins thought that must have been how she had survived all these years, by not allowing herself to become emotionally attached to Sokalov's demented fetishes. Instead, Maria had created, in a sense, an alter ego—perhaps that person who stares back at us in the mirror; that person who looks like us but lacks depth, morals, and ethics. In addition to the details, she assured Velikaya that she had many locations in Moscow where she had stashed photographs of Sokalov in various compromising stages.

Jenkins had the sense that Yekaterina Velikaya understood Maria Kulikova on a level the men in that room could never understand, that she understood Maria had done what she had done to accomplish what needed to be accomplished, that she had done her duty, without any emotional investment or attachment. She understood because,

Jenkins speculated, Velikaya had done exactly the same thing to survive for so long in a man's domain. When her father had been murdered, Yekaterina had been thrust into the role of head of the family, and Jenkins suspected she did what she had to do to preserve what her father had worked so hard to achieve. She met grisly violence with more grisly violence, and deadly force with more deadly force. Jenkins wondered if she, too, had created an alter ego—if Catherine the Great was that mirror image—but that she had never truly believed she was anything more than her father's *Malen'kaya Printsessa*. Jenkins met a movie star once at a charity auction in downtown Seattle, an A-list actor making $20 million a film. But that wasn't what drew him to the man. What had drawn him was the man's quiet intimacy and his humility. When asked, he told Jenkins acting was simply his job. A well-paying job, for sure, but still just a job. The job did not define him. He did not believe the accolades heaped upon him any more than he believed the assaults that ripped at the characters he portrayed, because it was just that—a character created to play a role in a film. It was not him.

When Maria finished, neither woman moved. No one spoke. A good minute passed. Then Velikaya stood. Maria followed. The two women stared at one another for a moment before Velikaya stepped forward and the two women exchanged a kiss on each cheek in a mutual sign of respect.

Velikaya looked to Federov and, without emotion, said simply, "I accept your counterproposal." Then she stepped toward Alexander Zhomov and considered him. "Do you know what they do with the scraps of meat and the sides of beef they do not sell?"

His mouth duct-taped closed, Zhomov could not answer.

"Let me tell you," she said.

—

After Velikaya and her men had left the hall, Jenkins said to Federov, "I'm assuming Matt Lemore got in touch with you?"

Federov let out a long sigh. "It seems that you are . . . how do you Americans say it?" He looked to the behemoth whom he called Peanut. *"Zhvachka na podoshve moyego botinka."*

"The gum on the bottom of my shoe?" Jenkins translated.

Peanut laughed.

"Did Lemore threaten you?" Jenkins asked.

Federov chuckled. "Let's just say he made the ramifications very clear if I failed to come forward and be of assistance. Your Mr. Lemore has a fondness for you. He can be very persuasive."

"I think he has a greater fear of my wife than a fondness for me," Jenkins said. "He made her a promise once that he would bring me home safely, and she made it very clear she expected him to keep that promise, and that there would be hell to pay if he fell short."

"Having been married, I can understand his motivation." Federov looked to Maria. "No offense intended to the present company."

Jenkins knew Federov could just as easily have walked away and not taken the significant risk of returning to Russia. He knew Federov didn't do it just for the money, or even the chance to spit in Sokalov's eye. His reasons also weren't completely altruistic. He was a complicated man. Jenkins was sure his reasons were just as complicated.

It didn't really matter.

"Thank you, Viktor, for what you did. I owe you."

"Do not be naïve, Charlie. As you may recall, I am a very good chess player."

"Da, no tvoy blef—der'mo," Peanut said. *Yes, but your bluffing is shit.*

"Nevertheless," Federov said. "Mr. Lemore and I negotiated a healthy donation to my retirement fund. It seems that saving you is a lucrative side business for me. But yes, indeed, you do owe me, and someday I intend to collect."

Jenkins knew Federov was just protecting his image. No doubt Lemore had threatened to expose Federov, but only to get him to the negotiating table. Russian men were steadfastly proud. They did not like to have their character, or their courage, impugned or insulted. Lemore, who had studied Russia in college and made the country his life's work, undoubtedly knew this. After the threat, he would have negotiated a payment amount to allow Federov to save face, and Federov had gladly accepted the money. But knowing Federov, Jenkins also knew he could not be so easily manipulated. His motivation for his actions went much deeper than dollars or rubles.

Simply put, Viktor Federov liked to win.

"I think, maybe you and I would work well together," Federov said. "In the future, perhaps."

Jenkins smiled. "Is that a threat, Viktor?"

"We are the same, you and I."

"How do you figure?"

"Why did you step in to help the prostitute in the Yakimanka Bar? You had to know it was the wrong thing to do, professionally."

"My head hurts too much for a deep conversation right now, Viktor."

"Very well. We will have this discussion on another occasion. Perhaps one in which I can meet this wife of yours. She seems, how should I say, to have a bull head."

Jenkins laughed and grabbed his side. When the pain eased, he said, "I'll be sure not to tell her that." He grimaced and looked to Maria. "Sokalov is in for one hell of a surprise."

She looked at Federov. *"Khotel by ya byt' mukhoy na stene doma Vasina."* *I wish I could be like one of the flies on Vasin's walls.*

Jenkins shook his head. "I don't understand."

Federov chuckled. "You will. Soon enough. We'll get you a doctor and let you rest for a few days before you travel . . . depending, of course, upon your condition."

"I think it best if Maria and I get out of Russia as quickly as possible," Jenkins said.

"Nonsense," Federov said. "To do so would be an insult to your host. Where I am taking you, no one would dare to follow. You will be in the good graces of Plato Vasin. You have already met his brother, my friend Peanut, and other men who work for him." Federov made a sweeping gesture with his hand to the others in the room.

Peanut looked down at Jenkins.

"Peanut?" Jenkins said to Federov. "I'm having a hard time picturing him as small."

"Peanut was never small. I suspect, like you, he was born big and just kept growing, always the biggest in our class."

Jenkins looked up at the man. "*Spasibo,*" he said.

Peanut smiled and spoke English. "You're welcome." He helped Jenkins to his feet, but they were stopped by the small man standing to the side. He stepped forward, speaking to the room.

"Excuse me," he said politely. "If everyone is done getting reacquainted . . ."

Federov stood. "A private conversation," he said. "Everyone clear the room but for Mr. Jenkins and my associate."

"I wish to stay," Maria said, holding a blanket around Jenkins's shoulders.

"Very well," Federov said, and everyone else left the room.

"Mr. Jenkins, my name is Arkhip Mishkin, chief investigator with the Moscow police." He paused as if unsure. Then he shrugged. "Good day. I recognize that you are in pain, but I have come a long way to ask you a few questions and would request your indulgence for just a bit longer." Jenkins was amazed that a Moscow investigator was present in a room filled with mafiya. "I need to know what happened the night Eldar Velikaya died in the Yakimanka Bar."

"You told Yekaterina Velikaya what happened."

"Yes," he said. "I did. But, you see, the videotape from the CCTV cameras has gone missing, the medical examiner's report is a fabrication, and every other witness is deceased. You are the only person remaining who can tell me the truth, so that I may close my file, my last file before I retire. I believe your testimony will contradict official reports and perhaps cost a few jobs."

Mishkin did not look happy at the prospect.

"That's your only motivation for being here?"

Mishkin looked at Maria Kulikova. "It was," he said.

Jenkins looked to Maria, then to Mishkin, and understood. "What is it you would like to know, Chief Investigator?" Jenkins asked.

"Only the truth."

Jenkins waited a beat. "Did you want to record our conversation?"

"Absolutely," Mishkin said. The chief investigator moved his hands, then stopped. "I'm afraid I don't have my notebook or an instrument to write with."

"One moment," Maria said, and she left for the door across the hall.

"Maria left the cabin at night on the train. Did she speak with you?" Jenkins asked.

"It seems neither of us sleep well," Mishkin said.

Maria returned with a pen and a pad of paper with "Irkutsk Meatpacking Plant" across the top. "This will do," Mishkin said. "Thank you." He looked to Jenkins. "Please. Begin."

Arkhip Mishkin put pen to paper as Jenkins patiently answered Mishkin's questions. When they had finished, Mishkin clicked the pen. He looked to Maria. "I will make my way back to Moscow. I do apologize again for not telling you who I was, but I hope that you can understand." He bowed slightly and turned to walk away. Maria's question stopped him.

"Do you travel, Arkhip?" Maria asked.

He shook his head. "I have never had the time. I was always working. Now . . ." He sighed. "It is one of my regrets. My Lada and I discussed trips many times that we would take when I had retired."

"Like the Trans-Siberian Railway?"

"Yes. That was one."

"Did you enjoy it?"

"I did," he said. "I enjoyed our evenings on the train, Maria. I enjoyed your company very much."

"Then it was a success. You said, if so, you might travel again."

Mishkin nodded. "I did. And I hope to."

"Have you ever had a desire to see the United States, Arkhip?"

Mishkin smiled. "Indeed. It, too, is on my long bucket list. I would like to see the national parks. The Grand Canyon, I think."

"As would I," Maria said.

Jenkins was in no position to make either a promise that they would be reunited. After weeks of debriefing, Maria would be given a new name, a new identity, possibly plastic surgery, and a new life. As long as Putin remained in power, her life would be in danger. Could the CIA find a way for Mishkin to meet with her? Mishkin had nothing to do with Sokalov or the FSB, and the FSB would know nothing of this budding relationship between Mishkin and Maria. Jenkins imagined that once Mishkin retired he could take a trip to the United States without garnering any FSB attention and, upon his arrival, arrangements could be made for him to visit Maria without giving away her whereabouts.

Mishkin bowed and gave a nod of his head. "I have no doubt that a part of America, at least, would appeal to me."

53

Dmitry Sokalov arrived at Lubyanka early the following morning, nervous. At his wife's request, and his father-in-law's insistence, Sokalov had spent the night at home, and off his work cell phone.

When he did retrieve his phone, Alexander Zhomov had not called since he had called to request the layout of the Irkutsk Meatpacking Plant, and informed Sokalov that he would take out the men who had abducted Charles Jenkins. Chairman Petrov, on the other hand, had called repeatedly. Petrov had left messages that he was getting considerable pressure from the Kremlin—with whom he had shared Sokalov's news that Alexander Zhomov was on the verge of arresting Charles Jenkins. Sokalov tried to stall the chairman, and when he no longer could avoid the chairman's calls, he had Olga advise that he was ill. Petrov, in turn, sent a terse text message demanding that Sokalov meet with him in person the following morning to update him on Zhomov's efforts. Sokalov's calls to Zhomov's cell phone all night and morning had, however, passed directly to voice mail, and Zhomov had not responded to encrypted e-mails or texts.

Things at home had also not been pleasant. With Sokalov's mind elsewhere, he struggled to pay attention and to remain engaged with

Olga and the children. They had all eaten together, including his in-laws. His wife had cooked fresh sausage and fried potatoes, but the meal, like Zhomov's silence, had not sat well with him. He really did feel ill.

Sokalov hurried into his office and removed his coat, hanging it on the coat-tree. He went directly to his phone and called his secretary, whom he had asked to come in early. "Any word from Colonel Zhomov?"

"No, Deputy Director."

"Let me know immediately if he calls; do not hesitate to interrupt me."

"Yes, Deputy Director. You did receive two packages, however."

"Packages? When?"

"They were on my chair this morning, Deputy Director. A box and an internal envelope. The box passed internal protocols." Which meant it had been inspected to ensure it did not contain a bomb that could blow up Lubyanka. "Do you wish for me to bring them in?"

Sokalov debated this. He checked his watch. "Yes. Do so now before my meeting with the chairman."

"The chairman is here, Deputy Director."

The door to Sokalov's office opened and Chairman Petrov entered carrying a two-foot-square cardboard box and the orange internal envelope. Sokalov quickly rose from his chair and took both packages. "Chairman Petrov, you didn't need to do this."

Petrov waved him off. Sokalov set the box on the coffee table and took the internal envelope to his desk. Petrov sat in a chair across Sokalov's desk.

"Would you be more comfortable on the couch?" Sokalov asked.

"I do not intend to be long . . . I hope. You no longer answer your phone?"

"My wife," he said. "She insisted that I spend family time with her and the children."

Petrov waved this off too. "You said you would have information for me on your efforts to arrest Charles Jenkins. What is that information?"

Sokalov moved back to his desk chair. "Yes, Chairman. I am still awaiting word from Colonel Zhomov on the status of the operation. I'm sure he will be calling any moment to confirm his success."

"You have not heard from him?"

"Not this morning, no."

"What did he say when you last spoke with him?"

"That he had knowledge of Mr. Jenkins's whereabouts in Irkutsk and would move to bring him in—"

"But nothing since then?"

The telephone on Sokalov's desk rang. To Sokalov it was like the bell rung at the end of a round, saving a boxer about to be knocked out. "Excuse me," he said to Petrov. "I asked my secretary to interrupt me were Zhomov to call."

"What happened to Ms. Kulikova?" Petrov asked.

"Still not well. I am told she has gone into the hospital."

"Have your secretary give my secretary the details so that I might send over flowers."

Sokalov picked up the receiver. "Yes."

"Dmitry Sokalov. Deputy director of counterintelligence." It was a woman, but Sokalov did not want to indicate this to the chairman.

"Yes. What do you have to tell me?"

"Your assassin and I have finally had the chance to meet," the woman said. "I must tell you that I enjoyed this immensely."

"I don't understand," Sokalov said. Across the desk Petrov's bushy eyebrows inched together.

"But you do. You see, I know that Alexander Zhomov is responsible for the death of Alexei Velikaya, that he shot him in broad daylight, and you then blamed another mafiya family for the murder."

Sokalov felt his knees go weak. Perspiration ran in rivulets down the sides of his body beneath his shirt. He could no longer maintain the game. "Who is this?"

"You know who this is, Deputy Director Sokalov. Though we have never met in person, we are well acquainted. One would say that you have intimate knowledge of my family, and now I have intimate knowledge of you and your sick perversions."

"Maria?" he asked, though it did not sound like her.

Petrov sat forward.

"I'm disappointed," the woman said. "To be mistaken for the object of your perversions."

Desperate, he asked, "Where is Alexander Zhomov?"

Now Petrov looked concerned.

"Is he missing?" The woman asked. "I arranged for him to arrive at your home yesterday, and in your office early this morning."

Sokalov did not answer. His eyes drifted to the box on the coffee table.

"You seem uncertain," the woman said. "Did you not unwrap your gift? It has been freezer packed, but you wouldn't want it to spoil. It is compliments of my father, Alexei Velikaya. I am Yekaterina Velikaya. Catherine the Great. Remember my name, for what little time you have left. One last thing. Maria Kulikova sends her regards. Look for an internal office envelope."

Velikaya hung up.

Sokalov held the phone to his ear, listening to the dial tone. Fear enveloped him, making his joints weak. His hands shook and he shifted his gaze to the envelope, then to the package on the table.

"Dmitry?" Petrov said.

Sokalov pushed back his chair, stood unsteadily, and stumbled to the package. He studied the shipping label.

The Irkutsk Meatpacking Plant.

His knees weakened. His stomach roiled.

"What are you doing, Dmitry?"

"I'm sorry, Chairman Petrov. I am not feeling well. Could we meet later? I think it might be something I have eaten."

"Who was on the phone? Why did you ask about Alexander Zhomov? I need to know if he has been successful. The president expects an answer."

Sokalov felt like he was traveling through a tunnel, the chairman's voice soft and distant. He turned and looked at the man. "I hope to have one for you within the hour, Chairman Petrov. I'm sorry. I don't know any details, but I will find out and I will inform you."

Petrov let out a sigh and pushed out of his chair. "Do so, Dmitry. I am receiving pressure from the Kremlin about how best to respond to the Ibragimov situation. I do not wish to give them a false hope, nor will I take responsibility if Zhomov were to fail. I warned you. The fault will lie with you."

"I will get back to you as soon as I can." Sokalov ushered Petrov out the office door, then closed it behind him. He turned and looked to the box as if the contents were rabid and might bite him. He walked slowly to the table. The tape across the top of the box had already been sliced open, per protocol. Sokalov carefully pulled open the lid. Inside he found a Styrofoam cooler. Again, he did not rush to open it. He recalled seeing a similar cooler at his home, though he had been too preoccupied to ask where it came from. He removed the Styrofoam lid. Inside he found multiple links of sausage, like the ones Olga had served the prior evening. The links were shrink-wrapped, six to a pack, with labels also identifying the source of the meat as the Irkutsk Meatpacking Plant.

Sokalov lifted the first pack and found a second beneath it. He removed the second pack, then a third. He lifted the fourth pack from the box and dropped it as if it burned his hands. Inside, the pack, vacuum sealed, were a thumb and four fingers, the index finger bearing a ring Sokalov recognized as the ring worn by Russia's elite Spetsnaz forces.

Zhomov.

At the bottom of the box he found a handwritten message.

Alexei Velikaya sends his regards from the grave.

Sokalov bent and threw up the contents of his stomach into the cardboard box, retching several times. Rivulets of perspiration ran down the sides of his face and dampened the collar of his shirt. He ripped at the tie, lowering it, and undid the button of his shirt, struggling to breathe. He felt a chill.

Think.

He needed to think.

Zhomov was dead.

But what of Maria and Jenkins? Did Velikaya have them as well? Could he negotiate somehow? Could he tell Petrov that Jenkins had somehow escaped, that his efforts to capture him had been well taken but had failed? Jenkins had escaped twice before. The chairman would understand. Would the president?

He teetered to his desk like a man on the deck of a ship rocking in high seas, clutched his chair, and fell into it. He could still get out of this. He would need help, but . . . His father-in-law. He could go to his father-in-law, tell him of his efforts to bring Jenkins to justice. If his father-in-law understood . . .

For the good of his grandchildren . . .

And the reputation of his daughter.

Yes. That would work.

He could still get out of this. Sokalov looked across his desk to the interdepartmental envelope. His secretary said it had been on her chair with the box when she arrived at work this morning. Given the hour that he requested she arrive, it meant the envelope had to have been hand delivered to the office by someone the prior evening.

Sokalov picked up the envelope and looked at the routing lines, but the envelope was new and contained no names except his own.

He undid the red string wrapped around the button at the top of the envelope and opened the flap. From inside he pulled out dozens of photographs, all taken of him in various stages of bondage. He flipped through them, dropping them onto his desk one by one. A few missed and fluttered to the floor.

In each picture, a woman, Maria Kulikova, though her face was concealed by a leather mask, loomed over him. She wore six-inch spiked heels, and held chains, leather whips, feathers, hot wax, and other assorted gadgets.

The phone rang. Sokalov stared at the photographs. Numb.

Reality set in.

The phone rang again.

He pushed the button as if on remote control.

"Deputy Director. I'm sorry to interrupt, but you have another visitor. I explained that you were not feeling well but . . . He has insisted that he see you immediately."

"Who is it?" Sokalov asked.

"Your father-in-law."

Sokalov felt his stomach drop. The room spun. He fought the urge to again vomit.

"Deputy Director, he is adamant that I allow him in to see you," his secretary whispered, the panic his father-in-law could evoke clear in her voice.

Sokalov opened his desk drawer and removed the pistol, setting it on his desk. "Tell him I need just a moment," he said. He disconnected the call and stared at the pictures on his desk, knowing many more existed and that a similar packet had undoubtedly been delivered to his father-in-law.

Maria Kulikova. The source of so much pleasure, and so much pain.

He reached inside the packet, but it contained no note or letter from Maria as Yekaterina Velikaya had said.

He put the gun in his mouth and shut his eyes. Then he pulled the trigger.

The gun clicked but did not fire.

He opened his eyes and pulled the trigger a second, then a third time. The gun did not fire. He removed the gun from his mouth and released the clip. The bullets had been emptied. Along the side of the clip, firmly taped in place, was a note. He recognized Maria Kulikova's handwriting.

You always did enjoy pain.

54

Vasin Estate
Irkutsk, Russia

Jenkins and Maria Kulikova spent five days as guests of Plato Vasin on his estate in Irkutsk, and Jenkins concluded the Fly and Viktor Federov had to be very good friends. If the man hadn't been a ruthless heroin dealer, Jenkins could have liked him. Vasin fed them all like royalty, though Jenkins ate little, with his busted teeth. His meals were pureed and he mostly drank them through a straw. He felt guilty lounging in the sunshine beside a pool. He wanted to get home to Alex, Lizzie, and CJ, whom he missed dearly; but he also knew he couldn't, not in his current condition. Alex would tell him he looked like the Frankenstein monster and was scaring the children.

So he waited, impatiently.

Over the five days, Vasin had medical experts brought in to fix Jenkins's nose, stitch cuts, cap his broken teeth, wrap his ribs, and otherwise heal his battered body—all of it paid for by the CIA. Jenkins had six cracked ribs, but he had not punctured a lung. For days, he had blood in his urine, but by the fifth day it had cleared; his bruises were better. He felt up for travel and was eager to get out of Russia. He knew he would have to spend time in Washington, DC, debriefing Lemore and getting Maria situated. He did not want to just abandon her, not when she was anxious about her new beginning. Jenkins also wanted to check in on Zenaida Petrekova, who Lemore said was going through the process but having difficulty with the fact that she could not see her son or her daughter, or her grandchildren, at least not until they were confident such a meeting could be done without endangering her life. It was another reminder to Jenkins of the sacrifices the seven sisters had made, and those sacrifices became even more prominent when Jenkins spoke to Alex and CJ and Lizzie on the telephone.

During his calls, Jenkins assured Alex he was fine, that while there had been a few setbacks, he was safe and preparing for his return. He knew his wife, however, and he knew she suspected there was more to the story when Jenkins declined to do the calls by FaceTime so the kids could see him.

Federov made travel arrangements to take them from Irkutsk by car to an airstrip in Mongolia. It was one of the Vasins' regular heroin runs, and Jenkins and Maria would be well protected on the drive. As they prepared to leave Plato Vasin's estate with their armed guards, the Fly called Jenkins into an opulent office on the ground floor. As with the other rooms, a colorful fly painted on the wall behind the Fly's desk dominated the décor.

"Vam u nas ponravilos?" *You have enjoyed your stay?* Vasin's English was not so limited that he couldn't carry on a conversation. This was his subtle reminder that they were in Russia and Jenkins was his guest.

"Dazhe ochen'," Jenkins replied. *Very much so.*

"You will tell your bosses about my hospitality, then."

"I have done so," Jenkins said. "And they are appreciative."

Vasin nodded but was not so easily placated. "The CIA has from time to time disrupted my shipments. This should no longer be a problem. Should it?"

Jenkins chose his words carefully. "My bosses are aware that I am alive because of you, and that you are transporting me and Ms. Kulikova out of Russia." *For which Vasin had been paid well,* Jenkins thought, but did not say. "I will emphasize this to them again when I am stateside."

"Khorosho." Good. "I believe we can have a mutually beneficial relationship. My contacts in this region of the world are numerous and widespread. You would be surprised how widespread. Viktor speaks highly of you, Mr. Jenkins. Because he does so, I will think highly of you. Do not disappoint me."

Jenkins nodded but did not verbally respond, and Vasin dismissed him.

Jenkins found Federov waiting in the roundabout at the front of the estate. Maria was not yet out of the mansion.

"This is where I must leave you, Charlie. I must say, you do add excitement to my otherwise carefree life. I am thinking now that I am too young to retire. There are only so many fine hotels, dinners, and golf courses one can frequent."

"I'd love to find out for myself. Care to switch? I didn't take you as a golfer."

"I stink. But I have learned that all golfers stink. It is just to different degrees." Jenkins laughed and looked about the estate. Upon his arrival he had marveled at the wealth—the house, the yard, the pool, the food. Plato Vasin could afford anything he wanted anytime he wanted it, but he was also as much a prisoner as Federov, maybe more so. Jenkins surmised from the armed guards that Vasin's life was fragile. Federov must have felt similarly at times, living large but alone in Europe's finest hotels and restaurants and on its golf courses. No doubt he filled that time with high-end escorts, but they, too, would eventually cease to be fulfilling. Jenkins wouldn't give up his home on Camano Island for five of these estates, and he wouldn't give up his family for all the hotels, meals, golf, and escorts in the world. He suspected Viktor Federov, a complex man for certain, felt the same, though he'd never admit it. It reminded Jenkins of something his father had once said: *When you can have everything, you appreciate nothing.*

"What are you going to do, Viktor?"

"I am thinking perhaps that what I do may depend on what you do."

Jenkins's eyes narrowed behind his dark sunglasses. "I don't follow."

"You seem to need help . . . often." Federov gave that Cheshire cat grin and raised his eyebrows. "I can provide that help, along with other resources. The Vasin reach, for example, is far and wide."

"I've been told. I'm not certain the CIA would look favorably on working with the Irkutsk mafiya."

"Don't be hypocrite. Your CIA is responsible for the deaths of many and engaged in affairs that would make the Fly pale, I am certain. Besides, if it was not for Plato and Peanut, you would be on someone's dinner plate."

"No doubt," Jenkins said. "And they were paid handsomely."

"And don't be naïve. Plato needs more money like the ocean needs more water. He did what he did because I asked him to . . . because I told him you were a friend of mine."

Jenkins could tell Federov had let the word "friend" slip unintentionally. Odd, that this former FSB officer now considered Jenkins a friend. Jenkins extended his arms. "Is this where we hug? I'm feeling a moment between the two of us, Viktor."

"You are jackass," Federov said, stepping away.

Jenkins stepped forward. "Come on, Viktor, bring it in."

"Bring what in?"

Jenkins lowered his arms. "I think of you as a friend also, Viktor. And I know you didn't do what you did for the money either."

Federov shrugged. "Actually, I did. My ocean is not as full as Plato's."

Two black Mercedes pulled into the roundabout, bringing the smell of diesel and the click of the engines. "Any word on Dmitry Sokalov?"

"My contacts within the FSB tell me he has disappeared, and no one knows where he is. His secretary said the last person to visit him in his office was his father-in-law."

"So, it's unlikely he got away."

"Very. People in Russia disappear all the time. Sokalov is likely sitting in Lefortovo, reconstructing what classified information he can recall divulging over the last three decades. Then he will be executed, rest assured. But we can't be too careful even with Sokalov and Zhomov out of the picture; the FSB and the Kremlin, the president, will want you all the more, knowing now Kulikova was one of the seven sisters. The Fly will continue to provide you with security until you have successfully exfiltrated her. Even then, word will spread quickly, and the FSB will adapt just as quickly. For every Sokalov and Zhomov, there are a dozen more."

"Then the sooner we are out of Russia, the better."

"On this I agree," Federov said. Maria appeared atop the steps, speaking to the armed guards, who smiled at her. "She is the last of the seven, no?"

"She is," Jenkins said.

"Good. Then let me give you piece of advice, Charlie. Don't return to Russia, under any circumstances. I can't take it."

Jenkins chuckled and felt it in his ribs. "I don't intend to do any sightseeing over here anytime soon."

"I am curious. What of the two assassins who tried to kill Fyodor Ibragimov?" Federov asked.

"I've been told that when I get back on American soil, the CIA will announce their capture and pin it on the Kremlin. The Kremlin will deny any knowledge of the incident, and the two countries will again begin that never-ending dance. One leading with an accusation, the other following with a denial and a counteraccusation."

"Perhaps the dance will change someday," Federov said.

"Both governments will have to change for that to happen," Jenkins said.

Two guards came down the staircase and nodded to Federov. One opened the back door of the first Mercedes. It was time to go. Federov checked his expensive watch. "I will say, until I see you again."

"See me again?"

Federov winked and slid into the back of the car.

Maria Kulikova came down the steps and watched the first car depart. "Where is he going?"

"I don't know," Jenkins said. "But I suspect this is not the last I will see of Federov, Viktor Nikolayevich."

"Consider it a positive," she said.

Her comment surprised him. "How so?"

"Viktor was one of the best FSB officers in the directorate. I did not know him to be a good person, but he is certainly a good person to have on one's side."

"Clearly."

The second car, with two armed guards, drove Jenkins and Maria from Irkutsk to Ulaanbaatar. The drive took almost fifteen hours, though it felt shorter because the drugs Jenkins had been given for his pain made him groggy, and he slept for most of those hours, awakening when they stopped to change cars or to pick up food, diesel, and other supplies. Each time he awoke, Maria Kulikova would be awake, staring at him from the other side of the car, a book in her lap.

"You haven't slept," he said.

"I wanted to be awake when we crossed the border into Mongolia, when I left Russia for the first time. A moment to consider."

"What are you considering?" he asked.

"What it feels like—to finally be free."

"And what does it feel like?" he asked.

She smiled as bright as a schoolgirl and looked ten years younger. "Like I am flying. Like I have wings and I am soaring above the ground."

"I'm glad," Jenkins said.

She wiped away tears. It was the first time Jenkins had seen her cry. "Do you think Arkhip will be allowed to come?" she asked.

"I don't know," Jenkins said. "But I think you will have some say in that decision."

She shook her head dismissively. "I don't want to get ahead of myself. I don't want to have hope . . . to dream. Too many times I have been disappointed."

"It's better to dream and be disappointed, Maria, than not to dream at all. Take it from someone who knows."

Jenkins thought of Alex. He wouldn't call her a gentle soul, but in her company he felt complete. He felt whole. When he was away from her it always felt like a part of him was missing. "My father once told me that love is not about who you can live with, but about who you cannot live without."

"He must have been very wise, your father. I like that sentiment. I like that very much."

The car pulled off the main strip of asphalt road and took a detour on dirt and gravel cut through a thick grove of trees. Though the expensive car was heavy and absorbed many of the bumps and rattles, Jenkins felt each one in his aching ribs. He leaned forward and spoke over the front seat to the driver and the second guard. *"Pochemu my svernuli? Kuda my yedem?"* Why have we turned off? Where are we going?

"My pochti na meste. Skoro uvidite." We are almost there. You will see soon enough.

Minutes later they came to a bend in the road, then to a clearing with what looked like a dirt landing strip, no doubt for the planes Vasin used to transport his heroin. A plane sat parked at one end of the runway, a Cessna from the looks of it, above it an inviting azure sky with thin white cloud streaks. Lemore had pulled some strings.

As the car came to a stop, a man exited the plane and walked down the airstairs. He was not tall, no more than five foot eight, but he had a presence about him. He wore a worn ball cap, his eyes hidden behind fighter-pilot, reflective sunglasses. It took just a moment for Jenkins to recognize the cocksure stride of the man's walk, one no doubt gained during flights Rod Studebaker had not just survived but enjoyed, like landing his wounded Cessna, with just one ski, on a frozen lake in Finland to deliver Jenkins and Paulina Ponomayova to safety. Studebaker removed the sunglasses and grinned as Jenkins exited the car and approached the stairs.

"Man, who hit you with the ugly stick?" Studebaker extended his hand.

"It's good to see you too, Rod."

Studebaker admired the plane behind him. "This should be a hell of a lot more comfortable than the last time we flew together."

Jenkins laughed at the recollection. "Let's just hope it lands a little more smoothly. Are you going to be bored without Russian helicopters and planes chasing us?"

"I'm older now," Studebaker said. "I'm starting to like the mundane. But it would get the juices flowing." He turned to Maria, who came around the back of the car. "You are anything but mundane. Good Lord, where did Mr. Jenkins find a beauty like you?"

She looked to Jenkins, not fully understanding Studebaker's comment.

"*On govorit, chto ty krasivaya,*" Jenkins said. *He thinks you're beautiful.*

"Thank you," Maria said.

"The pleasure is all mine. The name is Studebaker, like the car, but you can call me 'Hot Rod.'"

Again, Maria looked to Jenkins, uncertain.

"*Mashina yemu tozhe nravitsya,*" Jenkins said. *He likes the car also.*

"Have either of you ever flown on a bird this beautiful?"

Jenkins shook his head. "It isn't really English," he said to Maria in reference to Studebaker's slang. "But you'll get used to it soon enough."

"Somebody at home must like the two of you," Studebaker continued. "It's outfitted with food, drinks, and a place to lie down and sleep."

"Is it fast?" Jenkins said. "I'm just looking to get home."

"Then you are in for a real treat," Studebaker said. "This baby will *really* light your fire."

"He's quoting a song by the Doors, an American band," Jenkins explained to Maria. "It means the plane is very fast."

Maria nodded to Studebaker that she understood. "Yes. Then 'I'm on fire,'" she said. When neither Jenkins nor Studebaker responded, she added, "That is Bruce Springsteen. Yes? *Born in the USA.* 'I'm on Fire.'"

Jenkins laughed. "The Boss. I think you're going to do just fine in America, Maria. I think you're going to fit in in no time."

"Then let us go, Mr. Jenkins, and do like your mother says. Let us turn the page and see what happens next."

Epilogue

Camano Island
Washington State

Jenkins spent a week at Langley, just long enough for his pain to lessen considerably and his appearance to further improve. Langley doctors checked him over from head to toe and generally were impressed with the medical attention he had received in Irkutsk. Before departing he also spent time in the disguise department with a makeup specialist who showed him how to minimize his bruising, so he wouldn't scare his children. The makeup wouldn't fool Alex, however, though it might cause her to raise an eyebrow.

Jenkins had the chance to meet Zenaida Petrekova at a safe house near Langley. She was going through the process of debriefing, but also being educated on her new home. She remained distressed that she would not be able to see her son or her daughter or her grandchildren in person, at least not for a considerable time. If Russia searched for her, her children would be the first persons they put under surveillance. Langley had arranged for an encrypted call, and she had FaceTimed them, advised them that she was well, but provided no further details about her work on behalf of the CIA or her current whereabouts.

"Do you think they know of your spying?"

"They are smart. I'm sure they have figured some things out on their own and are coming to terms with it. My son says now he knows why he could never get away with anything." She smiled. "I miss them. I will miss them."

"I wish you the best," he said.

"And I you, Mr. Jenkins," she said.

"Charlie," he said.

"To use someone's last name is a sign of respect, Mr. Jenkins."

"Then I wish you the best, Ms. Petrekova."

She hugged and thanked him again.

Jenkins felt comfortable leaving Petrekova and Kulikova because both had been treated well and responded in kind. Maria seemed almost embarrassed at the attention she received and at the accommodations provided. Lemore ensured she had Russian food, television programs, books, and other amenities to help ease her transition to the United States.

Toward the end of the week, Jenkins spoke to Lemore about Arkhip Mishkin and about his possibly taking a "vacation" to the United States after he retired. "Maybe a cruise ship," Jenkins said. "He could get off in a port and simply disappear."

Lemore said there were no guarantees.

"Will I see you again?" Maria asked Jenkins before he departed.

"I don't know," he said. "They'll keep your location a closely guarded secret, but in time, and perhaps with a change in the Russian leadership, maybe those secrets will ease."

"Then I will look forward to seeing you again, Mr. Jenkins. And coming to your home to meet your wife and your children."

"I hope you can make a home here also, Ms. Kulikova."

"In Russia we say, *'V gostyakh khorosho, a doma luchshe.' A guest's house is nice, but it's better at home.* Thank you for all that you have done for me. All that you risked." She reached up and warmly hugged

Jenkins. He felt her tears on his cheek. After a moment, she pulled back and dabbed at her eyes. *"Do vstrechi." Until we meet again.*

"Do vstrechi," he said, and he hoped they had that chance one day. He hoped Maria Kulikova would one day be safe, and free to move about the world as she chose, but that seemed many years away.

—

A car picked up Jenkins at Paine Field in Everett and drove him home to Camano Island. The sun glistened off the Stillaguamish waters like diamonds, and it wasn't until he crossed the Camano Gateway Bridge that he felt that he'd arrived at home. He'd completed a mission that had started with lies, but he had completed the objective, rescuing Paulina, Maria, and Zenaida. He felt good knowing he'd left no loose strings. He wished he could have rescued the other sisters, before Carl Emerson had betrayed them. They deserved far better for the sacrifices they had made. He realized the extent of those sacrifices more than ever before, getting to know both Kulikova and Petrekova. What they had given up and what they would continue to give up saddened him.

Would he undertake future operations? Maybe. But for now he was content just to be home, with the family he loved.

Jenkins's new cell phone rang just as the car reached Camano Island on the other side of the bridge. He checked caller ID, but the caller was unidentified. He only had two numbers programmed into the new phone: Lemore and Alex. The area code, however, was for Camano Island.

Jenkins answered. "Hello?"

For a moment, there was silence. Then, "Dad?"

"CJ. Hi."

"Hi, Dad. Mom got me my own phone."

"I can see that."

"You're my first call."

Jenkins fought his emotions. Every time he left, he asked himself why he had done so. He had everything he needed on his little farm—a woman he loved and who loved him, two beautiful children, a home, a place to call his own. And yet he had that longing. That need to be needed, to help those who asked for help. Maybe it was something in his genes, passed down from his ancestor who spent her life freeing slaves. He hoped he could find a balance.

"Am I? I'm honored," he said. "Not one of your friends?"

"You are one of my friends. My best friend."

Jenkins might have thought CJ was buttering him up, but the boy no longer had a need. He had his cell phone. He could hear the hesitation and the softness in his son's voice. He missed his dad. Jenkins knew that feeling also. He'd lost his father at far too young an age. CJ might be growing, taller than his years, but he remained a boy at heart. Didn't all men?

"I was wondering, when are you going to be home?" CJ asked.

Jenkins smiled. "I'm not sure." He leaned over the front seat and directed his driver, using hand signals, to turn just past the Protestant church. "Why?"

"I was just missing you. I was hoping you'd be home soon."

Jenkins again directed the driver, this time to turn on the dirt-and-gravel road. They drove past the old barn and his pastures. "Well, then, why don't you look out the front window?"

"What?"

Jenkins stepped from the car. "Look out the front window."

"Dad! Mom, Dad's home! Dad's home!"

Jenkins heard the phone thud when it hit the ground. The front door flew open and CJ bolted out. The boy came full blast and Jenkins reached out to grab his son. When he did, he remembered his ribs. Too late. He winced at the pain, but he wasn't about to let go or to let this moment pass.

Alex came out the door smiling. She held Lizzie on her hip. She paused and said something to their little girl, who pointed her chubby fingers at the end of her chubby arm, which she began to flap up and down, excited. Alex put Lizzie down and she waddled quickly over to Jenkins, almost falling, but he bent and scooped her into his arms, again ignoring his pain. He lifted Lizzie into the air and she giggled and laughed, and in that moment, Jenkins thought of Maria Kulikova and hoped she could find not just a house, but make a home.

It was definitely better to be home.

Jenkins kissed Alex, who gave him a concerned look, no doubt picking up on his wincing and grimacing. "Welcome home," she said.

"It's nice to be home," he said.

She wiped her cheek. "Are you wearing makeup?"

Jenkins laughed and whispered, "I didn't want to scare the kids."

"Forget the kids. You're scaring me."

He looked to CJ. "Where's your new phone?"

CJ realized he didn't have it. "I dropped it," he said. "Phones are okay. But I like the real thing better."

"So do I, CJ," Jenkins said.

"Did you get it done?" Alex asked.

He nodded.

"They'll call again," she said. "You know that, right?"

"I know."

"Have you thought about what you might tell them?"

He had not. "For now, I'm content to be home."

"And we're content to have you home."

"You really should get a better cell phone, Dad," CJ said. "Did you know they have 5G now?"

"No kidding?"

"Yea. That way I could keep better track of you when you go away. In case you lost your wallet or got in trouble or something."

"Me, get in trouble? Never," Jenkins said, and he smiled at Alex.

ACKNOWLEDGMENTS

I had so much fun writing this Charles Jenkins trilogy. My goal was to make this installment different than the prior two novels, yet have Jenkins finish the mission he started in *The Eighth Sister* and continued in *The Last Agent*. That was no easy feat. I spent time with my editor, Gracie Doyle, and we discussed the things I had touched on. I told her I wanted to write a book where the lines between good and evil blurred. The Russian mafia is largely considered one of the most brutal operating in the world, yet it came out of Stalin's gulags as a means for men to survive. I envisioned a scene where these brutal men would somehow be on Jenkins's side, fighting against even more brutal men. But I never really understand a novel until after it's written. I also wondered about Siberia, which had once been Russia's massive wasteland but is now littered with cities. It is the primary area of recent protests against the government and considers itself separate from the country. A stroke of luck—Viktor Federov was from Irkutsk. Fate? Or good planning?

I'll never tell.

Much of my knowledge of Russia comes from a three-week visit that I detailed in the acknowledgments to *The Eighth Sister* and *The Last Agent*. Though I have traveled extensively, that trip to Moscow and Saint Petersburg remains a highlight for the sights I saw and the people I met.

For this novel, however, I had to become a book nerd and a computer nerd, something I truly enjoy. I read many books on many subjects including Siberia and the Trans-Siberian Railway: *Travels in Siberia* by Ian Frazier; *In Siberia* by Colin Thubron; *Midnight in Siberia: A Train Journey into the Heart of Russia* by David Greene. I read books on portraits of Russian spies and defected KGB officers including *Tower of Secrets* by Victor Sheymov; *The New Nobility* by Andrei Soldatov and Irina Borogan; *The Moscow Rules* by Antonio and Jonna Mendez; *Best of Enemies* by Gus Russo and Eric Dezenhall; *Red Notice* by Bill Browder. I read about Langley's disguise division: *The Master of Disguise* by Antonio Mendez. And I read about Russia's old and new mafia: *The Vory, Russia's Super Mafia* by Mark Galeotti. Not to mention enough magazines and articles to fill two four-inch binders.

Special thanks to those who helped me with the spycraft. I remain grateful for their generous help.

Again, I'm sure I made mistakes, but hopefully not too many.

Special thanks to my good friend and law school roommate, Charles Jenkins. In law school I used to tell Chaz that he was larger than life. In many ways he is. I told him I would someday put him in a novel, and did so in my first, *The Jury Master*. He was kind enough to let me continue the character in this trilogy, and I realized I hadn't dedicated a book to him. Chaz has never been in the CIA, or to Russia, at least not that I know of. He is a good man with a good heart, and I consider him a blessed friend.

Thank you to Meg Ruley, Rebecca Scherer, and the entire Jane Rotrosen Agency. A trilogy is always difficult, but my agents were there to lend support and advice. I'm so very grateful. I'm ready to keep writing the Charles Jenkins novels. I have an upcoming trip to Egypt, so . . . who knows?

Thank you to agent Angela Cheng Caplan, who negotiated the sale of *The Eighth Sister* and *The Last Agent* to Roadside Attractions for development into a major television series. I'm excited to see Charles

Jenkins and the crew come to life on the screen and hope they like this novel as well.

Special thanks also to the team at Amazon Publishing. From the moment I first met them, they have regarded me as a professional writer. They go to great lengths to treat me with respect and dignity, and to ensure everything that can be done is done to ensure the success of my novels. Thank you to my developmental editor, Charlotte Herscher. We've collaborated now on more than a dozen novels, and Charlotte is remarkable for making sure everything makes sense, and that the tension and suspense remain a priority throughout the pages.

Thank you to my copyeditor, Scott Calamar, who must get carpal tunnel fixing my manuscripts.

Thank you to publisher Mikyla Bruder; Jeff Belle, vice president of Amazon Publishing; associate publishers Hai-Yen Mura and Galen Maynard; and everyone on the Amazon Publishing team. I'm grateful to call Amazon Publishing my home. I've enjoyed getting to know each of you.

Thank you to Dennelle Catlett, publicist, for the tireless promotion of me and my work. Special thanks for handling the many requests for the use of my novels for charitable purposes.

Thank you to Lindsey Bragg, Erica Moriarty, Andrew George, and Kyla Pigoni, the marketing team that works to keep me and my novels relevant. And a special thanks to Sarah Shaw for all the fabulous parties and fabulous gifts that bring my family wonderful surprises and memories.

Thank you to Rachel Kuck, head of production; Lauren Grange, production manager; and Oisin O'Malley and Michael Jantze, art directors, who oversee the design of the amazing covers, including those for *The Eighth Sister* and *The Last Agent*. Each time I get to see the cover, I'm stunned. Like all the others, this cover was amazing.

Most importantly, thank you to Gracie Doyle, my editor at Thomas & Mercer. Writing can be a lonely profession, but I'm blessed to have an editor who collaborates with me from the start and helps me to be excited about each book. I look forward to placing many more books in your capable hands, and to renewing our Christmas celebrations.

Thank you to Tami Taylor, who creates my newsletters, and keeps me alive on the Internet. Thank you to Pam Binder, president of the Pacific Northwest Writers Association, for her support of my work.

Thank you to my mother, who gave me my love of reading and writing, and who is eighty-eight years old. She can no longer read this print, but she can hear the narration. I should be so blessed to reach the same milestone. You remain an inspiration to me.

I'm blessed to share today with a wife I love, a truly remarkable woman in so many ways it would be impossible to list them all here. She gave me two children who have grown to be two of the finest people I know. I'm proud to be their father. I love you all. Thanks for putting up with my imaginary friends, my mood swings, the long hours I spend at the computer, and the times when I've been away to promote my novels.

No man could be any richer or more blessed.

Until our next adventure, faithful readers, wherever it takes us, thank you for making my todays.

ABOUT THE AUTHOR

Robert Dugoni is the critically acclaimed *New York Times*, *Wall Street Journal*, *Washington Post*, and Amazon Charts bestselling author of the Tracy Crosswhite series, which has sold more than seven million books worldwide. He is also the author of the bestselling Charles Jenkins series; the bestselling David Sloane series; the stand-alone novels *The 7th Canon*, *Damage Control*, *The World Played Chess*, and *The Extraordinary Life of Sam Hell*, *Suspense Magazine*'s 2018 Book of the Year, for which Dugoni won an AudioFile Earphones Award for narration; and the nonfiction exposé *The Cyanide Canary*, a *Washington Post* best book of the year. He is the recipient of the Nancy Pearl Book Award for fiction and a three-time winner of the Friends of Mystery Spotted Owl Award for best novel set in the Pacific Northwest. He is a two-time finalist for the Thriller Awards and the Harper Lee Prize for Legal Fiction, as well as a finalist for the Silver Falchion Award for mystery and the Mystery Writers of America Edgar Awards. His books are sold in more than twenty-five countries and have been translated into more than two dozen languages. Visit his website at www.robertdugonibooks.com.